THE VERACITY OF LIES

ANNA WOIWOOD

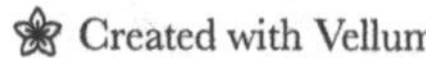 Created with Vellum

In honor of women.
And L.
You know which one.

Content Warning

This book contains dark themes that express the experience of women. It may not be suitable for all readers. Please note that there are references to alcoholism, domestic abuse, cancer, drug use, eating disorders, time period homophobia, and sexual assault.

Contents

Prologue

Kathryn

Hollywood, 1956

It was an obsession that had arisen out of thin air.

No, she thought as she smoked at her cigarette. It had not come from nowhere.

There had been a moment, or moments, that had drawn her to the precipice of it. Little things here and there. The intimately shared moments, the interested gazes, always seeking one another out during their days together at the studio. She served as a relief from the men who surrounded her, demanding so much from her.

Alice was a woman like herself. A vibrant, brilliant young thing. Life pulsed through her veins, and there was a sickly sweetness about her that had gone unbroken by the system. She sincerely smiled. She was thoughtful about herself, about others. She genuinely listened; she authentically cared. She did not make mistakes.

Kathryn hated her.

Until she hadn't.

It had been a dream some months before. Some strange deluded, drunken dream of auburn hair and gentle emerald eyes that had been so real to her. It had awoken something within her, had brought her to the edge.

The dream had forced her to see the other woman in a whole new light. It was teasing, tantalizing to have the vivid imagery of it when in life there was nothing between them, could never be anything between them. Colleagues, co-stars, yes, but something else…no.

Kathryn inhaled smoke, flustered.

She found herself backstage, hidden away in an alcove, the overhead lights blazing at full force only a wall away, the crew sprinting about, everyone's rapt attention focused on capturing the moment playing out upon the sound stage. It was a moment between her on-screen husband, Wes, and the downstairs neighbor, George, played by Larry Ackerman. The audience was in stitches about something, but Kathryn's attention was focused upon the silhouette of a feminine form slipping through the darkened backstage area, headed in her direction.

Kathryn inhaled shakily at her cigarette. Her heart pounded ever so when the woman came to stand beside her. She smelled of flowers and stage makeup. Her hair was perfectly set about her face, and her figure was trimmer than it had been only weeks before.

Kathryn turned to look at Alice in the dim lighting.

Alice looked back at her with wide, eager eyes.

How beautiful she was. Her blissful happiness made Kathryn long for a simplicity she had never known.

Alice drew closer to her, as if conspiratorially. Kathryn felt her body turning to match Alice's movement.

"Is my lipstick all right?" Alice whispered.

Kathryn's eyes fell to her full lips, painted a brilliant hue of red. There was not one bit of the rouge out of place, yet Kathryn lifted her ring finger to gently pass over the ridge of Alice's lip.

Alice's eyes widened, lips parting in a surprised pout. It was pretty.

She was very pretty.

"It's perfect." Kathryn clasped at Alice's chin, inspecting her lips further, catching the gentle blush that flared over the other woman's cheeks. Very pretty indeed.

And the urge overtook her sense. She leaned in and ever so lightly – ever so very aware of their differing shades of lipstick – pressed her lips to Alice's.

She heard the surprised inhalation, the gentle gasp that Alice managed before Kathryn stepped away from her, placed the cigarette to her lips and inhaled again before putting it out in a nearby ashtray.

Alice had not moved an inch.

Kathryn knew the script well enough to know that Alice's moment was approaching. It was time for Alice to transform into Kay, to go onto the set and deliver her lines. But Kathryn had bewitched her.

"Alice, darling, it's nearly your line." Kathryn whispered and a frightened look crossed over Alice's attractive features. Her cheeks flushed brightly red, and the moment before she was needed for the scene Kathryn caught a slight smear of lipstick and pulled her back to wipe it away before pushing her forward again, out into the light of the stage.

"Shit, shit, shit." Kathryn cursed under her breath, watching as Alice tottered onto the stage, a blank look of hesitation and confusion crossing her features. The audience was on the edge of their seats, everyone wanting to know why she had come bursting in.

Everything felt suspended in air, as if the clock had stopped moving forward, as if time itself had come to a halt.

And then, just like the professional Kathryn knew her to

be, Alice snapped to and had the audience howling with laughter.

Kathryn breathed a sigh of relief. "Fuck," she exhaled, lighting another cigarette to steady herself before she was to make her entrance and become Wes' adoring wife, Paula, and not Kathryn Anderson who had just kissed Alice Kincaid.

Part I

Chapter One

Alice

Los Angeles, 1981

"And up and down, four, five, six, we're going to ten ladies."

Alice's legs were screaming, but she lowered her pelvis down and then pressed it high again at the command of 'seven' the youthful leader Suzanne was demanding of the class.

"Can you feel your bodies coming to life?" Suzanne, tall and gorgeously handsome, asked before continuing the count, her voice dangerously near to Alice. And then Alice felt those gentle hands come to rest on her hips, guiding them ever upward at the command of 'eight.' "Good work, Alice." Suzanne murmured in intimate tones as she lifted Alice's hips higher to the sky for the louder call of 'nine.' Alice hoped that Suzanne could not feel the way in which her legs were trembling. "And ten." Suzanne was smiling down at Alice as she helped lower her to the ground. "Your stomach looks amazing." Suzanne whispered before returning to the head of the classroom for the cool down stretches.

Alice's heart was racing, her body more than alive by the end of the intimate maneuvers of the barre class. Sweat dripped from her brow when she picked herself up after the final stretch of the day. Her fifty-three-year-old body hummed with the rewards of a rigorous workout. Her filming schedule had kept her away from class for far longer than she would have liked, but she was certainly glad she had found the time to fit one in.

The young, blonde instructor appeared at Alice's side as she was pulling on a sweater. "I'm so glad you could make it today, Alice. It's been awhile." Suzanne leaned up against the wall, watching as Alice retrieved her water bottle from her gym bag.

"Yes, it's been far, far too long. The show keeps me too busy, I'm afraid."

"I'm loving this season, especially what they're doing with your character. Sharon is just so…ugh, I don't know, sexy." Suzanne eagerly admitted.

Alice gave her a crooked smile. "You think Sharon is sexy?" She laughed incredulously. "Honey, she's old enough to be your mother."

Suzanne flushed at Alice's insinuation and Alice wondered if she'd misjudged Suzanne's eagerness. It was hard to tell, especially amongst the barre set. The sexual undertones could make anything seem like a pass. "Oh, I don't…she's just strong. You know? We hardly have any strong females on television and I like her passion. You do such a good job with her."

Strong and passionate were words so far removed from Alice's own self-description. "I'm glad I can bring her to life."

"But, come on." Suzanne lightly touched her arm, voice going softer. "You're like her a little, aren't you?"

The place where Suzanne had touched pulsed. "Oh, I wouldn't say that. It's just a part I play. I'm afraid I'm rather boring compared to Sharon." Alice didn't want Suzanne to be blindsided by just how dull she really could be. Her life was her son and her show and every now and then a strange moment such as this one.

And speaking of her son, he was practically the same age as the beauty before her.

"I don't believe it." Suzanne had a rather unreadable smile on her pretty pink lips.

Alice shrugged and smiled. "I'd say I could prove it to you, but I'm afraid I'm running late for a rehearsal."

"I hope you can make it to class next week."

"I'll try not to miss it." Alice winked, letting her hand come to rest gently against Suzanne's toned arm and then was out the door. She had ventured far enough over the line that day, and she had to be careful.

Her car phone was ringing when she turned on the ignition. There was never a moment of peace, was there? "Hello?" She asked into the receiver.

"I know you're on the way to rehearsal, so I'll talk fast. Did you get the script for that TV movie?" Her agent's voice flooded the line.

Of course she had gotten it. Another overly dramatic romp where she got killed in the end. She was tired of the woman always getting killed. "You know, Alan, I'd like to play the role of someone who's still alive when the credits roll."

Alan laughed on the other end of the line. "Maybe you should start writing the pictures then."

She rather wished she had the knack for it.

"Listen, it's a quick shoot. You're in and out in a few weeks, make a few thousand and we're golden."

She didn't need a few thousand more, but her show *Different Threads* would be on hiatus and she hated down time. "I'll do it, but I do wish you'd get me something less gruesome, you know? Something I could live through. Do you think it would be possible for them to rewrite it?"

Alan did not sound hopeful when he said he'd speak with them. The movie revolved around the premise that she had to die.

So she resolved to die for the paycheck and be done with it.

She reached the studio and had a brief moment to freshen up before she was called to set.

It was the jangle of a wrist full of golden bangles that alerted Alice to *her* presence in the hallway. As she stepped out her dressing room door, she looked up to find the gorgeous Jeannette Jenkins passing by. The oversized leopard print sweater and black pants encasing her spindly little legs made her far more glamorous than Alice could ever hope to be on a rehearsal day.

Jeanette's dark, all-seeing eyes looked her over and then gave her a second, more scrutinizing glance. "Well don't you look like the cat who got the cream." There was a knowing smile that stretched across her lips, dimpling her dark cheeks.

"Oh, shush." Alice hit her shoulder.

"What were you getting up to this morning?" Jeanette looped her arm through Alice's as they walked down the studio hall.

"Not what you're thinking. But I hate to admit it, I wish it were that." Alice leaned into Jeanette to confess, remembering the feel of Suzanne's hands on her hips.

She wondered if Jeanette would understand that.

Jeanette's infectious laughter filled the hallway at the admission.

No, Jeanette was a woman who loved men. She was more than happily married to a very fine man. Even Alice could see the appeal and, based on their private conversations, he more than appeased Jeanette.

Jeanette turned to face Alice before they walked onto the

soundstage. "You need to find yourself a man and get laid, sugar." She squeezed Alice's hand and then laughed full and hearty again as she made her way to the stage, leaving Alice to try and play off the blush that crept over her cheeks with a bemused smile.

Chapter Two

Kathryn

Munich, 1981

The music was far too loud from the stereo in the corner, pounding deafeningly in her ears. Everyone trying to speak over the music only added to her annoyance as she made her way through the sea of people occupying their apartment. She stumbled, only a little, falling against someone as she passed through the hallway from having refreshed her drink in the kitchen.

It was so warm. She felt sweat pooling at her brow, beneath her arms, between her legs. Her heart was beating rapidly.

It was in the midst of the sitting room that she found Peter.

She'd done him up in her bathroom that evening after they'd watched the dailies. He'd said he wanted to have a few movie people over, which meant a party and the slinky gown he traded his director's jacket for, the blush comically placed in two bright, red circles on his pale cheeks. He was so very in his element on nights like these.

He, her husband, still so young and vibrant.

And at sixty she was fading.

She leaned against the doorway to steady herself, lifting the cigarette to her lips with a shaky hand and inhaling while she watched the jolly group around her.

"Mein Engel." He cried suddenly, coming to her, lifting her hand so that he could press kisses to it. "Meine Süße muse."

"Hör auf." She batted him away.

"My darling, but you are so pale." Peter cooed.

"It's nothing." She assured him.

"You're exhausted." He insisted. "Ah!" He held up his hand before reaching for her. "Komm her." And he pulled her into the center of the mismatched crowd of people about the room – lustrous young women, older men, men dressed as women, an older woman who smoked a pipe...

He cut a line of cocaine for her. A cure for all ailments, he insisted.

She inhaled the powder laid out for her, falling back onto the couch as she sniffed and wiped at her nose.

It was several minutes before the high came over her.

A light returned. At one moment she felt her husband's lips upon hers, at another there were soft lips pressed to hers and the whole evening scattered and shifted in a whirl of color and people and lights and sounds.

Until there was blackness.

Nothingness, for what seemed like hours. Sometimes, when this happened, she wondered if she was dead.

As if surfacing from a deep dive, though light fluttered into her consciousness and she found herself seated before a mirror. People fluttered about her, someone was patting her cheek, urging her back to the land of the living. "Aufwachen, Frau Anderson!"

Kathryn batted at the large make-up woman's hand. "Fass mich nicht an!" She hissed. "Get away!"

"Frau Anderson, I would ask that you not hit me. You're late as it is. We have to get the lashes on." The woman grabbed at her hands, held her firmly – she was a very strong, German woman – and another woman went to work on Kathryn's eyes, prying them open so that Kathryn was accosted with the sight of herself. The flash of blonde hair, the wrinkles that creased around bloodshot eyes, the deep creases around her carefully painted red lips. The lights were far, far too bright. She wanted to look away.

This was not her.

Once make-up was finished poking and prodding her and wardrobe had dressed her in the all too revealing little negligee, Kathryn began to nod off again. She slumped over in her set chair, giving up the fight to stay awake.

"She can't even keep her eyes open." She overheard one of the stagehands speaking in German before her.

"What is the problem here?" Peter's voice was heard.

"We can't work with her like this." The stagehand spoke in English.

Peter laughed this off. "Why, I can have her in working order in five minutes. She'll be right as rain. We'll roll in ten."

She felt his hands on her, shaking her awake. "Wake up, darling." He pulled her up and helped her to her dressing room. "What is it, meine Süße?"

"I'm so tired." She whispered.

"We have to get through the scene today. It's only a little bit more now, you see? And then we'll have ourselves another film." He slapped her cheeks and the force of it startled her eyes fully open. "Come now, we'll get you up and running."

She saw the line of coke he'd cut for her.

"Come on, darling. We have the crew waiting for us." Peter nudged her.

She sighed and leaned forward to snort the line, wanting, needing the pick-up.

Her nose felt numb.

The high hit and she was suddenly wide awake.

They returned to the set and Peter took his place in the director's chair and she, in turn, her place before the camera.

And her young, beautiful co-star Sabine – who could not be a day over twenty-three - looked at her with a curious little smile.

"Don't you look well today?" Sabine purred in her French accent.

Kathryn could not decipher if her tone was condescending or flirtatious. It was hard to tell with these young women Peter liked to pair her with for these horrifically confusing, albeit seductive moments.

Kathryn was playing the role of step-mother to the deliciously attractive Sabine as her youthful step-daughter. They were to hate one another. There was a struggle between them, Peter explained, but there was also something else to what they had between them.

"Action." Peter called out.

The scene unfolded. Kathryn stumbled over dialogue but Peter did not stop rolling. Sabine grabbed at her hair, pulling her head back and she called out in real pain.

The next take Kathryn remembered her lines until Sabine got too close to her and she faltered.

Peter cut a line of coke for her in her dressing room before the third take. "It's there, darling. You're fucking magnificent." He kissed her neck and it made her flush.

Peter called "Cut!" for the final time after the fourth take.

Sabine was panting atop Kathryn, who was sweating from the hot set lights. Sabine's crystalline blue eyes burned into her.

Kathryn thought, for some brief moment, that the young woman might kiss her right then and there, but instead the young woman's brow creased with concern. "Kathryn," Sabine cupped her cheeks in her hand. "You're bleeding."

Kathryn batted her hand away, putting a hand to her face. When she pulled it away she saw blood. It was seeping out of her nose.

Peter was at her side then, helping her to sit up and instructing her to pinch the bridge of her nose and to lean forward until it stopped. "The scene was Wunderbar, Kathryn. You reached that place that I know you can."

"I don't feel well." She confided, mind spinning.

"It was a beautiful performance. The two of you together are so very sensual." He assured her.

"Peter, I want to lie down."

He put her in a car that took her back to their apartment.

She took a bottle of whiskey and a pack of cigarettes to the bedroom and curled atop the bed, drinking until she passed out.

Chapter Three

Alice

"Mom!" She felt a gentle shove at her side.

Blinking, she realized that she had been out like a light.

"C'mon, you missed the end!" He shook her out of her slumber. "How could you possibly fall asleep?"

It was Sunday. The only day Jack had a moment for her, and he had shown up with a VHS copy of *Kramer vs. Kramer*. His obsession with the legal world was spilling into his appreciation for the arts.

"That Meryl Streep is really something. I don't know how she could do it, though. Leave her kid, just like that!" Jack exclaimed.

Alice rubbed at her eyes and sat up on her elbows. She'd seen the picture when it had been released and had gone home in a fit of uncontrollable tears. This new era of cinema was intense. It really said something, and usually what it said was not so flattering for the woman. Even if Meryl herself had exclaimed that it was feminism at its finest, Alice struggled to see it that way. Were a man to ever step up to actually care for his child, she might accept it more fully.

She looked at her son's large, expectant eyes – the most comforting of his features for they were the furthest from his father's. He had always been a naturally curious child, eyes wide open to the world.

"Oh, honey, you know it was fiction." Alice had not been prepared for this discussion, the parallels too close. It felt too raw still, too close to home. Even if her son was twenty-four and all of what had happened was far in the past.

"The guys at the firm told me they wouldn't have ruled in favor of her at all. Which is surprising, you know? I mean she's his mother."

"And don't you think a man should be able to raise a child? Isn't he capable?" Alice reached for a cold cup of tea.

Jack considered this. "Do you wish my father would have raised me?"

Alice nearly spat. "Of course not." That was the furthest wish from her mind. "No, it's only that in an ideal world you'd have a marriage of equals where both people are equally invested in raising a child. You don't know it, Jack, but this world we live in demands a lot from women. My God, we're only human."

Jack looked her over, a shy smile playing at his lips. She could never tell if she'd taught him what she wished she could. Things had changed, things were changing. But he was kind and he was sensitive, and he still came to see her on Sundays despite studying for the bar exam and working at a law firm so he had to have turned out mostly okay, hadn't he? There was no girlfriend, but it relieved her more than worried her.

"Oh, Jack. I'm so sorry I fell asleep. It's just...I'm so... exhausted."

Jack looked at her, worried. "You've been working a lot."

She laughed at that. "It never ends. But hey, I'm okay." She reassured him.

And just as if she had summoned it, the phone began to ring. She rolled her eyes to the ceiling; Jack laughed. Standing up, she started for the phone. As she went, she remembered that Jack had mentioned a new roommate several months ago and so she thought to say, "hey, why don't you bring your roommate some weekend? I'd like to finally meet him."

"Mom! You know how intimidating that can be!" Jack called over the ringing phone.

"Honey, I'm not intimidating." Alice laughed at the insinuation.

"But you're Alice Kincaid. They fall in love with you. It's awkward."

"It's not awkward. You bring him next weekend." She insisted before grabbing up the phone. "Hello?"

"Hello, Alice. I really hate to bother you on a Sunday, I know that it's your day off, but something just came across my desk that I thought you'd like to hear about." Alan's voice sounded unreadable. She was not sure if this was good or bad news.

Alice rubbed at her forehead. "Well, let's have it."

"Well, as you may know *The Wes Goodwin Show* has been doing so well in syndication that *The Holly Singer Show* wants to do a feature on where the cast is now. You know, like a little reunion."

Of all the things she had thought Alan might tell her, this she was least prepared for. Her heart began to beat rapidly. Her hand shook and she very nearly dropped the phone.

"Alice? Are you still there?"

"Yes…uh…what do you mean, Alan?"

"I mean, Holly Singer wants to interview the cast on her show."

"You mean…everyone would be…uh, has everyone agreed to this?"

"It's pretty much a go. We just have to work around your filming schedule, but I've already talked to the producers and they think it will work."

"You've already talked to the producers." She hummed.

So it was happening then.

Her chest was tight. Was this a heart attack? No, she was too young for that, wasn't she?

"Mom?" Jack was standing in front of her, mouthing 'are you okay?'

She nodded at him, held up her hand to put him off. "Alan, you mean the whole cast will be there?"

"Alice, is there something I should know?"

"No! Nothing…I just…it's hard to believe. You know? It's been, well, it's been a long time."

"Then I'm sure it will be wonderful to see everyone again."

She mumbled some incoherent agreement.

"Great, then it's all set. I'll let the show's producers know."

The phone slid from her hands.

"Mom, what's the matter?" Jack was before her, helping her as she slowly descended unceremoniously to the floor.

She didn't want him to see her like this, but she was helpless to stop the shocked reaction of her body. "I'm okay." She whispered.

"You're not." He insisted, kneeling beside her.

So she would see *her* again.

It would be on live television.

They had been colleagues. They could be collegial, surely. After so many years.

Couldn't they?

She reached for her son's hand, clasping it to stop him from his fearful questioning. "It was just a shock, is all. It was Alan. He just called to tell me about a reunion. You know for that show I was on. When you were born."

"With Wes Goodwin?" He questioned.

"Yes, that one." She patted his cheek, tried to smile.

Jack frowned. "Did he…did he try something…"

It took her a moment to figure out what her son was inferring and she nearly burst out laughing at the implication. Wes, oh Wes had been a good man. One of the only really good men in Hollywood she had ever met. Ridiculously devoted to his wife, Meredith.

"Oh God, no. Wes is a real gentleman."

Jack frowned at her. "That wasn't a normal reaction so something had to have…"

"Jack," she quieted him, nudging him to help her up. Her heart had abated its rapid beating. "Please, don't try out those attorney skills on me right now. Please." She pleaded.

He did not look convinced. "But if someone did something…"

"Honey, it was years ago. I'm okay." She assured him.

But even as she spoke, her words felt hollow. Was she really okay?

She wanted to be alone, but she had to put on a show for Jack to try and play the role of an okay woman. And she very well nearly convinced him as they ate dinner together — he insisted that he stay. She laughed so that he would laugh. Pestered him about his roommate. Worked it so that he might forget her momentary lapse and finally after they ate together, she insisted she had lines to learn and he should get back to his studying. So that he finally left.

She walked to her bedroom blankly. She did not know what to do so she sat on the edge of her bed and stared at the dresser drawer. She got up, went to pull the drawer open to locate the jewelry box, to open it and find, hidden deep in the furthest corner, the necklace. The jewel at the center of the pendant shone dark red in the overhead light of the room.

Deep, lusty red.

She could not bring herself to touch it, so she closed the

box, shut the drawer, drew herself a bath, divested herself of clothing and sank into the water and stared blankly at the wall before her.

So.

After all these years.

They would see one another again.

Chapter Four

Kathryn

The plane vibrated beneath her feet.

Turbulence nearly knocked her sideways, so that her elbow fell into the bathroom wall. She placed the burning cigarette between her teeth so she could reach out to steady herself.

Someone was knocking at the folding bathroom door.

"Just a goddamn minute." She breathed, working another line of cocaine on her compact mirror. She had to hold the mirror steady with each new dip and move of the plane, but she successfully snorted the line and righted herself, rubbing the excess powder she'd missed over her gums.

The person was knocking again.

"Fuck off." She whispered, putting away all evidence of what she had just done before looking herself over in the mirror. She grimaced. The overhead lights did little to make her look alive. Her eyes red, face pale, lines running ever deeper with each passing day in her forehead, and around her lips and eyes.

She bent down and splashed her face with cool water, slapping her cheeks to bring out some color before taking another drag on her cigarette.

The drug was beginning to run its course through her system, lifting her up again.

The knocking brought her back.

"All right, all right." Kathryn grabbed up her bag and unlocked the door, practically falling into the gentleman she'd noticed had been seated two seats ahead of her own.

He caught her about the waist and looked her over. "Why, aren't you that actress…why yes, Kathryn Anderson."

"The one and only." She smiled politely. "Would you like me to sign something for your wife?"

The man unhanded her. "Oh no, no. But, perhaps I might have your number. You're headed to Los Angeles, aren't you?"

She patted his arm. "Why, I don't think so. But it's flattering."

And when she turned away to take her seat, to allow the drug to fully overcome her and ease her unsteady nerves, she heard the man whisper "bitch" beneath his breath.

She sunk down into the seat and stared at her empty whiskey glass. When the stewardess passed by, Kathryn caught her. "Might I trouble you for a top off?"

"Why, of course, Ms. Anderson." The youthful thing flashed Kathryn a beauteous smile.

Kathryn smoked at the last of her cigarette, eyes upon the stewardess as she moved up the aisle to fetch her drink.

The infernal flight back to America felt as if it might never end. Another drink, a pill. She didn't want to think of what she was doing.

She passed out somewhere over the Pacific, only coming

to when the attractive stewardess roused her awake. "We've landed in Los Angeles, Ms. Anderson."

"Fuck." Kathryn cursed, wandered blurrily from the plane and was guided to a limousine where she sank into the leather seat and made quick work of snorting a bump of cocaine to wake herself up.

She was taken to a hotel near the studio and after the flurry of bell boys and handlers, she was left to herself in the suddenly all too quiet room.

She was warm, too warm. She removed her travel jacket and tossed it carelessly on the bed before unbuttoning the top of her shirt. There was perspiration on her forehead, her neck. She lit a cigarette and rummaged through the wet bar for a drink. Luckily, she was well stocked and the place was not on her dime.

She popped open a bottle of vodka and downed it as she sat on the edge of the bed, the world going sideways around her. She fished about in her purse for the baggie and pulled it out. Holding it up to the light, she realized she'd done one too many hits *en route* because her supply was waning.

She threw the baggie on the bedside table and groped for another drink.

She hated tedious hours alone, left to herself with nothing to occupy her time. And if she sat and thought about what it was she had come to do, she felt a tight pain wind its way across her chest, knotting her stomach.

Her heart was racing.

She laid back on the bed and lifted the phone on the bedside table. She had no earthly idea what time it was in Los Angeles let alone the hour overseas, but she called anyway. He picked up somewhere halfway through the monotonous ring of the phone.

"Hallo?"

"Peter, I can't do it." She hummed, feeling a headache coming on.

"Ah, my Süße. But it is in the middle of the night here."

She felt tears welling in her eyes. "Es tut mir leid."

"Nein, nein. Kathryn, this is wonderful for us. Think of the film. It's good, no?"

She rolled her eyes to the ceiling. He would see this as free publicity. Not knowing…but how could he know? She didn't wish to speak to him any longer. "Ja, I suppose, darling. Go back to sleep."

"But you have made it safely to America?"

"Yes. I'm here. I'm fine. Go back to sleep."

She hung up and felt more alone in the dreary hotel room than she had before calling him. She lit another cigarette and flipped on the television, accosted by the ridiculous American ruckus. Stumbling to the minibar, she drank another bottle of something before easing down into the recesses of the bed.

She willed sleep to overcome her.

There was blackness but suddenly a strange awareness of a voice. Clear and sonorous and far too familiar ringing in her ears.

She quite thought she was hallucinating.

Could she be there with her?

Studio audience laughter cut into the chimera.

Kathryn's eyes blurrily came open to see *her* on the television screen.

Gorgeous, long and leaner than she had ever been. Eyes bright in technicolor, voice as mellifluous as before.

A whimper escaped from between Kathryn's lips.

The image was too painful.

She fumbled for the remote, knocking things left and right off the nightstand before locating the device and changing the channel. Something unfamiliar, something less bright and brilliant and beautiful.

And she stared at the screen through hazy eyes and felt tears overtake her.

She could not do this. She hadn't the strength to face her.

After all these years.

Her finger betrayed her and the television flipped backwards and returned her to the show. She lit another cigarette and found herself entranced by what she had not been able to face for years. She couldn't look away.

Until her eyes grew heavy and the images on the television began to mingle with distant memories, and she almost could have sworn that time had rewound and that perhaps if she were to just open her eyes it could all go back to that distant utopia.

She dreamt fretfully, woven in and out of reality so that it all felt so very real to her and then all so very far away again.

If only she could grasp onto something.

Chapter Five

Alice

Jeanette leaned up against Alice's car door, lighting a cigarette.

"I've got to get home." Alice sighed, rubbing at her forehead where a migraine was threatening to come on.

"Ah ah ah, not so fast, my dear." Jeanette reached out to take her elbow. "You've been off *all* damn day."

"I'm just exhausted." Alice tried to play it off.

Jeanette blew a stream of smoke out the side of her lips. "You have that reunion show tomorrow."

Alice's stomach knotted. "Don't remind me."

"That bad, huh?" Jeanette's teeth shone brightly in the fading light of evening when she smiled.

"No, not bad."

"One of the guys fucked you over?"

Alice half-laughed at the guess.

"All right then, that Kathryn Anderson was a bitch to you."

Alice rolled her eyes to the sky. "Give me that cigarette."

"Oh my, now that I wouldn't have expected." Jeanette handed it over to her.

Alice placed it between her lips and inhaled but only succeeded in coughing out a cloud of smoke. The taste was revolting. "Jesus, how do you people smoke these?" She asked through coughs, handing back the cigarette.

"It's an acquired taste." Jeanette was laughing at her.

"I'm glad I've never acquired it. But really, I must get home. I don't want to look haggard on camera tomorrow morning. You know how puffy my eyes can be when I haven't slept." Alice spoke quickly, trying to make Jeanette's questioning gaze dissipate. She didn't want to talk any more about the show or about tomorrow or Kathryn Anderson.

The name made her knees buckle.

"You sure it's not something more?"

"I'm fine, Jean. I'm just fine." Alice assured her, leaning in to press her lips to Jeanette's cheek.

"Good night, sugar. You know I'm always a phone call away." Jeanette pushed herself from Alice's car door and made her way toward her own car.

"Thank you."

But instead of driving directly home, Alice made a pit stop at the local diner she usually tried to avoid. It had been nearly two years since last she'd come in. For this she had been very proud, but this evening her resolve had weakened. She ordered her usual cheat meal and made quick work of eating it, trying not to think, trying hard not to acknowledge what she was doing.

After she ate every last bite, she slid from the booth in the back corner and went to the bathroom. She checked to make sure she was alone before kneeling down in front of the not so clean toilet and then proceeding to vomit up everything she had in her stomach.

And for a brief moment – for the very briefest of seconds

she felt infinitely better. Better than she'd felt in months. Like she was walking on air, like no one could touch her.

Until the bathroom door opened.

She scrambled to her feet to hide what she had done.

She left a hundred-dollar bill on the table and made a hasty exit.

Shame, shame overtook her.

She drove home feeling lightheaded and awful.

She had been so good, she had been doing really well. Not one slip up. Not even an urge to do what she dreaded doing.

And then this.

What was she going to do? She couldn't stop the following day from coming. Would she be able to bear it? To face her again after what they had been through?

She wanted to call Jack, to have him come over and console her, but he was her son and she hated how he'd looked at her. How he still questioned her when he came to see her. And she kept having to reassure him that everything was okay – but she wasn't so sure that everything was okay.

Why? Why did she have to be entangled in all of this? Sure, the show had made her, had set her up to have all that she had now. But at what cost?

Alice divested herself of clothing as soon as she got home, ran a bath, and then slid into the hot water. She closed her eyes, trying to get ahold of herself, but it all felt like it was spinning out of control.

After her evening ritual of creams and potions, she took two aspirin and settled into bed, but she couldn't sleep.

There would be no sleep.

Even if she kept her eyes glued shut, her mind couldn't stop racing.

Suddenly she saw the dreamy rose of sunrise filtering in through her blinds, and she realized it was morning.

There was no stopping what would come next.

There were bags beneath her eyes, but her body looked slim.

The headache lingered. She took more medication.

She moved through the morning with a weight on her shoulders. Doing herself up, putting herself together as if she could face the day.

A car came for her at nine.

The driver was cordial, but she could hardly speak to him. Her heart pounding louder and louder in her ears the closer they got to the studio.

She could hardly hear from the ringing in her ears when she was escorted from the car and taken to an entrance. She braced herself as they stepped through the studio door. As if she expected the woman to be standing there waiting for her as soon as she entered. However, only crew members were running about. Alice was taken to a make-up room and placed in a chair and some rather chatty young blonde began doing her face over, smoothing out the lines of sleeplessness from her cheeks, making her eyes look bright and alive.

Alice listened, waiting for the first sign that *she* was also there, but there was nothing. Nothing except these young people swarming about her, talking and talking as if this was some joyous occasion.

A producer came to talk to her, explaining that there was a live studio audience. The four actors would wait back stage and would be called out on to set. Larry first, followed by Alice, then Kathryn, and last would be Wes.

Great – she would be standing backstage next to the very woman she hadn't seen in years. More than twenty years, she realized.

God, where had the time gone?

The make-up girl did a final touch up after the producer left and Alice felt like she might pass out. "You're so pale." The girl was looking at her strangely.

"Get her some water," someone else said.

Alice was handed a glass of water and instructed to drink it all down. A quick touch up of her lipstick and she was escorted out of the room.

It was then that she was led to the green room where she knew the unavoidable could no longer be avoided.

But it was only Larry who was sitting at the end of a couch and Wes, with his still very attractive wife, Meredith, standing opposite him.

Kathryn was nowhere to be seen.

"Why Alice! Look at you!" Wes exclaimed.

They embraced, kissing cheeks. She greeted Meredith with a quick kiss and hug.

Larry was on his feet, wrapping Alice in a hug.

They were all talking to her and she was attempting to speak to them, but her mind was a million miles away.

"Your son, he's doing well?" Meredith inquired.

"Oh, my son? Yes, yes. He's in law school." Alice hummed, feeling a tightness stretching across her chest. She wondered if she was going to vomit or simply fall over from the tension mounting inside of her.

"Law school! You must be very proud."

Alice just nodded and then felt the room shift. It was Wes who looked up past Alice and the deep, warm, oaky scent mixed with tobacco that alerted her to the presence. It was an energy that drove everyone to look toward the doorway.

Everyone except Alice.

"My God. Kathryn Anderson." Wes was the first to speak.

Alice felt her knees weaken and she groped for the chair near to her, to lean against it and steady herself.

Wes moived past her and began speaking to Kathryn in excited tones. Kathryn replied in a husky, deepened voice that Alice hardly recognized. Kathryn's smoky voice uttered forced greetings to Wes and Meredith and then Larry.

Alice finally had the nerve to turn, as if sensing that Kathryn was looking directly at her.

Their eyes met.

Alice slumped against the chair.

She could feel the others looking at them, could almost hear their wandering minds.

She wished they could have seen one another again – after all these years - alone and not before so many people.

"Alice," Kathryn's voice broke.

Alice couldn't speak.

Kathryn in the flesh was something else. Certainly, she had grown older, her features had aged, but she was still the same woman she had always been. Her eyes were so dark and shuttered and unreadable. Her blonde hair was coiffed and styled in her signature way. Her dress clung to her tall, tight body that seemed even smaller than it had all those years ago. And though she looked not so different, there was a fragileness that had formed, that made Alice suddenly want to embrace her, to protect her.

They gravitated towards one another, the others forgotten for the moment.

So close to the woman, Alice could see that Kathryn's wide, sleepless eyes shone with unshed tears.

They stood toe-to-toe and it surprised Alice how she had expected it to be different, yet it felt the same. After all this time she was as enthralled as she had always been.

Alice reached for Kathryn, put her arms about her and pulled her close for a hug. Kathryn's body was rigid in her embrace.

They stepped away from one another.

Alice felt the threat of her own tears. She wiped delicately at her eyes, afraid that she might ruin her make-up.

"You look well. Very tiny, but well." Kathryn spoke and Alice could smell the thinly concealed alcohol on her breath. Kathryn lifted a cigarette to her lips and, with an unsteady hand, lit it.

She had not changed.

They were called to places behind the curtain, the two parted, thankfully, before Alice could break down in front of everyone. The show was to begin momentarily.

They stood beside one another in the dark backstage, Wes whispered things to Kathryn, making her laugh that deep, warm, rich smoky laughter that made Alice's knees weak. Larry tried to speak to Alice, but Alice was acutely aware of only Kathryn.

"And now, please welcome George Harwell played by Larry Mitchell."

Alice felt her heart pounding in her chest as she watched Larry walk forward, out into the light of the set.

She felt a hand at the small of her back. A warmth pressed against her side. "I've missed you." Kathryn's voice whispered low and sweet into her ear.

"Oh." Alice whimpered.

"...Kay Bernhardt, played by Alice Kincaid."

They were calling her, but she didn't feel as if she could move her legs. The hand at her lower back urged her forward.

She plastered on a smile and walked toward the light, waving and smiling as the studio audience greeted her with wild applause.

Chapter Six

Kathryn

"And Wes' gorgeous wife Paula Peterson played by Kathryn Anderson."

The crowd's roar of applause was a deafening wall of noise, the blinding lights causing everything about her to swirl in and out of focus. She walked with careful steps, plastering on some semblance of a smile. Their hostess for the day, Holly something, an attractive enough brunette with full, brightly painted pink lips, was holding out her arms to welcome Kathryn. So Kathryn walked toward her, embraced her as if they knew one another.

Kathryn was grateful when Holly guided her to the chair designated for her. She sank as gracefully as she could manage onto its surface.

She realized she had been placed next to Alice. Alice who looked so very poised atop her chair. Alice, who was looking at her curiously.

Oh, how she had missed those gentle, curious eyes.

"And the one and only Wes Peterson played by Wes Goodwin!" The announcement pierced her ears and she remembered what it was they were here to do. She applauded along with the rest of the room.

The room seemed to tilt and stretch to the side.

She was warm under her collar; the lights were so fucking bright.

Perspiration had broken out on her forehead.

She wondered if her hearing was going. Holly's voice was speaking but it took every last effort for Kathryn to focus on the words that were fading in and out. Wes, she could tell, was laughing about something. When she turned to look at Alice, she saw that she, too, was laughing.

Their eyes met again.

Kathryn's foot tapped. Perhaps she'd overdone it on the powder. There was hardly any left, but she'd needed it. She'd been dead that morning.

"And Kathryn," she heard her name and looked at Holly, watching as her hot pink lips enunciated the words. "I hear that you came all the way from Germany just to be with us. You've been living there for several years now, haven't you?"

Kathryn nodded, re-crossed her legs. "Why yes. I've been there for a number of years."

"Still making pictures?"

"Oh, yes. My husband is a director, and he keeps me quite occupied."

"Now, some of us in America have been able to see these pictures and those of us who might have say that they're quite a departure from your role as Paula Peterson."

"Well, yes. I think you could say that." She could feel Alice's eyes upon her as she spoke. She wondered if Alice had seen the pictures. "Europe has very different values for their cinema. My husband is in the business of making art. Not necessarily feature films for the family."

Alice shifted, but Kathryn could feel that she was still looking at her.

Holly was looking at her curiously. "What did you think of your character on the Wes Goodwin show?" She was steering her back to safe territory. "We've just gone through quite a revolution in America in regards to women's rights. Paula was a good housewife which is very different from what most American women today want for themselves. Why do you think the show still resonates with so many?"

"Paula was a housewife, but she was much more than that. She was the brains behind everything Wes did."

Wes laughed at that. "She was my straight woman. Always righting my wrongs."

"And yes, she was a housewife, but what else could she have been on television in the 50s? That was a woman's place and Hollywood and America wanted women to remember it. Now, now I think women are more capable of making other choices."

Holly gave her another bemused smile. "And that brings us to Kay. Because she was not a wife on the show."

"But she wanted to be." Alice's voice came from beside Kathryn. "That was her whole objective."

"Do you think that's what made her acceptable to audiences?"

"I think it was the only thing that could make her singleness accepted, yes." Alice confirmed, shifting bracelets up her arm as she spoke. Her wrists were as small and delicate as Kathryn remembered them.

"Do you think her eventual marriage to George in the final season was what she would have wanted?"

"It's all she knew to want." Alice answered simply.

That ending had been such a copout. Total bullshit. Kay should have been allowed to stay single for the rest of her life. "It was a shit way to end the show." Kathryn blurted out.

All eyes went to her.

She felt Alice's hand cover her arm. Her glorious laughter filled the awkward pause. "I think she means that it was rather hasty. When the network decided not to renew the show they needed a tidy ending. I think the marriage made sense. Kay and George knew each other well enough and had a certain connection."

"Yeah, they really had a great connection." Kathryn snorted. What a laugh. Alice and Larry having any connection at all.

Kathryn pulled her arm away from Alice's, the touch far too intimate. Alice's fingers had been digging just a little too deeply, her hand too warm and soft.

Holly quickly shifted focus to the others, asking Wes and Larry about their favorite episodes and various tidbits about filming. Kathryn could feel her high receding. She felt Alice looking at her, watching her. And then she realized that her own foot was tapping incessantly. She placed a hand over her thigh to try and still the nervous tic.

"And that's commercial. Take five everyone." A producer called out.

Kathryn shot up from her seat, pulling at her mic. This show had been a terrible idea.

She moved hastily, not listening as the crew members asked what she was doing and where she was going. She handed the mic pack to someone and then disappeared into the green room she had been assigned. She closed and locked the door, placing a cigarette between her lips before fumbling through her purse for the baggie and mirror.

She just needed another line, just another hit to make it through. It was nearly over, wasn't it?

She snorted the coke and made sure that there was no trace of powder on her face.

Someone was knocking at her door.

She hid the baggie in her purse and opened it. A rather perturbed young-looking man was holding her mic, a make-up girl behind him. "Time for touch ups and then you have to get back out there. And no more outbursts. You're here to promote the show, not make it look bad." He instructed.

Kathryn rolled her eyes to the ceiling, then proceeded to smoke while the girl touched up her face, wiping the sweat from her brow, her neck, and redoing the powder about her mouth.

She caught sight of Alice in her dressing room mirror. The woman was standing at the door, looking at her with some indecipherable expression in her eyes.

But as soon as Kathryn turned to call for her, the apparition disappeared.

Had Alice really even been there?

"We have to get back out there." The man had returned to stick the mic pack back where it had been without even asking her if he could put his hand where he had.

Kathryn was rushed back to the stage and she took her seat again.

"Are you all right?" Alice leaned forward to whisper.

Kathryn took a sip of water that had been placed next to their chairs. "Just fine." She spoke without looking at Alice.

The cameras were rolling again in a matter of minutes. They were in the home stretch now, weren't they? This charade couldn't last all day.

"And now what the audience is really here for." Holly was speaking again. She turned and looked directly at Kathryn, then Alice. "Paula and Kay shared a very close friendship on the show. Our audience wants to know if you still share this same friendship today."

Kathryn's eyebrows shot to the ceiling. Well. "Sure."

"Yes." Alice spoke at the same moment. "Of course. We keep in touch. When we can." She was smiling as she spoke the lie.

Kathryn laughed. "I mean, it's rather hard. Me being on

a different continent and all. And things weren't always so picture perfect behind the scenes, you know."

Holly had a worried smile plastered on her face. "You mean that you didn't get along?"

"Oh, we certainly got along. We got along just fine." Kathryn smiled as she sat back in her seat.

"So you still call and write one another?" Holly worried her lip.

"Oh, yes." Alice sighed.

Kathryn's foot began tapping again. The interview could not end soon enough. The man from the dressing room was motioning at her, telling her to smile. So she plastered on the best award-winning smile she could muster. She spoke when acknowledged. She tried not to speak out of turn.

Her mind kept wandering back to the question: Did they still keep in touch?

"And that's a wrap." Someone called out.

Kathryn stopped smiling.

After the annoying man took her mic, Kathryn stood and exited the stage as quickly as possible. She was sweating profusely. She closed the dressing room door and did a quick bump of coke then lit a cigarette. She had to get out of there. She couldn't stay another minute in this insufferable place with that far too bubbly Holly woman and Alice…oh, Alice.

Kathryn opened the door to leave but found Alice standing on the other side, hand raised and poised as if to knock.

"Oh God. What?" Kathryn braced herself for this confrontation.

"Kathryn, are you…are you all right?"

Kathryn wiped at her nose and rolled her eyes. "Please, we don't have to do this."

"Kathryn." Alice shook her head, eyes filled with worry that Kathryn resented, did not feel she deserved. "You can't tell me…you can't tell me that you miss me and then…that was unfair." There were tears gathering in Alice's big, beautiful eyes. The same seeing eyes they had always been.

"Then forget I ever said it." Kathryn tried to brush past her but Alice grabbed her.

"No, you…don't do this. Don't run away."

"Run away?" Kathryn laughed. "I'm not running. I'm leaving."

"Damn it, Kathryn." Alice snapped. "You don't look well."

"What do you care?" Kathryn shot back, smoked furiously at her cigarette.

Alice looked stricken at this. "Jesus, Kathryn."

"Let's not drag this out. We made it through, let's leave it at that." Kathryn insisted.

"Kathryn…"

"Alice." Kathryn met her eyes and the intensity of contact made her chest hurt.

Alice's beautiful, sad face suddenly morphed into anger. "Fine. Fine. Let's go another twenty years without talking then. See if I care."

Kathryn sniffed. "Let me go."

Alice stepped back, leaning against the opposite wall.

Kathryn forced herself to move forward, to leave without looking back.

She couldn't look back.

But oh, how she wanted to look back.

It was not until she had been taken back to her hotel that she allowed the tears to overcome her, and she drowned them with the remaining bottles of alcohol in the room.

Oh, Alice.

Part II

Chapter Seven

Alice

Beverly Hills, 1956

Frank was watching television in the living room when the phone rang.

Alice startled at the sound, nearly dropped the package of fudge cookies she had finally grasped from the back of the pantry. Standing there indecisively as she had been for the past ten minutes, it felt as if fate were telling her to leave the cookies. But they beckoned to her, offering her some solace from her swirling mind.

The phone rang out again.

She settled the cookies atop the table and moved deftly to lift the phone from its cradle on the kitchen wall.

"Hello?" She asked, staring longingly at the cookies.

"Alice?" The voice breathed her name on the other end of the line.

Alice's knees went weak. She leaned against the wall to steady herself.

"Who's calling so late?" Frank called from the living room, his voice distracted, the television loud.

"Uh – it's, uh…" Alice called back, pressing her hand against the mouthpiece, but she could still hear the deep laugh on the other end of the line. "It's Kathryn." She nearly whispered the name, feeling a blush rising to her cheeks. She was grateful that they were in separate rooms just then.

Frank said nothing – as if he hadn't heard, or didn't care.

"I'm…I'm sorry." Alice whispered into the phone, unaccustomed to her co-star calling her at home and at such a late hour.

"Don't be. I didn't mean to intrude upon your evening." Kathryn's silvery voice flowed deeper over the telephone line.

"Oh, it's not so eventful." Alice eyed the cookies sitting out but felt a strange twist in her stomach that suddenly made them seem as if they were the least appetizing things in the world.

She hadn't been able to keep a thing down for days. Not since…

And here was the woman on the phone, calling her at home.

"I wanted to apologize." Kathryn's voice had grown smaller somehow.

"Apologize?" Alice pressed her forehead against the wallpapered kitchen wall, heart beating a mile a minute.

"It was – well, you see Charles and I had had a huge fight Friday morning. Just a really big, awful brawl, and I…I didn't mean, well I hope you weren't…upset that I…"

Alice felt her stomach knot. The thought of it, the way their lips had met in the darkness of the sound stage. It had not stopped playing on repeat for days. Kathryn's sad eyes, the way smoke curled from her lips, the feel of her hand as it had pressed against Alice's cheek. She felt it all as if it were happening again in the present. "No." Upset was the furthest emotion from her mind.

She needed to sit down.

"Oh." Was all Kathryn said in response to that.

They stayed on the line in silence, as if neither knew what to say next.

"Well, then." Kathryn sounded as if she might just hang up, and Alice did not want to lose this connection. Even though they would see one another the following day - as they always saw one another during filming on Monday mornings – they might never speak of what happened again and the thought sent a panic racing through Alice.

"Yes." Was all Alice could say, her throat dry.

"You…you're all right?" Kathryn asked and Alice was grateful for the continuation, grateful that she was not about to hang up.

"Oh, yes. I…I am." Alice sat down at the kitchen table, toyed with the edge of the cookie package. "Are you…all right? I mean with Charles…"

Kathryn's deep, throaty laughter carried over the line. "Of course. It's, you know, the ups and downs of marriage. Sometimes we love one another and other times, well, we certainly get into some real rows. But I'm fine, darling. Just fine."

The elegant endearment sent a wave of pleasure pulsing through Alice inexplicably.

"Listen, I'll let you go." Kathryn cut the conversation short, as if she were keeping Alice from something important. But it was only the cookies and her own meager will that Kathryn was protecting her from, and Alice didn't want to disconnect but felt foolish for this want.

She nodded as if Kathryn could see her from across the city.

"I'll see you tomorrow, Alice. Have a nice evening." And then Kathryn disconnected the line.

It hummed in Alice's ear.

Alice stared at the cookies before her.

Carefully she stood, hung the phone back on the wall, and reached for the package of cookies. She grabbed them up, moved through the kitchen, to the living room where Frank sat – half-sleeping, half-transfixed by the television before him – and then down the hall to the bathroom where she locked herself inside and slid down next to the tub on the tiled floor and opened the package and proceeded to eat every last cookie.

Kathryn did not directly acknowledge her the following day. When Alice arrived at the studio the woman was in conversation with their director, Stephen. It seemed they were discussing something about the script, Kathryn's hands leisurely in her slack's pockets, eyes following Stephen's face as he spoke. Alice stood hidden in the hallway, viewing the woman as if she had not been working with her for the past two years, as if seeing her for the first time.

Her blonde hair was swept up at the nape of her neck; she wore glasses and her face seemed hardened, focused.

As she spoke to Stephen she happened to glance up and for a brief, fleeting moment her eyes found Alice.

Alice colored a deep shade of red and turned on her heels to walk off to her dressing room, feeling as if she had been caught seeing Kathryn in the nude.

That thought made Alice color an even deeper shade of red. For heaven's sakes!

They worked through the new script that day – the reading followed by preliminary staging. Kathryn's plotline had her hardly interacting with Alice at all so they drifted around one another all day, but never had a moment more than to exchange a few pleasantries.

"I hope I didn't call too late."

"Not at all."

"Kathryn, we need you on stage left."

Alice was dismissed early. She drove directly home, thoughts all tangled.

How was it that Kathryn could go on unaffected by what she had done?

Alice's skin crawled at the memory of it.

She cooked for Frank that evening. He arrived home, as always, by six. They ate in relative silence. Five years and he felt more and more like a stranger with each passing day. He had believed in her, had pushed her to come to Los Angeles, to make a go at it on television. He had gotten her where she was, and now he seemed displeased with her. She couldn't understand him.

He returned to his usual spot after dinner, mindlessly watching television and smoking a cigarette.

She cleaned the dishes. She tidied the kitchen. She was grateful there was not another package of cookies hidden away.

She removed her script for the week from her bag and reviewed her lines at the kitchen table. In the midst of attempting to remember a line the phone began to ring.

She stared at the receiver as if it were a foreign object, afraid to touch it as if it might burn her.

It was nearing eight in the evening.

The phone rang again.

"Would you answer the damn phone?" Frank growled from the living room.

She stood and reached for it on the third ring.

"Hello?"

"I didn't get a chance to tell you how much I liked the necklace you were wearing today." Kathryn's voice, low and haunting.

Her necklace? She glanced down to see what it was she had worn. A simple emerald beaded necklace. She had thrown it on haphazardly at the last moment, not even thinking much of it. When had Kathryn even noticed it?

She'd hardly looked at her all day. And why was she calling her to tell her this now?

"Why, thank you. But it's not…well it's hardly anything of value."

"It's the color." She could hear a wistfulness in the woman's voice, as if she had been drinking. "It complements your eyes."

Why had she called? It could not have been to speak of a silly necklace. When had she paid attention to the color of Alice's eyes?

Alice, confused, accepted the compliment.

She could hear Kathryn light a cigarette on the other end of the phone, the exhale magnified by the phone receiver. "I hope you don't mind that I called. It's only – well, Charles is away."

Charles was away and Kathryn had thought to call her?

"He's never around long. Always working out of the damn New York office. There's a new show going up on Broadway next month." Kathryn explained. "It's all right, isn't it, if I call you?"

Alice looked toward the living room where she could see the light from the television playing on the wall. "Of course."

Kathryn laughed deeply. "That Frank of yours wasn't upset about last night?"

Alice laughed at this. "Are you kidding? He's not aware of the world around him when that television is on."

Kathryn exhaled on the other end of the line. "Best we keep him entertained, then."

Alice had the sensation in the pit of her stomach that she was doing something she should not. Alice had never felt remotely close enough with the starlet to count her as a close, personal friend even after all of their time working together. Kathryn had remained an elusive, closed off Hollywood star.

Yet, Kathryn had called her, had wanted to speak to *her*. Certainly Kathryn might have other acquaintances to keep her entertained, but she had chosen Alice for some inexplicable reason.

"Men, you know, are quite simple creatures when you come right down to it." Kathryn mused.

Alice agreed.

"Women, now women are a completely different breed. Aren't we? And we don't hardly get any of the clout we deserve. We just go along with whatever these men tell us to do. I mean, Jesus, Stephen just had no clue what the hell he wanted today, and I saw it all clear as day. But did he listen to me? Of course not." She exhaled again. "He tells me I'm being difficult. I mean would he say that to Wes? Certainly not. Wes can never do anything wrong."

Alice had never heard the inner workings of Kathryn's mind. Had never witnessed these moments of frustrations she spoke of. She felt as if she had been walking blindly for the past two years because she never questioned Stephen. She did as she was told.

"Oh, I don't mean to go on. I'm sorry to have mentioned it."

"No, I…uh, I don't mind." This, this was a revelation.

"Well, I shouldn't complain to you about it. It's not being fair. And Stephen adores you."

"Oh," Alice felt her cheeks flush. "I don't know about all of that."

"Well it's true." Kathryn spoke resolutely. "Maybe I've been around too long."

"I don't think so! You know," she settled down into the chair at the kitchen table. "I must admit that I saw you several times when you were in *Lady be Good* on Broadway." Alice conspiratorially admitted – as if this late-night phone call might give her the ability to say the things she had never been able to while at the studio. If Kathryn could confide in her, perhaps she might confide in her as well.

Kathryn laughed at this, a deep, real laughter that thrilled Alice down to her toes. "No; that was a horrible show!"

"You made it worth it." Alice smiled, traced the patterns on the tablecloth with her finger.

"Well, I certainly never knew you were such a fan." Kathryn chuckled.

Alice felt the flush return. "Please, forget I mentioned it."

"Well now I can't." And there was a smile in her voice.

Chapter Eight

Kathryn

Kathryn sat her script on the table and removed her glasses to pass a hand over her face. The words were all jumbling together. The plotline was a ridiculous mess, but George, the head script writer, had not wanted her suggestions of how to improve it. She let it go, gave in to the absurd so that she now struggled to make what was there work in her mind.

The house was silent around her. Mariella had left for the evening after bringing her a cup of tea.

She got up to pour herself a nip of brandy, as if it might assuage the oncoming headache.

Charles hadn't called.

She wondered just what - or who - he had gotten up to. She could only imagine one of those young things that threw themselves at him relentlessly might have captured his attentions for the evening.

Luckily, they never stuck. He was devoted to her, after all.

Kathryn sunk down into the chair near the telephone. She lifted the tumbler of brandy to her lips and drank it back.

And wasn't she devoted to him?

A sardonic smile curled itself on her lips.

She lifted the phone, dialed a familiar number.

It rang twice before the woman on the other end picked up.

"Kathryn, my God. Is it really you?"

"Helen, darling, it's been ages, hasn't it?" Kathryn lifted the ivory top off her cigarette box.

"Far, far too long."

Kathryn toyed with a cigarette, placing it between her lips. "Charles is away."

"I see."

She lit the cigarette. "He's opening a show on Broadway."

"Would you care for a drink?"

She would like nothing more.

They met at Bar Marmont, their favorite haunt. Kathryn had pieced herself together, slid into a black cocktail dress, pinned her hair up, and applied a deathly shade of red to her lips.

Though every eye was on her when she walked in the room, no one caught her eye the way Helen Laurence did. The woman was curled in a booth, smoking a cigarette between cherry red lips, flaxen hair curled about her face engrained with hints of age, eyes lined in black, wrinkling ever so when she smiled up at Kathryn.

She pressed her lips lightly to Kathryn's cheek in greeting. "Well don't you look a picture?"

"I could say the same about you, but I'm afraid it'd go to your head." Helen, the deliciously aging actress, deadpanned. "I haven't heard from you for months. I thought you'd forgotten all about me."

Kathryn laughed as she sat beside the older woman.

"How could I?" She ordered a drink from a passing waiter and then allowed Helen to light her cigarette.

"How's the show going?" Helen asked, turning so she could take all of Kathryn in, those dark eyes a warm retreat from the world which Kathryn so often liked to escape.

Kathryn shrugged. "Same as always."

"Staying out of trouble, I hope." Helen eyed her, seemed to know that Kathryn came to her for two things.

"I've been a saint." Kathryn laughed.

Helen's manicured red fingernail trailed back and forth against Kathryn's forearm. "Uh huh."

Kathryn downed the drink that was placed before her. Helen watched the action, a hint of concern etched in her brow. Kathryn ignored it.

"I have a room upstairs." Helen lowered her voice.

Kathryn tapped off her cigarette, nodding her consent.

They didn't touch, not even one accidental brush, until the hotel room door closed behind them. And then Helen captured her face in her hands and they were kissing.

Kathryn didn't make it home until the following morning. Her head throbbed. She downed two aspirin and spiked her coffee with a splash of vodka. She made it to the studio five minutes late, sunglasses hiding her tired eyes.

It was after she had rounded the corner to the set that she happened upon Alice. Alice glanced sheepishly at her at first and then gave her a more pointed, concerned glance.

Jesus, the woman was gorgeous. Kathryn had thought that perhaps a night with Helen might appease her, but upon seeing Alice - that look in particular that cut through Kathryn, made her feel impossibly seen – well, her night with Helen felt a far away, distant memory.

"Late night. With this Godawful script." Kathryn whispered, reassuring Alice.

She heard Alice laugh as she moved past her, catching a whiff of her intoxicating perfume as she did so. She moved to where Wes stood with Stephen. Wes grabbed her in a too tight hug. She felt like vomiting but made it through the rehearsals that day without a hitch – mindful of the shit script, doing her best to make something out of the farce.

Charles called that evening. "You went out last night?"

Kathryn baulked at this. "I saw Helen."

Charles' loud laughter rang out on the line. "Well, now, Kathryn. It's nice of you to give an old gal a good time."

"Yeah?" Kathryn waited for his laughter to die down. "At least she delivers."

"Oh, you wound me."

"Yeah right." Kathryn rolled her eyes. "Why the hell are you calling?"

"Because my wife didn't answer when I called last night."

"I figured you were busy yourself."

"I was. But I called when I got back to the apartment."

"Well then we'll chalk it up to my being asleep and call it a wash."

"Sure, sure. Hey, but I got you a deal, yeah worked out something real nice for when the show goes on hiatus. A picture."

"Yeah, a movie?"

"You betcha baby!" He explained the ins and outs of it, told her Howard would be by with the script. It sounded promising, but she would wait until she read the script to pass judgment on it.

They hung up and Kathryn lit a cigarette, poured herself another finger of whiskey and settled before the grand piano. Cigarette between her teeth, she began to play a Ravel concerto she had learned years ago, ash dropping everywhere as she did. The chords flowed clunkily, one from the other. She was not a great concert pianist, but there was some kind of solace in the feel of her fingers rolling over the keys. There was an enjoyment in the way the piano responded delicately to her indelicate touch.

She thought of Alice.

She fumbled a phrase. Stopped, tried it again.

She shouldn't call her as often as she did. It was crossing a line.

She trilled two notes and became fixated by the sound of it, lingering too long before flowing into the next phrase.

Alice. When had she taken notice of Alice? She was young. The studio had wanted someone young, fresh. And Alice had come to the show as a fresh faced twenty-six-year-old. Kathryn had snubbed her, kept her distance from her – because what could a twenty-six-year-old possibly know.

Two years later, she was older, she was coming into her own as an actress and as a woman.

Kathryn pressed heavily into a low note, letting the sound die out before allowing the next high section to move through her right hand. Heavy chords in the left were enunciated towards a dramatic climax of themes.

The concerto ended. She kept the sustaining pedal pressed firmly down, listening as the final chord rang out in the empty room.

No, she should not be calling Alice late in the evenings.

She sucked at her cigarette, tapping off ash on a nearby ashtray, and lifted her drink to her lips.

She released the pedal and the fading chord died out instantly.

The room fell silent again.

Oh, it was a terrible idea to call now.

She knew nothing of Alice's husband, Frank. Only what she had observed on Fridays when he would come to the tapings. The way he watched Alice, kept his eyes firmly fixed upon her as if afraid she might slip away. Kathryn had come across them quarreling one evening backstage. Alice had looked older than her years - so cross, shoulders taut with tension.

Kathryn knew men like him.

She slid into the chair by the phone, tapping her fingers against the table.

Another sip of her drink and she lifted the receiver, dialing the number she had committed to memory some nights before.

It rang three times before a man's voice answered the phone.

"Who the hell is this?"

And Kathryn promptly hung up the phone, heart pounding in her ears.

Chapter Nine

Alice

She was deep in conversation with Stephen and Wes, Alice noticed, when she glanced up from refilling her coffee cup. Alice watched as Kathryn stood, hand in slacks pocket, cardigan draped over shoulders, eyes hidden behind her glasses, cigarette in her other hand, listening intently as Wes discussed something animatedly with Stephen. Then Stephen responded before Kathryn shoved at him and laughed.

Alice felt something in her chest tighten and then release.

What was happening to her? Certainly she had appreciated Kathryn from the beginning – having known so much about her as a celebrity, but that admiration had faded away when Kathryn had become nothing more than a colleague. For the past two years they had worked side-by-side, day after day. The glamour and mystery had all but faded until...

It was as if it had all come back to her. The nervousness, the shyness, the admiration she had felt all those years ago upon first meeting the woman. As if she were awestruck by her presence, no longer able to simply walk up and greet her and the others, so Alice hung off in the wings, sipping coffee and reviewing her lines, waiting for the rehearsal to begin.

But as she glanced up from her script she caught Kathryn looking in her direction.

Their eyes met. Kathryn's lips quirked upward.

It was not until after rehearsing a scene together – Alice thankfully able to pull herself together enough to not flub her lines or act foolish in front of the crew (and *her*) – that they found themselves alone. Kathryn lit a cigarette as they walked toward their dressing rooms. Alice felt tongue-tied in her presence. She was being ridiculous.

"I like the direction you're taking our scene." Kathryn spoke.

Alice liked her use of the word 'our'.

"Yeah?" Alice felt her cheeks color.

"It's better than what George gave us to work with. I think it's the more logical way to play it, and if you do it like that again I think Stephen will have to agree. He knows it's better than what George wrote." Kathryn inhaled on her cigarette.

They were nearing her dressing room. She would disappear inside and Alice wouldn't see her again until after their break. Alice felt bereft at this but helplessly unable to keep up the conversation.

They slowed before Kathryn's door. Kathryn turned to face Alice, pinning her with a curious look. "Is something the matter?" She had graciously lowered her voice for people were always nearby.

Alice shook her head. "No, no...I..." Alice glanced around before lowering her gaze. "No, I just...did you call? Last night?"

Kathryn exhaled a stream of smoke. Her lips curled into a smile. "No."

Oh. Alice nodded. Then tried to laugh. "I thought, well… good. That's good."

Kathryn rested her hand against the frame of her dressing room door. "Did you want me to have called?"

Alice pressed her lips together, lost.

Kathryn was laughing as she brought the cigarette to her lips. "Jesus, darling."

"I – I've been enjoying speaking with you. I was worried that – well, Frank, he…"

"Well, listen, honey. How about if you want to hear from me, you give me a call. And then that won't be an issue?" Kathryn graciously suggested.

"I don't want to bother…"

"Oh, you won't be." Kathryn cut her off, looking off past Alice. "George, if you have a minute I'd like to talk something over with you."

And just as easily as Alice had thought she might have snagged Kathryn's undivided attention, she was dismissed.

But with a request. She had been asked to call her. Whenever she wanted.

Alice walked back to her dressing room, collapsing on the little couch in the corner.

Had she meant it, or was she simply being nice?

Everything seemed all mixed up, Alice no longer certain if she was meant to carry on their nightly conversations or if she should leave it. Kathryn had said that she had not tried to call the previous evening, but Alice had sworn she'd heard Frank answer the phone when she'd been in the bath.

She sighed. Perhaps it had been a wrong number.

Alice reached for the apple she'd brought, longing for a chocolate chip cookie instead.

It was later that evening with her hands soapy from doing the dishes after dinner that the phone rang and she felt her heart skip a beat. Kathryn, Kathryn would be calling. Surely the woman would call her again, for Alice did not want their nightly chats to dissipate into thin air. What had happened behind the sound stage all those weeks before already seemed like some far away, intangible memory.

Yes, Alice would be certain to answer this time, before Frank could reach the phone.

She lifted the receiver with renewed excitement.

"Hello there." She said.

"Well, now Alice, is that anyway to answer your phone? Were you expecting a call from someone? Is Frank out late?"

Alice felt her excitement wane, fade away into a terrible knot in her stomach. "No, Mother…I only thought…" but it was useless to explain - and how could she?

"It's no matter, dear. I'm glad I got you on the phone. You're so hard to reach nowadays! I call and you're on set, or I call and you're out and about. It's almost as if you were avoiding me, heavens."

Alice rolled her eyes to the ceiling, really wishing she'd stopped by the store to buy another bag of those cookies she really liked.

"Tell me, dear, are you well?"

"What do you mean, mother? Of course I'm well."

"You're looking rather out of sorts."

"What does that mean?" Alice pressed a hand to her forehead, nerves beginning to pinch together, signaling an oncoming migraine.

"It's just your weight, dear. Now, I only say this because I'm your mother. And I want you to look the best you can. You see, dear, the whole world is watching you now, watching my darling, sweet little Alice. And they've come to know you as you looked at the beginning of the show. And I've been watching very closely each Saturday evening, dear and it seems that you're putting on weight again. Have you not been eating well?"

Alice pressed her nails into the palm of her hand. "I've been eating just fine, Mother."

"I mean, is everything all right? Is it something with Frank? Have you been treating him well? You know how men can be. Especially in a situation like yours. Men are not used to watching a woman be successful. It could cause problems. I told you this when you got married. If he's upset with you — well, you certainly need to make sure you're taking care of him. Do you understand?"

Alice thought of the one too many nights she'd waited up until Frank had fallen asleep just so she might not have to do what it was her mother was now suggesting. Which only made her want to bury herself in something sweet and sinful because she *knew* that she was not doing her duty as a wife. Had not been good at doing it for some time now.

"Alice, you listen to me. I've talked to the doctor. He thinks you should be on a pill, this Dexamyl. You can get it prescribed to you, no problem."

"Mother! I don't want to be on a pill. Would you just leave it?"

"Alice, whatever is the matter with you? It's not like you to raise your voice at me."

Alice bit her lip.

"If you're not going to take care of yourself, then I've no choice but to come there and do it myself."

"No." Alice whispered, felt tears swimming in her eyes.

"Alice, dear, you're suffering. I can hear it in your voice. You *need* me."

Alice's grip on the telephone felt terribly strong. She had the horrible urge to rip the phone from the wall and hurl it as hard as she could into the kitchen window. She imagined the glass shattering and flying everywhere.

"Alice, I'll be on the next flight I can get."

It was Frank who found her fuming in the kitchen, slamming about in cabinets in search of something, anything.

"What the hell's happening here?" He demanded, watching her as she found a bag of chocolate chips she had forgotten about.

She slid down the wall, sat down cross-legged and stuck her hand into the bag.

"Mother's coming to visit."

Chapter Ten

Kathryn

"You've got to be fucking kidding me." Kathryn threw the script in Howard's face.

Howard looked up at her from his desk, catching the offending item in his hands, the pages folding every which way. "Now, Kathryn, it's a great part."

"I'm thirty-five, Howard! I'm not on my deathbed. I mean, it's rich. The role of the mother. And who, pray tell, is going to be playing my daughter?"

"Lillian Demille. She's already signed the contract." Howard straightened the edges of the script and sat it down on the edge of his desk.

"Lillian Demille? Why, but she's ten years younger than me! How the hell do you expect anyone to believe that I'm her *mother*. For Christ's sake." Kathryn sank into the chair before Howard's desk and fumbled for the cigarettes in her purse.

"Care for a drink?" Howard asked, as if to pacify her.

She grunted in response.

He got up to pour them both a dash of whiskey. "It's not your fault, doll. They're not casting for realism nowadays. Not in the films, anyway. It's an unfair market, everybody wants them younger and younger. Soon some twenty-year-old is going to be playing the mother."

Kathryn shrank into her chair, accepting the drink he offered. "It's offensive."

"Oh, come now. You're not getting any younger."

Kathryn eyed him through a cloud of smoke. "And neither are you."

Howard offered her a sad smile from his perch on the edge of his desk.

Kathryn leaned forward, resting her elbows on her knees. "Are you telling me, as my agent, that there is *nothing* else out there? Not a single goddamn movie I could play the title role in?"

Howard shrugged his shoulders.

"You think this is a good role?" She pointed toward the offending script.

"I quite thought you could do it justice. It's not some two-bit part, doll."

Kathryn sat back and eyed him as she smoked. "I oughta fire you."

Howard didn't even flinch. "Ah, come off it. I get threats all day long from actresses half as talented as you. But I'll tell you what I always tell them."

"Yeah, what's that?"

"You're all lucky to have me. Especially right now the way things are going in this business."

Kathryn downed the whiskey and slammed the crystal tumbler upon the table beside her. "Oh, go to hell." And she stood up, leaving Howard and the script behind.

She was rummaging through the liquor cabinet at home,

already unsteady on her feet, when she heard the unexpected voice come from behind her.

"Well now, there's my darling wife. I see you got a head start. I'm hurt."

Kathryn turned on him, cigarette clenched between her teeth, a bottle of vodka in hand. She eyed Charles through a hazy gaze and felt a spiteful smile form. "Well, well, well. Look what the cat dragged in. I wasn't expecting you."

"Nor was I expecting to be home." Charles pulled at his tie as he walked toward her. He took the vodka bottle from her hand and leaned down to press his lips against hers. "Had a little problem with a movie going up out here and had to come save the day. Thought I might stay the night. See my wife." He explained as he moved to pour the vodka into two glasses, handing one back to Kathryn.

"How nice of you to remember little ol' me." She fell into the chair near the window.

Charles collapsed into the seat opposite. He stared out at the pool. "Howard called me. Said you hated the script."

"It's a shit script." Kathryn lifted the glass to her lips and drank the vodka. "I mean you could have told me that they wanted me to play the mother to someone I would have had to have birthed when I was ten. Does that make any sense to you, Charles?"

Charles laughed. "I see. It's not the script then. The script is good."

"Come off it." Kathryn snapped, stubbed out her cigarette.

"Read it again. You'll like it."

Kathryn looked at her husband. He had always been right. Right about getting her on the stage, right about her first picture, right about dipping into television. She did trust his business acumen, knew he wouldn't steer her wrong. But this, it felt humiliating. "There's really nothing else, is there?"

Charles shook his head. "Right now? No." He scooted

forward on his chair, moving a bit closer to Kathryn. "It would be good for you."

"Why is that?"

"Oh, come now, Kathryn." He reached for her cigarette box to extract one for himself. She watched him light it.

"No, what is all of this about? I'm not good enough to get something else?"

"It's not that at all. People don't question your talent."

She felt the 'but' on the tip of his tongue. She glared at him, dared him to go on.

"They think, well, darling, to be frank, they find you rather difficult."

Kathryn laughed at this. "Difficult. Really? Difficult."

Charles watched her carefully. He had never spoken to her delicately. They had always been very open with one another and they did not mince words.

"They think I'm difficult because I'm a woman and they know I could do a better job than all of them. The studio executives, the script writers, the goddamn directors…*all* of them."

Charles was laughing then. Laughing with glee. "You know what, Kathryn, I believe you very well could."

Kathryn did not find it hilarious. She was furious. But when Charles put his arms about her, kissed her, she did not object. He kissed her with delight. And before he could undo her shirt he pulled back and laughed again. "It's too goddamn bad you weren't born a man."

She let him take her upstairs.

He passed out before nine, the time difference always making him exhausted when he got back to Los Angeles. Kathryn wrapped herself up in a robe and stole away from their bedroom. She padded down the stairs, staring out at the glittering pool that was illuminated in the night. It shimmered against the walls of the home.

She made her way to the wet bar, willing the disaster her mind had become to abate. Difficult. She was difficult?

No, she was right.

She poured herself another glass of vodka and then sat down near the phone. Her eyes danced to the clock on the wall. It was nearly nine. Not so late, but not so early.

Alice hadn't called her for days.

Kathryn lit a cigarette and lifted the phone from its cradle. She listened to the dial tone. Her hand shook as her fingers dialed out the number.

The phone rang twice, then a third time, then a fourth and Kathryn very nearly hung up the phone, but there was a need that burned inside of her. It was before the fifth ring that the phone connected.

"Hello?" A frantic, breathless voice came on the line.

"Alice, oh – Alice, am I calling too late?"

"No! No, not at all." Alice whispered gently into the phone.

"We can talk another time…I don't mean to disturb you."

"No, it's…" Kathryn could hear shuffling on the other end of the line, and then Alice was speaking to her like normal again. "Are you all right?"

Kathryn took a deep breath. She was very much not all right. "Yes, I just…wanted to hear your voice."

There was silence on the other end.

God, Kathryn was drinking too much. Had she just said that out loud?

"It's, uh, good to hear your voice as well." Alice finally spoke.

"Charles came back this evening." Kathryn spoke candidly.

"Oh, he's there?" Alice sounded panicked.

Kathryn laughed. "Passed out like a baby." She drank back another sip of vodka.

"It's nice, though, to have him home?" Alice attempted a cordial conversation.

Kathryn snorted. "If you say so."

There was a noise on the other end of the line, someone – a woman? - calling out Alice's name. She very nearly heard Alice curse under her breath. "I-I have to go. I'm so sorry! I'll see you tomorrow."

And before Kathryn could respond the dial tone flooded the line.

Alice had hung up on her.

Kathryn lowered the phone onto its cradle and sat smoking her cigarette. Irritation overcame her. She drank another tumbler of vodka before she passed out on the couch.

Chapter Eleven

Alice

Her cheeks burned red when she stepped on set the following morning.

Kathryn was sitting out in the audience bleachers, hidden away from the bright lights of the stage. Alice had spotted her out amidst the fray of crew members the instant she arrived. In turn, she could feel Kathryn's eyes upon her, watching her. Alice wanted to go to her, to apologize for the previous evening, but Larry caught her. He began discussing their scene for the day, and she could not get away from him.

Rehearsal began and Alice felt under a microscope, as if Kathryn were watching her every move as she went about her scene with Larry. It took nearly an hour for her to feel herself becoming Kay, really feeling herself in the character.

By the time break was called, Alice had nearly forgotten about Kathryn until she glanced to the audience seats and found the woman missing. She hadn't been watching the rehearsal at all.

Alice walked backstage, passing by the craft service table and eyeing the donuts that sat prettily atop a platter. She hadn't had a thing to eat all morning. Her stomach twisted in hunger.

"I heard the cherry ones are best." The voice startled her.

Alice turned to find Kathryn standing beside her, eyeing the same array of food. She watched as the blonde woman picked up a sandwich and an apple and then looked as if she were waiting for Alice to do the same. Alice knew her mother would disapprove, but she was ravenous. So she also chose a sandwich and an orange, and then Kathryn was beckoning for her to come with her.

"I apologize for having called so late last night." Kathryn spoke as they walked shoulder-to-shoulder down the hallway.

"Oh, don't…don't apologize." Alice felt her stomach knot. "I should apologize." They had arrived at Kathryn's door and came to a halt there. "My mother is here."

Kathryn looked at Alice, seemed to take her in. A knowing look crossed her features and she nodded toward her dressing room. "Why don't you eat with me?"

Alice was suddenly overcome with nerves. She had hardly ever set foot in Kathryn's dressing room.

Of course, there had been the occasional conversation through the door, a simple nod of acknowledgement as she passed, but they had never taken lunch together. Usually it was Kathryn who closed herself up – sometimes with Stephen or Wes or George or any other important person to have some sort of important conversation that Alice never seemed privy to. But now it was she who was invited inside.

Alice froze.

Kathryn's brow creased – was it in amusement or offense?

Alice, realizing that she had come to a complete halt, shook her head, willing herself forward. She followed Kathryn into the dressing room.

Kathryn closed the door behind them.

The older woman motioned for Alice to sit down, so she sat gingerly at the edge of the couch. She watched as Kathryn moved toward a cabinet in the corner of the room. She opened the door to reveal a well-kept liquor collection. "Would you care for a nip?" She held up a bottle of whiskey.

"Oh…no, no thank you. I don't…I've never touched the stuff." Alice felt her cheeks go red.

Kathryn gave her a curious smile. "Well isn't that precious."

Alice felt like a child then in her presence.

"So your mother's here, then."

Alice nodded, watching as Kathryn poured herself a small nip of whiskey. It was only a few minutes past noon.

"I take it you're not happy about that?" Kathryn sipped at her drink as she settled onto the couch, close to Alice, but not too close.

Alice shook her head and picked at the sandwich in her hands. "She means well, but she's…" Alice searched for the right words. "It's…it's suffocating." She finally whispered.

Kathryn reached out, patted Alice's knee ever so softly. Her hand came to rest, momentarily, briefly against her leg. "I can only imagine."

The touch sent fire racing through Alice's body. She continued to stare at the floor by her feet. There was a strange silence then and Alice felt as if she needed to fill it. "She was worried about me. She watches me on the show and thinks she knows what's happening, but she doesn't." She spoke without thought, realizing all too late that she was complaining and hadn't her mother taught her that no one liked to hear people complain? That it was not polite conversation?

Kathryn's brow furrowed. "Is something the matter?"

Alice looked up then, laughing as if to clear the air. "No, of course not. She just makes it up in her mind. Makes it seem like it's much worse than it is and then she wants to be a savior."

Kathryn continued to watch her over the rim of her tumbler. "The worst kind of mother."

Alice nodded in agreement.

"You should really eat that sandwich instead of playing with it. You have a long rehearsal ahead of you with Larry." Kathryn chastised.

Alice laughed. "Now you sound like my mother." Though she wished her mother would tell her to eat something instead of trying to force those stupid pills on her.

Kathryn groaned at that. "By Hollywood standards I'm probably old enough to be your mother."

Alice watched as Kathryn sat down her tumbler and took a bite of her sandwich. There was an anger simmering low in her eyes. "Just what does that mean? You're not that much older than me."

"Well, apparently Hollywood thinks I'm ancient." Kathryn huffed. "They want me to play Lillian Demille's mother in a movie. I mean, are they morons?"

Alice's eyes widened at that. Was this what became of someone who was loved and celebrated? Had the studios forgotten who Kathryn was? Sure she was older than she had been during all of those war pictures, but she had only gotten better and sharper as an actress. "It's a disgrace."

"Damn right it is." Kathryn lifted her glass to that and drank back the rest of her whiskey.

"Will you do it?"

Kathryn shrugged. And for the first time Alice watched the mighty woman shrink before her. "What else is there to do?"

Alice looked at her, truly taking her in. For as fierce as she was on set, there was a sadness to her, something that made her seem small and afraid. Alice recognized the look, knew it intimately.

Kathryn waved her hand in the air and the lioness returned. "Ah, hell. What can we do, right? We're just a couple of broads." Her words lacked humor.

Alice watched her take another bite of her sandwich, the subject dropped.

Alice looked down at her sandwich. Her mouth watered. She took one, tentative bite.

"You know, at some point in time you just have to stand up to your mother. You're an adult now. She can't run your life." Kathryn instructed.

Alice laughed at this. "If only it were that simple."

Chapter Twelve

Kathryn

Charles was buttering up the all too glorified actor Buddy Wilson for an upcoming role in a big feature film at the house that evening. Buddy had brought his new wife Ruby – a young slip of a girl who clung to her husband and had nothing interesting to say. He delighted in using her as a prop. Kathryn was bored to tears at the dining room table when the call came through.

Mariella looked flustered when she appeared in the doorway. "Ms. Anderson, there's a call for you."

Kathryn butted her cigarette, feigning irritation. "Can it wait?"

"It's your mother."

Kathryn felt the hairs at the back of her neck stand on end. "Would you please excuse me." She carefully took her napkin from her lap and placed it on the table beside her plate – catching Charles' eye in the process. He looked as perplexed as she felt.

She took the call in the sitting room, collapsing unceremoniously into a chair, taking a cigarette from the box as she spoke. "If it's about the check, Charles has already mailed it." She lighted the cigarette between her teeth.

"Katarina, Süßer, I am not calling about the money." Her mother's voice – thickly accented – tried to articulate the English words.

"Then what is it?" Kathryn rubbed irritably at her forehead. "And don't call me that. Jesus."

"It's your…it's Vivian."

"What about her?" Kathryn's skin prickled at the mention, a fear raced through her followed by anger. "I swear to God, if he touched her…"

"Katarina, please, Süßer, Warren er war krank."

"Gut." Kathryn exhaled. "What is it then? What about Vivian?"

"Well, it's almost her birthday. Her eighteenth birthday und ich dachte…"

April sixth. The date seared into her memory.

Yes, she knew it was approaching.

Eighteen years. Well, that was certainly something.

"Dachte was?"

"I thought you might come home. Ich möchte…"

"Nein, Mutter, nein Danke. Aber I'll be sure to put a little extra in next month's check." And with that Kathryn smashed the phone back into its cradle and wrapped an arm about herself, letting the smoke swirl about her head.

She stood to pour herself a splash of whiskey, then drank it while standing at the minibar, smoking her cigarette until she felt she could breathe again. Finally she returned to the dining room, apologized for her disappearance and settled back across the table from Charles. He gave her an inquiring look.

The droll conversation continued on. Ruby gave her

strange, furtive glances but seemed too afraid to strike up a conversation with her.

She drank to fill her boredom.

The following day at rehearsal she had a headache. She closed her door at lunch, made herself a drink and laid on the couch with a cool wet rag over her forehead.

She was thrilled when rehearsal ended that day, making a beeline for her car in the lot, wishing to have a drink and sleep off the pain from the day. But as she made her way to her car, she noticed Alice's car was still in its space. Inside the car was the woman herself, sitting motionless.

Kathryn watched her for a moment in the fading light of day, wondering just what was detaining her.

Kathryn's headache persisted, splintering her head with pain, so she got into her car and drove away, assuming Alice would do the same very soon.

But the next evening and the next as Kathryn left, she noticed Alice's car still in place, the woman sitting inside it, making no move to leave. In fact, as Kathryn drew closer to her car on the fourth day of this pattern, she discovered that Alice was sitting in her car reading a book.

Kathryn came closer, tapped against the glass of the window.

Alice nearly jumped out of her seat, the book falling from her hands, a hand moving to her chest in shock and surprise. It took her a moment before she was able to roll the window down.

"I didn't mean to startle you." Kathryn leaned against the window.

"I – oh, I didn't think you would still be here." Alice was laughing now, the fear rolling off her.

"I could say the same about you. Wasn't your rehearsal over an hour ago?" Kathryn mused, watched as Alice's cheeks colored a deep shade of crimson.

"Yes – but I…well…" Alice demurred.

"Ah," Kathryn stood, nodding. "Your mother's still here, isn't she?"

Alice nodded guiltily.

Kathryn smiled. "Would you like some company?"

She got into the passenger side of the car, reaching for the book that had fallen. "Well, I certainly enjoyed the film. Is the novel any good?" She turned *Rebecca* over in her hands, skimming the back cover.

Alice watched her. "I'm enjoying it. I feel the same way I did watching the movie. I want to see what she looks like, you know? Everyone is so in love with her so she must have been something."

Kathryn settled the book between them. "I suppose that makes it well written then. Or at least entertaining anyway."

Alice laughed before looking down at her hands. Kathryn watched as she took a deep breath. "I know I shouldn't just run away, but going home feels insufferable. My mother has taken over everything, and Frank's on edge all the time. He can't stand her being there but he won't say anything to her. He just lets me have it. But what can I do? She won't leave no matter what I say. So…I guess I'm just a coward."

"No." Kathryn could not stand the thought of her feeling that way. It was simply too much; it would be too much for anyone. She reached out and placed her hand over Alice's. "You're not a coward at all."

She watched Alice falter for the briefest moment, surprise coloring her cheeks.

Kathryn removed her hand, a certain pleasure coursing through her.

"You know, I met Daphne du Maurier once at a party. Yes, she was very striking, almost haunted looking herself. I caught her necking with an actress out by the pool." Kathryn watched Alice as she spoke, noting the rise of her eyebrows at the mention of this little aside.

"But she…with an actress?" Alice sounded surprised.

Kathryn swatted at Alice. "Oh, come now. We live in this fabulous world of make believe where anyone can be anyone or anything. You're telling me you've never considered that two women might…"

Alice was beet red. "Oh, well I…of course, I've known… back in New York every man I knew was a homosexual." She tried to laugh. "I'm not shocked, I only…well isn't Daphne du Maurier married to a man?"

Kathryn rested her arm against the back of the seat. The darling thing hadn't an immoral thought in her head, did she? "What of it?" Kathryn smiled as she rubbed at her temple. "Do you mind if I smoke?"

Alice shook her head distractedly as she stared out the windshield, lost in thought.

Kathryn tapped out a cigarette from her pack and lit it.

Alice turned to look at her. A question had formed at the tip of her tongue but it seemed to die there and instead of asking, she closed her mouth and looked back out at the studio lot. It was barren in the late evening hour.

Kathryn exhaled a cloud of smoke. "I should be telling you to go home and save that Frank of yours."

"I know." Alice sighed. "He knows what I'm up to."

"Well, don't let me keep you."

"You're not." Alice sounded momentarily panicked. For Kathryn knew that once she left her, she would be forced to go home.

If she cared less, Kathryn would take her out for a night. But that was not who they were to one another, and that was not what she *should* do with a colleague. She knew the rules.

So Kathryn opened the car door. "I know – but it's what's best." She patted Alice on the arm again and the woman gave her a sad, longing look. "I am just a phone call away, though."

Alice's face lit up with the hint of a smile. "Thank you, Kathryn."

"Any time, Alice." Kathryn winked and stood from the car. Shutting the door, she tapped the top of it and waited for Alice to start the engine and back away before taking herself home to an empty house.

And for the first time in a long while, she was almost grateful for the silence.

Chapter Thirteen

Alice

There was safety on the stage that Friday evening. As if when Alice were under the lights playing Kay, neither Frank nor her mother could touch her. She poured all her simmering anger and frustration into the comedy of that evening's taping. She was fierce, ruthless with her colleagues and it seemed the audience was taken with her beguiling performance. At the end of the evening, when they took their turns bowing before the studio audience – Alice very pointedly not looking in the direction of where her mother sat – she happened to catch Kathryn looking at her with what appeared to be a hint of admiration.

Alice was bereft when Kathryn disappeared behind the set, and instead of having a moment of time with her colleague, she was instantly accosted by her mother.

"You were wonderful, darling. Simply the most comedic of all of them, I must say." Her mother took her arm, pulling her close, conspiratorially.

"Great work tonight." Stephen passed Alice by, giving her a nod.

She tried to smile, but her mother took the compliment and ran with it. "Isn't she something? Just something!"

Alice was grateful that Stephen simply agreed, introduced himself politely, and then moved past them, not giving in to her mother's antics.

Her mother trailed her to her dressing room, yapping away about how wonderful Alice was and didn't she look spectacular and thin, and Alice stopped before her mother could follow her inside. "Please, give me a moment." Alice begged. She pulled the door closed in her mother's face, feeling horribly guilty, but she was beginning to feel panic rise inside of her.

She longed for a chocolate bar and a night alone.

Instead, she was driven home by a sullen, smoking Frank with her mother berating her from the back seat the whole way home for her ill treatment in front of her colleagues and the crew. "It's no way to treat your mother. Why, I raised you! I helped you become what you are. And don't you forget it. If it weren't for me, you wouldn't have looked so slim and attractive this evening. I'm helping you."

Her mother's voice droned on and on.

Frank was of no help. He left Alice in the living room with her mother and locked himself away in their bedroom. It was unfair that he could escape her mother while she was left to deal with her.

Her head was beginning to pound. She poured herself a glass of water, opened the medicine cabinet to extract the aspirin when she noticed the bottle of Dexamyl that her mother had positioned inside the cabinet. A reminder.

Alice poured two aspirin into her hand and then slammed the cabinet door shut. Her mother still talking to her. Words, accusations rolling off her tongue, rattling about emptily in Alice's brain. She downed the aspirin.

"…you're home late every night. I would hope that you're not…"

Her mother's words began to register in her brain again. She turned to look at the woman.

Her once vibrant mother had become stocky, her once-attractive face now beginning to sag with lines, her body loose beneath her simple dress. Here she was, berating Alice for having gained a pound or two.

And now what was she doing? Going on about how Alice had been home late for the past week?

"I would never. Don't you dare say that." She felt her cheeks burning bright red.

"I didn't say a word. Not one word. Why are you so upset, Alice dear? It only looks a certain way. Don't you think?"

"No, I don't think so. Rehearsals ran late this week. That is all." Alice spoke shortly, anger rising inside of her.

"Alice, dear. You have a husband."

"Don't you think I know that?" Alice's body shook as she spoke, her voice not above a whisper.

Her mother looked stricken.

"And yet here you are, clinging to me, keeping me from him."

"Alice, I'm doing no such thing. I…"

"Mother, I think it's time you leave." Alice clenched and then unclenched her fist.

"Alice, are you…"

Alice turned, unable to look at her mother a second longer. She reached for her purse, for her keys. "I am going for a drive and when I get back you better be gone."

Her mother continued to protest, telling her all the horrible things she was doing to her, how she was making her suffer.

Alice simply opened the back door and walked outside, her mother's voice drowned out by the night breeze as she got into her car and slammed the door shut. She had no idea where she was going, no idea what she was doing, only that she needed to get away.

She saw red as she drove.

What did her mother know? She hadn't done anything wrong. All of those nights when she'd sat in her car waiting for the hours to roll by so she could avoid too much time with the insufferable woman – she hadn't done anything wrong. Kathryn sliding into the car beside her, entertaining her for an hour or so several of those evenings hardly constituted some affair. Kathryn was her work colleague. Perhaps they had kissed, but that had not meant...

Alice thought of the way Kathryn touched her. On the hand, on the knee, her cheek.

She shook her head. It meant nothing. She was being ridiculous.

The Hollywood boulevards whirred past, colorful light from the local marquees and streetlights blurring together. She was driving aimlessly.

Though as she passed by a familiar locale, she realized she knew this place. She had been here before, after an awards show.

The house would be down the road, just there on the left.

And when Alice pulled before the sprawling white home, she realized the lights were still on. She cut the ignition and sat in the car. She should turn around and go back home. The woman inside had told her she could call – not show up in the middle of the night.

She should turn around and leave, go back to where she had come from, but the thought of seeing her mother again made her stomach knot. The worst that could happen, she surmised, was being turned away. Then perhaps she'd go to that diner that was open all night, buy a milkshake and while away the hours.

But now she was here.

She got out of her car, the aspirin soothing the dull ache

in her head as she walked closer to the imposing front entranceway. With a half-shaking hand, she reached out and pressed the bell, listening as it echoed through the corridors inside. She felt instantly afraid, thinking that perhaps she should turn and run away.

But before she could, the door flew open and a Hispanic woman appeared on the other side. "Yes?"

"Uh," Alice swiped a hand over her forehead. "I…I'm terribly sorry to show up so late, but I…well, is Kathryn here?"

The woman on the other side of the door looked her over, studied her features intently, and then gave her a surprised little smile. "Why, is that you, Mrs. Kincaid?"

Alice nodded. "Yes – yes, I'm Alice. Oh, please, call me Alice." Kincaid was Frank, his mark upon her and right now at Kathryn's house she did not wish to be known as such.

"Why come in. Ms. Anderson is in the sitting room." The woman opened the door wider.

There was no going back now. She followed the woman, who introduced herself as Mariella, into a little room off the back of the home that Alice did not remember from her previous visit during the party.

"Ms. Anderson, Mrs. Kincaid is here to see you." Mariella made the introduction and Alice shuffled uncomfortably behind her.

When she looked up she felt her cheeks go red at the sight.

For there she sat, cigarette dangling from her fingers, magazine open on her lap, glasses at the tip of her nose, robe sliding down her arms, a silky thin-strapped nightgown revealed beneath.

This was an image Alice felt she had no right to. It had been wrong to come so late in the evening when Kathryn was at home, enjoying a bit of quiet all to herself.

"Alice!" But the woman flipped her magazine closed, pulling her robe over a shoulder as she sat forward, fixing

Alice with a winning, welcoming smile. "What a pleasant surprise." She stood up, moving toward Alice.

Up close Alice realized that she was fresh faced. Not a lick of make-up to highlight her blonde eyebrows, so her eyes looked naked, and her lips were a pale shade of pink. And Alice felt as if she should not be seeing her like this, as if she hadn't the right to see her so exposed. But Kathryn was smiling at her. She pressed her lips to Alice's cheek chastely, reached for her hand and took her to the chaise lounge near the window and sat her down. Kathryn settled next to her, looking her over as she blew smoke from between her lips.

Alice was lost for words.

Kathryn exhaled a cloud of smoke and turned to extinguish her cigarette. "Well, you were quite the sensation this evening. It was a marvelous performance. You should certainly be feeling high."

Alice felt far from high.

She put her head in her hands.

"But what is this. What's the matter?" Kathryn let her hand come to rest on Alice's knee.

"I just snapped." Alice whispered. "I couldn't take it – she just talks and talks and talks and was accusing me of…well, I just left. I couldn't take it and I…oh, God. I told her to leave."

"Ah," Kathryn nodded.

Alice winced. "I'm sorry. I shouldn't have come here. I shouldn't have…"

"No, I'm thrilled. Pleased that you did." Kathryn rubbed her shoulder in consolation. "I'm happy to be a reprieve for you."

Alice felt a happy pain form in her chest. There was comfort in Kathryn's presence at her side, comfort in being here with her in the quiet of her home.

"Kathryn, did you see my briefcase?" A male voice bellowed from the hallway.

Alice's heart skipped a beat. She jumped away from

Kathryn and her comforting touch, nearly jumping out of her skin. For there appeared Charles standing in the doorway. He was holding a script, half paying attention until he looked up and locked eyes with Alice.

"Well now…who do we have here? Alice, I didn't know we were expecting you this evening."

Alice stood, ringing her hands. "No – uh, you weren't. I'm sorry. I must be on my way."

"Darling, you don't have to leave." Kathryn laughed, attempting to reach for Alice, but Alice slid from her grasp.

She hadn't known that Charles was home. Normally he came to the tapings when he was in town, but Alice hadn't seen him that evening. Unless she had been too preoccupied by her mother…oh, no. She needed to leave.

"No, I should go. I'm sorry."

"Alice," Kathryn caught her, turning to face her before she could run off. "You know you're welcome here any time."

Alice couldn't meet her eyes. She simply nodded, tempted to trace the line of Kathryn's nightgown where it rested against her freckled chest. "Thank you. But, I must go." She slipped from Kathryn's grasp, nodded to Charles as she passed, and then headed directly to the door, face blazing hot.

She was grateful when she made it home and her mother was nowhere to be seen but it was Frank she had to be leery of now. He was smoking in their bed, half-asleep.

"She left half an hour ago." He informed her. "Said she'd get a hotel room and then go back in the morning."

"Good." Alice slid from her shoes and went about unfastening the buttons on her shirt.

"Where were you?"

Alice's back stiffened. "Out driving."

She could feel his eyes on her as she undressed. She reached into her closet for a nightgown, but Frank's voice stopped her. "Come here."

She turned out the light.

Chapter Fourteen

Kathryn

Kathryn watched as Charles walked toward the wet bar. He tossed the script in his hand onto the wooden surface and uncapped a bottle of whiskey before pouring the liquid into two glasses.

Kathryn lit a cigarette, keeping her eyes on him as he moved toward her to hand her a glass. He settled into the chair opposite her.

She exhaled a stream of smoke and drank back the whiskey.

"You were expecting her?" He leaned forward, resting his elbows on his knees.

Kathryn shook her head.

He nodded, sipped his drink.

"It's a dangerous game, Kathryn."

"I'm not playing a goddamn game." She smoked angrily. "I didn't know she was coming this evening."

Charles looked as if he did not believe a word of what she said. "What has happened?"

She shook her head, let the liquid swirl about in the tumbler before sipping it again. "Nothing."

Charles laughed humorlessly and sat back in his chair. "Come on, I saw the way she was looking at you."

"I can't help that." Kathryn felt a certain elation overcome her. That Charles could see it. Well then, it was all but confirmed. Too bad he would ruin it somehow, wouldn't he? "Listen, I know the rules."

"Then I suggest you follow them." Charles eyed her, held her with his gaze.

Kathryn rolled her eyes to the ceiling. "Jesus."

"I'm serious. It's a liability to the production. Be smart."

"Like you're smart, sleeping with Sybil Matthews." She threw the name in his face, having seen the gossip column boasting his affair with the young leading lady of Broadway's latest hit.

"That's rich, Kathryn." He seemed to delight when she called him out.

"I guess it makes for better press, right? Young ingenue sleeping with the producer. Gets her name in the papers. And I know, I already know why you're doing it. I read the advance reviews and nobody likes her performance."

Charles was grinning like the cat who got the cream. "You're exactly right, Kathryn. I took her out for dinner and then stood in her stairwell consoling her and now New York thinks we're fucking. But I didn't touch her."

Kathryn laughed at this. "Sure."

"It was Clarice Perkins."

Kathryn frowned at him. "Who the hell is that?"

"The fourth dancer on the right. She's certainly something. In and out of bed."

"Well isn't that lovely." Kathryn smiled then, but it did not reach her eyes. Charles always had a soft spot for the underdog. "You want me to go fuck the boy grip on set? Think it wouldn't be such a big deal?"

"I don't want you fucking anyone close to *The Wes Goodwin Show*. You're the darling of America and those fans need to believe it." Charles was looking at her seriously.

Kathryn sat back and drank the rest of the whiskey. "God damn you."

Charles shot her a winning smile. "It's Hollywood, baby. It's the whole of these God forsaken conservative United States. I didn't invent the game."

Kathryn squinted her eyes and glared at him through a cloud of cigarette smoke. She was furious with him. Furious and annoyed by truthful logic. She was deflated and defeated.

She stubbed out her cigarette forcefully. "Take me to bed."

Charles downed the last of his drink and then was kneeling before her, buried in her silk covered chest, arms about her waist, warm, greedy lips pressed to her nipple.

She thought of Alice's golden eyes fixated upon the same spans of skin only minutes before. She held Charles close to her and let him have her there on the sitting room floor.

It was Sunday afternoon when Alice called.

She was on the veranda reading the week's new script and watching Charles swim. Mariella came to tell her she had a call. Kathryn retreated to the sitting room, having already guessed who it might be.

"Hello?" Kathryn asked into the phone.

"Kathryn." Alice spoke softly, bashfully over the line. "I'm sorry to bother you…"

"You're not bothering me at all. You must stop it with this apologizing!" Kathryn smiled, wishing she could assure her that her presence was never a bother.

"Well – but, I did want to apologize for just…for showing up the other night." Alice spoke softly. Kathryn wondered if that Frank of hers was home.

"Darling, it was no offense. You are welcome here any time you like. I meant that."

"But…"

Kathryn sighed, seemed to know her concern. "Listen, Charles doesn't mind a guest now and then. You see, he wasn't upset. Not upset at all."

Alice was quiet on the other line. "Oh."

"In fact, Charles is in town for another week. He would love to have you and Frank for dinner. How about Tuesday evening? It would give us all a chance to fraternize outside of work." She felt positively sinful making the request. She had been dying to see this Frank of hers up close and person, to know what he was like, what their marriage was. Dinner would be just the trick.

Alice seemed quite taken aback by the request. It was several moments before Kathryn received the reply she had been hoping for.

They spoke cordially for a moment more, Kathryn making several comments about the upcoming week's script, Alice agreeing with her, making several remarks of her own, and then they disconnected.

Kathryn walked back poolside, picking up her cigarettes to tap one from the pack. She picked up the lighter, flicking it in her hand several times, watching as Charles came to the edge of the pool, water rushing from his handsome features as he stood. "Who was it?" He called out.

"Why, dear, it was Alice. I invited her *and* her husband to dinner Tuesday evening." And she smiled a sweet, innocent smile and lifted the cigarette to her lips to light it.

Chapter Fifteen

Alice

Panic had splintered across her chest when the first course of the dinner was elegantly placed before them. Frank had worn a freshly pressed shirt reserved for nice occasions. He hated that shirt. As he lifted his fork and knife to cut into the steak set before him, Alice could not help but see how terribly out of place he looked in the elegant Hollywood home surrounding them. She despised him and then felt horribly guilty for despising him.

The food sat untouched on the plate before her.

She felt Kathryn's eyes upon her but did not dare to look in her direction unless conversation demanded it.

"Real estate's the future." Frank was saying, he and Charles trying to find some common ground.

Alice knew there was none.

Charles knew Hollywood. Names and faces and talents and what someone could do for another and what type of show worked and what type didn't.

Frank knew Hollywood by its numbers. The number of loans that crossed through the bank from the studios, the amount that was asked for and then lost and then somehow paid off in time to ask for more.

"Is that so?" Alice could detect a crack of boredom in Charles' well-practiced veneer. He was so handsomely charming, sitting across from his wife in his slightly dressed down gaucho shirt.

"You haven't touched a thing." Kathryn's low voice – intended only for her - was luring her away from the dull conversation Frank had gotten himself into with Charles – interest rates, business loans, the future of housing. Alice could only find it interesting to a point.

Kathryn was wearing purple.

A full skirt affair with matching jacket that fitted over her tall, slender frame, clinging to her at just the right places. Her wrists were sprinkled with bracelets that clicked together as she cut her steak with a knife. Her eyes were upon Alice, but Alice could not look at her. Not directly anyway.

"Are you all right?" Kathryn's fork and knife came to rest against her plate.

Alice knew she would have to say something, for Frank was giving her a curious look in the midst of his conversation with Charles.

"Yes, I'm just not hungry."

"You barely touched your lunch." Kathryn was frowning at her.

Had she been watching Alice during their lunch hour? She had seen Kathryn smoking and talking with several of the stage hands, but they had not shared more than a quick word with the other. There would have been no reason for Kathryn to notice her half-eaten salad and untouched apple.

Alice picked up her fork and knife and began cutting into the steak, watching as blood flowed from the meat. The image of it made her want to vomit, but the action served to appease Kathryn. Alice chose to eat the green beans at the side of the dish with a bit of mashed potatoes instead.

Kathryn was talking about stocks and bonds with the men then, as if she knew all about the world of business. They took to her points, agreeing with her about several rises and speculations.

Alice felt like a child sitting at the adult's table, as if she didn't belong in this dreadful conversation at all. Frank never let her know about finances. He handled everything. And as she listened to Kathryn discuss the market and post-war recovery boon she wondered if she needed to study harder, to not just let Frank do it all. Kathryn made it seem like the most fascinating subject in the world.

It was almost a relief when dinner ended and Charles invited Frank to the sitting room for an aged scotch that had been recently gifted to him by a studio executive.

Alice looked to Kathryn and their eyes met for the first time that evening. Kathryn smiled at her, motioning for her to come with her. She led Alice to the veranda that overlooked a well-lit pool. Kathryn lit a cigarette and surveyed her secluded backyard, the trees that had been imported and placed like a grove about them – as she explained to Alice.

Alice stood at her side, looking out at the curated scene before her, watching as the last rays of sunlight melted over the greenery.

Their shoulders were touching where they stood together.

Kathryn exhaled a stream of smoke that dissipated into the night about them. "Frank certainly knows a lot about banking, doesn't he?"

It seemed some sort of jab at her. She felt her cheeks color.

Kathryn turned to look at her. "You're very quiet this evening."

Alice looked down at the pavement beneath her feet. "I'm sorry – I…"

"No," Kathryn laughed and reached for Alice's wrist, guiding her toward a little path that wound its way to a sitting area at the other side of the pool. "Don't apologize." Kathryn settled into a pool chair and motioned for Alice to do the same on the one beside her.

Alice sat down but did not recline, as Kathryn did. She folded her hands, leaned against her knees and watched as Kathryn smoked. Kathryn watched her in turn.

"He hates get-togethers." Alice tried to laugh it off, worried she might offend Kathryn.

"Ah," Kathryn nodded as if she understood, then she laid back, blowing a smoke ring to the sky. "Things are good then? You have an amicable marriage?"

Alice folded and then unfolded her hands, peering at the windows at the back of the sprawling home. She could see Frank and Charles in the sitting room smoking and talking. She could tell Frank was being polite.

"He can seem rough around the edges, but he…he can be very nice. We met in New York, you know? I was in a show off-Broadway, and he came to see it. I guess he came several times and then one night he brought me flowers backstage. He was so…shy. It was as if he were afraid of me." Alice remembered the way he had asked if she might like to have coffee with him some morning and she had agreed. Because other men – well other men wanted dinner and… "He wasn't like the others." Until the wedding. And then…

Kathryn flicked her cigarette and ash went flying. "I see." Her body had gone rigid, her voice tighter.

Alice felt her chest tighten in fear, wondering if she'd ruined something.

Kathryn brought the cigarette to her lips and Alice watched the motion. The outline of her face was backlit by the light reflected from the pool. Alice followed the curve of it, a wavy line that rose in peaks and valleys. Until she reached the soft edges of her lips.

Alice remembered the feeling of them against her own.

The air in California was frigid in the evenings. Alice shivered.

"Are you cold?" Kathryn sat up, crushing her cigarette in a nearby ashtray.

"No." Alice spoke but found that she was chilly in her sleeveless dress.

She could feel Kathryn's eyes trail over her in the dark cover of night. They seemed to stop at her chest. "Perhaps we should be getting back inside?"

"Are you…upset?" Alice blurted out. Fear had gripped at her chest, paralyzing her. For she did not want to leave this moment without knowing just what it was that had happened.

Kathryn scoffed. "Upset? Why on earth would I be upset?"

Alice crossed her arms about herself. "I don't…oh, I just hope that you don't think I'm ungrateful for the invitation. It was such a lovely evening." Lovely was hardly the word for it.

Kathryn reached out a hand, placing it gently against Alice's knee. "Darling, you've done nothing wrong. I only wanted us all to get together and now we've done it, haven't we?"

Alice nodded, relieved at Kathryn's kindness toward her. Kathryn's gentle, reassuring voice soothed the fear that she had ruined something between them.

"Come on, you're freezing and I need a drink." Kathryn smiled as she stood, reaching a hand for Alice to pull her up. Then she wrapped an arm about her waist and pressed their bodies together as they ambled through the shadows of Kathryn's faux grove toward the too well-illuminated house. They walked so closely that Alice could smell Kathryn's faint perfume mingling with her cigarettes and something else Alice had noticed before that was all Kathryn. It was intoxicating, pressed together as they were. Alice hadn't a clue what it was they spoke of but they laughed together and she felt her chest ache deliciously.

But the moment they stepped into Kathryn and Charles' home, Kathryn released Alice before they could round the corner into the sitting room. Alice stood, watching as Kathryn said something to the men while pouring herself a glass of the aforementioned scotch. She draped herself on the back of Charles' chair and let her well-manicured hand come to rest on his shoulder. An intimate touch.

Frank was looking at Alice, his eyes narrowed.

"I so hate to do this, and you both have been so wonderful to have us, but I do think it's time for us to go. Frank has an early morning, and we have a rather early rehearsal ourselves." Alice mustered all the acting skills she could to get the words out convincingly.

Kathryn looked up at her from over the rim of her drink and gave Alice the most curious of gazes, but she did not protest Alice's abrupt departure. Like a gracious host, she showed Alice and Frank to the door, giving them a formal send off.

Alice felt the cold of California overcome her the instant the door was closed behind them.

Frank lit a cigarette in the passenger seat of the car. She could tell he'd had one too many by the way he tried to hold himself rigidly upright. "Don't you ever make me do that again."

She gripped the steering wheel tighter.

A headache began to form on the ride home. It only increased when they arrived.

Frank fell into a wall on his way to the bedroom. Alice felt a strange sense of relief, knowing he would pass out soon and let her be.

She opened the medicine cabinet for an aspirin and noticed the bottle of Dexamyl sitting next to it.

Chapter Sixteen

Kathryn

Charles had driven off without a word.

She'd watched his anger simmering beneath the surface all evening. The way he played his role to a T, acting the gracious host, entertaining Frank. All the while observing her, taking note of every intimacy between her and Alice. His jaw had been taut with suspicion.

She'd drunk herself silly, a momentary panic overcoming her in the midnight hours. A fear that he would not return made her chest splinter, until she drank more and eventually passed out, awakened by Mariella the following morning.

She was uneasy at the studio. She hid in the shadows, smoking and watching as the players moved about the stage.

And Alice – oh, she thought she might be sore with her, but Alice was on fire that day. As if their dinner had brought her some kind of renewed vigor. She had several crew members in stitches during their lunch hour. Kathryn watched her performance from the audience bleachers where she hid, smoking a cigarette, rubbing her throbbing head.

She hated Charles.

He did not call that night either.

She knew he was not due back in New York until Friday. He was somewhere in Los Angeles. Hiding away from her, most likely taking out all his rage on some strikingly beautiful young thing. Kathryn was forced to suffer in his absence. For calling his assistant to find out where he was would show a weakness in the united front they presented to the world.

It was not until Saturday morning that he called bright and early. He knew full well he was on New York time and she preferred to sleep late Saturday mornings after the show's Friday night tapings. Her head was pounding when she picked up the phone.

"You're signing the movie contract for the summer. It shoots in New York for two months." Charles spoke authoritatively, his voice all business. "I'm having Howard send over the contract for you to sign today."

Kathryn sat blurrily up, her eyes yet to open. She had wanted to demand a re-cast for the role of her daughter to someone perhaps younger, but the force of his words made it seem she had no choice in the matter now. "Okay." She groggily agreed, bracing her head in her hands.

"I hope you got what you wanted out of that charade of a night." Charles spoke pointedly.

She reached for her cigarettes. "Oh, please. I was being kind to my co-star."

"I don't know what the hell you were trying to accomplish, but I know a thing or two about men like Frank. And I wouldn't invite that kind of trouble if I were you."

"Charles…"

"How many times have I told you, Kathryn, that you shouldn't mix business with pleasure? The show is only in its second season, it's doing well in the ratings; you don't want to be the reason that Paula and Kay split up on screen, now do you?"

"Well now, darling, why do I get all the blame for this hypothetical split?" Kathryn trailed her fingers through her wrecked hair. "Besides, you're forgetting that nothing has happened."

"*Yet*. Nothing's happened yet."

"You make it sound like I bewitched her." Kathryn tapped off her cigarette ashes.

"You are very bewitching. But you are very much not available. Not for the looks she was giving you."

"What were these looks? She hardly looked at me." Kathryn spat back.

"All I'm saying is be careful. This isn't a game, not for her."

"I would never hurt her."

"Then don't get involved with her." Charles cautioned.

"Hypocrite." Kathryn punctuated the word with a cloud of smoke.

There was silence on the other end of the line and for the briefest of moments she'd thought he'd hung up on her. Until she heard the flick of a lighter. "I fully expect you to sign that contract today. And you know, it might just be good for you to get out of Hollywood for a while." He hung up.

She let the phone fall to her shoulder, listening to the dial tone as she smoked the rest of her cigarette.

She spent the weekend quietly. Reading, taking a mid-day swim, moving things about, signing the movie contract, playing the piano, going through her stretches and a light weight routine, sending Mariella away to restock the mini-bar, drinking and smoking in the evenings while listening to melancholy classical music on the radio with no one around at all.

The only flicker of light in all of this was the thought of seeing Alice at the table read on Monday morning. She dreamt of her, dreamt of Alice's auburn hair, her large, clear eyes, her smooth skin, her soft lips. Her hand was between her legs when she awoke at some ungodly hour and she did not stop herself from indulging in the wistful fantasy.

She arrived early to the studio. Script in one hand, cigarette in the other, feeling, perhaps for the first time in a longtime, well-rested and clear-headed.

She sat at her designated seat and greeted each of her colleagues as they arrived. Wes pressed his lips to her cheek, asking after her weekend and she returned the same sentiments.

But the one person who she wanted to see did not make an appearance.

Stephen walked to the table with a furrowed brow. "Alice is indisposed of this morning, but if things turn around she will try to join us later today. In her place, Cynthia will be reading Kay's lines." He pointed distractedly to an awkward female assistant who shyly took Alice's seat at the table.

What the hell was wrong with Alice? Kathryn wanted to get up, to race to her, to find out, but she was confined to the rehearsal so she slid her glasses on and picked up the script, feeling uneasy and concerned.

Cynthia was no Alice. Relief overcame the cast when right after lunch Alice appeared looking herself, as if nothing bad had happened at all.

Kathryn stood back and observed as Larry and Wes asked her how she was, if she was all right, and filled Alice in on the morning's table read. Kathryn could tell Alice was putting on an amicable front for the men – half-present to them but her eyes would briefly flutter to where Kathryn stood.

It was not until the afternoon rehearsal had commenced that she found herself near enough to speak to Alice, who was twisting a pencil about in her hands, looking far away.

"You're feeling better then?" Kathryn spoke quietly - for

Stephen was directing Wes through a scene on the sound stage before them.

"Yes, but how embarrassing! I've never missed a rehearsal before in my life." Alice seemed antsy. "Do you think they're upset?"

Kathryn shook her head, reaching out to slide an errant lock of hair behind Alice's ear. The woman's eyes looked bloodshot up close, wide and afraid. "No, they were concerned."

"I just feel so out of it. I've never felt like this before." Alice shifted back and forth on the balls of her feet.

"Darling," Kathryn reached out to steady her. "I know that Stephen would not be upset if you went on home for the rest of the day. If you're still feeling poorly."

"No, I can't let him down. I can't let *you* down." Alice insisted.

Kathryn chuckled, a bit surprised. "You wouldn't be letting *me* down at all. Nor anyone else here. If you're unwell, then you're unwell."

Alice shook her head. "I just needed the morning, I swear. I'm as good as new."

"Kathryn?" It was Stephen calling her to the stage.

Alice was far from good as new. She was different some-how, less grounded, possibly still delirious from a flu? Kathryn wanted to insist that she go see a doctor, go on home and let it be for the day, but Stephen was calling her. So she had to go, she had to leave Alice to twirl her pencil and stare off into space.

The rehearsal was painful. It was as if everyone could see that there was something wrong with Alice and yet no one spoke a word about it. They seemed to accept that she was feeling unwell and let her be.

Alice seemed to disappear as soon as the rehearsal was over. Kathryn thought it wise and assumed she would go right on home to get some rest.

She did not expect, however, on her way out of the building, that she might find Alice still in her dressing room, leaning against the make-up counter, head hanging between her arms.

"Alice?" Kathryn stepped into the room.

Alice moaned in pain.

Kathryn closed the dressing room door. She let her bag fall to Alice's couch, moving ever so much closer to her. "What's the matter?" Her hand reached out to gently touch Alice's shoulder.

Alice inhaled shakily.

Kathryn watched as she lifted her hand, swiping at her face.

"What is it?" Kathryn stepped closer, urging her to look at her.

Alice turned to lean against the counter. Kathryn was looking down at her, could see how her eyes were bloodshot and wide and looking everywhere but at her.

"Are you…late?" Her voice dropped to a whisper.

Alice groaned. "No, it's not that."

Kathryn was relieved by this confirmation.

Alice's eyes were fixated on Kathryn's neck.

Kathryn's hand had instinctively gone about Alice, bracing the small of her back. Holding her close enough to feel the heat that radiated from her body. Kathryn's thumb grazed absently over the material of Alice's shirt.

As alone as they had been since that night…

Alice's tooth sank into her bottom lip as she contemplated something.

Kathryn bent her head.

Alice turned her face upward, a hand lightly clasping at Kathryn's hip.

Their lips met.

Inevitable.

Strawberries and beeswax, lipsticks smearing together as their lips moved in a delicate dance.

There was a noise outside the door, someone passing.

Alice gasped.

They parted, staring at one another, wide-eyed.

Fear had grown large in Alice's dilated pupils. Her chest was heaving up and down, her body working overtime to pull in air.

"Why don't we sit down?" Kathryn realized then that she was fully supporting the other woman's weight.

Alice's face was growing more pale with each passing second. She was a ghostly white when Kathryn attempted to help her to the couch.

Alice clung to her before her body went limp.

She collapsed, dragging Kathryn down to the floor with her.

"Alice!"

Chapter Seventeen

Alice

There was the beep of a machine.

Everything before was a blur.

She had no recollection of the time nor date or where she was. All she could hear was the steady beeping of a machine that echoed her heartbeat.

The lights were dim. She looked about, found a window and took note of the darkness outside. It was late. She could sense this.

And then her eyes narrowed in on a sleeping form beneath the window, deformed and uncomfortable in a chair, his body slouched down, arms crossed about his chest, head at an odd angle.

Frank. What was Frank doing there?

Where was she?

Then a gentle brush of fingers against her own alerted her to another presence in the room.

And suddenly everything began to come back to her.

The Dexamyl, the sickness, the kiss…

Her throat was raw.

Kathryn was standing above her, sleepy-eyed and disheveled.

"You're awake." Kathryn whispered.

Alice tried to speak, but her throat felt impossibly tight.

"Shh," Kathryn smoothed her fingers over her forehead. "The doctors said it might hurt to speak for a while. Do you want some water?"

Alice felt her eyes tearing. She could only nod her head.

Kathryn helped her drink from a cup and then sat at the edge of the bed, wiping at the tears that streaked down her face. "You should get some rest."

Alice could only stare up at Kathryn, afraid. What had happened to her? Why wasn't Kathryn telling her?

She looked to Frank. He was out like a light.

She wished he wasn't there.

Why was Kathryn still there?

Kathryn was stroking her hand, fingernails sliding up her arm. The motion was lulling her back to sleep. Her body was so tired. Her stomach hurt. Her throat hurt.

She looked up at Kathryn, gazing into her eyes, watching them until she fell asleep.

It was the sound of a discussion that roused her again.

Sun was filtering in through the blinds.

She laid with eyes half-open, half-closed, wondering if Kathryn had been some late-night apparition.

She had wanted her there. Had it been a dream?

From her spot in the hospital bed, she could see Frank standing with his hat in his hands. He looked so fragile in that moment, as if he had no idea what to do with a sick wife. He was listening to a doctor, but his eyes were not focused.

A strange tightness twisted deep in her chest.

He was a good man. He had taken her away from New

York and helped her get into Hollywood. He had helped support her.

He had stayed with her all night. He had been concerned about her.

And she had kissed Kathryn.

"She's awake."

Alice's eyes blinked fully open.

Kathryn was there. Had she really been there this whole time?

"Alice, oh, darling." Kathryn came to her side. Those dark eyes peered down upon her, relief written in her irises.

To look at the woman above her too intently made Alice feel exposed. She could not look at her a moment longer, not when she could feel her husband's presence so near.

Frank was beside her then. Alice looked up at him and he down at her, his hat still in his hands, running the brim of it round and around in circles.

"Hello Mrs. Kincaid." The doctor introduced himself. She looked from Frank to the man in a white coat. He was a plain man with little cheer in his eyes. Alice wasn't sure if she was dreaming it or if he seemed to be regarding her disdainfully. "Please, don't try to speak. You've had a tube down your throat. It will be very irritated."

She looked from the doctor to her husband.

"They say you took something." Frank spoke after clearing his throat. "It didn't sit well." His voice had gone soft with each passing word.

"Dexamyl, from what we could tell. Your body couldn't handle it. Just a bad reaction to the drug, was all it was. I would suggest, Mrs. Kincaid, that you look for some other way to curb your anxiety." The doctor looked rather smug in his delivery.

Alice felt her cheeks go red. Who was he to go about airing her secrets? She hadn't taken the pills for anxiety. She wanted to open her mouth and say as much to him, but her throat was too constricted, too dry to even consider it. So she looked away from the doctor, disgusted.

"We'd like to keep you here the rest of the day, Mrs. Kincaid. Just to make sure nothing's amiss. I'll have the nurses come to check on you." And then the doctor made his exit.

But then the feeling of Frank above her, Kathryn there at her side…

She looked at Frank. He did not reach for her. He had never been outwardly affectionate, but she longed for him to make some grand gesture in that moment.

She felt Kathryn's hand brush against hers. "They had to pump your stomach. Thank God I got you here when I did."

The pieces were being put back together for her.

Because the last memory she had was of kissing Kathryn.

She could feel her cheeks going rouge again.

Frank continued to shuffle beside her, furtively glancing at the clock on the wall.

And then it dawned on her that it was Tuesday, wasn't it? What about the show? It would be another day of missed rehearsals? She couldn't very well afford that!

And as if Kathryn had seen the panic flash in her eyes, she patted lightly at Alice's arm. "They did a rewrite last night. Kay is going off on vacation for the episode. You needn't worry a thing about it. If you feel up to it, you'll be at rehearsals later in the week."

Alice fumed quietly. The episode had been good that week. Her part had been good. And now they were re-writing her out of the episode because of this one ill-conceived choice? She felt rage, burning rage at her mother for having ever even brought the damn pills into the house in the first place. She had been managing just fine before… so what if she threw up a little bit now and then? It was better than this!

"Don't you worry, Alice. You'll get an A plot next week." Kathryn tried to console her.

Frank was checking his watch again. "You're all right, Al?" He asked her, the words foreign to him.

She was looking ahead, unable to look at either person hovering above her. The man she was married to and a woman whom she had kissed. Both there in one room.

She nodded up and down.

"I hate to…but I've got to get to the bank. I have a meeting, you see, a real important meeting." He sounded apologetic about it, and Alice very nearly felt bad for him. He was a very by-the-book, never-missed-a-day-in-his-life man. He did what was asked of him. He did not diverge easily from his daily routine.

This had been something altogether different for him.

She lifted her hand for him, reassuring him. He took her fingers, held them with a tenderness she had never known him to have. And for a brief moment she could see the concern in his eyes.

He had been genuinely worried about her.

"I'll, uh, be by to pick you up after work. You should be cleared by then." He let go of her hand and placed his hat on his head. And before he left, he tipped the hat to Kathryn, who politely acknowledged him.

Alice felt the hospital bed shift. Kathryn sat beside her. Fingers reached out to smooth hair from her forehead, to run down the curve of her cheek. It was much too intimate. "I don't know what you were thinking." The woman whispered as she stroked Alice's cheek. "You scared me half to death."

Alice felt frustrated tears well in her eyes. She was so angry at herself.

"Oh, now darling. Don't cry." Kathryn wiped at her eyes. "It was all an accident. A silly, ridiculous accident. You would never intentionally…no. So you see, it's all okay. You're okay."

Alice looked up to see that Kathryn had tears in her own eyes.

Kathryn wiped at her eyes, standing up to turn away from Alice. "Damn."

Alice watched her, watching as she went to her bag, rummaged about inside of it before pulling out her cigarettes. She sat in the chair that she had presumably occupied the whole of the previous night and lit a cigarette. "You know I'm due at the studio in a half hour, but I hate the idea of leaving you." Kathryn pointed the cigarette at Alice, as if in a threat. And then she smoked, holding Alice's gaze through a cloud of smoke.

Alice did not look away.

Chapter Eighteen

Kathryn

"You don't have any more goddamn whiskey?" Kathryn slurred over Georgia Gibbs singing on the record player.

"Did you look to the left?" Helen called back.

Kathryn squinted, for without her glasses she was practically blind. And when she finally turned and looked hard enough, she found the label she was looking for right before her. She took the bottle down and poured a generous helping. She drank as if she had just discovered water after walking parched through the desert. Then she placed her burning cigarette between her lips and inhaled.

She turned to look at Helen who was draped naked across the bed.

Kathryn watched as Helen French inhaled.

She felt dizzy. Her hip fell against the wet bar. She drank more.

"Come back here." Helen beckoned to her.

She obeyed, laying on the bed, stretching her naked body out beside Helen's.

"What's going on in that head of yours?" Helen shoved at Kathryn's forehead before puffing on her cigarette again.

Kathryn sighed and drank back another sip of whiskey.

"Lay off that, would ya?" Helen took the glass from her and drank it herself.

"Hey." Kathryn protested but didn't have the coordination to grab it back.

Helen laughed at her, leaning over so that her breasts hung in Kathryn's face as she extinguished her cigarette and settled the empty tumbler on the bedside table. Kathryn's hand reached up instinctively, cupping a breast in her hand. She delighted in the way Helen's body responded to her.

"Distracting me, I see." Helen's deep voice thrilled Kathryn. Always had since the first day she'd met her on set of her first ever movie in some bit part as a secretary. Helen, then the leading lady, had taken her under her wing, shown her everything she knew, took her to bed... "I mean if you're not going to tell me what's going on then I'll have to guess. And you won't like that much, now will you? But well, let's see. You've met someone new and you thought it was going well, but you've had a little lover's quarrel, or perhaps Charles is on to you about this person...I'm assuming she's a woman because you haven't mentioned her."

Kathryn pinched Helen's nipple.

"Jesus." Helen cursed, rubbing her breast.

Kathryn rolled onto her back, crossing her arms over her chest. Her lips pressed tightly together.

"Well, you hardly tell me a thing anymore." Helen scolded, propping her head up on her hand, looking down at Kathryn. "Who is she?"

Kathryn's hands flew to her face as she groaned. "There is no she. There is no he. There's Charles. And there's you."

Helen remained silent. Waiting.

Kathryn flailed, turned to face Helen. "It's useless. I've been forbidden."

Helen's eyebrows rose. "Forbidden."

"Yes, so it's pointless."

"Not if it has you going on like this. Just tell me who it is."

"No, I'm not going to tell you who it is. It's no one." Kathryn huffed.

Helen studied her. "I'll bet it's that darling what's her name…on that show of yours…that very lovely girl who plays Kay?"

"Helen!" Kathryn sat up, irritably reaching for her cigarettes.

"Oh my God. It's her, it's that Alice…Alice Canard?"

"Kincaid." Kathryn snapped as she flicked her lighter.

"Mmm," Helen was smiling. "She is scrumptious, isn't she? But certainly not a queer…I would highly doubt."

Kathryn blew a stream of smoke pointedly. She rubbed at her forehead. She stood up, swaying as she retrieved the tumbler again. "Was I queer when you first met me? Was it written all over my face or something?" Kathryn snapped as she picked up the whiskey bottle to pour herself another glass.

"My goodness, Kathryn. You've already seduced her, haven't you?" Helen's voice was far too knowing for her liking. As if she actually knew what had or had not happened between her and Alice…

"No." Kathryn choked out through her sip of whiskey.

"I can see why Charles might be concerned. I mean, darling, that is risky. Even for you."

"Oh, don't you give me that too." Kathryn sank into the lounge chair beside the mini bar, away from Helen.

Kathryn watched the older woman through a cloud of smoke. Helen had lost her mirth and was no longer laughing at Kathryn. Instead, she was wrapping her silk robe about herself, the fun of the evening diminishing. Kathryn traced the outline of the tiger that decorated Helen's right shoulder, stared him right in the eye.

"Don't you think I know?" Kathryn picked ash from her

tongue. The muscle felt heavy when she spoke, as if it were in her way. Her mind was hazy from drinking too much, smoking too much, trying to forget too much.

Alice, the darling idiot, had come back. Had made it beautifully through the show that week as if nothing had happened to her at all. As if she hadn't been in the hospital for pills.

Why had she taken pills?

Pills – oh, they killed you faster than anything. And they were everywhere in Hollywood. Kathryn knew far too many people who swallowed those damn things up. Helen, for example. Helen, who was now opening up a pill bottle for her nightly sleep remedy.

"Are you sure you should be taking those?" Kathryn spoke as she watched Helen through blurry eyes.

Helen looked at her and laughed. "What? These? Oh, they're nothing. Just a little something to help me sleep."

Kathryn stood on unsteady legs. She walked to Helen, snatching the bottle from her hands. Veronal. "I mean what is this shit?"

"For sleep. A woman my age needs sleep." Helen took the bottle from Kathryn, placing it on the bedside table before laying on the bed.

Kathryn sat down on the edge, smoking the last of her cigarette before stubbing it out. "God, I feel like all I do is sleep. I walk around half-asleep!"

"Then maybe you need the other ones." Helen quipped.

"The drinking I can handle but the pills…" Kathryn looked at the bottle. She knew it would be far too easy to fall down that rabbit hole. She had watched it consume people.

"Are you just going to sit there?" Helen asked sleepily.

Kathryn laid down beside Helen, curled into her side. "Tell me…tell me how you knew…"

"Knew what?" Helen's eyes were closed.

The record had stopped playing and all Kathryn could

hear was the sound of the night out beyond Helen's window-panes. The chirping, the stillness, the quiet. She felt the strangest sensation that it would all just swallow her up.

"About me."

Helen chuckled at this. Her fingers began to stroke Kathryn's scalp. "Well, you were so fucking green. I mean you didn't even know a goddamn thing about movies. You didn't know where to stand or what to do with yourself…"

"I wasn't…it wasn't that terrible." Kathryn muttered indignantly.

"It was the way you looked at me."

"What way?"

"Like you wanted to eat me up." Helen smiled in the lamplit room. "I'd catch you looking from across the room and Charles told me to make it stop."

"Charles?"

"Yes, he wanted me to help you get over your little infatu-ation." Helen rubbed at her eyes. Growing sleepier by the minute.

"I wasn't infatuated."

Helen laughed at this.

"He…he told you to…"

Helen shrugged. "He knew my proclivities and probably assumed his new bride harbored the same feelings. And lucky for me, she did."

"That shit." Kathryn cursed, laughed, and lay so that she was side-by-side with Helen.

There was silence. A distant clock. The rustle of palm leaves outside the window.

Helen's breathing had evened out.

Kathryn knew she should go home but also knew she was in no state to drive. So, she put out the bedside lamp and laid in the nearly dark room.

"Hey, kid." Helen's raspy voice came out muffled.

"Hmm?" Kathryn hummed.

"I'd listen to Charles about that Alice."

Kathryn rolled her eyes. "What, are you jealous?"

Helen laughed at this, tired and rough. "You'd like that."

The room fell silent again.

The California night air had cooled.

Kathryn felt chilled to the bone. She reached for the sheets to cover her naked body.

Didn't Helen know, didn't Charles know that Kathryn was not considering a fling with Alice? She wished that Charles and now Helen would leave her alone. She had done nothing wrong – save for that kiss, that idiotic kiss she had stolen all those weeks before.

That Alice had kissed her again…well…

No, she could never go near Alice.

"I can't have her." Kathryn whispered, ignoring the lump that tightened her throat. "I wouldn't…Helen, I wouldn't…She's not like you or Charles…" Kathryn turned to look at Helen, needing her to understand.

She could see the woman's face illuminated in the soft light from the mini bar. Her eyes were closed, face relaxed, breathing deeply.

"Helen?"

She was out like a light.

Chapter Nineteen

Alice

The more the days went on the worse it became.

She caught herself fixated on the most minute details; the way the flaxen haired woman would touch her neck with index and middle finger whilst listening or when deep in thought. It was an unconscious gesture, but to Alice it became bewitching, to see her fingers pressed against the delicate skin of her neck.

Or it was the way she would play with the gold band about her ring finger when she didn't have a cigarette between her fingers. As if her hands needed to stay busy, as if she was never quite certain of what to do with herself. Alice found these quirks most endearing.

Or when she might be deep in conversation with someone, she would flick her lighter so the flame would flicker and then die over and over again. All while she didn't pay the flame or the lighter any heed until she brought it to the end of her cigarette, her eyes narrowing in on the blaze, connecting it delicately with the paper between her lips.

There were tiny wrinkles – so small they might not have been noticeable to anyone in respectable range – around her lips. Lips that were always the same muted red that complemented her eyes, the eyes that wrinkled when she lit a cigarette or smiled (so rarely that happened). But when she smiled, oh those tiny wrinkles about her eyes - always hidden behind stage make-up to the world - were visible.

They reminded Alice that Kathryn was older than her.

That fact in and of itself drove Alice mad.

It was embarrassing – the thoughts that crossed Alice's mind.

Still plagued by the embarrassment of her stint dabbling in pills, she feared making another untoward mistake.

The pills had been flushed down the drain. Never to be taken again.

Kathryn had not addressed the kiss. It remained unacknowledged between them.

Alice began to wonder if it had happened at all. She circled about Kathryn, afraid to enter her orbit. Afraid to approach her. Afraid that it had all been some strange dream she had awoken from and now it was all over.

She sat at the back of the audience bleachers, legs hugged to her chest, script on the seat beside her, pencil firmly between her teeth as she watched.

Kathryn was on the stage, along with Wes and Stephen. It was a domestic scene, Stephen giving direction to the happy on-screen couple. But all she could see was Kathryn, whose eyes focused on Stephen as he spoke, script clasped in hand, arms crossed over her chest, head tilted to the side, listening.

Alice bit the pencil harder.

Kathryn's gaze had shifted. The woman had spotted her hidden away as she was.

Their eyes met.

Alice could have sworn she saw Kathryn's lip quirk upwards, a smile shimmering in her eyes.

Then, like the professional she was, Kathryn's attention returned to Stephen.

Alice felt her stomach knot. She had not eaten all morning. She was suddenly ravenously hungry. When they called lunch, Alice raced for a sandwich, eating two.

The days went on like this – a never ending ache welling up inside of her, a hunger she could not sate. Her attention was split between acting and Kathryn.

The phone calls had ceased. She did not hear from Kathryn in the evenings. She ate chocolate cookies. She thought about Kathryn at night while sitting on the couch watching whatever it was that Frank was watching beside her, but her mind was a million miles away.

A blonde woman on the screen would evoke new images that raced through her mind, thoughts of the way Kathryn's body had felt pressed to her own, the way she smelled of cigarettes and perfume, the softness of her lips when they kissed.

"I'm going to bed." Frank had shut off the television, but Alice was lost.

It was the inside of Kathryn's dressing room. The woman was removing make-up. First it was the foundation that they wore caked on each Friday evening for tapings. Then Kathryn pulled off one and then the other of her false eyelashes, making her eyes look smaller. With one wipe her red lipstick was gone and it was only the natural deep pink of her lips left.

Their eyes met in the mirror.

"Why are you over there?" Kathryn asked, as if she expected Alice to be standing there watching her. As if it were the most natural thing in the world. Kathryn beckoned to her warmly and Alice came.

Kathryn's hand appeared before her, an invitation. She could see the age in her skin. The slight tremor as she waited for Alice to take it.

Kathryn's hand was warm, and it felt nice where it rested in Alice's palm. She clasped tightly, and then it was dark eyes looking deeply inside of Alice's being. As if they could see all of who Alice was. Seeing her as no one had ever seen her before.

Her hand cupped Alice's cheek and Alice could feel the pressure of it, the heaviness where it rested, how her thumb stroked patterns against her skin.

Then relief in a feather light kiss.

Lips brushing against one another, turning into a heated, open-mouthed lip lock.

The warmth of skin burned her. The want for more and more had her reaching out, grasping at anything and everything she could touch.

She was practically crawling out of her skin with this fierce want, a desire that might destroy. Kathryn held her close and tight, until Alice no longer knew where one began and the other ended. Close, far too close. It was irresistible.

Until she opened her eyes.

She realized it was not Kathryn that she had taken in her arms, but Frank. Frank was on top of her, inside of her. He had want burning in his eyes.

The wind was knocked out of her lungs.

"It's never been like that." Frank was saying as he laid down beside her, breathing hard.

She couldn't look at him. Her cheeks grew red and hot and her throat swelled with a lump, unable to stifle a muffled sob which Frank took as a sound of pleasure.

Oh, it should not be like this! And this chimera, this dream had done nothing to quell the overwhelming feeling of want that had mounted unnaturally within her. She was left crying into her pillow because it had felt so real, because it was not Frank she wanted. It was not Frank who could soothe this ache.

She could not look at Kathryn the following day at rehearsal.

Chapter Twenty

Kathryn

Alice eluded her.

And yet…and yet…

At the studio during rehearsal, she felt her eyes, watching her every movement. The stares bore into her, making her feel entirely too self-aware of her movements. It became exhausting to know she was being watched, and yet the watching aroused in her pleasure.

Stephen moved toward her, telling her something about Paula, how she might react to the news that her husband was telling her. She listened, digesting the gist of it – had already decided how Paula would react – so she simply nodded her head in agreement, while very consciously playing with the ring on her finger. Slipping it from side to side, pulling it to the bend in her digit and then back into place again.

The scene commenced and she acted with total aware-ness, a sureness coloring her actions because there were eyes upon her. Watching. Elevating her performance in a way she had not tapped into for a very, very long time.

There was suddenly a strange flurry of excitement that broke out before the soundstage. A young secretary with wild curly hair had bounded in, was trying to get someone, anyone's attention. Stephen waved a hand for the rehearsal on stage to halt and looked pointedly at the young woman. Words were exchanged, Kathryn watched this, but felt her eyes drift upward, up and away, daring to meet the eyes that were watching her.

Alice straightened in her seat and looked away.

"Kathryn." Stephen was trying to get her attention.

She moved towards him.

Something was wrong. Something had happened.

"Kathryn, you have a phone call." Stephen irritably informed her.

Kathryn turned to the young secretary. "Can it wait until our break?"

The secretary hopped from foot to foot, uncertainty and fear furrowing her brow.

"Well, who is it?" Kathryn snapped. Annoyance rose within her. Whoever was calling was cutting into their rehearsal time. Stephen was staring at her with displeasure. Alice was looking at her again.

"It's…it's your mother. She said it was…well, it was important." The girl stuttered.

Kathryn felt a stabbing pain in her side. How dare she call the studio?

Eyes were upon her, watching her.

She straightened her shoulders. She apologized to Stephen and told the secretary she would take the call in her dressing room.

"Mother, I told you never to call…"

"Es tut mir leid, Katarina. Es ist …it's Warren." Her

mother's voice wavered on the other end of the line, the English language eluding her. She had been crying.

"Was ist mit ihm?" Kathryn felt her chest tightening.

"Er ist tot, Katarina, dead."

Kathryn felt the pressure suddenly release from her chest. She closed her eyes and exhaled.

"Es war sein Herz, his heart." Her mother went on.

Kathryn reached for her cigarettes. "Wann?"

"Heute Morgen."

She inhaled deeply on the lit cigarette, a strange mix of panic and relief swirling about inside of her. Why was her mother mourning his death? She wanted to shake her, to see that she was free, that she should be celebrating.

"The funeral will be dieses Wochenende."

"No." Kathryn shook her head. "I will not…"

"Katarina…"

"Stop calling me that!" Kathryn snapped. "I will not attend his funeral. And don't call the studio again." She slammed the phone back down into its cradle.

She sat on her dressing room couch smoking, staring blankly at the wall before her.

He was dead.

Well then.

She crushed out the cigarette and stood, went to the little cabinet in the corner, removed a bottle, poured a drop of vodka into a glass, and drank it down. She straightened her hair in the mirror, reapplied a fresh coat of lipstick, wiped mascara from the corner of her eye and then returned to the stage.

"I apologize for the interruption. Please, let's resume where we left off." Kathryn addressed Stephen, Wes, the others about them, and Alice, who sat with a new look of concern off in the audience bleachers.

Stephen looked at her curiously before he called places. "Take it at the top of the scene again."

The rehearsal went by in a blur.

It felt as if no time had passed at all when they called for a break. Kathryn stumbled from the stage, made a beeline for her dressing room, tossed her script to the make-up table and found her cigarettes. She lit one, smoked, rubbed at her forehead, and returned to the cabinet for another nip of vodka.

There was a light knock at her door. She downed the stinging liquid, coughed. "Who is it?"

She moved nearer to the door, expecting Stephen to come berate her.

But it was Alice who stood shyly on the other side. "I… uh, is everything all right?"

Kathryn reached out and pulled Alice into her dressing room, closing the door behind them. Alice ended up pressed against the wall beside the door. Her breathing shallow, eyes fearful.

Kathryn smiled. "You needn't be scared of me."

"I…I'm not." Alice whispered.

Kathryn had not moved away. There were warnings that rattled about in her head, but there was Alice before her, looking at her with those wide, innocent eyes. Wanting to know something.

"I'm all right. It was a small matter of no great concern." Kathryn scratched her neck, watching as Alice's eyes followed the motion.

It was no good, this. Whatever it was they were dancing around.

Kathryn wondered if others could see it.

The door was closed now so no one would see. No one would know.

The vodka had warmed her.

Alice's lips parted as if she might say something.

Kathryn smoked from her burning cigarette and exhaled out the side of her mouth.

Alice watched the smoke as it flowed from her lips.

Kathryn reached up, cradling Alice's cheek in her hand, pulling her closer.

Alice met her halfway, stretched up on her toes so that their lips could meet. And it was not the innocent kisses of before. It was pointed, direct, and very intentional. Alice kissed her with a fierceness, a longing that both surprised and delighted Kathryn.

She pushed at Alice, ever so slightly, parting them. Smiling.

Alice's brow furrowed; a fearful look crossing her features.

"Easy, easy." Kathryn smoked.

She had mis-stepped. The news earlier had caught her off guard, and now she had just involved an innocent bystander who looked as if she might start crying at any moment.

"Oh, Alice." Kathryn sighed, trying to reach for the woman, but she ducked out of her grasp.

Alice was shaking her head. She looked as if she might run away.

"I'm afraid I only make things worse for us. Don't I?" She stepped away from Alice, gave her some space to catch her bearings.

Alice leaned back against the door.

Kathryn looked into the mirror and straightened her hair, used her pinkie finger to fix her smudged lipstick. She caught Alice staring at her in the reflection of the mirror. "Oh darling, you couldn't possibly want to take up with me."

Alice whimpered, as if Kathryn's words of warning had only served to rouse her further.

She turned to face her. "No, I'm not..." she shook her head. How could she do this when she had just indulged her yet again? "I'm not worth all of that, you see. Listen, come... come here." And she held out her hand, offering a truce between them.

Alice stared at her hand as if it might burn her if she

dared to go too near it. "I can't stop..." Alice whispered and then closed her mouth again.

Kathryn sat down at her make up table. "I didn't mean to cause you any distress."

Alice shook her head. "I don't understand."

Kathryn turned, looking up from where she sat. Alice seemed so fragile, so frightened by it, by her. She had the power to break Alice, to rip her to shreds. And she didn't want that but she wanted...oh, what was it that she could possibly want? "What?"

"I don't understand....this." Alice whispered.

Kathryn wanted to tell her that this was not wrong - but she knew better than that. This was right but what this led to...well, that was wrong.

"Please, forgive me, Alice." Kathryn lowered her eyes. "I shouldn't...well, I shouldn't do this to you. To the both of us."

"But I want..."

Kathryn crushed out her cigarette. Her head was starting to pound. She wanted another drink before they would both have to return to set.

She needed Alice to not want; she needed her to leave.

She shook her head. "Please."

Alice looked as if she might cry, but then her eyes glowed with something Kathryn had never seen before - an internal rage that took Kathryn by surprise.

"Then don't..." Alice swiped a hand across her face. "Don't do that."

And she turned and left the room and Kathryn felt sick to her stomach. She reached for the bottle of vodka and downed a splash or two more than she should have. If she slurred her lines a little the rest of the day, what did it matter?

And when she got home that night she drank straight from the bottle alone in her darkened bedroom.

Chapter Twenty-One

Alice

The dream had shattered, split in two.

The kiss was relived again and again. The way it had played out between them. This time deliberate unlike the previous two encounters.

It returned to her subconsciously at night. As if she could alter what it was that had happened, that she might have brought about a different outcome.

Instead, she was left with the truth in the light of day. Kathryn existed. Kathryn was at rehearsal. Kathryn smelled of fragrant perfume and cigarettes. Kathryn's lips would curl into a smile if she saw Alice, but there was a lack of recognition in her glances. Kathryn laughed with Wes, with Larry, with Stephen, with the others.

Alice walked about as if a ghost.

"Alice," Stephen had caught up to her in the hallway.

She was eating a bagel.

Was she in trouble?

Her heart pounded as she turned to look at the director.

"Mind if I walk with you?" Stephen fell into step with her as they walked toward her dressing room. "You know, the producers have really been pleased with you. They like what you're doing."

"Oh," Alice felt a warmth welling inside of her, breaking through the funk she had fallen into. They came to stand in front of her dressing room. "Gee." Was all she could think of to say.

"Even I have to admit, Alice, you're doing really well. These last few weeks Kay has been incredible, really on the mark." Stephen – who almost never seemed enthusiastic about anything – looked pleased with her.

"Why, thank you." Alice smiled.

"I just wanted to say that I wouldn't be surprised if there was something in the works for you." He winked and then walked off.

Alice watched him go, stomach fluttering.

She had had no idea they were even watching her. She had always felt a wallflower and here they had been paying attention. She closed the dressing room door and ate the whole of the bagel, then rummaged for a package of cookies she'd stuffed away in a cabinet.

The show was coming to an end for the season. There was a theatre company in Los Angeles that her agent wanted her to perform for during the show's hiatus. She studied the script while the last of the television season taped. The weeks of filming flew by and she shared scarcely any pleasantries with Kathryn outside of rehearsal. They existed only as Kay and Paula those final few weeks of taping.

Their onstage chemistry had not waned. In fact, it only seemed to intensify. The comedy became more comedic. The looks Kathryn gave her – oh, those were not for an audience, but Alice could not accept them as anything more than what their characters asked of them.

A party was to be had after the final taping. A rather casual affair at Charles and Kathryn's home on Saturday evening after the final episode filmed.

Frank did not wish to attend.

Alice felt unnecessarily guilty attending, but it would be expected of her. Everyone would be there. *Everyone.*

She arrived at the familiar home. She felt as if everyone might know how she had shown up, uninvited one evening, then had been invited back for a disastrous dinner. The only consolation was that she would not be the only other guest this time.

Mariella opened the door to grant her entrance and they greeted one another cordially. People spilled into the main corridor and out to the back patio, wrapping about the pool that shone brightly in the fading evening light.

Alice took a deep breath and made her way through the others about her. She saw a generous spread of hors d'oeuvres, stopping briefly to survey a rather large cake that made her hunger surface.

It was familiar laughter that carried over all the other noise about her that caused her to look up. Her eyes came to focus on the vision dressed all in white, smoking a cigarette and laughing about something, the center of attention. Those about her were equally enraptured. She was smiling, poking at a man's chest as those dark eyes looked him up and down, and her red lips spoke something that made him look flushed and then had him and those around them laughing. She could drag anyone down; she could kill with words.

"Would you care for a drink?" A voice asked at her side, breaking her line of focus.

She turned to find Charles at her side.

"Oh, no thank you. No, I don't drink." She smiled politely, feeling a flush rising on her cheeks. Had he seen where she was looking?

"Frank's not with you this evening?" Charles asked, sipping his own drink.

She shook her head. "No, no. He doesn't like parties."

Charles nodded. "Smart man."

And then his attention diverted and he moved to greet someone else.

Alice took a deep breath, feeling out of sorts. She filled a plate with the garish offering of food and carried it out to the patio, to sit on the lounge chairs that she and Kathryn had sat quietly upon all those nights ago.

Her eyes darted about, finding Kathryn in the crowd again.

For a brief moment their eyes met.

Alice looked away and noticed Larry ambling towards her. He sat down in the lounger next to her, starting into some conversation that Alice only half listened to while eating every last thing on her plate.

Larry faded away at some point, replaced by several others.

The evening began to fade, darkness overtaking the outdoor events.

She had lost Kathryn in the fray of people.

She felt she didn't need to stay any longer. She felt unwanted and unsocial. Returning home and eating her way through a package of cookies while sitting beside Frank as he watched television and smoked – well, that might be a better way to spend her time.

She moved through the party, noticing that it had begun to thin out.

She knew she should not leave without speaking to the hostess. A deep hole in the pit of her stomach had opened itself up, for this would be the last she saw of Kathryn for the rest of the summer. She had no reason to keep in touch with her until the show went up again (there was at least a small relief in knowing it had been renewed for another season – at least this would not be the last she saw of Kathryn).

But as she made her way through the party she noticed a familiar woman in red. Why, it was that famous actress Helen Laurence. Alice had idolized her on screen, and here she was in the flesh.

Alice fell shy in the realization that she was only steps from the woman who looked surprisingly taller and more perfectly aged than she ever had on screen. Her features in person were softer; her smoky laughter charming.

Alice found herself hiding from Helen's line of sight, wanting to simply observe her. For who was Alice to talk to the woman?

From her vantage point she watched Helen, noticing when Kathryn appeared from the throng about her. Helen lifted a fresh cigarette to her lips and Kathryn turned to her, eyes shimmering as she cupped Helen's cheek in order to light the older starlet's cigarette.

It was the way they looked at one another. It was the way Helen furtively placed her hand on the small of Kathryn's exposed back. Red fingernails lightly scratching at the skin.

Alice's stomach sank. She wanted to vomit up all she had just consumed.

She was foolish. But of course…

She wanted to leave then. She wanted to forget this night had happened.

She moved through the crowd, determined to make her exit.

But before she could reach the door, she felt a hand reach out and grab her, pulling her into a stately little room off the side of the main foyer.

Kathryn was standing before her in the deafeningly quiet space.

"Leaving so soon?"

Chapter Twenty-Two

Kathryn

She'd been circling her all evening. Watching. Waiting for her to approach. And yet she did not. It was as if she didn't wish to speak to her at all.

Kathryn had ruined it before there was an it to ruin.

She'd watched Alice take flight, darting through the crowd as the party dwindled. And Kathryn knew she couldn't leave it like this.

She needed to speak to her.

Now she had her cornered in Charles' study, and Alice was looking up at Kathryn with fear in her eyes.

What did she fear? That Kathryn might try to kiss her again?

"I...no, it's late. I..." Alice fumbled for an excuse as to why she had been about to leave. "Frank..." it was the first time she'd attempted to use his name between them. She looked down, not believing herself either. "Well, it's late."

"I've hardly seen you all evening. Why were you hiding

from me?" Kathryn demanded. As if they were not about to spend nearly three months apart. Three months of not seeing one another almost every day. Perhaps they needed the time, but Kathryn didn't want to contemplate it. Not just then.

"I wasn't...I was *not* hiding." Alice spoke firmly. "You seemed otherwise occupied."

Kathryn's eyebrow rose at this. "There were guests to entertain, dear, but you were more than welcome to join in."

Alice shuffled.

Kathryn knew Alice was not one to just 'join in'. For as fun and outgoing as she appeared on television, she was a quiet thing who enjoyed solitude in her real life.

"I should be going." Alice did not try to mince words.

"Alice." Kathryn did not want to let her go.

"You should go tend to your guests. It was a lovely party." Alice was trying to stay even keeled, kind, but there was something simmering in her eyes.

"Don't you leave like this." Kathryn whispered.

"I don't know what you want from me." Alice quietly but firmly responded.

Kathryn whispered "oh God" under her breath and turned to Charles' desk, fishing for a cigarette out of the Bakelite box. She lighted it with his Dupont lighter and settled atop the corner of his desk, looking at Alice, who had pressed herself against the edge of a bookcase. She looked ridiculously gorgeous, auburn hair curled about her face, a simple green dress that hid all of her best features.

Alice crossed her arms over her body. "When you told me about Daphne du Maurier you were telling me about yourself."

Kathryn felt a strange twisting pain in her chest. "What?"

"You implied that she lives a life outside of her marriage. That she has lovers...female lovers."

"Yes." Kathryn blew a stream of smoke from the corner of her lips.

"And you as well?" Alice's cheeks turned a charming shade of pink.

Kathryn could only laugh. "Well, yes." She wondered if her own face had warmed. For of anyone to know who and what Kathryn was, she had not expected Alice to be so forward about it.

And Alice looked as if she might cry. "I'm…oh."

"Does that shock you?" Kathryn tapped her cigarette in a golden ashtray. Her hand shook as she did so.

Alice shook her head. "I should have…well…no."

"Alice, you don't think less of me, do you?"

Alice's face looked pained.

Oh, it had all gone wrong.

"No." Alice shakily exhaled. "I don't know what I was thinking."

"Thinking?"

"You kissed me. You kissed me and I wanted…but I'm just…I'm just a toy to you. Just one of a thousand others."

Kathryn stood from the edge of the desk. "No. No, that's most certainly not true. Alice…"

But Alice slunk away from her again.

"Alice…"

"Then why did you do it? I hate that you did it. I hate it because I can't stop…Why?" Alice covered her face with her hands, as if she just wanted to disappear.

Kathryn's legs weakened. She wanted to take Alice into her arms, but all she could do was stand there. Smoking. Uselessly. "Alice, please." She whispered.

Alice peered at her from between her hands.

"Alice, you're not like me. You should run far, far away from me."

"But I can't!" Alice half-whispered, half-yelped. "It's unfair. You keep pulling me in and then pushing me away. How am I supposed to feel?" She was pacing, unable to look at Kathryn.

How gorgeous she was. All riled up from the knowledge that nothing had been innocent between them.

"I don't know." Kathryn sat against the desk.

Alice finally looked at her. Her hands by her sides, stance defiant. "I don't want to be a part of your harem."

"My harem?" Kathryn laughed incredulously. "I'm not so dastardly as all of that. Jesus, Alice."

"Well I don't know what it is that you do or don't do." Alice countered before covering her face with her hands again. Overwhelmed. "You know, I think it's good that we won't see one another for the summer."

"Oh, Alice. You don't mean it."

"No, I won't be a part of this. I can't…not the way I…oh, Kathryn." A tear slid from Alice's eye and she wiped at it furiously; she was looking right at Kathryn with such longing. With such pain.

How had she hurt her so terribly even before it began?

Charles would murder her if she'd already fucked it up without even…

And then Alice was kissing her. Arms about Kathryn's body, hands coming to rest on the exposed skin of her back, warm where they touched.

And then Alice cursed and stepped away. "I have to go." She turned and fled the room, fled Kathryn's home. Leaving Kathryn to finish her cigarette, attempting to reel in her racing mind.

What was it she had just been accused of? What had just transpired between them?

Alice saw and knew more than Kathryn had suspected.

"Shit." She cursed under her breath, lifted a shiny envelope opener from Charles' desk so she could inspect her smeared lipstick.

"What are you doing alone in here?" Charles had appeared in the office doorway.

Kathryn startled, the knife slipping from her hands.

"Nothing." She smoked the last of her cigarette and crushed it in the ashtray before reaching down for the knife.

Charles continued to watch her, staring as she smoothed back her hair, ran a hand over her dress, and made sure she was straightened out as she walked toward him.

"Alice left rather hastily." He spoke knowingly as he lightly wiped at the edge of her lip with his pinky finger.

Kathryn hummed, shaky. "Did she?"

"Yes, raced right on by. I suppose you wouldn't know what that was about?"

Kathryn shook her head slowly as they walked into the foyer together. "Not at all."

Charles clasped his hand about her wrist. Tightly. Pressing the golden bracelet about her wrist into her skin. "Don't be stupid." He whispered into her ear and then smiled at Gordon Nielson – another producer of *The Wes Goodwin Show* - who happened by just then. Charles dropped her wrist, sauntering off to take up a conversation with him.

Kathryn disappeared into the living room to pour herself a real drink – not some frou-frou cocktail they were serving - from the mini-bar and inspect her reddened wrist.

The rest of the evening passed by in a daze.

She remembered not seeing Charles again for the whole of the night and had only a vague recollection of ending up in her own bed with Helen between her legs, fueled by disjointed thoughts of Alice's lips pressed against her own.

Chapter Twenty-Three

Alice

It was easier. The distance between.

There was a rhythm, a repetition that she fell into that summer. There were the rehearsals that preceded the two-month run of the play. She had come from theatre, remembered what it was like and yet this time it was different because she was Kay from television. They gave her a white glove treatment that she was not familiar with at all. She felt left out when the others, who were not on television, congregated, and she was left to herself. As if she were some porcelain doll who couldn't be touched.

After the performances began, she would perform in the evening, receive gracious accolades from the critics and the public, and then quietly drive to an all-night diner where she sat alone in a corner booth, unrecognizable without make-up, dressed down so nothing might call attention to her. So that she might not be Kay from television while eating a burger and a plate of fries and a milkshake all alone.

Sometimes she would drive home, and, on the way, there was a gas station with a dingy little bathroom out back where she'd occasionally vomit up all that she had consumed.

And by the time she got home, Frank would be passed out asleep.

Their schedules were off.

He left early in the morning. Alice slept until noon most days.

She ate to pass the tedious boredom of time between mid-morning and evening when she would drive to the theatre and prepare for another performance.

In the meantime, her waist began to fill out.

Her costumes stopped fitting three weeks in.

A seamstress was called to alter her dresses.

It was humiliating, but instead of feeling as if she could break the habit of what she was doing to herself, it only made it worse.

Her agent wanted to talk to her. He set a lunch meeting at Musso & Frank's. She put herself together, wore black, and did up her face.

Nathan greeted her with a kind smile, kissed her cheek. He was so young, so very young, but the agency had recently promoted Alice to his care. They said he was the hottest young agent who knew what he was doing with his clients. He was hungry; her career was going well.

"How's the show going? You've gotten nothing but praise for your role. I think it was absolutely the right thing to get you back on stage now. They think you can do anything. That's just what we want them to think." He spoke quickly as they settled across from one another in the red booth toward the back of the restaurant.

"Well," Alice watched the young man as he lit a cigarette, eyes glancing away and then back at her. "It's going well. I would say."

"Yeah, you're really good in the part. It might as well have been written for you."

"I identify with her." Alice moved the knife atop a napkin from side to side.

Nathan nodded enthusiastically. He ordered a drink and asked if she wanted one. She politely asked for iced tea.

He looked at her again after the waiter had gone, as if he'd used up all his pleasantries. He fiddled with the gold watch about his wrist. "Wes' show starts up again soon." He drummed his finger against the white tablecloth.

Alice felt her stomach twist in a knot. It would be less than a month. It seemed too soon and yet not soon enough.

The waiter brought their drinks.

Nathan drank his back then looked at Alice. He leaned in close. "You're not, uh…" he smoothed a hand over his tie, looking about the restaurant as if afraid someone might overhear. "You're not you know, in the family way? Are you?"

Alice frowned. His question took a moment to register.

He was asking her if she was pregnant?

She wanted to cry.

"No." She shook her head. "No, I'm not." Her cheeks warmed.

She would know if that were the case. And it most certainly could not have been because it had been weeks - had it been months? – since Frank had last touched her. They had used protection. She knew what the contract for Wes' show explicitly stated. There would be no pregnancies on camera.

The tension that had mounted in Nathan's shoulders released. "Good, that's good. Really good."

How had she allowed this to happen?

He ordered himself steak and potatoes and a salad for Alice.

She knew what he was telling her.

She drove home in tears, absolutely humiliated. She did not touch another morsel of food until after the performance, when she drove to the all-night diner and ate through another burger and fries and milkshake meal. This time she didn't get rid of it.

The next morning, she awoke to the sound of the television mumbling in the living room.

She had forgotten the day. Saturday.

She felt ill from the previous evening's unneeded activities. She ended up vomiting in the toilet before she groggily stumbled to the kitchen, but before she could reach the kitchen for a cup of coffee to wake herself up, Frank reached out and grabbed her wrist. He pulled her towards him.

She stumbled, dazed and confused.

"The show gets over at 9:30." Frank looked up at her from his spot on the couch.

She felt as if she did not recognize him, as if she were looking at him for the first time in years. His face was older in the early morning light that came through yellowed blinds. His eyes bore into her. He smoked, looking up at her. Her stomach twisted.

"You know I can't sleep after a show." Alice said tiredly.

Frank regarded her, seeming to not believe something about what she was saying. "You're my wife."

Alice's brow creased. "Of course, I am." What was this?

"What is it you do from ten to well past midnight then?" Frank pulled her closer. Her knees pressed against the edge of the couch. "Huh?"

Alice was not awake enough for this. "Nothing. I just..." she shrugged. "I just drive around."

"You just drive around." He'd sat up, sliding his hand beneath her nightgown.

"Frank," she tried to push at him, but he held her tighter. "I just drive around, go to a diner. It's nothing. I can't sleep, oh..." Her hands were on his shoulders as he pulled her closer.

And she thought about Kathryn, about the way Kathryn's

bare skin had felt beneath her fingertips when she'd kissed her all those months before. And she thought about the way the woman's lips had tasted of cigarettes and alcohol and she'd smelled of her expensive perfume and that little bit of herself that drove Alice wild.

"Don't, Frank…don't." She warned him because they couldn't be careless.

But he didn't stop.

Chapter Twenty-Four

Kathryn

New York, NY

From the moment the plane touched down at Idlewild, Kathryn was hardly sober a moment in New York. Charles sent a car to fetch her at the airport that took her to their Apthrop apartment.

Charles was not there, but he had left a message with the doorman that she should meet him that evening at the St. Regis for dinner. She lit a cigarette, slid out of her heels, poured herself a glass of brandy and proceeded to drink as she clumsily moved from room to room. The apartment was as she remembered it. But she was not a part of it. It was so very much Charles' domain, and she would be forced to fit into it for the coming weeks.

She searched for clues, rummaging through his things to see just what he got up to when he was on the opposite side of the country without her. She sat on the side of his bed and opened the top drawer of the bedside table, surveying the abundant supply of condoms, the numerous pornographic photographs, tissues. She placed the cigarette between her lips and picked up one of the photographs, admiring the curve of the woman's hips raised high as a man's dick entered her from behind.

She was half an hour late to meet Charles. He was entertaining business men. He greeted her with curious eyes and a kiss to her cheek. Loose from alcohol, the whole affair was not so awful. The men found her charming. The drinks kept coming. She found the men charming.

Charles had to hold her upright when they left, his arm bracing her firmly.

"You have the read through in the morning." He cautioned her when she reached between his legs in the safety of the bedroom. Her dress was half off, and she was swaying.

"Don't you want to fuck your wife?"

"You're drunk." He enunciated as if she couldn't hear.

"So are you." She laughed at him, her hand finding that he was not as opposed to her as his words attempted to imply. "You can do whatever you want." She whispered against his ear.

He shoved her face first onto the bed.

She was hungover at the first read through and the subsequent days of early morning production.

If she fumbled over some lines, well what did it matter? The script was shit.

She couldn't stand the Demille girl who, when the cameras weren't rolling, looked at Kathryn with disdain, dismissing her with disinterest. If there was not any onscreen business between them, Lillian would otherwise ignore Kathryn, acting as if the entire picture was centered around her and no one else mattered.

It was exhausting.

The only person Kathryn could stand to be with was her onscreen husband.

Dick Garrison.

Invariably they ended up in his hotel bar after filming wrapped each day, since Charles scarcely had time for her, despite the fact they were living together now. He seemed absent most evenings, gone out to wine and dine and appease the whole of the New York entertainment world.

Dick, however, had time on his hands. He had grown handsome over the years, since their first picture together. She remembered finding him attractive then but unapproachable, nearly ten years prior. His dark hair was now peppered with gray, the pronounced wrinkles around his steely eyes creased deeper when he smiled, and it annoyingly suited him.

She wondered if he could see the same tells of age written on her own visage.

He was nearing fifty. At least his age matched the age of their on-screen daughter.

He was married again, as he had not been the last time they had filmed together. Though his wife was back in Los Angeles, a hot young thing making a name for herself in some A pictures.

He lit Kathryn's cigarettes as they sat at the bar.

"That blundering Stevenson doesn't stand any more of a chance now than he did four years ago. He hasn't the balls of Eisenhower." Dick lamented.

"Balls enough to try again." Kathryn smiled.

Dick snorted.

Kathryn drank back more of her brandy. How many had it been? Oh, did it matter anymore? "Stevenson's too smart for his own good. Besides, he's not a leader. Not a real one anyway." She tapped off ashes and smoked again. "And, if you really look hard enough their campaigns aren't any different."

"The devil you know and all of that?" Dick laughed, waving down the waiter for another round.

Kathryn raised her glass in a salute, downing the last of it. "Why the hell are we talking about politics?" She winced as the alcohol burned. And yet she didn't feel nearly as far gone as she wanted to.

"You're about the only woman I can discuss politics with." Dick was grinning, boyish charm twinkling in his cool, blue eyes.

"That wife of yours doesn't have a head for it?" Kathryn extinguished her cigarette.

Dick gave her a dangerous half-smile. "She wasn't even old enough to vote for Eisenhower the first time."

Kathryn rolled her eyes to the ceiling. She reached for her golden cigarette case and opened it, lifting another to her lips. Dick leaned in closer this time when he lit it for her. Kathryn could see the blue of his eyes. Two pools. Kathryn blew off a cloud of smoke. "She's good in bed then?"

Dick had the decency to blush. "Well now."

Kathryn shoved at his shoulder. "I bet you can't even keep up with her."

"You wound me." He feigned hurt, laughing good naturedly as he drank back the alcohol before him.

"A hot young thing like that." Kathryn inhaled sharply and drank again.

"You speak as if you could do better." He laughed heartily.

"I could." Kathryn spoke assuredly.

Dick's hotel room was on the tenth floor.

He shoved her against the door as soon as it shut.

He was drunker than he had appeared moments before.

His face was rough, kisses pressed chaotically to her lips in a comical prelude to something.

She didn't even particularly like him. He'd played one of Helen's paramours in a movie. She'd remembered watching, feeling ridiculous jealousy and something akin to intrigue splintering through her chest when he'd kissed Helen on screen. Now she felt his real kisses, and they were not as intimate as the camera had made them appear.

He couldn't get hard. No matter what they tried.

He passed out not long after.

She put herself together and hailed a cab to the Apthrop.

Charles was sitting in the living room when she arrived.

Her shoulder fell into the hallway wall as she attempted to slip out of her heels.

Charles watched her as she moved to the minibar in the corner of the room and, with much focus, poured herself another drink.

Charles came up behind her, slid his hand beneath her skirt. "Not Demille, I presume."

She snorted at that, setting the empty tumbler roughly against the bar top. "Not that nit-wit." She turned to face Charles, supporting herself against the surface behind her.

She met Charles' all too sober face.

He was familiar to her. For fifteen years they had played at this marriage. They knew one another inside and out. She felt an odd comfort, his hand cupping her behind as he held her close.

She thought he might kiss her, but he pressed his lips to her ear. "You know I don't give a shit what you do after hours with yourself, but cut it out on set."

Kathryn frowned at this. "What are…"

"You're not stupid." Charles cut her off. "Drinking in your trailer, snubbing Demille…"

Kathryn snorted at that. "The girl barely acknowledges my existence!"

"The forgotten lines, the slight slur, the tremor in your hand…" He kept right on at her.

"Hey buddy, I'm not the one who agreed to this." She shoved at his chest.

He looked unamused as he took the tumbler from her hand. He drank it back before slamming it down atop the bar. She watched him, wondering if she had pushed him too far this time.

Though they had an amicable marriage – arrangement perhaps -, she knew where she stood with him.

There were limits.

"Just lay off it, would ya?" He gave her a wry smile.

She nodded, feeling far more sober than she had only moments before.

"I brought you here to be with me." He pulled her closer. "To keep an eye on you."

Kathryn snorted. "You haven't been home the last three nights."

"But I'm here now."

"You just want me because someone else showed interest." She taunted him.

He grabbed her tighter, looking into her eyes. "You're my wife, aren't you?"

He took her into the shower, washed her clean and then took her to bed.

Afterwards, Kathryn sat in the darkened bedroom, smoking a cigarette, watching him as he slept, head in her lap. She ran her fingers through his sandy-brown hair.

She had not had a drink for hours. Her mind was razor sharp and her thoughts crystalline in a way she had grown unaccustomed to.

She smoked uncomfortably.

She listened to a passing siren wailing just outside the window, reminding her where she was.

She looked at the clock with illuminated face on the bedside table.

1:36.

It would be 10:36 in California.

Charles snored lightly, shifting closer to Kathryn.

She lifted the phone quietly from the bedside table. She dialed the numbers she had memorized and then felt her heart pound when the phone began to ring in her ear. She pressed the receiver close, wondering if Charles would hear, too.

But he did not stir.

It was the sound of a phone picking up that made her heart leap into her chest. And then that darling, timid voice came on the line. "Hello?"

Alice.

Kathryn's lips moved to form the name on the tip of her tongue, but she couldn't make a sound. Not one sound.

"Who is it?" Alice's voice grew bolder.

Kathryn inhaled shakily on her cigarette, eyes slipping shut, head falling back to rest against the headboard.

"Hello?" Alice whispered again and Kathryn wanted to speak, wanted to ask her how she was, how the play was going, if she was all right... but the words all died on her tongue.

Charles snored again.

Kathryn could hear Alice breathing.

She exhaled a cloud of smoke.

"Hello?" Alice tried again, and Kathryn feared Alice would hang up. Until she heard her name whispered. "Kathryn...is that you?"

Kathryn's eyes flashed open. Caught at her own game.

Alice continued to listen.

Kathryn covered her mouth against the receiver and whispered "I'm sorry" before hanging up.

She crushed out her cigarette and felt a tear lodge itself in her eye.

Chapter Twenty-Five

Alice

An apology could mean many things.

Cryptic as it had been.

Alice finished her calisthenics and longed for a piece of bread.

Had Kathryn's apology meant she was unable to reciprocate?

Alice looked into the refrigerator and saw only the vegetables she had purchased and nothing she wanted to eat. She closed the door.

Perhaps Kathryn wanted to be with her? But then why couldn't she say it?

Alice rummaged through the cabinet, feeling lightheaded.

And did Alice want it? Knowing who and what Kathryn was? Was Alice like that? Could Alice be the same?

She found a hidden box of crackers. She guiltily slunk off to the bedroom to lay on the bed and flip through daytime television shows, attempting to distract her racing mind.

Before she realized what she had done, she had eaten every last cracker.

She vomited in the toilet, hid the box down at the bottom of the trashcan, and then prepared a salad. Wasn't salad supposed to be good?

But it did not taste good.

Could she be with Kathryn knowing Kathryn could not be with her fully?

Could she be with Kathryn fully knowing that there was Frank?

She checked to see if her period had come.

It had not.

She was two days late.

It happened occasionally this way and she tried not to worry, but this time she supposed there was cause for worry.

She stood on the scale and made note that she had lost five pounds. Five pounds in a week. Well, wasn't that something?

At least her costumes fit again.

The show ended that weekend, and she was more upset by this than she had expected to be. It had been a good run. She enjoyed the character, the whole show.

But the end meant a new beginning for *The Wes Goodwin Show*. It meant seeing Kathryn again.

What had Kathryn meant?

"I'm sorry."

But sorry for what? Calling so late as she had? Could it have been so simple?

The days dwindled downwards.

Her period did not come.

The final night of the production came. Everyone cried and then attended a party, and Alice made a brief appearance for the sake of the press but then went home to Frank. She looked at him sitting in his chair, watching television. And she could not see what she had once seen in him. He seemed like every other man. She wanted to smack him. Because her period had still not arrived.

He had been selfish.

"What're you lookin' at?" Frank asked finally.

She realized she'd been standing frozen in place, staring.

Huffing, she walked down the hallway, showering away the last remnants of stage make-up and sweat and then curled into a ball on the bathtub floor and cried.

Would it be better to have a piece of Kathryn than nothing at all?

It would not improve a thing for her, perhaps only satiate a need that burned inside of her.

But there was more to it than that, wasn't there?

They could never be together. At least not in the public's eye.

Oh, Alice was being very presumptuous. As if Kathryn even wanted to be with her! Oh, who was she to think she could have a place in Kathryn's heart?

The first day of rehearsal came all too quickly. Alice was still ten-pounds overweight. She wore all black, as if it might help conceal what she had done to herself. She felt self-conscious and nervous.

And she longed to see Kathryn. She needed clarification.

Sorry for what?

But as she sat at the read-through table, anxiously leafing through the script, she felt suddenly shy at the first sight of Kathryn. Kathryn in slacks and a clean white button-up shirt, hair pulled back in a French twist, glasses framing her dark eyes. She was looking right at Alice, clasping her own script to her chest. Her eyes appraised Alice, looking her over.

Alice blushed at the brazenness, at the way that she looked *too* deeply.

Kathryn's red lips twisted into a smile.

But there was not time to speak because the rehearsal commenced almost immediately.

Alice kept her head down, only stealing furtive glances in Kathryn's direction, watching smoke swirl about her head as she sat listening while the other actors read through their scenes. Alice watched Kathryn as she recited lines animatedly from her script.

They only spoke to one another as Paula and Kay.

The read-through offered a kind of protection from one another.

Kathryn caught her looking and offered her a small smile.

Was it all right now between them? Had anything changed?

Alice's stomach knotted.

An assistant called for break and Alice stood, fearfully.

Kathryn was caught by Wes, who pulled her into a conversation.

Alice raced to her dressing room and locked herself away in her bathroom, discovering that her period had come.

She smiled at herself in the mirror.

She was still free.

She could not be certain how she managed it, but moments later she slid inside Kathryn's dressing room and closed the door behind her.

Kathryn looked up curiously from where she sat, eating lunch at her make-up table. A pleased smile played at her lips as soon as she registered Alice's face.

"Alice." She turned to greet her. "Look at you. How is it possible you became more gorgeous in only a few months?"

Alice's cheeks burned red. "No, I…I'm…grotesque."

"Don't say such a ridiculous thing. It suits you." Kathryn spoke seriously.

Alice pressed herself against the wall behind her, needing the support.

Kathryn was looking at her curiously.

Why had she come to her so boldly?

"I'm sorry."

"What if I am like you." Alice whispered.

Kathryn's studio sculpted brow rose in amusement. "Like me? Why…I wouldn't wish that on anyone." She opted for humor, as if she could sense Alice's discomfort in the confession.

"Kathryn." Alice groaned.

"Come, come here." Kathryn stood and motioned for Alice to follow her to the couch.

Alice peeled herself unwillingly away from the wall, moving to sit on the opposite end of the couch.

"What is all this about?" Kathryn lit a cigarette, eyeing Alice.

Alice looked at her hands folded in her lap. She could not look at Kathryn. "You said that I couldn't be…that I wasn't… but I…" she closed her eyes, took a deep breath. "I've felt it before. I was…curious. I had a roommate in New York before Frank. We used to, you know…just a little kissing, petting, nothing…and I never thought…but now…" Alice watched as Kathryn's hand came to cover her folded hands.

"It's all right, Alice." Kathryn's voice was gentle.

Alice liked the weight and the feel of Kathryn's hand against her own. She turned one hand upward; Kathryn's fingers slid between hers.

"Charles is in New York this weekend. Come to my place Sunday afternoon. We can talk more about this." Kathryn's tone was unreadable.

Alice looked up. "But Frank…"

"Tell him you're going shopping, anything…"

Alice bit her lip, felt Kathryn's thumb stroke the back of her hand.

And then she nodded. "Yes, all right."

Chapter Twenty-Six

Kathryn

New York had reignited something within Charles. Passion returned. As if he could not get enough of Kathryn. He followed her back to Los Angeles once the movie wrapped. He attentively stayed home with her in the evenings. It felt as if their relationship had slipped backwards, to a more innocent time between them. Her body reacted sweetly to him.

This happened between them.

A fissure, a splintering apart followed by passionate days of coupling and rekindling.

But this time, Kathryn felt an unfamiliar uneasiness. She yearned for Charles to go back to New York, though she realized this passionate interlude could serve her well. She could make him happy, very happy, and then he would never suspect, might never know if she were to...

Alice's confession haunted her. Every day at rehearsal when she saw Alice from across the room, nights after rehearsals when she was drinking with Charles, sleeping with Charles, then watching Charles sleep...it was Alice. And her words and this new understanding that had come between them.

Charles left Friday after the taping. He looked almost sad when he kissed Kathryn goodbye in her dressing room after the show. It should have been endearing, that he could love her so much and she him after all that they did to one another… Instead, she felt guilty and almost pulled him back toward her to tell him of her plans.

Instead, she let him go and felt an unjust relief in his parting.

She saw Alice with her husband talking to Larry when she left later that evening. Alice looked at her and seemed lost. She tried to offer her furtive encouragement. *Only two days more, my darling.*

Alice did not seem reassured.

Saturday was uneventful. Kathryn had Mariella instruct the housekeepers to leave no space uncleaned and informed her that she could take the following day off.

Kathryn sat in her bedroom, smoking, reading, drinking, thinking. She passed out far too early for a Saturday evening but awoke Sunday feeling refreshed.

She made herself a decadent breakfast of scrambled eggs and bacon and toast and a drop of champagne in some orange juice. She luxuriated in a bath until her skin smelled of roses. She dressed carefully and then waited without waiting with a novel.

It was sometime after noon that a car turned into her drive.

Kathryn peered through her blinds, watching as Alice emerged from the car, eyes shaded behind large, dark glasses, hair gleaming red in the sun, a gentle yellow dress encasing her beautifully filled in figure. She looked nervous, anxiously smoothing herself out.

Kathryn extinguished her cigarette and met her at the door.

Alice slid the dark glasses from her eyes, uncertainty coloring the motion.

Kathryn pulled her inside, closing the front door so that they were shielded from the outside world. Alone together now.

"My, my. What a picture you make." Kathryn looked her up and down.

Alice stood in her yellow dress, hands folded in front of her and then down at her sides.

"Come on. You needn't be frightened." Kathryn reached out a hand for Alice, pulling her toward the back of the house. "I made us some lemonade, since I know you won't have a real drink." Kathryn winked. "I thought we could have it outside on the patio. It's such a nice day in the shade, don't you think?"

They sat near one another at the shaded patio table. Kathryn poured the lemonade into two glasses, tossed in some ice, and then lit a cigarette. Alice watched her every movement. She became intensely self-conscious. She swiped a stray strand of hair from her forehead and looked to Alice.

Alice's head bowed. She held the lemonade clasped between her hands, appearing to stare into its surface as if she could jump into it and disappear.

Kathryn exhaled a stream of smoke to the sky, tapping off her cigarette.

"I've never…" Alice whispered, as if she felt Kathryn had lost patience with her.

"It's all right." Kathryn assured her.

Alice nodded, sipping the lemonade that matched the yellow of her dress and then settling the glass atop the table. "You and Helen Laurence?"

Kathryn choked for a moment. "Helen? What about Helen?"

Alice held her gaze. "It seemed that you were…intimate with her. At the party…"

Kathryn's brow furrowed. Intimate with Helen at the party? Why Helen had been there, Kathryn remembered. But what had happened between them that evening had certainly happened after Alice had taken her leave. How could she possibly know a thing about that? "What do you mean?" Kathryn tapped off ashes and inhaled again.

Alice watched her. "Her hand…it was on your back." Upon speaking the words Alice's eyes glazed over. As if she had replayed the very image of it a thousand times over and over.

My, the woman was perceptive.

Kathryn could not deny Alice this. Perhaps if she were to come clean, perhaps if she told her the truth of it then she might leave and whatever was bubbling up between them might burst at the seams and rip them apart for good. "I've known Helen for years." Kathryn looked at the table before her, at the pool that flowed from the back patio, to the trees that surrounded it. "Yes, we have been intimate."

Alice exhaled through an O shaped mouth, as if trying to formulate a response. Instead, she reached for the lemonade, drinking it.

"Does that bother you?" Desperation suddenly clutched at Kathryn.

Alice turned the lemonade glass in her hands. "No." She sighed.

She was so good, she was so kind, she was so pure and innocent to all of this. What was Kathryn doing to her?

Alice should have gotten up and left then. Perhaps it would have changed things.

Instead they finished their glasses of lemonade. Kathryn stubbed out her cigarette, staring out at the glistening pool. It seemed so inviting.

"It makes it worse." Alice finally spoke.

Kathryn turned to look at her, puzzled.

"What?"

Alice took a deep breath. "That she's…that you and her have…It makes me want…well, it doesn't help."

Kathryn felt her cheeks flush, wondering if she could blame it on the late summer California heat.

"I think I know how it is. I read the papers enough to know that Charles does what he wants and it seems you do what you want and…well, that seems very strange, very foreign to me. But it doesn't make it go away…"

"Alice, what do you want?" Kathryn folded her arms atop the table, leaning closer to Alice.

"Oh, what do I want?" Alice wrapped her arms about herself, looked blindly around at the world about them. "What do I want? Well, I want to go inside. It's so warm out here."

"Yes, of course. It's cooler in the sitting room."

They moved inside, into where a fan blew cool air and the house protected them from the sun. Kathryn got Alice a glass of ice water. And they sat on a couch near to one another.

Alice pressed the cool glass to her forehead, closing her eyes as they sat together. She looked about the room, anywhere but at Kathryn. "Do you play the piano?" She asked.

Kathryn followed her line of sight and saw the giant instrument that sat grandly in the middle of the room. "Yes. Would you like to hear something? I'm not very good." Kathryn prefaced.

Alice nodded.

Kathryn got up and sat at the piano, racking her brain for something easy to play. A Haydn sonata she'd learned years ago came to mind and she began playing. The notes flowed from her fingers in the sticky hot afternoon and occasionally she fumbled but began again, delving into the curves and twists of the trills, careful to fall harder on her right-hand notes than left hand so that the melody came out somewhat clearly.

And at some moment she was aware that Alice had stood from the couch, had moved towards her. She was watching her intently and then somewhere in the B section of the piece she felt Alice's fingers ghost over the exposed skin on her neck.

Her hands stilled on the piano and the sound died out around them.

Alice seemed suddenly frightened and Kathryn reached up to cover her fingers with her own. Holding Alice's hand against her shoulder.

"It was beautiful. I didn't mean to interrupt you." Alice spoke softly.

"You didn't." Kathryn released her hand slowly. Turning, she glanced up at Alice who was looking down at her for a change.

Neither moved.

And then Alice reached out and cupped Kathryn's cheek with her hand.

Kathryn was afraid to move, so she sat still.

Alice's thumb began to slowly ghost over Kathryn's lips.

Kathryn's lips parted.

Alice's thumb slid between her teeth.

She bit down on the nailbed.

There was the ticking of a clock, the sound of their breathing.

Alice shifted ever so. Her hand retracted from Kathryn's mouth, moved gently to Kathryn's shoulder, beneath which was the strap of Kathryn's dress. Her fingers toyed with the material.

Kathryn watched her face, afraid to move, scarcely able to breath as if afraid the slightest sound or movement might frighten Alice away. And she did not want Alice to go away. She felt a pleasant sensation warming her.

She dared to place her hands around Alice's waist, feeling the softness of the yellow dress beneath her fingers.

Alice stepped closer to her. "Please." She whispered.

Alice's breasts were pert, pink nubs, revealed from beneath the yellow material. The weight of them was perfect in Kathryn's palms. The left nipple hard when Kathryn pressed her lips to it.

Alice's fingers worked at Kathryn's dress until she was free from it.

Their lips found each other.

Alice's dress fell to the floor.

They barely made it to the couch where Kathryn laid Alice down.

Alice's whimpers were mellifluous, her gasps, the way she grasped at Kathryn intoxicating. And she was willing, so very willing.

Her body convulsed and Kathryn held her close, pressed kisses to her neck, to her cheeks, her lips and Alice wrapped herself about Kathryn, holding her close.

It was only moments – hours? – later that Kathryn stumbled from the couch for a cigarette and a drink.

Alice looked up at her with hooded, emerald eyes and Kathryn, tumbler pressed to lips, could see the fire that burned brightly in Alice's gaze. The want had not been extinguished.

Alice cleared her throat, covering herself awkwardly as if ashamed of her glorious figure. "I should leave." But Kathryn knew she wanted to stay.

Kathryn shyly nodded, not wanting her to leave.

Alice began to put herself back together.

They stood at the door, the sun no longer high in the sky.

"Will we…" Alice looked at her, worry lacing her words.

"Yes."

They kissed in parting.

Part III

Chapter Twenty-Seven

Alice

Wanting, to want.

Her mother called, wanting her to come to Christmas dinner. She told Alice she was looking far too thin.

Which was it? Too fat or too thin?

Alice ruminated on this question, half listening as her mother unloaded her long list of concerns and complaints. She became fixated on a piece of lint that had come to rest on her bodice. She flicked at it, the image of Kathryn licking her nipples coming to her so that she was completely lost to whatever it was her mother kept saying.

"No, mother, we can't make it this year. I'm sorry." She finally said at what seemed to be an appropriate moment and then hung up on her mother's continued protests.

She ignored the phone ringing as she walked to her bedroom. She closed the door behind herself, muffling the incessant ringing, and fell atop the bed. She tried to fight off the urge, but it won out.

Sex. Sex had always been a chore. Something that was to be endured. She had been told that what a man and woman did together was sacred and beautiful and holy. A perfect union.

But sex with Frank had only ever felt stifling to her. Frank had been her only point of reference.

Now there was Kathryn. Kathryn who could caress her and make her insides melt. And it was never enough, never enough time, touching, fucking, caressing, kissing. She wanted more and more.

But because it was Kathryn, another woman, it could not be enough. There were weeks that might pass with only a brief stolen interlude in Kathryn's dressing room bathroom, or - even worse - only a simple, small touch, a gentle, furtive caress that would have to carry them through days and weeks of nothingness.

Charles was home more often than not now – Kathryn told Alice he was putting up a new show that required him to be in Los Angeles more – and Alice could not disturb the delicate balance of time at home with Frank and work at the studio.

Frank. Frank wanted her more.

Some nights he was careful with her. Sometimes he used a condom.

But other nights it felt as if he were doing it on purpose. He'd corner Alice, he'd whine and tell her it felt better this way. He wouldn't give her time to get the diaphragm. He was inside her, his body larger than hers. She'd try to push at him, but he'd wrestle her down until he'd come inside of her. The wetness dripping between her legs.

She'd go to the bathroom and clean herself up and feel tears welling in her eyes. Because she couldn't be reckless like this. She would lose her contract. He knew this.

But he kept at her. As if he suspected something, as if he might know…but how could he know? When it was so infrequent? When it was so perfectly kept hidden away, a little secret at the back of her mind that she'd bring out to comfort herself.

Sunlight playing in mussed blonde hair, the long, lanky length of her smooth body, the feel of a pert, dark nipple between her teeth, the way she felt like satin against her fingers, her tongue… The thoughts came to her when Frank was passed out in the dark night beside her. It was the only solace she could find in a life that was caving in around her. The walls of the room felt as if they were moving inwards every morning when she awoke until it made her feel like she was suffocating.

Until…until she was inside the large, white expanse of the room Kathryn called her own. She kept it sparse, tidy. A vase of red flowers atop a white vanity. The ceilings so high above their heads, their bodies naked as they dove for one another atop the soft bedding. Always in the light.

Kathryn lit a cigarette and pulled Alice close to her, so that she might rest her head against Kathryn's thigh and look up at her. She smelled distinctly of her sex, and it was this smell that Alice liked most. Alice let her fingers curl about Kathryn's nipple and wondered if this was what heaven was like. She thought, in that moment, that religions had it all wrong.

"What will you do for Christmas?" Kathryn ran her fingers mindlessly through Alice's hair.

"We'll be on a flight to Vermont the minute we finish filming the Christmas episode. I'll be with Frank's family." Alice watched Kathryn smoke jealously, uncertain whether she wanted the cigarette or Kathryn's lips.

The plans seemed too far in the future to touch her, so she did not think about how miserable the whole affair would be. Frank's mother was a cold woman and his father was forever knocking Frank down. His brother was friendly, but his wife was often cold-shouldered to Alice and their two sons were young enough that they did not care to engage with the adults. Alice would spend the holiday alone.

And this year – oh, this year there would be the guilt. Surrounded by his family…when she was…

"Vermont, well isn't that idyllic?" Kathryn hummed. Her eyes seemed far away.

"Will you be here with Charles?" Alice could picture how Kathryn would spend such a holiday. Exchanging gifts with Charles, sharing a decadent Christmas breakfast together. She did not imagine there would be other family involved and how ideal that seemed!

"No." Kathryn tapped off the ashes from her cigarette. "He'll be in New York."

Alice moved to better look at Kathryn. "You don't want to go be with him?"

Kathryn shook her head. "He flies back the following day. It would be ridiculous. No, I'll enjoy the evening alone. It's not so terrible." Kathryn smiled down at Alice's concern, tapping Alice's nose with her finger. "Don't you worry about lil' old me."

Alice frowned but then caught sight of the clock upside down. The numbers unscrambled in her brain and she realized how late it had become. "Oh, it's nearly four."

"My, how the time flies."

Alice kissed her way up Kathryn's body, reluctantly standing from the bed to collect her things. This was always the worst part. If only they could have more.

Kathryn watched her through a haze of smoke. "I suppose this shall be it before the holidays, then."

Alice stopped mid-redressing and looked up at Kathryn. "Oh, is that so?"

"I do believe it shall have to be. Charles comes home tomorrow."

Alice felt foolish, frustrated tears gathering in her eyes.

"Now, now. No tears. Come here. You see, I thought it

might be, so I've gotten you something…just a little something." Kathryn pulled a box from her bedside table.

Alice, sitting half-dressed on the edge of the bed, took the box that Kathryn handed to her. "Oh, Kathryn." Her fingers played over the soft suede of the small square box.

"Open it." Kathryn marveled at her, biting the side of her thumb as she often did, Alice had realized, when she was uncertain about something.

Alice lifted the top of the box. The light shone on the sleek gold of a chain, a round ruby pendant glittering up at her atop a satiny white bed. "Oh…it's beautiful." Alice sighed, having never received such a present before. Sure, Frank had purchased a gold watch for her their first Christmas together and her simple wedding band was nice enough, but this – oh it was simple in its elegance and yet was the most precious thing she had ever seen.

She felt a stabbing pleasure splinter in her chest at the thought that Kathryn might do such a beautiful thing.

"You like it?" Kathryn crushed out her cigarette and sat forward, taking the box from Alice so she could untangle the necklace and place it about Alice's neck, sealing it with a gentle kiss.

Alice shivered. "It's beautiful." She caught sight of the pendant sparkling around her neck in the mirror across the room.

"Good, I wasn't sure, but…yes, I like it. It suits you." Kathryn sat back and admired Alice.

Alice fingered the necklace and felt a sudden rush of fear and happiness. "I…I love it."

Kathryn looked at her with shy fear.

Alice leaned forward, pressing her lips to Kathryn in thanks, as if she needed to reassure her of something. "I haven't gotten you a thing." Alice looked at her in horror.

Kathryn laughed off whatever had clouded her visage

only seconds before. "Please, I didn't expect anything in return. I just wanted you to have something…"

Alice smiled, enjoying the delicate weight of the necklace about her neck. An invisible embrace.

"You should be going." Kathryn tried to break the tension that had come between them.

Alice nodded softly, not wanting to go.

And as she drove home that day – admiring the necklace in the rearview mirror as she did – she wondered what she might tell Frank if he were to notice.

Kathryn had chosen well. It was not showy and could be worn discreetly.

But Frank might wonder and what would Alice say? A little Christmas present for herself since the show was going so well?

But as she stood before him, his eyes glazed over as he watched the television, he did not seem to notice.

Neither the necklace nor her.

Chapter Twenty-Eight

Kathryn

She supposed it could be tragic. Tripping through the living room for another splash of alcohol. Alone on Christmas Eve.

She sat down at the piano, letting her fingers improvise over the keys.

Mariella had left a fire blazing in the hearth. Kathryn stared into the flames as she drank from her tumbler, smoking at her cigarette, messily toyed with dissonant melodies that flowed from her fingers in broken, incohesive phrases at the piano before her.

There had been a time when she would have preferred this to hosting some wild party, entertaining Charles' family or clients.

But this year it felt cold to be all alone.

Charles would see his brother in Boston. Kathryn had assured him it was better this way, that she should stay home all by herself. He asked her if she would really be alone and she had looked him dead in the eyes. "Yes, alone."

Helen had called to invite her to some festive event with that wild husband of hers, but Kathryn had declined. As she had declined all of Helen's recent invitations. "It's the girl, isn't it?" Helen had spoken after a long, dejected silence.

Kathryn hadn't responded.

"Well I certainly hope you get over that little crush soon." Helen had sniped before hanging up.

She played a long scale before slamming her hands down on the keys.

The phone rang, startling her.

She stubbed out her cigarette, standing to go to the receiver. It was probably Charles, calling to wish her well.

She lifted the phone from the receiver. "Hello?"

There was silence on the other end for the briefest of moments and Kathryn sat forward, wondering if *she* would dare to call…but then a small voice spoke. "Kathryn?"

Kathryn felt the wind knock out of her lungs. "Vivian?"

"I…I didn't know if you would answer or not." Vivian's feminine voice had matured. She was no longer a little girl.

"Well," Kathryn fumbled for a cigarette, "here I am."

"I just wanted…well, you didn't come home. For daddy's funeral."

Kathryn felt sick to her stomach, that the girl called him that. Daddy. "I was terribly busy. With the show…" Kathryn flicked the lighter.

"It's really good. The show. All my friends think I look just like you." Vivian confessed shyly.

Of course she looked just like Kathryn.

"They can't believe you're my older sister." Vivian went on.

Kathryn inhaled deeply on her cigarette. "How…how are you? Doing well in school?"

"Oh yes. I've already been accepted to Bryn Mawr."

Kathryn's eyebrows rose, a pain in her chest. "Congratulations are in order then."

Vivian laughed and it was joyful, free. Her lightness made Kathryn feel a bit like she was drowning. "Thank you."

"Why aren't you celebrating Christmas Eve?"

"Oh," Vivian's voice quieted. "Mother wanted things to be quiet this year. It's not the same. Not without…Oh! She doesn't know I called you. I hope you don't mind that I did."

Kathryn wiped at an errant tear that had formed in the corner of her eye. "No. I'm glad you did."

"Will you…well, will you come visit us?"

Kathryn shook her head. "I…I don't know. It's so hard to get away." She pressed a hand to her forehead, willing her voice not to shake.

"I understand." Vivian sounded as if she did not.

"Listen, I must go. But it seems that things are going well for you. I'm…I'm proud."

She hung up and sat in the near silent room. Listening as the fire crackled in the fireplace, lifting the tumbler to her lips again and again until it was empty.

Kathryn hadn't even finished high school.

Well then.

She wiped at her face and stood up shakily. She returned to the minibar and refilled her glass. There was a pain in her side, a horrible pain that felt crippling. She half-walked, half-crawled her way to her upstairs bedroom, bringing a bottle of bourbon along with her.

She curled into her white sheets, watching as candlelight danced on the walls around her.

At some point she drifted off and then awoke to a coughing fit, quelled only by a cigarette.

She was startled when the phone rang.

Almost afraid to answer − for she felt as if she were in her own Dickens nightmare - she let it ring until she could not stand it any longer and then lifted the receiver to her ear. "Hello?"

There was the sound of life, a party happening in the background, people talking. It must be Charles.

"Kathryn?"

"Alice? Oh!" Kathryn tried to sit soberly in bed but she was too far gone.

"Are you all right?" Alice's voice was soft.

"Just fine. Are you? All right?"

Alice laughed under her breath. "You sound far away."

"I'm right here." Kathryn breathed.

"I miss you so terribly...I...oh, anyone could be listening, but I can't stop...I wish it could be different."

"I know." Kathryn wrapped an arm about her middle.

"Everyone's having a wonderful time and I just feel... lost." Alice confided.

Kathryn had never heard her speak so candidly. So forwardly. It was intoxicating in the moment. "I know how you feel."

"A million miles away." Alice whispered. "They think I'm sick. They think there's something wrong with me, but they don't know..."

"Be brave, darling. It's only a few days more."

"I wish I could see you now." Alice lamented.

Kathryn felt heat welling up inside. "The feeling is mutual, dear."

There was a surprised gasp on the other end of the line. Then noise growing closer. "Oh." Alice sighed, sounding as if she might be crying. "I have to – I told him I was calling my mother – I have to..."

"It's all right. Soon. I'll see you very soon." Kathryn assured her. "Merry Christmas, Alice."

"Merry Christmas, Mother." Alice spoke firmly before the line went dead.

It scared her. This want.

She buried herself in her sheets and pulled the comforter over her head, wishing she could disappear.

Why did it have to be so difficult?

Some days she wished to be innocent to the world. To have not known what sex was. To be completely pure like the heroines she had once portrayed on screen.

But Hollywood was not real life – no matter what the actors and studio executives tried to sell the world. It was not *real*.

She groaned when the phone began to ring again. Her head was starting to hurt. She drank straight from the bourbon bottle and then picked up the phone from beneath her cocoon of sheets. "Hello?"

She heard his full laughter on the other end. He was as drunk as she. "Having a good time, then?"

"The best." Kathryn closed her eyes.

"I've got a girl here. Mary…"

"It's Meredith." She heard the titter of a young woman on the other end, correcting Charles.

"Right, Meredith. She's a big fan, you see, a great big fan of you, Kat."

"I see." She rolled her eyes. He was meant to be with his brother, but knowing the two of them they'd found a bar still open on Christmas Eve. Despite the fact his brother's doting wife would be home putting their three children to sleep.

"I'm gonna put her on."

The phone switched hands. "Oh gee, I didn't put him up to this." The Meredith girl laughed nervously.

"It's all right." Kathryn sighed.

"I just…well, I'm just such a big fan of yours. I love watching you on television. You know? You're a real inspiration."

"Why thank you." Kathryn sat up to find her cigarettes.

The girl went on for an excruciatingly long time, and Kathryn offered a few words of thanks until the girl finally gave her back over to her husband. Charles came on the line, laughing. "Thanks, Kat! She really appreciated it."

Kathryn puffed at her cigarette. "You're going to fuck her?"

Charles howled with laughter. "Who knows? The night's still young."

"She sounds like a child."

"Prettiest little thing I've seen in a while. Might have to get her in a picture."

"Good night, Charles."

"Merry Christmas, darling."

Kathryn hung up the phone and drank more bourbon.

She drank until she passed out.

Chapter Twenty-Nine

Alice

She opened the car door and leaned as far out as possible, just in time to throw up all over the street. When there was nothing else to heave, she spat and then eased herself up again into a seated position. Messy, undignified.

She was two blocks from the Hollywood home.

Her heart was pounding in her chest.

She wondered if she might be sick again, so she waited until the horrible feeling passed.

What could she do? What was there to do?

It was all over, wasn't it?

It would all disappear.

Kathryn met her at the door – their first meeting after so many days apart and now it felt ruined. As soon as the door closed behind Alice, Kathryn moved to kiss her but Alice had to push her away, shaking her head, and darting for the powder room beneath the stairs.

Kathryn was kneeling beside her, pushing back her hair,

wiping her cheeks, pressing hair away from her warm fore-head. When there was nothing else to expel, Kathryn flushed the toilet and helped ease Alice back against the wall, Kathryn rubbing a hand over her back. "There, there. You're all right." Her voice was sweet.

Alice closed her eyes and shook her head. "I'm not."

They were silent. Sitting side-by-side on the bathroom floor.

"How far along are you?"

Alice felt tears trailing down her cheeks. Messy and untamed and broken. "Three months."

"Does he know?" Kathryn took Alice's shaking hand in her own.

Alice shook her head. "I just came from the doctor's office." She turned, looking fully at Kathryn, needing to know if she was upset with her, if she was disappointed, if this had ruined everything. "It's all over, isn't it?"

Kathryn's lips quirked upward. "Over? No. Not over." And she pressed her lips to Alice's knuckles.

"I violated the contract."

"It takes two people to get into this predicament, Alice."

"But he doesn't have to deal with the consequences!"

"It's unfair." Kathryn agreed.

Alice buried her face in her hands. "He knew! *He knew.* It's in the contract. And he…oh God." Alice sobbed. "I won't be able to work."

"Not necessarily." Kathryn patted her on the back.

"What do you mean?" Alice messily wiped at her nose. Kathryn got some tissue paper and handed it to her.

"I mean that the studio likes you. A lot. They'll figure something out to keep you. The show isn't good without you. Everyone knows it."

Alice balked at this. "The show's not about me."

"But you're an integral piece of it." Kathryn insisted firmly.

They held the other's gaze.

Alice had missed Kathryn during their holiday away from the show. She no longer felt alone for the first time in days sitting beside Kathryn. And there was comfort in the fact that though Alice was a mess on her bathroom floor Kathryn did not seem to mind.

"Alice," Kathryn stroked a strand of hair behind her ear and then cradled her cheek. "Do you want this?"

Alice, in all the time she had worried over it happening to her, pondered the question. "I don't…I don't know."

"Because it can be taken care of…"

Alice's stomach sank. But that wasn't… "No!"

Kathryn rolled her eyes. "For heaven's sake, Alice."

"Isn't that…illegal?"

Kathryn laughed mirthlessly. "There are no laws in Hollywood."

Alice detected a knowing sadness that lingered in the corner of Kathryn's eye. "You…"

Kathryn took a deep breath. "It doesn't matter." And a wall went around her. "You have options." Kathryn reiterated.

"I can't lose…I don't want to lose it all…" Alice let the tears stream down her cheeks. "I don't know what to do."

Kathryn comforted her and gave her space to feel what it was that she needed. But nothing seemed to make it better in the span of the afternoon. The puzzle pieces remained broken, scattered all around her. Indecipherable.

She went home to Frank. She was resolved to not mention it at all, not to say one word to him, but when he came to the bedroom that evening and she was changing into her night-gown, he grabbed her and was about to push her face first onto the mattress. He wanted her legs spread apart, but she fought back at him. "I'm pregnant!" She cried when he wouldn't let her go.

That seemed to stop him cold in his tracks.

He backed away from her. "We're...we're going to have a baby?" He shoved a hand through his hair, looking like the shy young man he had been when they'd first met.

He kept repeating it, over and over, his voice getting smaller with each revelation. He had planted something inside of her and it was now growing. He was thrilled, excited. He crawled gingerly into the bed beside her and rested his head on her stomach. He did not touch her.

She had been made into a saint, something sacred to be cared for, looked after, protected. He would not hurt the child growing inside of her. He vowed. And he hoped it would be a boy.

Alice let silent tears slip down her cheeks as she consoled him.

Where Frank cooed at her, treating her like she was a porcelain doll, that she might shatter and fall apart at any moment, Kathryn remained firm and levelheaded.

"You can take care of it and not mention it. There are options, Alice." Kathryn was pacing her dressing room, smoking furiously.

"He won't hear it. He won't understand." Alice pleaded, feeling a headache coming on. And then the horrible urge to vomit overcame her. She stood up, rushing to the bathroom.

"You don't look well." Kathryn ushered her to the couch after she'd cleaned herself up and washed out her mouth. "Have you been eating at all?"

Alice shook her head. Food had been her last thought. She had been under-weight at the doctor's. They were worried about the baby. When had everything become about the baby? What about her?

"Eat this." Kathryn unwrapped a half of her own uneaten sandwich.

Alice took one look at it and shoved it away. "No, I can't."

"You have to take care of yourself." Kathryn chastised.

"The meeting is this afternoon. Frank will be coming

soon." Alice hiccupped back tears, closed her eyes and pinched the bridge of her nose.

"Jesus." Kathryn cursed, but did not sound as if she believed it when she added "they can't kick you off the show."

Alice no longer knew what *they* were capable of. *They* held the power to make or break her. *They* had the power to get her pregnant, or not get her pregnant.

Why wasn't it ever her own decision?

She felt Kathryn's arms about her, and it was the only thing that made any sense. She opened her eyes and looked into Kathryn's. A moment of serenity. Their lips met, Kathryn tried to breathe reassurance into each kiss. Alice clung to her until there was a knock at the door and they were being called back to set where they pretended as if nothing was happening.

Frank arrived some time toward the end of her rehearsal. He watched her intently, hat in hands. He did not fit into the scene.

She felt Kathryn's eyes upon her when Frank gave her a gentle kiss and put his arm about her. They were ushered to a studio office. There were men all around the table. Charles was present. Alice wished Kathryn could be present, but Kathryn was not in charge at the studio. Kathryn, she began to realize, mattered very little to the studio.

The men in charge looked at Alice and waited for her to tell them the news. Her voice shook when she spoke. "I recently found out…well, you see, I'm pregnant."

The room was silent. The men looked at one another, then began to speak amongst themselves as if she were not even present.

"We can't have Kay pregnant on the show. She's an unmarried woman."

"It's a violation of the contract."

"We can have this taken care of if she wants to comply with her contract." One man looked at Frank.

Frank's cheeks colored a deep shade of red. "What are you saying?"

"Just that…we can have it taken care of. She doesn't look pregnant yet. There's still time."

"It's my child!" Frank's voice rose in anger. "You can't do that."

"Listen, she can't be pregnant on the show. The audience doesn't want to see her knocked up. Kay is a docile, pretty girl who goes on harmless little dates. She doesn't have sex. She can't be pregnant."

"Why can't you marry her off to George?" Frank tossed out.

The men took up another conversation amongst themselves.

Alice looked down at her lap. She wondered if she was even still present in the meeting. No one looked at her. No one acknowledged her. Yet, they were talking about her, weren't they? And this thing…this thing she had growing inside of herself.

If only she had just taken care of it…

Did she even want it?

She mindlessly fingered the ruby about her neck, thinking of Kathryn. Thinking of how Kathryn wouldn't let the men talk *about* her. No, Kathryn would insist they talk to her. Alice wished she could be more like Kathryn.

"This is a huge inconvenience to the show." A man finally looked directly at Alice, making sure Alice knew how horrible her actions were. It was, after all, her fault. Wasn't it?

"She cannot be on television like this. It is not decent or moral for us to broadcast it. You're lucky, very lucky." The man speaking turned to look at her, and she felt as if she were not lucky at all.

Charles was looking at her strangely, unreadably. She could not look at him.

"The audience resonates with Kay. The ratings are high.

And you are very talented, unlike the other players on this show." The same man went on.

Did they not find Kathryn talented?

"We will continue to honor your contract until you're showing. At that point, Kay will disappear from the show and you will go without pay until the pregnancy is ended and then we will bring you back next season. But this cannot, do you understand, *cannot* happen again. This is your first strike. And you only get one."

Alice felt a strange sense of dread and relief wash over her.

It was only then that the realization began to dawn on her.

She was going to have Frank's child.

Chapter Thirty

Kathryn

Charles was looking at her over his newspaper as they sat catty-cornered from one another at the breakfast table.

She raised her eyebrow, catching his gaze. "What?" She lifted the coffee cup to her lips and then inhaled from her cigarette.

Charles tapped the ashes from his cigarette. "Alice."

Kathryn's stomach flipped at the name, but she covered her reaction with another smoke. "What about her?"

"She's in the family way." Charles eyed her.

Kathryn raised her eyebrows. "Are you trying to shock me?"

"You knew." Charles put his newspaper down.

Kathryn put out her cigarette. "Well, don't look at me. I didn't get her pregnant."

Charles brow creased. "You better not have had anything to do with her."

Kathryn lowered her eyes. "I'm glad they are keeping her under contract."

"The studio would be idiots to fire her. She's the goddamn best thing on that show."

Kathryn felt the stab at her in the statement. "I see." She picked up the newspaper she had been reading and tried to focus on the little black words. Bombings somewhere, expelling of Communist literature, a mass murderer put to death in a gas chamber.

As soon as Charles left for New York that day, Kathryn called for Alice to come to her. Alice arrived soon after. Kathryn looked her over, wondering if she had changed, but she looked the same as ever. The child was still too small inside of her to show. And somehow her body had grown smaller.

There was a fire that burned in her eyes. "He won't touch me anymore." She announced, both amused and relieved and aroused. "He's afraid he'll hurt the baby." She rolled her eyes, removing her cardigan from her shoulders as she kissed Kathryn up against the stairway banister.

Kathryn laughed, thrilled by the thought of it.

"I've never been more turned on before in my life. It doesn't make sense." Alice was fumbling with Kathryn's pants. "All I can think about is touching you and you touching me. I *need* you to touch me."

And Kathryn did. She coaxed Alice into her bedroom where they landed between the sheets and it was unlike any time that had come before. Alice was insatiable. Kathryn buried her fingers inside of her, as if wanting to tempt fate, to do the thing a man was afraid to do. And Alice welcomed her, delighted.

They laid together afterwards. "Did you ever want a child with Charles?"

It was an inevitable question. Kathryn would have

preferred it never be asked, but she could not blame Alice for wanting to know. "Perhaps, for a time."

Alice turned to look at her, legs rubbing together, restless. "What happened?" Her innocent eyes asked, demanding that Kathryn tell her.

"I…well, by the time we were ready to have a child…I couldn't." Kathryn shrugged.

Alice frowned, reaching out to take Kathryn's hand. Their fingers played together.

"It wasn't really a choice." Kathryn found herself going on. "He wanted to make me famous and a baby would have ruined the image." Kathryn felt ridiculous tears come to her eyes. All the things that she had tried to push to the back of her mind, to forget. They were now forced again to the surface.

"Oh." Alice seemed to understand. "You have been pregnant."

Kathryn nodded. "Several times." She tilted her head at the admission.

Alice sat up a little straighter.

Kathryn eased up further in the bed. "Now, Alice. You know how this business goes."

Alice shook her head. "It's awful."

"Oh, shh." Kathryn reached to pull Alice to her, to bury her face against her stomach so that she wouldn't have to look at the pity in Alice's eyes. "I did what I had to do."

"Men are infuriating." Alice's muffled voice was heard.

"Don't I know it." Kathryn reached for her cigarettes. "But I don't think I'm any worse off. I wouldn't have been a good mother anyway."

"I don't think that's true."

"It is." Kathryn lit a cigarette, knowing.

Alice pressed her cheek against Kathryn's stomach. They laid in silence. Kathryn smoking, lost to the distant memories, thoughts she had kept hidden away. Lost to the time no one else had ever known about, save for Charles. And now she had very nearly told Alice.

A want for Alice to know everything overcame her in that moment, and the thought frightened her. To be so vulnerable was to be weak.

Kathryn had never been weak.

And yet when she felt Alice's tears – tears for her – trailing down the skin of her stomach, she wondered why it was so wrong.

She sniffled, wiped at her nose. "I hate this." Alice whispered.

"What, darling?" Kathryn trailed her fingers through Alice's hair.

"Being pregnant." Alice sighed. "I hate the idea of something growing inside of me. I know – I know everyone says that it's the most wonderful thing in the world, to be a mother, but I never thought…well, it certainly was not something I wanted. Not now anyway. Not when everything is going so well…"

Kathryn knew these sentiments well, felt them innately in her own body.

"It must have happened around the time we first…" Alice spoke quietly, playing with the edge of the sheet. "It was like Frank knew and he… when he slept with me, it felt like he was trying to claim me. And I wish…" Alice's voice petered out, as if afraid to say what it was she wished. She laughed dryly.

"Wish what?" Kathryn encouraged, needing to know.

"It's stupid." Alice muttered. "Impossible really, but sometimes…sometimes I pretend that it was you, and not him. It's the only thing that makes it better."

Kathryn inhaled shakily. "Oh, Alice." And she held her closer, fighting back tears because it was so beautiful. This idea. That they could possibly conceive a child together. And a pain ripped through Kathryn, a possessive ache welling inside of her. She wanted to protect Alice and this growing being inside of her from everything and everyone.

But how could she when she was only an outsider with demons of her own? How could she want to love this child when she had not been able to love her own?

When Alice left that afternoon, Kathryn buried her fears in a bottle of bourbon.

Alice saw good in her.

Kathryn was beginning to believe Alice was blind to who she truly was.

She thought – halfway through the bottle - that she should end it between them.

Alice might just be better off without her.

But the thought of severing what they had hurt all the worse, and she knew she would be selfish and she would hold on.

Chapter Thirty-One

Alice

The doctors were worried she was keeping off too much weight. She was well into the second trimester looking trimmer and thinner than ever before.

That she rarely ate, despite being hungry most of the time, helped.

As long as she could keep going for as long as possible on the show… She dreaded what would come when they deemed her too far along to continue.

So when she became lightheaded at rehearsal and the whole world around her went black, she was surprised to find this regimen might not be the most effective. She awoke on Kathryn's dressing room couch. Kathryn was pressing a cool, damp cloth against her forehead and fighting off Stephen and the other faceless crew members attempting to crowd in.

"Just leave her alone for a bit. She'll pull out of it." Kathryn spoke, flustered.

"I'm calling the studio doctor." Stephen warned. "She

can't be holding up rehearsals like this. She's wasting my time."

"Look, she's waking up. She's going to be okay. Just give her a few minutes and she'll be as good as new." Kathryn's face came into focus. She was looking intently at Alice then to Stephen. "Please, Stephen. Just give her some space."

"I didn't know you were in charge around here." Stephen was looking at Kathryn with a mean glint in his eye.

"Please." Kathryn pleaded, her voice unnaturally strained.

Stephen sneered at her and then at Alice and then called off all the men who had been surrounding them. "Five minutes. And then you'd both better be out on that stage, back at the top of the scene." He slammed Kathryn's dressing room door shut behind him.

Alice felt anxious tears in her eyes. Kathryn redoubled her efforts to soothe her, wiping at her forehead, reassuring her. "You were just a little faint. When's the last time you had something to eat? That baby needs food, Alice." Kathryn was speaking quietly.

Alice couldn't remember the last time she'd eaten.

"Here, I have some things left over from lunch. Eat this. You'll feel better." Kathryn held out a half of a sandwich and an apple.

And Alice ate because she could not pass out again. If she faltered, she'd be out.

"You're wasting away, darling. You're smaller than ever and you should be getting larger. It's natural, dear." Kathryn was sitting beside her, coaxing her to eat.

But how could she tell Kathryn that if she got written out too early they would struggle to pay the mortgage? She needed the work, even if Frank insisted that he could support them. He felt he had enough because he was in the world of banking, but he scarcely made what she made on the show.

And besides that, it would mean less time with Kathryn. She wanted all the time in the world with Kathryn.

She ate and watched as Kathryn stood from beside her to light a cigarette and then pour herself a nip of vodka with a slightly shaky hand. "Christ, he's an asshole." She spoke to no one before downing the drink as if it were water. It seemed to have a steadying effect. Once she'd calmed herself, she returned her attention to Alice. "Do you feel better?"

Alice nodded, the sustenance returning her to the living world.

There was a knock on the door. Kathryn cursed under her breath. "We're coming."

They returned to set, but Kathryn kept an eye on Alice. Alice could feel her watching her, making sure she did not look ashen or pale or as if she might faint at any second.

Where Frank did not seem to mind if Alice skipped a meal, Kathryn began patrolling her eating so there would be no other mishaps. Kathryn brought fresh baked muffins, egg sandwiches, sometimes even pancakes each morning and would sit with Alice until she finished every last bit of food and then would do the same for lunch.

The few and far between days Alice managed to spend an afternoon alone with Kathryn, there was always a feast ready and waiting her, so that after they rolled around in bed, Kathryn, picking at the food whilst smoking, would watch to see that Alice ate.

And Alice felt, for the first time in her life, a strange happiness with food, that Kathryn shared this with her, provided it for her, told her that it was good.

Afterwards they would lay atop a couch, Kathryn stroking Alice's swollen stomach, happily searching for signs of life beneath the surface. And sometimes, sometimes the touch would lead to more. And Alice would be lost to Kathryn until she had to go home to Frank.

Frank gave her the white glove treatment. He could not

look at her while naked. He even began sleeping apart from her, as if afraid he might hurt the child.

By the seventh month, she could no longer hide herself.

It was fortunate, however, for the show only had four more episodes left to film for the season. She would only miss a month of pay. She was relieved she could keep it under wraps, especially to the press. Nothing was said, and they wrote her off so effectively that she was convinced the general public didn't even notice her absence.

Save for her mother.

She had taken to eating whatever it was she pleased, for there was no more reason to conceal herself. She had been told to stay out of the public eye, to lay low. So she was eating freshly baked cookies straight from the oven when the phone began to ring.

"Hello?" She yearned for the person on the other end to be Kathryn, but Kathryn would be at rehearsal.

Her stomach sank in knowing before she heard the voice on the other end. "Have you lost your job?"

"No, mother." She licked melted chocolate from her fingers and felt the guilt descend. Oh, how she had dreaded this moment. How she wished she could just simply not tell her at all.

"Then what is it? And my goodness, Alice. You've really been putting on the pounds. You know for a while I thought you were looking too thin, but those last few episodes..."

"I'm pregnant, Mother." Alice spoke over her.

For a moment she thought the line had gone dead.

"Mother?"

"Alice." Her mother gasped. "Alice, this is horrible timing. Why would you do this now when things are going so well? How far along are you? How could you have kept this from me?"

She listened to the torrential downpour of questions that followed.

"I'll be on the next flight out."

"No, mother." Alice put her foot down. She could not stand the idea of her mother living with her until the baby came. "No, you can meet your grandchild after it's born. You'll be the first phone call."

"But Alice, we both know that, now don't take this as a criticism, Frank is a wonderful man, but he is not capable of caring for you in this state."

"I don't need his help and I don't need yours." Alice held firm. "Please. Please, just let me be for now." She did not listen to her mother's protests as she hung up the phone.

Chapter Thirty-Two

Kathryn

Alice waddled now. Kathryn marveled at it, this new way that she moved, as she watched the younger woman emerge from the pool and then walk toward her. Water gleamed in the sun on her skin, rolled off her body, curved over her enlarged chest and around the convex stomach covered in a tight one-piece swimsuit. Kathryn slid her sunglasses from her eyes, watching. The silhouette made her warmer in the summer heat.

Alice frowned at her as she reached for her pool towel, wrapping it about herself. "What are you looking at?"

Kathryn pushed her sunglasses back into place and reached for her sweating gin and tonic. "It's attractive."

Alice huffed and lowered herself into the pool chair. "It certainly doesn't feel attractive."

Kathryn smiled slyly, putting her newspaper down. She swung her legs over the chair and went to Alice, helping settle her comfortably back into her seat before leaning over her to look into those intoxicating verdant eyes. She cupped Alice's cheek.

"We're outside." Alice whispered.

"No one's around." Kathryn responded and leaned in to press her lips to Alice's. "God, I've missed you." It had been weeks since they had last seen one another. Charles was either home or Kathryn was called to set for a minor B film where she had been cast as an aging starlet who was losing grasp of reality.

She felt as if she could relate to the character intimately most days.

There had finally been a day Frank and Charles were both away, that nothing was keeping them apart and she'd called for Alice who came, incognito, to her home looking more pregnant and filled out than before. She couldn't recover from the image, how it struck her as so intoxicating, arousing. Their foreheads pressed together, Kathryn let her hand trail from Alice's cheek, down over the new curve of a breast, surprised by the weight and heft of it.

Alice inhaled shakily. "Kathryn."

The phone was ringing. Somewhere far off in the distance.

Kathryn ignored it.

She pressed her lips again to Alice's. The warmth of the day, of her second or third gin and tonic, of Alice's very real, very full presence made her feel emboldened. She wanted her more than ever and the way Alice moved against her made her feel that Alice wanted the same.

The phone started up ringing again.

"Should you get that?" Alice moaned, arching her back upwards as Kathryn kissed at her uncovered nipple.

"No." Kathryn tasted pool water and Alice against her tongue.

But the phone began ringing again. It seemed more urgent this time.

"Christ." Kathryn returned the swimsuit to its rightful position and kissed Alice. "I'll be right back." And she grabbed her gin and tonic and went inside.

The phone was ringing a fourth time when she reached for it. "Hello?" She asked.

"Kathryn?! Oh, Kathryn." It was Helen's husband.

"Ernie, what is it?" Kathryn had never heard him so upset.

Fear curled itself low in her stomach.

"Kathryn…it's Helen."

"No…" it was as if she already knew. She didn't need him to tell her. "No."

"I found her this morning."

"No." Kathryn heard ringing in her ears.

"…overdosed…completely accidental…I wasn't home…I can't believe…"

It was not until Kathryn felt something pierce her foot that she realized the tumbler had slid from her hand. Glass scattered all about the floor. There was a mix of ice and alcohol and blood smearing the ground. "No." She moaned, her knees going weak. She needed to sit down, she needed… the blood was getting worse.

"I'm so sorry, Kathryn. I'm so sorry." Ernie was saying in her ear.

She could only mutter something incoherent before she dropped the phone, before she walked over the glass and then sank into a chair, lifeless. She didn't even see Alice appear in the doorway. Nor come toward her.

"Kathryn? Kathryn, what is it?" Alice was trying to reach for her, but she could only stay still, motionless.

Helen. Helen was dead.

"You're bleeding. Kathryn!" Alice was crying.

Kathryn was not quite sure what happened then. She saw only blackness. It was as if she had completely left herself, as if she was not in the world, not present to anything. She briefly registered noises somewhere in the distance, someone talking to her, but she found she could not respond.

It was only when she heard the phone ringing again that her mind cleared.

No, she didn't want to answer the phone. Not again.

She looked down and found that Alice had bandaged her feet and the floor had been swept clean. "Alice." Kathryn's eyes focused.

"Kathryn, what is it?" Alice looked at her with worry in her eyes.

Kathryn sat up, reaching for her cigarettes.

The phone rang again.

"Helen Laurence is dead." Kathryn's mouth was dry, her voice cracked. She exhaled a stream of smoke and then lifted the receiver from the nearby phone. "Hello?"

"Kathryn, I just heard the news." Charles was on the other end of the phone.

"They did this to her!" Kathryn cried. "They ruined her."

"Kathryn, speak sense. She did this to herself." Charles chastised.

"No she didn't. The studio had her hooked on those damn pills for years. She couldn't stop." Kathryn hissed.

"Kathryn, you're hysterical right now. Just calm down. Do you want me to come home?"

"I am *not* hysterical." Kathryn hissed. "Are you trying to console me or belittle me?"

"I knew you would be upset, but come now, Kathryn."

"No, no...I don't want you to come home." Kathryn hung up on him because he could not understand the pain coursing through her just then.

And when she looked at Alice, she realized that perhaps she might not understand it either.

Alice was wide-eyed. Confused. "Should I go?"

"No!" Kathryn sat up, reaching for Alice. "Please, don't go."

"Frank will be home…"

"I need you." Kathryn puffed at her cigarette. If Alice left her now, she wasn't sure what she would do.

Alice bit her lip. "I'm sorry…I…I'm so sorry. It's horrible."

Kathryn nodded. "I need a goddamn drink." She attempted to stand, but her feet suddenly hurt like hell. The cuts had sliced deep. "Shit." She cursed and fell back on the couch.

"You don't need a drink." Alice whispered but pushed herself up and went to the wet bar. She mixed a fresh drink for Kathryn. Kathryn wondered if she did that for Frank.

"Are you upset?" Kathryn could not understand the unreadable expression on Alice's face.

Alice shook her head but did not sit down again on the couch. "No. But I should go."

"Alice, what is it?" Kathryn demanded. She had just lost Helen. She could not lose Alice, too. And for what? What had happened?

Alice settled into a seat across from Kathryn. She looked at the ground, played with the hem of the dress she had put back on. "You loved her."

Kathryn felt her brow furrow. "What?"

"You were in love with her."

Kathryn shook her head. "No." Oh, how could Alice ever know? How could she understand? "No, Alice. It wasn't like that. Not at all. She was…oh," she was so many things. She had always been so many things to Kathryn.

"How many." Alice's voice did not rise above a whisper.

"What?" Kathryn focused her eyes upon Alice's face, her chest tightening.

"I mean, how many other people are you involved with?" Alice folded her hands in her lap, unable to meet Kathryn's brazen gaze.

"Alice," Kathryn laughed hoarsely. "Don't be ridiculous. It's you…it's only you."

"And Charles and Helen and….?" Alice kept her eyes downcast.

"Alice." Kathryn gasped, feeling the worst pain of her life tighten at her chest. She thought, for a moment, that she could not breathe.

"I never thought I was the only one, I just…I'm sorry. You've just heard this awful news." Alice apologized.

"Alice, don't you dare think that. Don't you dare…"

"I can see it on your face. You loved her." Alice looked at her then.

"Of course I loved her. But we haven't….not since you… oh, Alice. I…" Kathryn sank back into the couch, felt as if all the fight had left her.

Alice looked as if she might cry. "I should be going."

"Please don't leave like this." Kathryn begged, feeling like a child. She'd spoiled it all, ruined things, hadn't she? Alice was not like the others one could just fuck around with in Hollywood. Alice was so much more than that.

"I have to go, Kathryn." Alice moved to stand, to leave her.

But something happened in the movement. Kathryn could see it on her face. Something was wrong.

"Alice!" Kathryn put out her cigarette, sat her tumbler down and stood on shaky, aching feet to go to Alice.

Alice grasped at her, looking up at Kathryn with wide, fearful eyes. Her fingers pressed tightly into Kathryn's arms, her eyes welling with frightened tears. A wail escaped from between her lips. And when Kathryn looked down she saw liquid pooling at Alice's feet.

"Oh God." Kathryn gasped. "Alice, we have to get you to the hospital. You're in labor."

Chapter Thirty-Three

Alice

She stared down at the bundle in her arms.

Jack Henry Kincaid. All of six pounds and four ounces.

His eyes were closed to the world. She wondered if she could keep it that way.

He did not fuss much; he had let out a few wails to greet his new world, but generally he seemed to remain quiet, calm.

Alice wondered if she should feel something more for him. He seemed a stranger to her. The weight of him in her arms was foreign. She did not know if she should cuddle him closer or talk to him or rock him. She only knew that she was to feed him every two hours. Her breasts would become full, as if on cue, and she would need him to relieve her.

It was uncomfortable, strange even, to have this small being attached to her so intimately.

The sun shone through the hospital window. It had been less than a day that Jack had existed in the physical world. He did not seem to express whether he was pleased or displeased about this.

Alice wished she could keep him as innocent and unknowing as he was now.

Frank had been so pleased, so overly ecstatic that it was a boy.

Alice pitied him for his sex.

She stroked his cheek and he opened his mouth. She removed her breast from her robe and held Jack's eager lips to it. And she thought of other lips pressed to her and felt her cheeks burn.

Frank had gone to work after a sleepless night on a chair in the corner of the hospital room.

Alice had been awakened for feedings so she felt exhausted, her body tired from all it had endured.

And all she wanted was to see Kathryn again. All she had wanted during labor was Kathryn. Kathryn, who had gotten her to the hospital just in time and then had been instructed to contact the father. They had been separated and Alice had no idea where she had gone or what had happened to her.

It was then that she heard a light tap at the hospital door. She looked up from staring at Jack and found the woman from her thoughts had materialized.

She was holding a bouquet of roses in one hand and a little teddy bear in the other.

Her eyes, Alice could see when she came closer, were puffy and dark. She looked exhausted. "Well, how did you do?" Kathryn moved closer, curious to see the baby.

"You look terrible." Alice commented, finding that Kathryn reeked of alcohol and cigarettes when she came closer.

Kathryn shrugged, "I slept in my car."

Alice's brow furrowed.

"Well, I sure as hell wasn't going to leave. I had to be here."

Alice felt tears prick at her eyes, and she felt ridiculous. The exhaustion was doing her in. She uncovered her chest and revealed the baby to Kathryn. "His name is Jack. Jack Henry. Henry after Frank."

"Thank God it's not Frank Jr." Kathryn chuckled, looking down at the baby in Alice's arms. "And thank God he looks like you."

Alice frowned, looking down at the boy. Did he look like her? He seemed to resemble no one at all. Just a concerned old man, perhaps.

"Oh, Alice." Kathryn sat on the edge of the bed so she could look down at Jack, so she could stroke his cheek and watch as he suckled at Alice's breast. "You're really a mother now."

Alice sighed. She wondered if she would grow to like this distinction. Mother. She felt not ready, not at all right for the title. But he was here now. He needed her. "I suppose I am."

"God, I want to kiss you." Kathryn whispered.

And Alice wanted that in return. But a nurse appeared in the room, looking rather surprised by the guest now inhabiting the space with Alice.

Kathryn moved from her spot on the bed, busying herself by placing the flowers in a vase, the teddy bear on the table beside the bed, then retreating to the chair in the corner where Frank had slept. She extracted a cigarette and lit it.

Alice was fixated upon her every movement as the nurse helped ease Jack away from her. She was going to take him back to the nursery. "Wait," Alice stopped her from doing so. "Can he stay? Just a while longer."

The nurse looked nervously at Kathryn and then back to Alice. "I can come back in ten minutes."

"Thank you." Alice offered a slight smile.

Kathryn smiled at Alice when the nurse left.

"May I?" Kathryn sat her cigarette in an ashtray and moved toward the bassinet.

"Yes, please. I want to see him with you." Alice felt suddenly as if she needed them to know one another.

Kathryn lifted Jack into her arms with practiced ease. She cradled him, rocking him as she spoke to him. "You're the luckiest little man in the world, do you know that? You get to suck your mommy's gorgeous tits whenever you want."

"Kathryn!" Alice cried.

Kathryn laughed. "Well, it's true." She looked down at Jack and the image was gorgeous. Jack cooed contentedly in her arms, happy to be near to her. "You're a beautiful little thing, aren't you? And you'll be different from all of those other boys. We'll see to that, won't we?"

Alice wrapped her arms about herself, longing for that intangible future. Kathryn was a natural with him, but there was a sadness about her.

"Isn't it something? One life ends and another begins. Just like that." Kathryn spoke, and there were tears in her voice.

Alice sat up. "Oh, Kathryn." And she reached for her to come closer.

Kathryn sat on the edge of the bed, cradling Jack closer to her. Tears slid down her cheeks messily. "I'm sorry." She whispered.

"No, you've just had a terrible shock." Alice reached out to caress her cheek.

Kathryn caught her hand, pressing her lips against her palm. "I wish you could have known her. Really known her." Kathryn sighed, holding Alice's hand, looking to Jack in her arms. "It's not – it was never what you thought. Helen was the first woman in Hollywood who took care of me. But what we had was not what *we* have. Alice, I *need* what we have." She whispered, a sad half-smile tugging up the corner of her lips.

And Alice knew she needed Kathryn too. A pain wrapped itself about her at the thought of this need.

Kathryn seemed to notice. "What is it?"

Alice shook her head, looked down at Jack. "What does this mean?"

"What?"

"For us."

Kathryn shook her head. "Darling, nothing has to change."

"But it's different now." Alice wiped at her cheeks.

"It doesn't have to be."

"I have to think about him…"

"Alice," Kathryn's face fell. "Alice, please. We're always careful, aren't we?"

Alice nodded.

"We can continue being careful. No one needs to know. Except us." Kathryn cradled Jack closer, as if afraid both he and his mother might be taken from her. And Alice wanted to take her in her arms and hold her close and assure her it would never happen.

But instead, the door opened and the nurse returned, taking Jack from them.

Alice watched as Kathryn retreated to the corner of the room, wiping at her cheeks, lifting her burning cigarette from the ash tray to smoke at it. She inhaled roughly, as if needing to steady herself. "I can't lose you." She whispered as she stared out the window.

Chapter Thirty-Four

Kathryn

It was rare she awoke beside Charles, but that morning she had.

Drenched in sweat and sleep, naked save for a silk robe that was tangled about her torso and arms, she found the space between her legs sticky from whatever it was Charles had done to her the night before.

The world was quiet around them. The sun cast a hazy pink hue on the walls. A headache had surfaced, throbbing relentlessly at her temples. The room still seemed hazy from the cigarettes they'd smoked the previous evening, and the smell of alcohol permeated everything.

Charles shifted in his sleep. She thought he might wake up, but his breathing soon evened out again.

She was as alone as always.

The quiet morning felt as if it were caving in around her.

There was a tear in her eye and she did not understand her melancholy.

Ah, but there had been dreams.

She remembered them in fragments. Like puzzle pieces floating back into place. A meadow, a forest, far away mountains, a place familiar yet distant. An uneasy feeling of home.

And there had been Helen. Helen as real and alive as she still seemed. Despite the fact Kathryn had watched them lower her body into the ground some weeks before.

She twisted in the bed, reaching blindly for a cigarette. There was an empty pack of hers that she tossed to the ground before she found one of Charles' preferred brand. She hated the way they tasted, but she hadn't the strength to move in search of her own.

The flick of the lighter seemed loud in the static morning.

Smoke curled from her lips. She French inhaled for fun.

She did not notice that Charles had awakened until he reached over her for a cigarette. His limp dick pressed into her thigh. He used her cigarette to light his own.

"I think it's good." His voice was rough when he spoke.

"What?" Kathryn leaned back in the bed.

Charles laughed hoarsely. "That that husband of her's knocked her up."

Kathryn turned to look at him. "What are you talking about?"

"It's kept you away from her, hasn't it?" Charles laid back down, looking like the cat who got the cream.

Kathryn squinted. "What the hell are you talking about?"

"Oh, come now, Kathryn." Charles puffed at his cigarette looking nonplussed. "I knew you were fucking her. But you can't have her as much now, can you? That's why you were so wet for me last night." He tried to touch her and she hit his hand away.

"You're an ass. Get away." She sat up in the bed, rearranging her robe to cover herself. "I haven't done a thing. Not one goddamn thing."

"You're so full of shit, Kathryn. You're not in love with her so give it up." Charles fell beside her on the bed.

"How do you know?" She felt tears threatening to fall from her eyes, having not been prepared for this. What had led to this? What had she done the night before? She had submitted to Charles after another long day of rehearsals in which Alice was a million miles from her. Right there beside her and yet too far away to grasp.

It was not the carefree and reckless affair of her formative years. It was not nights spent luxuriating at Helen's for an evening and sometimes the morning after. It was not a few rolls in the hay like it sometimes was with others. No, this was something else entirely. Something that was now blocked, stalled because of Jack's arrival, because Alice's mother had barged into her life and taken over the care of her grandson as if she owned him, and, inadvertently, Alice.

Jack's arrival into the world heralded a new epoch to their already tangled affair.

There had been exactly one, very dangerous, irresponsible liaison one evening after rehearsal in the back of Alice's car off Mulholland Drive somewhere in Laurel Canyon. Her breasts had been full of milk and Kathryn had helped ease her pain. She had been more sensitive than before. It had been too rushed.

"Just wait. Just let it all settle." Kathryn had tried to assure Alice when she'd turned up in her dressing room during a break in their rehearsal.

"I can't wait." Alice had sighed.

And yet to the rest of the world, Alice was her normal self. She came in knowing all her lines, she performed as she was instructed, and she didn't miss a beat. But behind the scenes...oh, Kathryn could see it all unraveling and she was helpless to fix it.

Charles was looking at her now. "My God. You can't be serious." He nearly laughed.

"What if I am?" Kathryn attempted to sit up in the bed. She rummaged about the too full ashtray, the empty liquor bottles, searching for a bottle of aspirin. She needed a clear head if she was going to have this conversation with Charles.

"Kathryn, be reasonable."

"I have been reasonable. All I ever am is reasonable." She found the bottle and downed them with the remnants of a whiskey bottle. "And careful. At least, I thought I was being careful."

"It's a disaster waiting to happen. And even worse if you have the silly notion in your head that you love her. You've just charmed her. Like you charm everyone, Kathryn. She's no more in love with you than you're in love with her. It's going to ruin everything. Mark my words. And I might just not be there to pick up the pieces. Why should I help my wife's whore?"

"Don't you call her that. Don't you dare call her that!" Kathryn turned to face Charles and would have punched him right in the face for saying a thing like that if he weren't so much bigger than her. And filming was only a day away for the week and she didn't like when the make-up people had to cover bruises.

"That's probably right. Because it's you who is the whore. Always giving yourself away to whoever might have you. I know about your little stunt with Dick Garrison. Good thing he's an honorable man and pushed off your advances."

"Oh, please." Kathryn laughed at that. "He just couldn't get hard. At least get your stories about me straight."

Charles was thrilled by this.

"I mean, what is all of this about?" Kathryn hated the smug look on Charles' face.

"I just want you to know," Charles sat up and caught Kathryn's arm, "that I'm your husband, see. And I know more about you than anyone else. I can ruin you. So don't you go and ruin my show."

Kathryn shrugged out of his grasp and stood on unsteady feet from the bed. "Fuck you."

"You already do, baby." Charles laid back in the bed and Kathryn saw what their early morning sparring match had done to him.

She stubbed out her cigarette as he began touching himself. "You're disgusting."

She showered off the remnants of the previous night and left for the studio early, downing vodka as she drove. It was a feeling of unease that plagued her, running on repeat in the back of her mind. Charles could leave at any moment.

Who was she without him?

But who was she with him?

She wanted to leave him but had the nagging feeling that he might be right, that she was nothing without him. He had made her.

She smoked furiously in her dressing room, ruminating on this as she stared blankly at the script for the week.

There was a knock at her door. She looked up to find a tired yet radiant Alice standing in the doorway.

"You're here awfully early." Alice spoke breathlessly.

"Close the door." Kathryn whispered.

Alice closed it.

She came to Kathryn, worry furrowing her brow. "There's a bruise…" her voice trailed off.

Kathryn looked in the mirror and noticed that the back of her arm was turning purple. "Fuck." And she reached for a cardigan and put it about herself.

"He hurts you."

"No." Kathryn shook her head. "No, it's always very mutual." And she looked to Alice and saw want in her eyes. "Jesus, Alice. How is Jack?"

"I don't want to talk about Jack." Alice murmured as her arms wrapped about Kathryn and her lips pressed to her forehead.

Kathryn tilted her head up and Alice leaned down to press her lips to Kathryn's.

"I can't go on like this." Alice closed her eyes. "I can't stop this want. My mother is always around, the baby's always crying, and I feel like I'm going insane. And the only thing that makes sense is you. I need you, Kathryn. I lo..." Her voice died on the word.

But it existed between them.

"Don't talk like this, Alice."

"I know, I didn't..."

And then there was a knock at the door. Alice slid from her grasp and the day commenced and they were hardly able to speak more than two words to each other the rest of the day. But just before Alice left, Kathryn reached for her and drove them out to the little turn off on Mulholland Drive and gave what the younger woman so desperately needed.

Chapter Thirty-Five

Alice

She pulled a smiling, relieved looking Jack up into her arms, holding him close, inhaling the fading newborn scent of him.

"Where have you been?" Alice's mother was hot on her heels, having followed her from the kitchen to the nursery, inundating her with questions.

It was well past six.

Alice knew how recklessly she was behaving, but she couldn't stop it. She wondered if Jack could smell it on her, what it was she had been doing in the backseat of Kathryn's car. She held him closer, as if he could protect her.

"We ate without you, you know." Her mother spoke as if this was some kind of punishment. As if she hadn't been controlling everything Alice ate for the past six months since Jack had arrived. "He's your husband, Alice." Her mother's voice lowered to a deadly whisper.

"Don't you think I know that?" Alice whispered back,

bouncing Jack so as to not let him know how irritated her mother's incessant reminders made her.

"I went through the same thing with your father. It wasn't pleasant after your birth or your brother's birth, but I knew I needed to do it for him. Men have needs, Alice. We have to keep them happy or else…"

Oh, how Alice wished there could be an 'or else'. Sometimes she fantasized that Frank might leave her for some young bank secretary. She'd been to see him at work a time or two. She knew how attractive those women were. Yet, Frank scarcely looked at them, seemed bent only on her.

She had put him off as long as she could until she'd gone to the doctor in search of something, anything that could prevent what had happened before. Because she could not have another Jack. Not with Frank. Her doctor put her on a pill, something called Enovid, that was meant to control her menstrual cycle, but told her that it might just help out with the other thing, too.

"I don't know what's going through that head of yours, Alice, but you have a family now." Her mother continued to chastise.

"I just went for a drive, mother." Alice railed against her. "Just a drive. I needed space, I needed to think, I needed…"

"Oh, please, Alice. I am here *helping* you care for your son. You wouldn't be able to still have that fancy television job without me."

"I could hire someone, Mother." Alice covered Jack's ears, pressed her lips to his soft head.

"He needs his family." Her mother's cheeks colored.

"He needs peace. Just like I do." Alice found it harder to bite her tongue with each passing day.

"I have sacrificed half a year for you, Alice. I left your father to fend for himself."

"I didn't ask you to." Alice's voice quivered.

Her mother looked at her as if she did not recognize her.

"You know, when you kicked me out the last time, I thought you were just going through something, but now I see what this is. You don't love me." Her mother's cheeks were bright red, tears pricking her eyes. And before Alice could attempt to take any of it back, her mother left the room and closed herself up in the guest bedroom.

Alice cradled Jack closer to her body. He cooed at her as if in consolation.

She stayed with him as long as she could. Feeding him from her swollen breasts, changing him, and then rocking him until he fell asleep on her chest.

Frank was in the living room smoking when she emerged into the too brightly lit room. Her shoulders tightened.

"Where were you?" He asked before she could reach the kitchen.

"I went out driving."

"You can't just go out driving. We have a son now. He needs you." Frank spoke firmly.

"I know that, Frank." Alice sighed.

He put out his cigarette and sat forward.

She let her hip fall against the wall, looking at him as she crossed her arms over her chest.

"I need you here." He looked pointedly at her, as if he knew.

And for that moment, Alice felt a chill race through her. That he could know.

So she let him fuck her that night and it seemed to appease him.

Daphne, a bright young girl from Saint Kitts, was hired on as Jack's nanny. Neither Frank nor her mother, at first, took kindly to having a 'colored' girl in the home, but Alice held firm. Daphne had come highly recommended and Alice liked her immediately; she saw something in her she could relate to. And she adored Jack, and Jack adored her.

Alice's mother left in a huff over this betrayal.

"Good riddance." Alice had whispered under her breath so that only Daphne had heard and she had laughed behind her hand until Alice turned and shared in the laughter.

She needed her mother gone, however, because it was becoming quite clear her mother saw things more clearly than Frank did.

Daphne did not question Alice if she got home later than usual. Alice would press several extra dollars into her hand and send her on her way.

It became more uncontrolled. Alice's body had impulses all its own that she felt incapable of stopping. Sometimes if Frank had his way with her she might derive pleasure from it in a way she had not before. And she wondered what was happening to her. That this affair that was consuming her might make her so wanting that her husband could satisfy her. So wanting that one Saturday afternoon, when Frank went golfing with some businessmen he was attempting to strike a deal with, she phoned Kathryn.

"Please, come." Alice's body felt as if it were on fire, humming and sizzling.

"Alice, it's not smart."

"He'll be gone for hours. Please." Alice pleaded, for it had been days if not weeks since they were able to escape together.

And, as if Kathryn could not keep away either, she arrived thirty minutes later. "This is risky." Kathryn berated between kisses.

"You came to see Jack." Alice reasoned, the boy napping in his nursery.

Kathryn had the buttons on Alice's dress undone, hand beneath her bra in a matter of seconds. It was messy, Alice falling into a wall before she led Kathryn to the guest room and laid her on the bed before straddling her.

There was a tension to it. A fear Jack could wake up, that Frank could come home at any moment. But these fears only heightened the arousal to a point Alice had never reached before and she came beautifully twice before she moved between Kathryn's legs to taste what she had done to her.

They lay in silence afterward. Kathryn stroking Alice gently.

They both heard the cry pierce the air.

Alice kissed a path from Kathryn's breast to her lips and then pulled herself up. She half-pieced herself together, certain her hair was ruined, but it was only to get Jack. He called out for her, a mix of syllables and cries.

"Ma! Ma!" He cried when he saw her appear in the room, and she pulled him up into her arms, nuzzling him.

"Jack, Jack." She replied.

"He's gotten so big." Kathryn's voice came from the doorway. More pieced together than Alice, hair brushed right back into place. "May I?"

Alice smiled and brought Jack to Kathryn. "This is Auntie Kathryn. Do you remember her?"

Jack looked at Kathryn. He seemed to instantly remember her, warmed to her presence there in his room. He looked at her bashfully then hid his face in Alice's chest before peering through his fingers at Kathryn again.

"I think he's flirting with me." Kathryn chuckled, then held out her arms. "Come here, come to Auntie Kat."

And Jack held out his arms for her and she took him into her embrace, cuddling him close to her chest. She inhaled him, cradling him with a maternal instinct Alice found intoxicating.

They both heard the door opening in the distance.

Their eyes locked, a fear raced down Alice's spine and she saw the same reaction course through Kathryn.

"I just came to see Jack, remember?" Kathryn whispered.

Alice cursed, looking into a mirror to smooth out her hair and finish buttoning up her dress.

Alice looked to Kathryn for reassurance but felt her heart pounding in her chest a mile a minute. It had been risky.

Could they salvage this?

Alice slid past Kathryn, closing the door to the guest room because the bed was in disarray, and then walked to greet Frank who was lighting a cigarette in the kitchen.

"Who's here?" He asked, looking through the window to Kathryn's car that was parked in the street.

Alice felt her throat go dry.

"I stopped by to see little Jack. I hadn't seen him for weeks and couldn't stand being away for so long." Kathryn appeared with a giggling baby in her arms. Rescuing Alice.

Frank looked from Alice to Kathryn and then back again.

"What's going on here?" Frank asked of Alice.

"What – what do you mean?" Alice stuttered.

"It's like I said, Frank, I came to see Jack." Kathryn insisted firmly, cradling the boy closer to her.

Frank looked at Kathryn. Alice had never seen him so stoically silent. She was afraid of him then.

He started walking down the hallway, pushing open the nursery door and peering into the room and then disappearing down the hall to their bedroom.

Alice stared at Kathryn and Kathryn stared back. Neither moved a muscle.

She heard Frank open the guest bedroom door.

There was silence for what felt like ages.

And then Frank appeared again. Rage filled his eyes, his hands curled into fists and Alice wondered if he'd beat her right there in front of Kathryn.

"How could you? How could you do this to me?" Frank's voice seethed at her. "Get out. Get the fuck out of this house, you fucking dyke."

"Frank, please…" Alice tried to reach for him, tried to console him, but he evaded her reach.

Had she brought about her own demise? Had she wanted

this? When he grabbed her roughly she felt a thrill race through her.

"Get the fuck out of my house." He shoved her toward the door. "Give me my son." Frank ripped Jack from Kathryn's arms and the boy started crying.

"Frank, please…let me have Jack." Alice gasped, racing back for her child.

But Frank held her off. "Don't you dare touch him, you lying bitch. He deserves a hell of a lot better than a dyke, whore mother." Frank held the wailing boy awkwardly in his arms. "Leave, before I end you."

And she knew he could. Knew where he kept his gun. It would be easy for him.

She felt Kathryn's arms about her, pulling her toward the front door. "Come on, let's leave it for now. We'll work something out." Kathryn was whispering.

"But Jack!" Alice cried, attempting to fight her way out of Kathryn's strong grasp.

Kathryn held tighter, leading her into the light of day and away from her crying child and her cold husband.

Kathryn put her in her car and drove away from Alice's home. Kathryn smoked cigarette after cigarette, Alice whimpering in the seat beside her.

Chapter Thirty-Six

Kathryn

Kathryn was drunk.

Charles' angry face came in and out of focus.

She pressed the tumbler to her forehead, wondering if she might just pass out or if she could just disappear.

"Pay attention." He knocked the tumbler from her hand and it went scattering to pieces on the ground around them.

"Jesus, Charles." She cursed.

He grabbed her roughly, shoving her against the desk and then lifted the receiver that had been pressed between his ear and shoulder to his mouth and started speaking to someone on the other end and Kathryn half-listened. It was a studio lawyer or someone in public relations that he was barking orders at.

Kathryn shrugged out of his embrace and walked carefully around the broken glass to retrieve a cigarette.

"Don't you go anywhere. I'm not finished with you!" Charles' gruff voice barked at her and she slunk down into his office chair, puffing away at the cigarette. Thinking of Alice holed up in a room upstairs, knocked out with a sleeping pill Kathryn had offered her. To take the edge off. To help her forget if only for a little while.

She waited, in and out of conscious awareness of what Charles was saying.

"…no, don't let him get to the press…don't let him talk to *anyone!*"

She smoked, blowing angry puffs to the ceiling. Had she wanted this to come collapsing down around them? She knew going to Alice's home had been a terrible idea. And now here they were.

She wasn't paying attention until Charles slapped her cheek. It stung, and she pressed a hand to the hot surface, tasting blood in her mouth.

"What did I tell you? What did I tell you would happen? Hmm? You think you can just pull these little stunts and get away with anything you want, but you have no idea what this will cost me. Better yet what this will cost you. It was stupid, absolutely idiotic. Reckless! You can't do these things, Kathryn. You can't mess with other people's lives. He is her husband. He owns her and he might not realize it, but he has a hell of a lot more rights than he knows. And you better hope to God he doesn't realize it or else Alice is sunk. This isn't over for you, either. You'll pay for this all right. You won't know when and you won't know why, but mark my words, Kathryn, you will pay."

Kathryn's hand shook as she brought the cigarette to her lips to inhale, to steady herself. It was no use fighting back. She knew that much. She could bear the brunt of his anger and then lick her wounds in private.

She would not give him the privilege of seeing her break down before him. What kept her steady in that moment was the intimate knowledge that only a week ago Charles had sent a young, nubile actress, Miss Mary Danvers, to a special hospital to have a special procedure to cover up something *he* had done.

Charles took another call and then slammed the phone down in the cradle, collecting the jacket and hat from where he'd tossed them on the desk. "God damn you." He looked as if he might strangle her before he put on his hat. "I have to go to the studio to handle this in person. I'll be back to deal with you later."

She smoked the last of the cigarette, listening as his heavy footsteps receded into the distance. The opening of a door. His car starting up, backing away.

Kathryn stubbed out the small remnant of cigarette and stood shakily. She was careful of the glass but fell into a bookshelf. Steadying herself, she managed to clean up the mess of glass and liquor on the floor. As she washed her hands in the sink she saw blood mixing in the water and realized a glass shard had cut her palm. She stared at the gash, watched it bleed, dripping cherry red liquid into the sink basin.

She could taste the blood in her mouth. She spat redness into the sink and then washed away the taste, cleaned the gash on her hand, bandaged it, and then studied the bruise forming on her face.

It was only the beginning, she reasoned.

She crawled her way up the stairs, turning to the room where Alice lay blissfully unaware, sleeping. Even breaths belied her current disconnect from the world.

Kathryn stood over the bed, looking down upon Alice's angelic, sleeping form. She looked so beautiful, peaceful, content in sleep.

Tears welled in Kathryn's eyes, frustrated, angry tears. For why couldn't this always be how Alice was in her woken state?

She felt her knees give out and had to sit at the edge of the bed to stop the room from spinning. She realized she was crying. "Alice, oh, I'm so...I'm so sorry." She whispered, leaning over Alice's sleeping form, wrapping herself close to her. "I'm so sorry." And she pressed her ear to Alice's chest, listening to the slow, dull beat of her heart beneath. "Oh, Alice. I love you, damn it." Kathryn whispered against Alice's chest that rose and fell with each even breath.

She was unaware of time then. Sliding in and out of consciousness. It was delirious, delicious.

Until she heard the slamming of a door and she sat straight up in the bed, fear coursing through her veins. A headache had formed behind her eyes.

"Kathryn!" Charles bellowed.

She stumbled from the bed, turning quickly to find Alice was still sound asleep. Good, she thought.

Kathryn slunk her way down the winding staircase, pressed up against the wall.

Charles was in the sitting room, pouring himself a drink, already smoking a cigarette.

She watched him from her spot in the doorway.

"We shut him up for now." Charles growled after downing a glass of bourbon. "You should be fucking glad of that because he was not easy to shut up."

"Jack…what about Jack?" She whispered, voice hoarse.

Charles laughed out loud. "Why the fuck do you give a shit about the kid? You played with fire. You had to know this could happen. The courts don't take kindly to dyke mothers."

"Charles." Kathryn pleaded.

Charles poured another shot of bourbon and drank it down, slamming the glass on the top of the bar. "He's being sent to the mother for now."

"Alice's mother? Does she…"

"No, she doesn't know the full extent of it. But I'll tell you what, she seemed to know." Charles shook his head. "Said she'd suspected her daughter was stepping out."

Kathryn swallowed. "Can she get him back?"

Charles looked at her as if she had two heads. "What do

you care about the kid? You certainly were happy to get rid of your own."

Kathryn clenched her fists behind her back. "That was different, Charles, and you know it."

"What is he talking about?" A small, quiet voice surprised them both.

Kathryn turned to find a sleepy-eyed, fearful Alice standing in the hallway.

Charles looked from Kathryn to Alice. "Of course. She didn't tell you about her daughter, did she?"

"Charles." Kathryn snapped.

"She doesn't say much about herself." Charles went on. "Like how she likes to fuck everyone she works with."

"That's not true."

"Man, woman. She doesn't care."

"That's enough!" Kathryn shouted.

Charles poured another drink.

"Kathryn, what is he talking about?"

"I'll tell you later." Kathryn hissed.

Alice looked at her, pained. "What is going on?" She cried, and tears slid from her eyes. Kathryn longed to give her another sleeping pill and make it all go away before she could wake again.

"Your child is going to be with your mother and for now Frank's going to keep his mouth shut about what he witnessed. But at a great cost to you I'm afraid."

Alice looked so small standing in the grand foyer, folding in on herself. "What cost?" She whispered. It was almost Faustian, as if she knew she was making a deal with the devil.

"It'll all come out in the wash, don't you worry your pretty little head about that. But for now, you see, you'll be out of a paycheck. I presume the studio will put you up somewhere, some nice little bungalow and you'll have enough money for food."

Alice folded her arms about herself. Kathryn longed to go

to her but knew she could not, trapped between Alice and her husband. Her penance.

She pressed herself tighter against the wall.

"What about my son?" Alice's voice was less than a whisper, more a strangled sob.

Charles shook his head. "Don't know what to tell you about that."

Alice bowed her head, seeming to accept all of this. "Thank you for…for doing this…for me."

"Oh, my dear, it's not for you. It will never be for you." Charles stubbed out his cigarette and grabbed his coat and hat. "I'm going out. Don't wait up for me." He placed the hat on his head and brushed past Kathryn so that she fell back against the wall.

He left them both standing in silence.

When Kathryn dared to look toward Alice she saw the younger woman had taken on the appearance of someone much older. Her face tired, her body defeated.

There was a lack of recognition on her face as she stared blankly past Kathryn.

Chapter Thirty-Seven

Alice

She was allowed one supervised visit with Jack. The day before her mother was to take him back to Michigan with her.

At that point she had not eaten for a day. It hadn't necessarily been on purpose, she just hadn't felt hungry. She was lightheaded but delirious to see Jack, to be able to wrap him up in her arms and hold him close, and the thought crossed her mind that maybe, just maybe, she could slip away with him and take him far, far away and start all over. For the first time, her celebrity felt like a punishment. That she could not just go anywhere and escape because she was Kay from "that show." There was no hiding.

Her mother stared at her coldly. For the first time in thirty years, her mother kept a stiff upper lip, not uttering a word. Her silence was disarming, uncomfortable.

Alice cradled Jack close, tears slipping down her cheeks despite her even keeled disposition.

"I wish you'd say something." She hissed at her mother.

Her mother bristled.

"I know what you must think of me." She prodded further. Needing *something*. Not this silence.

"No." Her mother breathed.

Alice looked at her.

"No, Alice. I'm afraid you don't have any idea what I think." The way she spoke was as if to a passing stranger whom she had never met, with whom she had no relation at all.

Alice watched as her mother looked down at her watch, as if she could not count down the seconds to the end of the visitation.

Fear grasped at her chest, for Alice had no idea when she would be allowed to see her son again. They were precious seconds; she resented her mother's impatience.

The thought made her choke outright on her tears and it startled Jack and he clung to her, threading his little fingers into her hair and holding her close. "Oh, my Jack, Jack. I love you. Do you know that?" She whispered, holding him ever so away from her so she could peer at his face – he already looked so different, and it had only been a few weeks since she had last seen him. She would miss the next few days, weeks, months…could it be years? "Oh!" She held him tighter. "I love you." And she had never meant it more, had not expected to feel this for a child she had not even been certain she wanted in the first place.

But now he was being taken from her, and she realized all that she felt for him and all she was about to lose.

Had she wanted this?

Her mother left the room, as if she could not stand it a minute longer.

Alice clung to Jack and began sobbing when the man who had supervised everything from the corner of the room came to take Jack from her.

Jack began howling and Alice fought for him, but the man was stronger and he simply pushed her away. She watched as Jack, crying and reaching for her, was handed to her mother. Her mother, in turn, gave her a chilling glance and then carried the boy from the building.

Alice cried, letting out an inhuman howl, and then she was running toward her mother and son. It took the strong man grabbing her, holding her off in the parking lot, to stop her from chasing her mother down. She could only watch as her mother put her crying child in a car, closed the door, and drove away without looking once in her direction.

Her legs buckled. She fell to the concrete ground and sobbed uncontrollably, with no dignity or care for civility.

Afterward, she drove through Hollywood aimlessly as the sun started going down. She stopped at a diner and ordered a large meal and proceeded to eat half of it before she ended up puking in the diner's bathroom. She tossed a few bills on the table and left, anxiety not quelled.

She clasped the steering wheel tightly, eyes blurred from tears.

She did not want to return to the dingy, grimy little place they had found for her. It was nothing more than a little studio apartment. The sink had a leak that dripped all night. The only relief was that she could go to bed by herself most nights and not have to fend anyone off. But the too bright lighting and the empty walls and lack of her son made it the last place Alice wanted to be.

But it was all she had.

Her headlights caught the sleek green polish of a familiar car and for a brief moment she was relieved at the sight of it.

She made her way up the stairs to her apartment, put her key in the lock and pushed open the door.

Kathryn was at the table, smoking a cigarette, a glass of something in hand, the newspaper folded out before her. She stood, unsteadily, at the sight of Alice. "My God, where have you been? I was about to send out a search party."

Alice slid from her heels, tossing her purse and keys atop a table and sank down on the puke green couch. She curled her legs up, wrapped her arms about them and rested her head on her knees.

"Oh, Alice." Kathryn came to her, sitting carefully on the seat beside her. She smelled of liquor, despite the fact that Alice kept none in her new home. But what did it matter? Kathryn always had a stash of it hidden up her sleeve.

"It was awful." Alice whispered.

"I know." Kathryn let her fingers trail down Alice's back. It delighted her skin, almost soothed over the prickly sensation of the past few hours.

"How could you possibly know?" Alice snapped before she could stop herself.

Kathryn's hand stilled on her back.

She could tell Kathryn thought she had forgotten what had been said all those evenings before.

A daughter. Kathryn had a daughter, and she'd told Alice nothing about it. They hadn't come close to it again because life had become about managing the damage done. Keeping everything hush hush, keeping the reporters and lawyers and everyone else who had been brought in at bay, on the verge of knowing the truth without ever actually knowing it.

Alice looked to Kathryn. She had gone silent, practically shrinking beside her. "I spoke out of line." She offered, not wanting to get into another brawl that evening.

Kathryn slunk from the couch. Alice watched her as she went to the kitchen table to take a cigarette from her case, lighting it with the flick of a golden lighter. The elegance of it all did not belong in such grim surroundings. Kathryn did not fit here. With her.

"No, how could you know." Kathryn shook her head. "I had a baby." Kathryn puffed at her cigarette, considering her words. "Or rather, I *have* a daughter. She was born when I was seventeen and I was gone the minute she arrived." Kathryn laughed without laughter at this.

"My God, Kathryn." Alice stared at her in disbelief.

"Go on, berate me for my teenage recklessness." Kathryn leaned against the table, as if waiting for Alice's chastisement.

Alice shook her head. "How could you leave her?"

Kathryn inhaled raggedly. "I couldn't stand the thought that she existed. And anyway, I wouldn't be where I was today if I hadn't left her. She's had a better life without me."

Alice stared, confused, at Kathryn. There were pieces missing, holes in this story.

"But it's not the same as what you have." Kathryn insisted. "Not at all. You will see him again, Alice. They can't keep you from him forever."

Alice shuddered, remembering what a lawyer had told her several days prior. That her behavior was immoral and judges did not side with the immoral party.

"We haven't done anything wrong." Kathryn half-whispered.

"Haven't we?" Alice felt fresh tears welling in her eyes.

Kathryn stubbed out her cigarette. "Does it feel wrong to you?"

Alice considered the sick feeling in the pit of her stomach. Where once Kathryn had felt like a haven away from everything, she now seemed like the reason for the void. For this blank, darkness all around.

But there she was, kneeling beside Alice, looking at her with those glorious dark eyes. Pleading with her.

And, after all, Kathryn was there. She had been there for her through it all.

Alice shook her head, letting the tears overtake her and Kathryn's lips pressed against hers. They found themselves entangled atop the couch, Kathryn cradling Alice as she cried until there were no more tears to cry.

They must have fallen asleep like this. Alice drifted in and out of consciousness, at moments dreaming of her previous home with Frank, at others she was at the sound stage in a rehearsal, forgetting lines, and then in another moment she was in her childhood home, running through that field down the road…

Her shoulder hurt.

She awoke to the dim kitchen light and a silhouette sitting at the kitchen table. The image frightened her until she made out the glowing cherry of a lit cigarette.

She watched in silence, as a flask was unscrewed, its contents carefully poured into a glass. The glass was lifted, lips caressing the rim like a lover.

Alice closed her eyes to the image, wondering if it were, in fact, a dream as the others had been.

Chapter Thirty-Eight

Kathryn

Charles had laid out the red dress on the bed. He liked that dress.

It should have been the first sign.

She dressed without question.

Charles escorted her to his car, ushered her inside.

It became clear to her the instant they drove through the ranch's front gate.

It was evening. She longed to be able to stay outside and savor the remnants of warmth from the day. There had been the chirp of cicadas and the night was warm after California's brief attempt at winter. Palm branches whispered together in the quiet evening breeze.

Charles took her by the arm, leading her through the wide, double-doored entrance into the rustic home. Her knees nearly buckled, but Charles kept her upright with a stiff embrace.

Men, a sea of men. The room filled full, all eyes on her for she was the only she, the prize for the evening.

There were men she recognized and men she had never seen before. Their faces all blurred together. She was handed a cocktail and her cigarettes were lit.

Until Charles motioned for her and she was led to a secluded room.

Inside which sat men.

There was Gordon Nielson, offering her a cigar with a somewhat apologetic look on his face as he ushered her to the edge of a bed in the center of the room.

She took the burning cigar and inhaled, holding the luxurious smoke in her mouth.

The door was closed and locked.

Charles took a cigar for himself, cut it, lit it delicately and then stood by the window smoking it.

Kathryn took another puff, looking from Charles to Gordon Nielson to Ken Martin to Ben Carter to Maxwell Rockhill to another few men she did not know at sight. Their faces blurred together and the cigar was replaced with another cocktail.

No one spoke.

Charles stood stately at the window.

Kathryn felt her vision going blurry at the edges.

"Take off your dress." Charles' voice cut through her cloudy mind.

"I'd like it to stay on." A hand was caressing her collarbone.

She flinched but did not brush the touch away.

A belt buckle clicked, then the rush of the belt dislodging from its place in the belt loops.

It sounded so far away.

She closed her eyes, her body sinking down into the warm recesses of the bed.

She was somewhere else, she was not here. Her mind

clouded with images of other places, other times, other worlds. There were flowing streams and magnificent water-falls. There were fields and fields of flowers, all different sizes and shapes and colors, colors she had never before seen. There were tall, tall trees and lush, verdant landscapes and dark, inviting caves. There was a small shack near a stream with a woman inside, and she welcomed her with open arms and she held her and protected her from a sudden thunder-storm that burst forth out of nowhere and there was lightning in every color that illuminated the sky like fireworks.

"Kathryn." She felt someone shaking her awake.

She turned over and then moaned, body sore.

When her eyes opened, light was streaming into the room.

Day had come without her knowledge of passing through the night.

Blood and other substances clung to her skin. She was unclean. She wanted to bathe, to make it all go away.

Charles escorted her home, put her in a hot shower and then left again. Off to New York or wherever it was he went off to.

It had been done, the debt paid.

She crawled into her bed wrapped around a bottle of gin.

She was cognizant of the phone ringing several times but she hadn't the strength to answer.

The days passed and she felt she was half of what she used to be. She went to Alice, but could not let her touch her.

She relied on the alcohol to wake her up enough to go to rehearsal.

"She hasn't been sober for weeks."

Kathryn pressed herself into the dark recesses of the soundstage. She could hear her heart pounding in her ears.

"I heard they had to slap her awake the other day after lunch."

"I heard that she had something to do with Alice's divorce."

"You think they were fucking?"

"How hot would that be?"

Kathryn grimaced, wondering how she might be able to slip past these nosey stagehands so she could get back to her dressing room and that bottle of gin.

"What are you doing in the dark?" Wes appeared before her, fresh from the stage. His smiling face held strange concern. Was everyone concerned for her nowadays?

"No-nothing." She stuttered.

"Hey, you all right there, Anderson?" Wes caught her arm, as if she needed to be steadied.

"Right as rain." She saluted.

Wes laughed tightly. "Come on, let's get you to your dressing room." He looped her arm through his and escorted her through the set, past the men who had just been talking about her, and to her dressing room. He closed the door behind them as she slumped down on the couch. "What the hell are you doing, Kathryn?" His tone shifted from its usual friendliness.

"What are you talkin' about?"

"Everyone knows you're drinking." He came closer to her, as if he were threatening her. "Get it together, Kathryn."

She sobered, feeling a dull headache surface, a dire need for that gin.

"Be the professional I know you are. Stop drinking on my set."

He left her in the room and she heard him laughing with someone on the other side of the door, as if he hadn't just bawled her out.

Her hand shook.

She stood and after falling against the couch and then the wall, found her way to the cabinet where the bottle of gin was. She reached for it only to find there was no bottle to grasp.

Where had the gin gone?

"Fuck, fuck, fuck."

She cursed.

The rest of the day was a blur. She was forgetting her lines left and right, her mind racing a mile a minute. She had to excuse herself to vomit. Her hand was shaking so terribly that she shoved it into her pocket.

Stephen was looking at her with fury in his eyes.

But the worst of it was the fearful glances Alice gave her.

She fumbled a line and Stephen snapped.

"Get off my set!" He screamed, and Kathryn threw her script in his direction, sulking off the stage.

Alice was on her heels in a matter of seconds.

"What are you doing?" Kathryn cried. "Get back there."

"I told them I was going to make sure you got home safely. I was already done for the day anyway." Alice spoke shortly.

Alice drove her to her apartment, put her to bed, made her tea and told her to rest.

Kathryn fluttered in and out of consciousness, awaking at one moment to find Alice perched at the side of the bed with tears in her eyes.

"I wish I knew what was going on with you." Alice whispered.

And Kathryn wished she could tell her. It felt, however, as if it had all been a bad, terrible dream.

There was a part of her that knew she had deserved it. Knew she had needed to bear it to keep Alice safe.

Kathryn wanted to protect her, wanted her to never know the dark recesses dwelling inside of her. But how could she do any of that when she couldn't even protect herself?

She rolled away from Alice, curled into a ball and closed her eyes.

Chapter Thirty-Nine

Alice

It felt strange now, to be sitting across from Charles in his ornate studio office.

She could not lift her eyes to meet his face. They had not been alone together since before, and the discomfort made Alice wither.

He had called her in to meet with him. She supposed she had expected it, for everyone else had been spoken to that day, and the hush hush and long faces of the whole ordeal seemed to mean one thing for the show.

"It's over, isn't it?" She spoke at her manicured nails, trimmed into perfect ovals, luminescent in the dim lighting.

"I'm afraid so. The network thinks it's too similar to other shows, and the ratings have been steadily dropping for months." He spoke without rancor.

"I see." She felt as if she could cry, but she refused to do so in front of him. So she balled her hands into fists and shoved them into her skirt.

"But," the happy lilt to his voice surprised her. "The audience loves you. In fact, you had the highest ratings of them all, according to a recent survey. The network doesn't want to lose you."

"What?" Alice frowned.

"The network has you in mind for something."

The 'however' was tangible in the air between them.

Alice unfolded and then refolded her hands.

"Of course, since your involvement with my wife has rather unsettled things for you, we have some damage to take care of." Her cheeks flared red and hot at the mention of this. "The network wants your image to be squeaky clean, you see," Charles continued. "All of our stars have pristine images. Marriage, home life, it matters to our viewers. Your behavior on and off screen serves as a patriotic example to all women of America. Do you understand, Alice?"

She did but wished she did not.

"If you would like to take advantage of this *more* than generous offer that the network is extending to you, then there are several concessions to be made. You see?"

"Concessions." Alice's throat was dry.

Charles smiled and sat back, folding his hands over his stomach. He looked far too smug. "You want your son back, don't you Alice?"

Her heart began to beat faster, pounding deafeningly in her ears.

"That would require that you prove this little liaison, this dalliance on the wrong side, was simply a misstep and you really do love men. Because, let me tell you, Alice, men love you. Those fans of yours, they're men. They like you. They want to know that you like them back."

Her stomach sank.

"Alice, we're going to get you a show, hell, we can even get your son back, but you've got to do something for us. Do you see?"

Alice looked up at Charles. What would she possibly have to do to have all of this?

Charles tossed a headshot across the desk. A young man. She briefly recognized him from some picture, or had it been a television show? He looked like he could have been any man.

"This is Ken Parker. His real name is Kenneth Pastorek. He's sweet, real sweet, from the Middle-West like you. I think you'd have a lot in common."

She looked at the brown-haired boy and then up at Charles. "What is this?"

Charles tried to hide his smile, but she could see it wrinkling the corner of his lips. "An eligible bachelor."

Alice felt her skin crawl, wanted to get up and race away from the room, but her legs felt like lead.

"You think about it. We're offering you something big, Alice. Your own show." He shoved the picture toward her, and she wanted to vomit. "But don't take too long to think about it. The network's whims change like the weather. One day they love you, the next…"

Alice rose unsteadily from the chair and made her way from the dimly lit office back into the light of day that fluttered in through the lobby windows. She made it only a bit further to a restroom where she vomited up in the toilet all she had consumed that day.

That evening Alice watched Kathryn pace the spans of her living room restlessly. A lit cigarette hung in her fingers, ash dropping messily atop the wooden floor as she moved.

Alice rubbed her forehead, feeling a headache coming on. She wanted to grab Kathryn and pull her to her, to make her stop pacing, but she hadn't the strength to move in that moment.

Kathryn cursed. "The asshole didn't even have the decency to tell me ahead of it. You know, he used to tell me things. He used to warn me, but I suppose he's still punishing me. He probably couldn't wait to tell me after everyone else knew. The smug bastard." Tears clung to her lashes.

She finally stopped pacing and stood, staring at Alice as she brought the cigarette to her lips, inhaling deeply as she regarded her.

"Why aren't you upset?" Kathryn snapped.

"I am. I am upset." Alice sighed quietly, reaching for a throw pillow she could wrap her arms about.

"Well the fucking show is all over, and you're oddly quiet." Kathryn poked. Provoking Alice, as if she wanted a fight with her.

Wasn't that all that had been going on between them? Fight after fight. One pushing, the other pulling. Never on the same page anymore. The fact that they hadn't touched for weeks only added to the dissonance.

Alice played with the edge of the pillow.

Kathryn continued to look at her through a cloud of smoke.

Alice closed her eyes. "He…he offered me a show." She whispered the words.

"A show?" Kathryn's voice took on piqued curiosity.

Alice nodded.

"They offered you your own show?" Kathryn guessed without having to be told.

Alice nodded again.

Kathryn laughed, "Good. That's good. You'll have your own show then." She spoke with forced sincerity.

Alice could understand what it was she might feel. But Kathryn did not fully understand what the offer of the show meant for her. "Oh, but it's not." Alice took a deep breath and watched as Kathryn kneeled on the opposite side of the coffee table.

"Why is that?" Kathryn tapped off her cigarette in an ashtray Alice had placed on the coffee table.

Alice looked at Kathryn.

Kathryn had a sad, knowing look in her dark eyes.

"What do they want?"

Alice held the pillow closer, the weight of it comforting, familiar. "There's an actor..."

Kathryn slowly pieced it together.

Alice felt tears threatening to fall. "He said I could get my son back." Her voice was a strangled whisper.

Kathryn scratched her forehead, smoking irritably. "Surely you don't have to do *that* in order to get your son back."

"What else am I supposed to do? I've lost everything, Kathryn. Everything. I don't want to lose my career too."

"No," Kathryn stubbed out her cigarette. "No, and you shouldn't." She moved to sit beside Alice. Alice wanted so badly for her to reach out, to hold her, to tell her it would all be all right, that it might all just be some bad, horrible dream. But Kathryn did not touch her; she merely sat beside her as if in solidarity. No physical comfort was extended. It had not been for days, as if an imaginary wall had come between them.

"What am I supposed to do?" Alice asked without hope of answer. There seemed to be only one solution.

"It's terrible." Kathryn's hand was shaking, Alice noticed, when she reached for another cigarette. "It's all my fault, too." She breathed smoke.

"It's not." Alice shook her head.

"Yes. Yes, it is." Kathryn clasped her head in her hands, fingers wrecking her blonde curls.

"Kathryn, I wanted this." Alice tried.

"You shouldn't have." Kathryn shook her head.

"It's the only thing that's felt *real* to me...I...Kathryn, I lo..."

"Don't. Please, Alice." Kathryn sat up abruptly, looking into Alice's eyes. "Don't say that. I think it will make it worse. For the both of us."

"Kathryn…"

"Damn it." Kathryn stood up. "I need a goddamn drink."

"Kathryn, please."

"You're right, Alice. You need to save yourself and I can't…I can't stand in the way of that. You go on and marry the nitwit. You'll have a show and your son." Kathryn spoke as she moved to gather her things together.

"I don't just want that…"

"Alice," Kathryn sighed, "Don't you see? I'm only going to get in the way. You've got to let this go."

"Kathryn, don't leave." Alice was standing there before her, not knowing what to do, except to clasp at her wrists, to hold her close. "I can't lose you, too."

"Alice," Kathryn twisted out of her grasp. "Don't make this harder than it needs to be." There were tears in her eyes as she spoke resolutely.

"Where are you going?" Alice demanded.

"A bar. It's as dry as the prohibition in here."

"Kathryn, don't go."

"Alice, please. It's better we leave it. I want you to have your life."

"I want you in my life."

"I told you, Alice, from the beginning, that I'm not worth all of this."

"You are, damn it, Kathryn. You are."

Kathryn looked at her with a strange, unreadable expression. Alice saw the lone tear that slid its way down Kathryn's cheek, but the sad vulnerability lasted only a fleeting second before her expression changed back into something unreadable again. And she pushed at Alice. "Don't make me be mean about it."

"Kathryn…" Alice tried to reach for her again, and the two ended up in a strange tug of war. Grasping, pushing, pulling, shoving, until Kathryn's hand connected with Alice's cheek. Alice gasped. Shocked by the sensation, even more so when she could taste blood on her teeth.

Kathryn looked at her, startled and surprised.

They both stood, the only sound between them their labored breaths. Kathryn was a stranger to her. She did not recognize her at all. Something had shifted, and she was no longer the person Alice had once known.

"I'm sorry, Alice." Kathryn reached for her, but Alice stepped away.

There was a sad smile on Kathryn's face, as if a great burden had been lifted from her shoulders, as if she were relieved to be getting away from Alice.

The pain in Alice's chest intensified.

So it would end here. Terribly unfinished.

But what else was there to do?

Alice opened her mouth as if to say something but then closed it again.

Kathryn collected her items and stole away into the night to drink herself into oblivion. And Alice collapsed on the ground, wrapping her arms about herself.

The tears came when the shock wore off.

Part IV

Chapter Forty

Kathryn

Los Angeles, 1981

The restaurant had not been her idea.

Howard sat across from her. He had gotten fatter and uglier. He looked like a bloated whale about to burst. There wasn't a wrinkle in his aged face because of it.

He smiled at her over his steak, a mocking smirk on his reddened jowls.

"Howard, listen to me. I want to work again. In America. After all this time…there has to be something." She tapped her cigarette against the ashtray as if in punctuation.

"I've gotta be honest with you, doll, in this market if you're not twenty-five with big tits, America doesn't want you."

"Howard, I was just on that Holly…Holly whatever her goddamn name is' show. That was fucking free publicity. And,

and the American public still loves Wes' show. That has to count for something."

Howard laughed and bowed his head as he continued tearing into his steak. "I'm afraid it doesn't quite work like that. You vanished to Europe and made yourself some pretty questionable pictures with that eccentric husband of yours. He's still dressing like a lady?"

Kathryn lifted her wine glass to her lips and inhaled the drink. "I don't see how that's any of your business." Her foot was tapping incessantly beneath the table. A sheen of sweat had formed on her brow. She wiped absently at it.

Howard looked at her again. "This isn't about breaking back into America's Hollywood is it."

Kathryn's brow furrowed. "What the hell are you talking about? Of course I want to work in America again…I…"

"You're not making money on those pictures, are you?"

"Well, now…" she played with the edge of her napkin. Fuck. "It's not that at all."

"Sure, sure. But we both know art doesn't equal money." Howard pointed a piece of steak at her.

"Excuse me." Kathryn stabbed out her cigarette and grabbed her purse, making a beeline for the restaurant's restroom.

Fuck. Fuck Howard. Of course he'd just wanted to dine out with her because he didn't take her seriously as a client any more. She was dead to him. If they'd met in his office then maybe they could have actually talked business. "Fuck." Kathryn slammed closed the bathroom door and sat on the toilet seat, fishing about in her bag.

When she pulled the baggie from her purse, she realized she only had a line or two left. There would be no more after this.

Panic welled inside of her.

She still had a flight back to Germany to suffer through. This couldn't be the last of it.

And she knew, oh fuck, how she knew what their finances looked like. Screw Howard for seeing through her.

They were up to their necks in debt.

As she looked further into her purse for a rolled up American bill, she realized it was only a dollar bill and the rest of her cash consisted of a five and a twenty.

"Fuck, fuck." Panic was rising by the second.

She cut a line and snorted it, sniffing and sniffing. It hurt. But when it finally settled she felt infinitely better.

Putting everything away, she had the strangest feeling it would all work out. She would find a way.

This was Los Angeles after all.

She cleaned herself up, made sure her nose had nothing noticeable on it nor was it bleeding.

The panic had receded into a dull hum.

She tucked her bag beneath her arm and fluffed her hair. She didn't need Howard, the fat fuck.

And she exited the bathroom, running directly into the chest of a tall man.

"Sorry," she stepped away, but then felt the man's arm pull her back.

"My God. Kathryn."

She looked up and felt the blood rush from her face. "Ch-Charles? What the hell are you doing here?"

"What the hell are you doing here? I thought you were off cavorting around Germany with that queer tranny husband of yours."

"Fuck off." She shoved at his chest.

He grabbed her arm and held her up to the light, looking her over. He laughed. "I thought you said you'd never get into that stuff. Not after what happened to your brother."

"Take your hands off me!" She cried, attracting attention from those seated near to them. How dare he?

Charles removed his hand but did not step away. "I saw you on the show. You were high out of your mind."

"I was not." Kathryn tried to laugh.

Charles looked over her head, scanning the dinner crowd. His eyes came to rest on the table she was about to return to. He laughed again. "I see. You think Howard can get you back into the good graces of America. Well that's a laugh. The guy is living off syndication and young hot blondes. He can't do anything for you."

"How do you know?" Kathryn felt the panic returning with each passing second. She needed to deflect, hating how he always knew. "How's that wife of yours? Still a teenager?"

"Good, Kathryn. We're just great. Want to see pictures of the children?"

"No." She searched for a cigarette, needing something more to calm her frayed nerves.

Charles, ever the gentleman, lit it for her. "Get yourself together, Kathryn." And he leaned in to press a kiss to her cheek. "That stuff will kill you."

He left her there. She fell against the wall, lifting the cigarette with an unsteady hand to her lips until she could walk again. She wiped at her eyes, at her nose and then walked back to her table where Howard was waiting.

"You know, I thought about it, Kathryn." He said as she sat back down.

"Hmm?" She asked, tapping off ashes, lifting the refreshed wine glass to her lips.

Howard leaned forward conspiratorially. "There is a picture that has been looking for an older woman. It's just a bit part really, but I think…if you were to do something for me… just a little something, I might just be able to —"

He couldn't finish his sentence because she splashed the remainder of her wine in his face. "That's vile, Howard! I would *never*. I will *never*. You sick fuck." She hissed and stood up, storming out of the restaurant, leaving curious onlookers in her wake.

Chapter Forty-One

Alice

The phone was ringing.

A migraine had overtaken her. She moaned, shifting the ice pack on her forehead to peer out into the darkened room.

The phone rang again. Her heart leapt at the possibility...

Her answering machine picked up the call. She listened attentively when it beeped.

"I know you're home, sugar. Pick up or else I'm going to come over there myself."

"Oh." Alice groaned and shifted on the couch to rummage about for the phone. She lifted it to her ear and closed her eyes again. "Jeanette, please..."

"Alice...I've got to tell you that I've certainly suspected it a time or two, but on national television..."

"What are you talking about?" Alice sighed.

"Now, I'll hand it to you, I don't think the common viewer would suspect it. Maybe it's only because I know you so well..."

Alice covered her forehead with her arm. "Please don't say it."

"It's safe with me, Alice. I won't say a word."

"It's not whatever you're…it's not…"

"Cut the shit, Alice." Jeanette spoke firmly.

There was no hiding from her. She always saw through Alice.

This, this Alice had tried to keep locked down, hidden away, tucked back in a secret, hidden corner that could not be accessed by anyone.

But it seemed Jeanette had figured her out. All from one interview.

Had it been so obvious? She'd hardly even spoken to Kathryn, hardly even looked at her…

"It was written all over your face every time she spoke." Jeanette said, as if she could hear Alice's thoughts.

"Oh God." Alice felt a lump rising in her throat, tears tugging at her eyes. She couldn't cry any more. "Please don't…"

"Honey, I just told you I wouldn't say a thing. Your secret is safe with me."

And Alice burst into tears. "I don't know what to do. I mean, there's nothing *to* do. There were words exchanged afterward and it…well it's very clear that she doesn't want anything more to do with me."

Jeanette laughed at this. "I wouldn't be so sure. But, Alice…there are other *people* out there."

"No…I couldn't." Alice wiped at her tears. Had *she* been looking at her? "I couldn't. I'm not, uh…you know, I'm not, not really…"

"Uh huh." She could hear Jeanette lighting a cigarette on the other end of the line. "Why don't you let me take you out."

"Oh no. No, I don't think so."

"Come on. You need to cut loose. Get her out of your system. You deserve that, sugar."

Alice protested, but she found herself at a smoky jazz club in the middle of Los Angeles drinking a club soda with lime the following evening. She longed for home, for an excuse out of this attempt at getting her back out into the world of sex and delusions. She wanted nothing to do with it.

She watched the pianist run his fingers over the piano with a frenzied flourish, the music the only soothing balm to the smoky bar around her. The drums beat wildly, and she could feel each pound reverberating deep in her being.

Jeanette turned her gaze to Alice, shifting her eyes as if to allude toward someone and Alice followed her unsubtle motions toward a rather handsome black man who was looking right in her direction. Their eyes met, and he nodded his hello.

"Oh, Jeanette. I couldn't." Alice whispered against her ear.

"Because he's black or because he's a man?" Jeanette shot back.

"Stop it." Alice rolled her eyes to the ceiling, a pain forming in her chest. She excused herself from the bar, making her way through the crowd to the restroom. And once inside she leaned up against the cool, tiled wall and tried to remember how to breathe.

Kathryn would be miles away by now.

So that was it.

She had spent years trying to forget, years pretending as if she had never known the woman at all.

But now after having been in such close proximity the protective shell had all but cracked and Alice could not get the sight of her, the smell of her, the feel of her, out of her mind.

She had been before her in the flesh. She was not an apparition.

It had all really happened, hadn't it?

"Oh." Alice sobbed, the tears falling hot and thick down her cheeks.

She'd managed to keep it together all day. She'd managed not to think. But now – how was she supposed to go on as if it all hadn't mattered? As if it all hadn't happened?

"Are you all right in there?" A voice called out.

"I'm fine…I'm…I'm sorry." Alice was shaken out of her thoughts. She made quick work of wiping at her face and flushing the evidence away. She stepped out to peer into the vanity mirror and noticed a woman at the other mirror, reapplying an attractive shade of red to her lips.

"Didn't sound like you were fine." The woman spoke again as she smacked her lips together, wiping at the corners before clicking shut the lipstick canister and slipping it back into her purse.

"It's been a long day." Alice exhaled.

The woman looked her over in the mirror, and Alice could see the very instant she recognized her. But Alice was grateful when the woman simply smiled at her and held out her hand. "I'm Robin."

"Alice." Alice took the hand and shook it.

"Well, Alice, I'd say you deserve a drink. Would you let me buy you one?"

Alice's heart hammered in her chest. Was it customary for a woman to ask another woman such a question? "I…I don't really, well I don't drink." Alice tried to laugh.

The woman looked at her curiously. "And yet you're at a jazz club."

"Not my idea." Alice reached for some paper towels. "I'm here with uh…uh with a friend."

"Ah," Robin smiled prettily. "Perhaps you'd feel more comfortable somewhere else."

"If you mean at home then yes. Yes, I would." Alice

wiped at her brow, looking herself over in the mirror. Her eyes stared dully back at her, her face pale in the dim light.

"There's a diner around the corner." Robin was still looking at her. "Would you care to join me for a bite to eat before you run along home?"

Well that seemed innocent enough. Perhaps this dark-haired beauty was politely attempting to mingle with a television personality. It would not be the first time Alice had run into such a situation.

It most certainly was not the other possibility that Alice had considered.

She returned to the bar to retrieve her jacket and purse, and Jeanette's eyes landed on the woman who now accompanied her.

"I'm going to get out of here." Alice spoke against Jeanette's ear.

"With that hot thing?" Jeanette whispered back, eyes trained on Robin, who stood patiently waiting at Alice's side.

"It's not what you think."

"Oh, sugar, it's not what you think. But you have fun." Jeanette pressed her lips to Alice's cheek that burned hot red. She was thankful for the low lights about them.

Robin's hand went to the small of her back as they wove through the throng of people to the exit.

Chapter Forty-Two

Kathryn

She stumbled down the Sunset Strip, tipping ever so slightly so that she had to brace herself against the brick of a building. She pressed herself against the wall. Eyelids heavy, heart pounding in her chest, she couldn't seem to catch her breath.

Fumbling about in her purse, she fished out a cigarette and lighter. With unsteady hands she managed to light the end of it, puffing away as if it could ease her racing mind and pulsating chest.

The flight missed that morning. Having awakened fifteen minutes after its departure. A frantic call to Peter, an afternoon spent at the hotel bar drinking and waiting for things to be sorted out. It felt a lifetime ago.

She looked up and for a moment had the sense that she was nowhere at all. Reality distorted, lights blurring into darkness, faces obscured as bodies hurried past her. The once stately buildings of Sunset Boulevard were now hovels of noise and youth. This was not the Los Angeles she had known. Everything had changed. Progress marched ever forward, obliterating the past.

Kathryn liked the idea of total obliteration.

She pushed off from the wall and walked toward the sounds of a wailing heavy metal band coming from a nearby bar. Some tall man stood at the entrance, but after looking her over, he allowed her inside.

She didn't care for it at all - this heavy metal sound was a sad reduction of music, but it was not the noise she had come for. Nor the ridiculous mess of youth that darted around as if shot by arrows, bouncing off the walls, knocking into her as she went. No, the only part of it that she wanted was the cocaine she could see dripping from their noses.

She could feel eyes on her. She was not their normal patron, fellow party-goer, celebrant. She was an older woman who did not belong and yet they had no idea how much she belonged.

The music blasted at her eardrums, everything becoming muted and dull to her. She walked without knowing where she was going. Looking over the bar littered with drinks, scanning the dancing crowd, and finally moving toward an alcove of tables and lounging chairs.

And she came to a halt, stood, watching as a pretty young thing, hardly eighteen, leaned forward over the table and snorted a line of coke while a young man sat nearby, watching. He patted the girl's head as his eyes came to rest on Kathryn.

They looked at one another.

"Hey! That's Kathryn Anderson." A young man sitting near to him exclaimed over the loud music.

"What the hell is she doing here?" Another chimed in.

"Who gives a fuck. She's hot as shit."

The man was still looking at her.

He shoved roughly at the girl beside him and she crawled away. He patted the empty spot and Kathryn drifted forward, sinking onto the couch beside him. His features blurred into the room around them.

"You want some blow, don't you?" He whispered against her ear.

She placed her purse atop her lap and peered about at the curious onlookers.

The girl beside her was staring at her with wide, wondrous eyes. "I've seen you on television before." She chattered away as the man beside her cut a line.

Kathryn stared at the wondrous powder. Just like a pile of snow. Her memory slipped for the briefest of moments and she could see the view from her childhood window, the snow-covered forest that stretched out for miles. How beautiful it had been on those frigid winter mornings. How it had snowed the first time he'd come to her...

Someone was nudging her. The man was handing her a straw.

She leaned forward and inhaled.

Sitting back again, her hand came to her nose and she sniffed until a rush overtook her. It had been far, far too many hours without. It was intoxicating, the room spinning out into nothingness around her.

Was this what death might be like? To be so detached, so free from everyone and everything?

She basked in the sensation as it washed over her. Someone lit her cigarette. The girl was talking to her, words falling on deaf ears.

She was warm. The bar was stiflingly warm. She wanted to get away, to experience this sensation alone, but when she moved to stand she felt an arm pulling her back.

"Where do you think you're going?" The man was laughing at her side.

Ah.

"Come on, you're a celebrity, aren't you?" He turned on her.

She felt a cold sweat break out on her brow. But she could not show her bluff if she was to get out of this without a fuss. "What do you want?"

"Depends on what you need." He smiled.

"A gram." And she sensed that if she played her cards correctly she could get it.

The man cut a line of cocaine for himself and sniffed it before downing the rest of his beer. "Come with me."

He pulled her to her feet, and she tripped her way through the crowd as he led her toward the back of the bar, out an exit and to the back alley where a car sat parked. He chivalrously opened the passenger door and guided her inside.

Her heart beat loudly in her traumatized ears as the silence around her became deafening.

The driver side door slammed shut and she felt him beside her in the silent interior. Leather crinkled as he shifted, lighting a cigarette before unzipping his pants. "I suspect you're going to have to pay another way."

She stared at his lifeless dick as he began fondling it.

Was she always to come to this?

There were fleeting thoughts - thoughts that she was certainly old enough to be his mother, she was certainly too old to be doing this, she needed the cocaine so badly that all of it didn't matter - as he guided her hand towards him. "We're gonna go for a little drive to get you that gram." He started up the ignition, the engine purring.

He was a fast driver, weaving in and out of the Hollywood traffic. It was terrifically exhilarating and yet the sense of danger was missing from her mind.

He was warm in her hand. He yelled if she stopped for a second.

He sped away from the city, driving like a racecar driver up through the canyon. Her stomach somersaulted and she was on the verge of vomiting when he flipped the car into an alcove and killed the ignition.

He grabbed for her, pushing her down so that her mouth was level with his sad, pathetic member.

"You pay your debt and I won't leave you stranded up here." He leaned back and lit another cigarette.

She closed her eyes and put her mouth on him.

And when he finally finished, she sat up and opened the car door to vomit.

He was laughing, laughing at her or with her. She couldn't be sure.

He nudged at her knee and pulled a flask from the glove compartment. After taking a swig, he handed it to her.

"Woo!" He howled like a wolf. "Kathryn fucking Anderson. Well damn." He cut them both lines of cocaine and she inhaled hers greedily before lighting up a cigarette, wiping at her mouth and her nose.

"I'm gonna get you that gram, baby. You're really something, aren't you?" His eyes were wild.

He started up the ignition.

There was a thrill that shot through her, heart racing as the car went lurching along the dangerous terrain that wove through the canyon. He was moving up, up, up. Further and further away from the city, speeding. The world obscured as they rushed by.

The crash hardly registered in her mind. There was simply blackness.

Chapter Forty-Three

Alice

Alice ordered a coffee, and Robin ordered a glass of wine.

They sat at a back-corner booth, Alice grateful for the dim lighting and the sparse number of patrons littering the diner.

There was no reason to feel uncomfortable – Robin was easy to talk to and rather quite lovely – and yet Alice did feel uncomfortable. As if she were on display for everyone to see this thing she had worked hard to never show.

Robin's perfectly manicured hand came to rest atop Alice's for the briefest of moments. "No one's paying us any mind, Alice."

Alice removed her hand so she could lift the coffee cup to sip it, peering again around the room. Her eyes landed back on the woman before her, and she smiled uneasily. Robin's red lips quirked upward in amusement, eyes gleaming. She was a very attractive woman.

"I'm sorry, I've never..." Alice looked down at her hands

that rested about the coffee cup. "Well, I'm certainly not in the habit of going out."

Robin laughed at this. "Don't worry, Alice. We're simply talking, right? I've told you about myself, and now I'd like to know more about you."

It was Alice's turn to laugh at this. "Oh, come on…you know who I am."

Robin did not laugh. "But I don't know you."

Alice played with a ring on her finger.

"Of course I know you're an actress. A rather good one, at that. You've won some awards, you made some good television shows. But selling homes to the stars of Hollywood makes me rather bored, you know, with celebrity. They're just people. Usually rather obnoxious when you're up close and personal with them. But you – you seem different. You don't wear it like a badge of honor."

Alice watched Robin raptly as she spoke. A shock of awe overcame her, that someone could so instantly define her. "I guess I never thought to." She simply muttered.

Robin sat forward and a lock of raven hair fell over her shoulder. "So tell me something I don't know."

"There's not much to know." Alice shifted in her seat. "I've done well in the industry, it's true, but I never take it for granted. You never know when it could all come crumbling down."

"Ah." Robin sat her wine glass down and tapped at its pregnant surface.

Alice smiled shyly. "What?"

"Only someone who knows what it is to lose everything could know that." Robin said.

Alice felt tears sting her eyes. She wiped at her dry cheeks, lifting the coffee cup to distract herself.

"I didn't mean to upset you." Robin apologized.

"You didn't. I…I only just recently brushed up against my past." Alice shrugged.

"Thus the tears in the bathroom." Robin filled in the blanks.

Alice nodded, staring down into her empty coffee cup.

Her eyes shifted forward and found that there wasn't a drop left in Robin's wine glass. Robin declined a refill when the waiter came to check on them, and instead asked for the bill.

Alice didn't want to leave it so soon. Had she bored Robin so horribly? Was she really nothing more than a personality on television? But Robin didn't seem concerned with all of that.

Robin was looking at her as they waited for the waiter to return with her card.

"Perhaps we could speak more freely somewhere not so public."

Alice's heart pounded in her ears, cheeks warming.

Robin invited her to her home.

This was not like Alice at all, not one bit. But because it was not like her and because she decided to pretend as if she were someone else entirely, she followed Robin to a rather gorgeous Mercedes and climbed inside. "Don't you worry – that was my first drink of the night. Cross my heart and hope to die." Robin promised as she peeled out into the Hollywood traffic, aiming south toward Palos Verdes.

Her home was a simple white villa with ocean views out the back windows. Alice sat at a marble bar staring at the enormous body of water enshrouded in darkness while Robin boiled water for tea. She could feel her body trembling. She was out of her depths.

"Are you cold?" Robin was looking at her.

"N-no." Alice shook her head. "I'm just not...not used to...this."

Robin's eyebrow rose curiously. "You mean you're not in the habit of going home with attractive women you meet at jazz bars?"

Alice blanched.

"Oh, Alice." Robin laughed to ease the tension. "You mean you're not…"

"Are you?" Alice bit her lip.

Robin lifted the whistling kettle from the stove and poured it over two tea bags. "Men, women. It doesn't matter so much to me. I prefer women, of course, but I'm sure you know how difficult it can…"

"I don't." Alice looked away, her brave façade wilting. She couldn't do this.

"Well if that's so, then why did you come here with me?" Robin's gentle voice inquired.

Alice found no good answer to this question, could not even move her lips in an attempt at an answer.

"Oh, come. Come into the sitting room. Have some tea with me." Robin nudged her, mugs in hand as she left Alice sitting at the kitchen counter.

Anger, anger overtook her then. Anger at herself, at Jeanette for having suggested this whole ridiculous evening out in the first place. Alice could be home now, licking her wounds and trying to forget the whole thing had even happened, but here she was.

"I'm not like that." Alice spoke as she rounded the corner in search of wherever it was Robin had gone off to.

She found the woman curled up on a couch, mug in hand, blowing on the steam. "All right then." Robin patted the spot beside her.

Alice's bravado fizzled. She moved to sit on the couch, not too close but not too far, and lifted the mug Robin had left on the table for her. It smelled of vanilla and roses. "Perhaps…" Alice kept her eyes trained on the liquid's surface. "Perhaps I was once, but I…"

"It's perfectly normal."

"If it were so normal then we wouldn't have to tip toe

around it." Alice sipped her tea. "All it does is bring pain, so what's the point of acting on it?"

"It doesn't have to." Robin offered.

Alice turned to look at the woman. To truly take her in. She was a good ten years her junior. It appeared she was unmarried and had no need for such a contract. She was well off enough on her own as a real estate agent. So how could she possibly know?

"So what…what is it that we do, hmm? Kiss a little and then fall into bed together and then in the morning we just… pretend it never happened?" Alice curtly spelled it out.

Robin chuckled. "Well don't you just have it all figured out? But it doesn't have to be like that."

"No?"

"No, because you see I had no plans of taking you to bed with me." Robin half-smiled.

"Oh really." Alice laughed.

"Honest, I didn't have any objectives other than offering you some tea and a friendly shoulder to cry on."

"How chivalrous." Alice commended.

"But I must confess there is a part of your plan I am tempted by."

"And which part might that be?" Alice asked before sipping her tea.

"I can't get the idea of kissing you out of my head. I must admit I've been thinking about it since you stepped out of that bathroom stall with your eyes all puffy."

"That was a turn on?" Alice marveled.

Robin shrugged and took the tea mug from Alice's hands, placing it atop the table before them. Robin was closer to her on the couch than she had been only moments before. Her lips upon her own were for a moment shocking and then a sort of consolation.

Gently, a forgotten thrill coursed its way down her spine.

A knot in her shoulder unleashed its tight grasp, her body unwinding as Robin's lips pressed against her own.

When Alice awoke with the rising sun, she found herself tangled in a strange bed, Robin curled away from her.

Alice shifted, wondering just how she might steal home to shower and piece herself together before she was due at the studio. She was grateful when Robin awoke and gave her a gentle smile. "I'll send for a car." She made Alice coffee in her beautiful kitchen and Alice sipped it while staring out to sea. It was tranquil. When Robin put her arm about Alice it felt both natural and frightening.

Robin slipped Alice her business card, kissing her goodbye when the car arrived in her driveway. "I hope you keep in touch."

Alice daydreamed the whole ride back to her Santa Monica home of what keeping in touch might entail. And a hazy, disconnected comfort warmed her at the thought of it.

She walked as if in a daze into her home. But the sight of it began to tear into her false sense of reality. What she had tried to escape the previous evening began to come back to her, bit by bit.

The phone was ringing.

She looked at the clock on the wall. It was only eight-thirty in the morning. Who would be calling so early?

She lifted the phone from its receiver. "Hello?"

"Mom, mom – have you seen the news?" Her son's all too alert tone filled the line.

"What news, baby?"

"Your friend from the show…she's been in an accident."

Alice's pulse quickened. "Jeanette?"

"No, mom. Kathryn. Kathryn Anderson."

Chapter Forty-Four

Kathryn

She groaned.

Something was beeping incessantly. Rattling about in her smarting head.

It wouldn't stop.

Her body shook, cold. So dreadfully cold.

A hand was pressing something warm against her forehead. "It's all right, Kathryn." That voice flowed through her like honey wine.

The pain seeped back into her consciousness. The torn knee, the crushed rib, the broken nose. It overwhelmed her, this excruciating discomfort she found herself in.

She was overcome with the urge to expel everything from her system. It came in fits and waves. She hoisted herself up just in time for a pan to be placed at her side, and she painfully twisted to throw up. The throbbing in her side made it all the worse. When the feeling finally passed, she lowered herself back against the bed and felt tears trailing down her cheeks.

Someone wiped at her mouth and then gently at the corner of her eyes.

"Cigarette." She whispered.

The bed was adjusted so she could sit up ever so slightly and her eyes came open as a cigarette was placed between her lips. She met Alice's eyes when the lighter flicked in the dim hospital room.

It startled her. A ghost standing before her.

Was she delirious? Was she dreaming it all?

She could not be so certain anymore what was real and what was not.

She had not had a drink for hours now so everything seemed a little hazy and uncertain.

And then her body shook, her hand unsteady as she brought the cigarette to her lips.

Alice's form did not disappear but simply stood there. Watching her.

"What are you doing here?" Kathryn brushed ash from her lap with a sore hand.

"I had to see you." Alice's voice was unreadable, her face lost to Kathryn's poor vision so she could not make out her expression. "I…" Her voice faltered. "I had no idea." Alice whispered, lifting the ashtray for Kathryn to tap off her cigarette.

The smoke burned her chapped, cut lips. The damaged rib making it hard to inhale and exhale. The whole of it exhausting, but if she wasn't allowed a goddamn drink then what else did she have? The pain medication - oh it was heavenly when they'd give it to her.

"Why should you?" Kathryn's voice was rough from vomiting, from sleep, from screaming at the doctor for medication, for a drink, for anything. She remembered her deplorable behavior from earlier that day. How frightened she'd been when she'd awakened in the hospital. All those lights, all those people around her.

A scared animal cornered and caged.

Why hadn't she died? It would have been so much easier.

The pain was enough to wish she could simply drift off and never wake up again.

She blew a stream of smoke from her lips.

She hated this - Alice Kincaid standing over her, seeing her like this, knowing…

"You didn't have to come." Kathryn spoke coldly, wondering if she could drive her away, make her somehow forget.

"Didn't have to come." Alice choked, and Kathryn could tell she was crying. "I thought you were dead."

"I wish I were."

"Is that what you really wanted?" Fear laced the rapid-fire question.

Kathryn shrugged and smoked again. "What does it matter, anyway?"

"It matters." Alice whispered. "To me. It matters." And she leaned back against the window ledge, crossing her arms over her chest.

Kathryn did not want to acknowledge the tears that pricked at her eyes, nor the one lone drop slipping down her bruised cheek. She smoked and wiped at it. She was over-taken by an intense cold again and began shaking.

Alice immediately came to her, draping another blanket over her body and tucking it about her frame. "You need help."

"I need a drink." Kathryn crushed out her cigarette.

Alice slammed the ashtray on the table beside Kathryn. She did not find this humorous. "My God, I wish you'd take this seriously."

Kathryn jumped at the noise and then grimaced at the pain that shot through her whole being.

"Cocaine." Alice muttered, pacing then. "You had cocaine in your system. Do you know how dangerous that is?"

"Please, Alice. Save your lectures for someone else."

Alice turned on her heels, affixing Kathryn with a glare she could feel intensely. "Do you really not care?"

Kathryn's pulse quickened, chest splintering in a tightness.

"My God." Alice huffed, retreating to a chair in the corner where she'd left a bag and her jacket. "I can't believe I wasted my time."

"Please…" Kathryn tried to sit up but the pain in her side forced her backward. "Please, Alice. Don't…don't leave me." Her voice broke and she realized she was crying, she was shaking, she was afraid. The thought of being alone in this place…

Alice stopped mid-way from picking up her jacket. "Why?"

"Because…" Kathryn's voice was a hoarse whisper. "I'm…scared."

Alice did not move for a moment.

She hesitated.

Alice was going to leave her.

Panic welled inside of her, fear wound tightly in the pit of her stomach. She had finally succeeded in pushing her away, and she would never see her again, death had been a better option than this…

But Alice lowered her purse back down to the chair and turned to face Kathryn. "I won't leave." She sank down on the seat instead, pulling her legs up beneath herself, looking at Kathryn. "I'll be right here."

She was not there the following morning when the sun forced its way into the room and the nurses and doctors poked and prodded at her and she screamed and wailed. Didn't they know she was in pain?

And a call came in that morning. A nurse held the phone for her.

"Who is it?" Kathryn demanded.

"Someone named Peter?"

Ah, the news had finally stretched itself across the ocean.

She didn't want to take the phone, but she allowed it. For a brief second feeling not so alone in the world anymore. Betrayed as she had been by Alice leaving her.

Had she even been there the previous evening?

"Hello?" Kathryn asked into the phone.

"Meine Süße, what has happened?"

"A little accident."

"Why yes. But when can you make it back? We have post-production – I need you."

When could she make it back? When...well, as she was confined to the bed with a non-working leg she doubted it would be any time soon. And shouldn't he know that? "Not for a long while." She slammed the receiver down, not wanting to talk to him anymore.

The phone rang again, but Kathryn told the nurse to silence it and laid back in the bed, closing her eyes, wishing she had a drink to get her through, the pain too intense.

She dropped in and out of consciousness – for it was better when she was asleep, when she couldn't feel a damn thing. But when her eyes opened for a brief second and she found that day had descended into night, she found the same familiar figure standing over her.

Alice.

Alice had returned.

Chapter Forty-Five

Alice

"You look like shit." Jeanette was standing in her dressing room doorway, startling an eye pencil from Alice's hand so it dropped and rolled from the vanity to the ground.

"Jesus." Alice cursed, leaning down to pick it up.

"Late night?"

"You could say that." Alice straightened in her chair. She brushed her hair from her eyes. Her eyes were rimmed and puffy, her body stiff. She groaned when she moved. She hadn't made it to her barre class since before…

"Kathryn?" Jeanette had the decency to lower her voice.

Alice stiffened at the name spoken between them. "She's not doing well."

"You don't have to…"

Alice turned and fixed Jeanette with a pointed glare. "She doesn't have anyone else."

Jeanette held up her hands in mock defense. "But she is not your responsibility, sugar."

Alice worried her lips together as she returned to covering her haggard face. "I know that."

"Do you?"

Alice caught Jeanette's eyes in the mirror. "Why are you giving me the third degree?"

"I'm worried about you. One night you're off disappearing with a very attractive woman and the next…"

Alice sighed, head rolling forward, fingers coming to rub at the tension in her brow.

Jeanette was behind her then, hands rubbing at her tense shoulders. It felt magnificent.

"It was really nice." Alice whispered.

Jeanette nudged her. "Good for you. Are you going to see her again?"

Alice laughed at that. "How the hell would I do that now…"

It was Jeanette's turn to sigh. "You deserve more, Alice." And she pressed her lips to Alice's cheek. "I'll see you out there."

Alice drug herself through the day of rehearsals. It was treacherous because her part was rather robust that week. Lots of monologues that she stumbled through with the distinct promise she would have them down by the next day.

Jeanette eyed her warily as she slipped out the door that evening.

Alice drove home to shower and grab a change of clothes. She stared longingly at her bed.

She didn't have to do it.

She got in her car and drove to the hospital.

She made her way down the too familiar corridors, waving at the night nurse who now recognized her, and then slipped into the room. She expected it to be dim as it always was, but a bedside lamp was alight and Kathryn was sitting up in her bed, glasses on the bridge of her nose, cigarette in hand, reading a newspaper.

Kathryn looked up, her eyes startled and clear. Clear as Alice could never remember them being.

She looked, surprisingly, well.

"So it really is you." Kathryn spoke, exhaling a cloud of smoke before stubbing out her cigarette.

"Of course it's me." Alice dropped her bag in the corner chair and came to Kathryn's side. "You seem better."

Kathryn laughed humorlessly as she folded the newspaper. "I feel like shit."

"I've no doubt." Alice took the paper from her. She folded it and placed it between a book and the lamp.

"Why are you here?" Kathryn was eying her curiously over the rim of her glasses.

Alice could detect a hint of trepidation in the inquiry.

"Do you want me to go?" She crossed her arms over her chest, knowing just as well as the other woman that she wasn't going anywhere.

Kathryn took her glasses off and rubbed at the bridge of her nose. "No."

"Well then." Alice patted her arm and looked her face over. The bruising was receding, but her nose was still bandaged. "It's not as bad."

"It's mortifying. Thank God the press can't get in to see it in the flesh. I've already read what they've written. They've really painted quite a flattering picture of me, don't you think? Desperate, dried up, old, coked-up, movie-star angling for some attention." Kathryn sighed as she reached for the water. Her hand shook and Alice took over, holding the bendy straw to her lips. "Thank you." Kathryn whispered and then reached up to rub a hand beneath her eye. "But who cares about that, right?" A spooked look flashed in her eyes. "That man – whoever he was – he's...he died."

She was only now processing.

Alice could see it. Could see it in the shake of her hands and the way her eyes darted about. Kathryn fumbled for another cigarette and Alice stopped her, tapping one from her pack, placing it between her lips and lighting it for her.

"But what can I do?" Kathryn exhaled a cloud of smoke. Her eyes finally focused on Alice's face. "You're awfully quiet."

Alice played with the edge of Kathryn's blanket.

"I don't know why you've been coming here every night to check on little ol' me. You look exhausted, dear. Have you eaten anything today? You're far too thin." Kathryn went on as if she were the one caring for Alice. "No," Kathryn decided after another puff of her cigarette. "I don't suspect you have." And she was reaching to phone the nurse before Alice could stop her. She ordered up the hospital cafeteria's finest and then hung up with a laugh, "it's nothing special, but it's certainly edible enough."

All this talking, all this going on. All this avoiding. "Kathryn…" Alice whispered.

"Alice." Kathryn caught her with a piercing glance. "I am…happy you are here."

Disarming. So terribly disarming she was. Alice resented the thrill it gave her to be bestowed with this gratefulness. But steeled herself enough to ask, "are you going back to Germany?" She moved the ashtray to the bed where Kathryn could tap off her ash.

Kathryn exhaled, groaning. "Oh, Alice." She shook her head and frustrated tears welled in her eyes.

Alice marveled - for how the slightest thing could shake her now. "What will you do?"

"How the hell should I know?" Kathryn's gravelly voice snapped.

Alice flinched, no longer accustomed to Kathryn's outbursts.

"I'm sorry." Kathryn grew small and timid. "Jesus, if only I could have a drink so I could think straight."

But a drink would not help, and both of them knew it.

Alice took a deep breath. "A nurse told me about your heart."

"Did she." Kathryn smoked absently.

Alice leaned against the window ledge. Kathryn sober was about as unpredictable as Kathryn soused. It was as if she didn't have a care in the world. As if her high blood pressure and weak arteries were of no concern. But by her blatant coolness about it, Alice knew it mattered a great deal to her.

Kathryn tapped off her cigarette. "They want me to go somewhere. A facility for addictions."

Alice's heart hammered at the idea. Would she do it, though?

"I'd be locked away for weeks. Sounds miserable." Kathryn pondered the wall across from her. "Of course, Peter - you know, my husband - wants me back. We've just finished a picture. A real art house thing - quite lesbian all of it, but then he prefers me that way." Kathryn laughed darkly. "He'll be pissed if I don't come back soon."

Alice bit her lip to keep from commenting.

"He's a real gem, Peter. Wanted me to look glassily alive - thinks it makes my acting better - so he kept coking me up." She smiled wryly at this.

There was a knock on the door and a young man entered with a rolling cart piled high with covered dishes. "You're a darling, Mark." Kathryn winked at him as he left. "What a cute young thing." Kathryn teased as she glanced at Alice and then motioned towards the cart. "Please - eat something. You're making me hungry just looking at you."

Alice felt as if she might be ill; she was in no mood to eat a thing. But Kathryn was looking at her so hopefully.

"Kathryn," Alice spoke once she began eating what looked to be a salad. "Don't go back to Germany."

Chapter Forty-Six

Kathryn

She sat in an alcove smoking.

The world looked brighter around her, the greens of trees vibrant, the sky blazing blue, the sun's rays casting intense golden light on everything. Kathryn's mind was clear. Clearer than it had been in decades.

She exhaled shakily.

The discomfort that came with a clear mind overwhelmed her.

A figure appeared before her, blocking the sunlight.

She flicked ash from her cigarette and shielded her eyes.

Flowing dark hair leapt in the wind, a loose caftan whipped about curves.

"Dr. Nakai." Kathryn exhaled a stream of smoke on the name.

"Mind if I bum one of those?" The doctor inquired, and Kathryn reached for the pack in her breast pocket, tapping one out to hand her along with her lighter.

The doctor placed the cigarette between her lips, lit it, inhaling joyously once it caught.

Kathryn turned her eyes away, blushing inexplicably at this show of pleasure by a woman who spoke to her weekly from behind a desk. This was different. She was not a professional then but a woman. An attractive woman enjoying her cigarette.

"You don't mind if I join you, do you?"

Kathryn shrugged, motioning toward the chair beside her.

Dr. Nakai sank down beside her.

Kathryn noticed the doctor's exhaustion for the first time in the three weeks she had known her.

"We must really do a number on you." Kathryn said around smoke. Her only vice left. The one she would hold onto for dear life.

Dr. Nakai laughed, the sound warm and comforting.

Kathryn had hated the woman, resented her from the first day of arrival at the rehabilitation facility. And here she was acting as if she were just someone ordinary sharing a smoke with someone else who was rather quite ordinary.

But they were both far from ordinary, weren't they?

After being released from the hospital, hardly able to stand on her own, she'd checked herself into the facility. Whether she had done it to piss Peter off or if she had done it for her own good was still unclear, even to herself.

She was quite uncertain as to her own motives.

Dr. Nakai had asked her why. Kathryn had not been able to supply a why.

"You're too smart for all of this, aren't you?" Dr. Nakai said then.

Kathryn's eyebrow arched at the statement. Her hand fluttered ever so as she lifted the cigarette to her lips. "Well, certainly not smart enough to avoid ending up in a place like this."

The sleepless nights. The incessant screaming down the hall. The desperate want that clawed at her in the dark.

"But haven't we had enough therapizing for today?" Kathryn crushed her cigarette roughly in the littered ashtray.

"Yes, I certainly have." Dr. Nakai crossed her ankles and reclined back. Her lips were a soft pink, skin tanned. Her eyes wrinkled as she smoked.

Kathryn wondered if they were the same age. What had she been through? Did she know what this hell was like?

"I drank myself into a place like this. Nearly lost my license. Doesn't help that alcoholism runs in the family." Dr. Nakai spoke as if she could read Kathryn's mind. "So sometimes it doesn't help to be smart. Sometimes being smart makes it worse."

Kathryn's eyes were wide before she fumbled for her cigarettes, extracting another.

Well then.

"Do you think you'll do it again when you leave?" Dr. Nakai looked at her over her cigarette.

Kathryn shrugged as she lit the one between her teeth. "How can we know? This is a relatively safe place. Gives you the illusion of stability, but it's not the real world, is it? It's not being on set dead tired with another scene to film and only an hour of sleep in the past two days. So how can I know?"

"Do you want to?"

"God, every second." Kathryn smoked and eyed the doctor. "Do you?"

Dr. Nakai turned and gave her a curious smile. "What do you think?" She put out her cigarette and stretched before standing up. "Thanks for the smoke."

Kathryn watched her curiously – recognizing something in her that she had not before. "Any time."

The doctor walked away, disappearing back inside the facility.

Kathryn pulled at her cigarette.

That evening she was given the great privilege of calling someone. An honor granted her once a week.

Since she had to stand in line in order to receive this prized treat, she had to listen to everyone else's conversations before her.

She pretended not to.

Dr. Nakai had informed her that her husband, Peter, had been calling almost non-stop. Begging and pleading with those in charge to release his ill-captured wife and return her to Germany. She was *needed*.

Dr. Nakai told Kathryn it was best that she not contact him.

Kathryn had had no such plans anyway, grateful for the safety and cover this stint in rehab had given her. Away from him and the drugs.

She sniffed.

Besides, her nose was still ruined.

He'd have to shoot it into her veins if he wanted her high again.

She laughed to herself and wondered if she might be insane now.

She found that she was at the front of the line. The phone number was written on a well-worn piece of paper in her pocket. She memorized lines for a living, but could not for the life of her remember ten numbers in a row.

She lifted the receiver and dialed the ten numbers scrawled in a hand not her own. She turned away from the on-lookers in line behind her, pressing herself against the wall.

The phone rang once, then twice and she wondered if it wasn't a good time. That would be just perfect, wouldn't it?

But on the fourth ring there was a click and then a voice. "Hello?"

"Am I catching you at a bad time?" Kathryn let her hip

sink against the cinderblock wall, relieved at the sound of that greeting.

There was a laugh. "I just got in. I'm – it's good to hear your voice."

"Yours as well." Kathryn sunk her hand into her pocket, fishing for a cigarette.

"I'm glad you caught me when you did."

"Thank goodness for waiting in line to use the phone." Kathryn flicked the lighter and inhaled. "It's just maybe one step above a prison around here."

She heard a stifled laugh.

How she had missed that laughter. How she had thought she might never hear it again.

"Alice," Kathryn thumbed some ash from her tongue. "You didn't need to do it."

"Do what?" Alice inquired.

"I got curious to know what happened about the hospital bill, seeing as how I no longer have American health insurance, and it turns out the bill was already paid in full."

"Oh." Alice said.

"Yes, it baffled me as well until I realized what had happened." Kathryn inhaled and caught sight of the nurse in charge, giving her a wrap-it-up warning glance. "Alice, you didn't…"

"Now Kathryn, don't be cross with me." Alice's voice was strained.

Kathryn longed for the warmth of the beginning of the conversation.

"I will pay you back."

"I won't let you." Alice insisted.

Kathryn did not want to be someone's charity case.

"Stop whatever it is you're thinking. Let me do this for you." Alice spoke.

Was Kathryn so readable that everyone could tell what she was thinking?

"I don't like it." Kathryn rubbed at her forehead.

"How many more weeks have you got?" Alice ignored her.

"Two." Kathryn inhaled unsteadily. Two more weeks and then what? A flight to Germany? Back to Peter? Back to the films and the drugs and death?

It scared her suddenly, making a cool sweat break out beneath her arms and on the back of her neck.

"I want to see you. Will you see me?" Kathryn asked suddenly.

"Yes." Alice spoke .

"There's a – a visiting thing. This weekend. Can you get free?"

"I'll be there." Alice promised.

The nurse was giving Kathryn the indication it was time for her to hang up.

She gave Alice the details and rushed through a goodbye before slamming down the receiver, glaring at the nurse before stomping off to her room.

Chapter Forty-Seven

Alice

She was late and the Los Angeles traffic was doing little to help her.

She wondered if the rehearsal that had gone too long had made her miss the moment.

A part of her almost wished it so.

Did she want this or not?

She had been as uncertain as ever since that night.

She pulled into the parking lot a half hour late, checked herself in the mirror and then took a deep breath. She hadn't had much time to think about it prior to then. Rehearsals and life had gotten in the way. But now that it was upon her she felt the nerves creeping in, making her unsteady.

What if she had come too late?

She forced herself out of the car and through the doors, heart beating wildly. This was reckless of her. Anyone could see her here.

She should leave, but it was too late now, wasn't it?

There, sitting across the room, was a pair of eyes looking at her.

She was still there.

Someone was trying to ask if they could help her. Alice turned, apologized, saying no thank you and then slipped across the room.

"I didn't think you'd wait."

The woman across the table from her pulled a cherry from a plastic sword between her equally cherry-red lips. She'd finished her drink. She laughed. "I have a pretty good idea how you Hollywood-types operate. Always saying one time and then showing up whenever it suits you."

"Well, now, I'm not like that. Not really. It was rehearsal. It went long this evening, I am very sorry."

"Alice, you don't need to apologize. I enjoy people watching. What are you drinking? Coffee?" Robin. Robin turned and waved down a waiter and ordered for Alice.

Alice watched her profile, marveling at the fact that while she seemed still a stranger to Alice, their bodies had shared unspeakable intimacies. And the memory of it made Alice blush, her pulse quicken. She looked down at her lap, smoothed out her slacks.

Robin was looking at her again, chewing carelessly at the plastic sword. "I didn't think you'd call."

Alice shrugged, smiled sheepishly. "I wasn't…sure I would either." She fidgeted with the edge of her napkin.

Robin laughed at this. "You flatter me."

"Oh," Alice realized her careless words. "No – it wasn't about," her eyes darted around, wondering if anyone recognized her, if anyone was watching, if anyone could hear. "It wasn't about that. I," she lowered her voice, "very much enjoyed that."

Robin smiled prettily. "So, what then? You've got

someone else up your sleeve? You mentioned a brush with your past."

Alice startled. The woman had been paying attention, hadn't she?

The waiter settled a cup of coffee before Alice and a refreshed cocktail before Robin.

Alice's throat was dry. She sipped water before toying with the stem of the glass. "Yes, I suppose that's it."

Would Robin leave now? Alice didn't want her to go.

But Robin was still smiling. "All right," she leaned forward, conspiratorially, waiting.

What could Alice say? "It's not – well, it's a friend. An old friend. Who is in a bad way." Alice picked up her coffee cup and drank its dark liquid. So much better than the studio coffee, she noticed.

"Something happened between you and this…friend?" Robin sipped her drink, eyes sparkling beautifully.

Alice didn't want to talk about her *friend*. A primal urge she was not used to was overtaking her. It was not something she was accustomed to, not since…

Wasn't she too old for all of this?

"Yes." Alice swallowed roughly. "A long time ago." A lifetime ago.

It was surreal to be here now. Straddling something new when the old was so tangible now.

"Alice," Robin had crossed her legs. Her foot brushed at Alice's shin lightly. "You know I'm not asking for a lifetime commitment."

Alice hummed into her coffee. After insisting that she pay for their drinks, she followed Robin to her home in Palos Verdes, body throbbing and alive.

When she arrived home the following morning for a quick shower, she saw a familiar car parked in her driveway.

"Shit." And she guiltily stepped into her house, wondering

if she could play off the smear of make-up from the previous evening and soiled clothing she'd put back on, not anticipating her morning guest.

He was laying on the sofa in the sunroom, the television hazily accompanying the morning calls of birds. She turned off the television and looked at his peaceful, sleeping face. And it brought back all the memories of returning to him late in the evening in a similar state. How guilty she had been then and how guilty she felt now.

He stirred and she realized she'd missed her moment to hide the evidence of her night.

"Mom?" He was looking up at her.

"Yes, baby." She sat on the edge of her coffee table and stroked his hair, his cheek. He was older now. Hardly her baby anymore.

"You never came home last night." The accusation came easily.

She nodded up and down. "I wasn't expecting you."

He blinked, his eyes warming to the light of day. "I didn't know you…"

She laughed. "It's not…" well it was. He was certainly old enough to know she might partake in adult pleasures. "But why are you here?" She tried to turn the blame from herself, to distract from any awkwardness this predicament put them in.

It was Jack's turn to demur now. He sat up and rubbed at his eyes. "I had an argument with Bobby. Just a disagreement and…I don't know, just ended up here."

Bobby, the roommate Alice had yet to meet. "Are you all right?"

"Yeah, just needed some space." Jack yawned and smiled to reassure her. "I have to get to class. I'll make us some coffee before I go."

Alice wanted to know more about this argument, but if he

wasn't going to press her about her night then she wasn't going to press him about his.

She floated through the day, Jeanette catching her mid passing backstage with a suggestive look in her eyes. "Well then."

Alice flushed.

"Those porcelain cheeks of yours sure do speak volumes."

"Oh." Alice scowled.

Jeanette smiled her knowing smile. "Good for you."

Was it good?

It was not until filming the following evening that Alice completely fell apart as the two thoughts began to collide in her mind.

What was she doing?

"Why Sharon, I didn't know you had it in you." Jeanette, as her on-screen persona Cassandra, was angling towards Alice over the set desk.

"Have what in me?" Alice, as Sharon, looked up into dark eyes and instantly lost her spot, mind diverging from the scene they were playing out to the realization that the following day she would see Kathryn again. That several days before she had spent an evening with Robin. It played out languidly in her memory and somehow the thought of Robin mixed and melted with that of Kathryn and Alice had the strangest feeling of guilt.

"Cut! Cut! Alice – where did you go?" The director was crying from the side of the stage.

Alice had missed her next line. What was the next line? "I'm so sorry, John." She rubbed her forehead and stared past the bright stage lights and out to the curious audience waiting, watching. She was letting them down. This rarely happened to her. This should not be happening to her now.

Jeanette was looking at her with concern. "Are you all right?" She whispered.

Alice waved her off, took a deep breath and searched her memory for the moment that was supposed to be playing out between Sharon and Cassandra.

The script came to her again, Kathryn and Robin fading back into the hidden recesses of her mind. Ignored, forgotten. "Let's go again from the top." Alice spoke firmly and did not miss another cue for the rest of the evening.

"Why Sharon, I didn't know you had it in you…"

The audience laughed – she had not lost them.

Alice left that evening before Jeanette could leap on her and try to make something out of it. It had been nothing, hadn't it?

But afterwards she couldn't sleep. She tossed and turned and finally made herself a cup of tea and sat wordlessly on her couch staring out the back windows into darkness. When she opened her eyes night had transformed into rosy daybreak.

She moved lethargically through the morning. Making coffee, eating toast. She showered and put herself together meticulously, nervously.

At half-past noon she left her house and drove to the address Kathryn had given her.

Her palms were sweating when she parked.

Why was she here?

She had promised.

She watched as others emerged from their cars and moved toward the entrance.

But she had promised.

She took a deep breath, steeled herself, and got out of the car.

She entered amidst a group of other visitors, and they were ushered toward a large hall littered with occupied tables surrounded by reuniting friends and families.

Alice peered around, feeling self-conscious and seen, as if

eyes were upon her and yet no one seemed to be paying her any mind.

She did not see Kathryn at first, but upon a second glance about the room, she caught sight of the woman hidden in a corner near a tall weeping fig, smoking a cigarette, looking right at her.

Chapter Forty-Eight

Kathryn

The shake in her hand was not perceptible to anyone but herself.

She brought the cigarette to her lips to steady it, to give her hand movement that could mask the slight tic. Anxious.

Alice moved with an unaware grace through the crowd. She looked like no one else in that room, seemed to be another species entirely. She did not belong here amongst these broken, dejected humans.

Kathryn should not have asked her to come.

But she smiled at Kathryn as she approached, she leaned down and pressed her lips to Kathryn's cheek — she had a new scent. Floral and rich and Kathryn inhaled it, drank it in.

Alice settled into a chair. "You're looking well." She spoke softly in the noisy room, taking in the lightly bruised bridge of Kathryn's nose, the healing cut on her lip, her cheek, her forehead. That was only her face. Kathryn wondered if her eyes would like to appraise the bruise running across her ribcage or the angry deep purple of her knee hidden beneath her clothing.

How it thrilled her to think about stripping down bare before Alice and asking her to see all of her. How she wanted that in this moment.

Kathryn could not take her eyes away from Alice. Marveling at her presence before her. "You're really here."

"Of course I'm here." Alice echoed the same sentiment from all those nights ago in the hospital room. When she had been there over and over again.

But it still surprised Kathryn.

Kathryn put out her cigarette and reached into her breast pocket for another. "I'm happy, really happy you're here." She spoke before placing the cigarette between her teeth.

Alice looked around as Kathryn lit the cigarette, quietly observing her surroundings. "Is it nice here? Well...I mean is it...all right?" Alice played with the edge of her fingernail, painted a deep maroon.

Kathryn exhaled a cloud of smoke. "Well it's certainly not the Ritz, but sure...it's all right."

Alice's lip quirked upward. "How are you?"

Kathryn took a deep breath and leaned back. How was she? Well, she had certainly been better. She shook her head. "Well I can't say I'm well. More like bored out of my mind. I think I've read my way through their entire library, which mainly consists of books on addiction and recovery. So you could say I'm well informed."

Alice did not laugh but seemed amused at her candor.

"Is it...hard?" Alice kept picking at her nail as if she didn't know what to do with herself.

Kathryn tapped off ash from her cigarette and brought it to her lips. "Hard? Sure. I'd love to bury myself in a nice bottle of bourbon, but alas..."

This did not amuse Alice.

"What will you do? In a week you'll be done here."

Kathryn shrugged. "I haven't a clue." She pulled deep and hard at her cigarette, rubbing at her brow. "My husband keeps calling and calling, but I haven't spoken to him since the hospital. He needs me for the film, but if I...if I go back there..." her voice trailed off, broke.

Alice watched her smoke. Silent. Worry creasing her brow.

Kathryn sat up straighter. "What choice do I have?"

"You can stay here. With me." Alice spoke then.

Kathryn gave her a curious look. Laughed. "Oh, Alice. No, I think you've done quite enough."

"No, I insist." Alice was being serious. Very serious. "I'm sure you could find work here."

"Ha!" Kathryn laughed humorously. "I tried. They don't want to touch me with a twelve-foot pole. They've deemed me indecent for the American public, and besides, this whole accident business has probably driven the nail in the coffin. No, there's no work for me here."

"Just think about it then. I have plenty of room." Alice was insisting, a fierce, protective glint in her eyes.

"I wouldn't want to impose."

"It's no imposition."

Kathryn looked at Alice through the smoke of her cigarette. They stared at one another.

After all that she'd put her through...

She couldn't.

She wanted to.

But she couldn't.

"Alice, there's the movie..."

Alice looked down, defeated, as if she'd been punched in the gut.

"Hey," Kathryn nudged Alice ever so slightly. "The doctor wants me up and about every hour. Help me take a walk. It's nice outside."

Alice rubbed at something in her eye and nodded. She

went to Kathryn to help her up. Kathryn did not like being an invalid but could not deny the aid, nor did she wish to deny the way Alice wrapped an arm about her waist and held her close as she stiffly moved them away from the crowd, toward the door in the rear of the room.

Outside was deafeningly quiet. It was only the sounds of birds, a slight wind in the trees, of nature and sunshine which happily greeted them.

"It's nice here." Alice said.

"It is." Kathryn exhaled a stream of smoke away from Alice.

"It hurts?" Alice asked as they moved slowly down a path.

Kathryn nodded. "Only a little." It hurt a hell of a lot more than that, but she kept limping along as if it didn't hurt a bit because she had Alice's support.

"It will heal?"

"Supposedly." Kathryn sighed.

They came to stop at a little pond and stood staring down into its shallow, clear recesses. Koi swam lazily to and fro.

Kathryn stubbed her cigarette on the ground and reached for another.

Alice was eyeing her curiously.

"It's all I have left. They encourage it in the beginning, see. It's only a substitute, of course, but it helps." Kathryn explained as she lit the cigarette. "I know you've never liked it, have you?"

Alice was watching her smoke. "No, I don't suppose I ever have."

Kathryn coughed then – almost as if for effect. "It's a nasty habit, isn't it?"

"They've been helpful here?" Alice let her fingers lightly tickle over Kathryn's back where her hand rested. Kathryn wondered if she were consciously aware of it.

"Yes, I suppose they do their best." Kathryn agreed. Thought about just what it was they had helped her with, what it was they had pulled out of the dark recesses of her troubled mind. What they had made her relive, driven her to ruminate on; the reasons, the whys of things. The thoughts had become dark and terrible and made her feel empty and defeated and disgusting. How could she ever tell Alice any of this?

Did Alice even want to know?

She was still looking at her. Her fingers still moving against the material of Kathryn's shirt.

"There's so much…" Kathryn began but stopped.

Alice looked at her encouragingly.

But she hardly knew her anymore. It had been years, hadn't it? What had Alice done? Married that ridiculous man? Stayed with him until he'd met someone else, but then what? Had there been others?

She wanted to know everything.

"How is Jack?" Kathryn could still see the boy in her mind, just a baby the last time she'd held him in her arms. And then not again after that day…

Alice looked surprised by this question. "Well, he's just fine. He's nearly twenty-five. Can you believe it?"

"No." Kathryn could not.

"He's in law school. He'll be a lawyer soon." Alice beamed with pride for him.

They had reconciled; she had raised him. For that, at least, Kathryn was grateful. Felt as if she had done something right.

"Can I see a picture of him?" Kathryn scratched at her forehead, smoked.

"Oh, yes. Here." And Alice's hand moved away from her and Kathryn shuddered at the loss of it. Alice pulled a wallet from her purse and extracted a photo of a handsome young man, who did not look like Frank, thank goodness, but a handsome version of Alice with dark hair and kind eyes.

"He's very good-looking." Kathryn appraised. "I'm sure he's very popular with the ladies."

Alice laughed at this. "Well…I'm not sure I would say that…"

"Oh," Kathryn seemed to understand.

And Alice's cheeks flushed ever so. "I'm not sure, but I…"

"Well, that's better, I think." Kathryn smiled.

Alice smiled. How beautiful she was in this afternoon light and how much Kathryn wanted to stay in this place with her.

But she felt their worlds splintering and breaking apart again.

She knew it could not be so easy.

Alice slid her arm about her waist as they walked back to the rehabilitation center. The throng of people was beginning to disperse; time had run out. Visiting hours were over.

Kathryn felt a tightness in her chest – wondered if she might be having a heart attack, it hurt so terribly.

"I suppose I have to go now." Alice was saying.

Kathryn grasped at her wrist, startling the both of them. "Alice, I'm…"

Alice's eyes, she realized, were full of unshed tears.

"Can I see you again?" Alice whispered.

"I…I don't know…I'm supposed to be finished Thursday, I…" Kathryn's world was swimming around her. Dipping in and out of reality. She wanted a drink. She wanted Alice to stay.

Alice pulled them close together and pressed her lips against Kathryn's cheek. "Don't do this."

And then she was walking away.

Leaving Kathryn.

Don't do this?

How could she not do this?

Kathryn fumbled for her pack of cigarettes, felt a big, wet tear slip down her cheek.

I'm sorry, Alice. I'm sorry.

Chapter Forty-Nine

Alice

Kathryn had gotten on a flight Thursday evening for Germany.

She'd called Alice one last time to tell her this.

Jeanette was sitting on Alice's couch.

Alice was curled in a ball, eyes blood-shot and red from crying the tears she'd kept at bay all day at rehearsal. Until Jeanette found her collapsed in her dressing room, distraught and crumbling.

Jeanette had driven her home, made her some dinner, some tea, and sat with her.

Alice didn't want to talk about it, but it was all she could think about.

One misstep and Kathryn would slip from her forever.

She could feel it in her bones more now than ever before.

Before she had not imagined Kathryn as she was now.

Her heart was weak, the doctor had said. The alcohol had wrecked her and the cocaine would do her in.

She had not promised Alice anything – not that Alice could ask her to make a promise. Because she couldn't do it for Alice, or because of Alice. It would have to be her decision.

Jeanette was looking at her, blowing on her steaming cup of tea.

"You should go home to Daryl." Alice sputtered.

Jeanette gave her a raised eyebrow *no way* expression. "I'm worried about you. You haven't even touched your dinner."

Alice stared at the plate of food Jeanette had generously prepared for her. "I know, I'm sorry...I'm not...I'm not hungry."

"Alice..."

"It's not...I'm okay." Alice tried to reassure her friend. Who knew far too much about her after they'd spent the last two years working side-by-side on the show. "I'm sorry – I... don't mean to keep falling apart like this." She was sorry she kept pulling Jeanette into her wreck of a life.

Why? Why had she ever had to become fixated on that woman?

She would be in Germany the following morning, so far away that Alice could do nothing to pull her back.

"Don't you apologize to me, sugar." Jeanette admonished.

She helped Alice to bed and crawled in beside her that night.

Alice slept in fits and spurts.

They filmed the following night – Alice had never been more distracted before in her life – and then she uncharacteristically took off for the weekend. She drove up the coast, rented a room at a beach-side resort and laid in bed and let the feelings wash over her.

She had been there – within reach. She had touched her again. Her fingers had stroked at Kathryn's unforgotten lower back. She had pressed her lips to her cheek, she had felt the tension in the other woman when she'd grasped at her wrist.

She wasn't going to stay for Alice.

Alice had been foolish to think she would.

She laid in the resort bed, staring idly at the ceiling. Wondering what she was running from now.

Everything had upended after that reunion show. Could she go on as she had before? Pretending like it didn't bother her? Wishing it could have been different?

It had been easier before seeing Kathryn again.

Kathryn had made it worse. Far worse.

Alice nearly starved herself that weekend, until she almost fainted standing from the bed. She had promised herself, her son, Jeanette, her agent, that she would not do this to herself again and so she ordered room service and ate until the faintness dissipated. Then she ordered a coffee, put it in a paper cup and drove back to Los Angeles.

But instead of taking the normal exit off the highway that would return her to her home in Santa Monica, she traveled onward.

It was late when she arrived and she had no way of knowing if the woman would be occupied or not.

There were lights on that she could see through the front window.

She rang the doorbell before the nerves settled in and she wondered what it was she was doing here. Of all the places…

"Alice." The woman had appeared on the other side of the door. Smiling, fresh-faced, glasses sliding down her nose, hair piled atop her head. Gorgeous, as she was. She kissed Alice on the cheek and guided her inside. "I wasn't expecting you."

"I'm sorry." Alice's throat felt dry. Why had she come here?

"Are you all right?" Robin asked as she helped to settle her onto the couch where they had first kissed.

Alice tried to say yes, tried her hardest to act as if nothing were wrong – as if she hadn't just spent the weekend running away. But the tears that slid down her cheeks betrayed her yes.

"What is it?" Robin wiped tears from her cheek.

Robin made them tea and brought some refreshments, and Alice curled into a ball on the couch and thought that this was the worst place to fall apart.

"I shouldn't have come." She apologized to the floor.

"Alice, think of me as a friend, all right? Please, you can speak to me as a friend."

Alice fought it, did not want to utter a word, but then it all started flowing out of her in bits and pieces so that she couldn't stop it. She had no idea how long it was they sat there, but each piece came out in terribly accurate detail and she knew what she was risking by saying it, but it could not be held in any longer.

At the end Robin sat there looking at her as she had always looked at her and took her into her arms and held her. "That's an awful lot to carry." She finally whispered against her hair.

Alice, having expelled everything, felt it leave her. Her body, usually so tense, released into Robin's chest. "I'm sorry, I'm sorry…"

"Shh," Robin consoled her. "You have nothing to apologize for."

And Robin sat with her until dawn broke out across the glittering ocean and Alice had to leave.

Her message machine was flashing when she returned home the following morning. For a brief, fleeting moment she hoped that one of those messages would be long distance.

She played them as she made coffee, heart beating wildly.

"Mom, I've tried you a few times now – haven't heard back. I hope you're okay…"

"You're really worrying me. I mean – I get that you can have relationships too, but just call me. Oh my God. I sound like I'm your mom."

"Hey sugar, give me a call when you get in. You just disappeared after filming Friday...I'm worried."

Her son. Jeanette. Alan had called about a script.

Nothing. There had been nothing.

Alice pushed the panicked feeling in her chest aside and called her son to let him know she was still alive. She'd assure Jeanette at rehearsal that day.

And another week began. Another week of rehearsals and meetings and life.

A gossip magazine would catch her eye in the supermarket and she'd scan the surface furtively until she was certain that nothing was mentioned.

The news would play somewhere in the background and Alice would half-listen while sitting in make-up or sitting in traffic on the freeway. As if waiting, waiting for the inevitable to happen.

But nothing happened.

Weeks went by.

Weeks of nothing.

She listened out in the background for any sign, for any clue, but none came.

And though this lack of news should assuage her, it never brought relief when she crawled into bed in the evening because there was always tomorrow nagging at the back of her mind.

She saw Robin intermittently, feeling ashamed that she should know and yet Alice felt a sense of protection, of peace with her. But she felt guilty when she could not be present because a part of her was always tuned into that faraway chimera – waiting, waiting, waiting.

It was months later.

The show was nearing the end of the season.

There was news that it had been renewed, that they would be back again for another season and normally this would make Alice feel elated, but she could only half-process the announcement.

She dragged herself home from the rehearsal that evening, made herself a cup of tea and curled on the couch, turning on the television – as had become her habit – and sat eating cookies and watching. Waiting.

She had gained weight. She was aware of it, but she promised herself that with the end of the show she would take care of it. She would return to her barre class, she would get herself together. But there was something holding her back, preventing her from doing it now.

Now she sat on her couch, eating, sipping the tea, staring at the screen as the news anchor detailed a shooting in downtown Los Angeles, a wreck on the 101, a new bill being passed for women workers and what it might mean for big business.

Nothing. Nothing. Nothing.

She fell asleep on the couch.

She had no idea what time it was when she heard the phone ringing somewhere far away. It was, at first, an interruption of her dream. Some terrible dream of a desolate city of fire. An alarm was sounding and she couldn't save someone. Someone trapped in a building and she was stuck on the ground. Helpless, useless.

The phone kept ringing until it registered in her mind what was happening.

Her eyes opened and she wiped the drool from the side of her mouth, passing a hand over her feverish forehead, and then slowly – slowly crawled toward the ringing phone.

She lifted the receiver to her ear, fearing the worst. Her son, or else…

"Alice?" The voice slurred on the other end of the phone.

Her heart skipped a few beats.

"Alice, I can't…uh…I can't…stay…here. I ca-can't be he-here." It was fear that dripped from her voice.

"Kathryn, Kathryn, oh, Kathryn!" Alice was fully awake then. "Kathryn, are you all right?"

"I can't be…shit…help me, please! Damn, damn it!" Kathryn whined.

"Kathryn, can you make it to the airport? I…I can have a ticket waiting…oh, Kathryn. Please, come here. Please come."

"Alice, I love you." Kathryn was crying, disoriented.

"I know, I know it." Alice cried. "Please, Kathryn. Come here. Come here to me."

Chapter Fifty

Kathryn

It was a blur. The entirety of the last twenty-four hours.

It came to her in broken moments of clarity, but she washed it away with the mini-vodkas the airline offered.

Peter. A party. A fight. The needle. A call. Confessions.

Oh, she didn't want to think about it. She just wanted it all to go away.

The plane dropped from the sky, and she drank to mask the fear.

What was she doing? What was she doing here?

She had not intended on returning.

But the way her heart had beat so rapidly that she thought she might die – oh, that had scared her shitless.

The plane taxied to the gate and Kathryn could barely stand on her own. A young, attractive air hostess caught her and helped her up the ramp. They emerged into the light of Los Angeles day. Blinding.

And there.

Standing there, red hair illuminated like a beacon, offering her safe harbor in the storm.

She held her arms out to Kathryn, welcomed her into her embrace.

There were people watching, but Kathryn melted into her.

"You're here…you're really here." Alice whispered, tears of happiness, of sadness, of fear welling in her eyes as she held Kathryn close.

Kathryn nodded, let Alice lead her to a waiting car. They sat in the back seat and Alice was careful with Kathryn. Offering her water, helping her light her cigarettes.

"I'm sorry." Kathryn whimpered, wondering just how haggard and worn down she looked. There was alcohol and cocaine coursing through her system, and she could not hide either from Alice yet Alice held her hand, offering her assurances.

They drove to a quaint bungalow in Santa Monica. Alice helped her inside, took her to a room down a hallway and put her to bed. Alice sat on the edge and tucked Kathryn's hair behind her ears.

"Sleep it off. Just sleep it off. I'll have someone come in to check on you soon."

"No." Kathryn whimpered – the humiliation of it all beginning to dawn on her.

"Now, Kathryn, I've hired a nurse. You can't just…well it wouldn't be safe. So she'll be here to check on you. Just sleep for now." Alice assured her.

Kathryn reached for Alice. Even though she knew she had no claim over her, no reason to deserve any comfort or consolation from her at all. Yet the woman crawled into the bed beside her and held her, and for the first time in days Kathryn fell asleep. Simply slipped into a deep, quiet state of utter peace and relaxation.

She, for one brief moment, marveled at the fleeting idea that this should be the first time they actually slept together.

She awoke some time later, sick to her stomach.

Alice was there and a black woman who helped her into the bathroom where she vomited.

"You're all right." Alice assured her, stroked her back, and her arm until her fingers discovered the marks.

Kathryn watched her look and felt tears stinging in her eyes because she didn't want her to see what she had done.

Alice looked at Kathryn. Looked into her eyes and leaned down to press her lips to the angry red marks.

"Alice," Kathryn breathed through tears and then had to vomit again. Finally she sat back and Alice placed the towel the nurse had handed her over Kathryn's forehead.

Why had she done this to herself? So that she could go through all of this again?

She would have been better off if it had just ended her.

And yet Alice's clear green eyes shimmering, looking at her – well hadn't that been worth holding on for a moment more?

But she was being selfish. Selfish as always.

Alice helped her back to the bed and the nurse, Chantelle, went about looking her over. She was very gentle and kind with Kathryn. It only served to infuriate her further.

But she knew the fury was misguided. The anger was meant for herself.

She smoked a cigarette before falling back to sleep.

Time went on like this – hours and days became foreign to her. Time no longer seemed to matter because her body was in so much pain.

It was only in the moments that Alice slid into the bed beside her and held her against her that it all, momentarily, went away.

Until one morning, Kathryn awoke and heard birds chirping outside the window. The bed beside her was empty.

She remembered Alice had come to see her the previous evening after a rehearsal but was now gone in the early morning.

For the first time in a long while Kathryn felt awake. Awake as she had not felt since her stint in rehab.

She sat up, her body creaking and groaning. She massaged her knee to get it to bend enough for her to stand and then stretched her arms above her head. Reaching for her cigarettes and lighter, she decided to wander from the bedroom.

The hallway was illuminated by the dawning light of day. She moved towards the light, balancing herself against the wall because her body had grown unaccustomed to being upright.

There was a kitchen overlooking a backyard of palm trees and a crystalline pool, with a sitting room and sun room off of that. Kathryn looked at the coffee maker but deemed it too complicated to figure out so she ended up slipping out the back door and settling on a patio chair.

The birds had grown louder overhead. She searched for them as she lit a cigarette, the fresh air of day hitting her, warming her, making her skin tingle where it was exposed.

She sat, smoking and listening.

She did not belong here and yet she did.

She watched the sun rise higher and higher in the sky — early morning mauve melting into brilliant blue skies all around her. And the birds chirped and flew from tree to fence to roof to tree. She watched them, transfixed as she lit another cigarette and then another.

It was the scraping of the back door that startled her from this reverie.

She turned to find Alice standing with two steaming cups of coffee and a blanket tucked over her arm. "I'm glad to see you up." Alice smiled as she sat the cup of coffee next to

Kathryn and then draped the blanket over her legs. "It's chilly in the morning."

"I was all right." Kathryn murmured, but she was grateful for the care.

Alice settled beside her in the neighboring patio chair and sipped her coffee.

Kathryn studied her through a haze of cigarette smoke.

She seemed the same and yet different.

The wrinkles about her eyes had deepened, the sleepless nights made her cheeks puffy, she'd gained weight and yet – as always – it suited her.

And though she smiled at Kathryn, Kathryn felt a distance from her. A wall had been placed between them.

Well, Kathryn thought. She deserved that, didn't she?

But it enraged her, making her want to grasp at Alice, to pull her back from whatever it was that was preoccupying her mind.

Kathryn knew that at least a part of whatever was bothering Alice was her. The problem was her. Had always been her.

"We film today. I'll go into the studio later, but Chantelle will come by to make sure you have dinner." Alice explained.

Kathryn hated being treated like she was incapable of caring for herself.

But her track record so far made it seem as if she wasn't so good at it.

"You know you don't have to do this." Kathryn sipped her coffee.

"I know." Alice didn't look at her when she spoke.

Kathryn continued to stare at her.

It wasn't as if she had thought they might fall into one another's arms again and everything that had happened might just disappear, but she wanted...oh, how she wished and wanted.

"I want to." Alice whispered into her coffee cup. "I'm…I feel better knowing…"

Knowing…knowing what? That Kathryn was there? That Kathryn was still alive?

"Well," Alice turned to her with a guarded smile. "I'm happy you're here. I want you here."

And there was that look in her eyes that made Kathryn burn.

"Well." Kathryn had to look away. She smoked the last of her cigarette and stubbed it out before lighting another.

Chapter Fifty-One

Alice

"You're not sleeping, are you?"

Alice looked up from the script for their evening show to stare at Jeanette – already done up and gorgeous – in the mirror.

Alice laughed dryly. "I don't think I've slept a full night in months."

Jeanette's lip quirked in a concerned smile. "How is she?"

Alice shrugged. "She seems better, but I don't..." she shook her head. "I don't know. I don't know what she'll do or want to do next."

Jeanette crossed her arms. "I said it before, but I'll say it again. She's not your responsibility."

"All right, you don't have to keep telling me that. I know! I know." Alice held up her hands.

"And the other one?"

Alice's cheeks burned bright red. "Oh, Jeannie."

"Okay, that's good, isn't it?"

"It doesn't feel good." Alice shook her head. "She's so… wonderful and I…"

"You've talked to her about…"

"She knows." Alice nodded.

Jeanette laughed, moved closer to Alice, lowering her voice so anyone passing by might not hear her. "But you're still…"

"Yes. Not often, but yes." Alice whispered as she searched the counter for the lipstick that would go with the blouse they put her in that day for filming. Her fluffed hair was already beginning to fall flat. She'd have to call in Rochelle for last minute touch-ups.

"Does Kathryn know?" Jeanette was closer then.

Alice shook her head. "I can't talk about this now."

"All right, all right. But perhaps you need to get away for a weekend because you look exhausted. I'm not sure they can smooth out that much puffiness."

"Go away!" Alice shooed her off and then stared in the mirror at her tired features. "Jesus."

The show went off without a hitch – Alice far too adept at turning off everything else and just letting her character take over. For that evening she was consumed with Sharon's fictional issues and not her own.

But all too soon she had to become Alice again. She wiped off the make-up and changed into her own clothes and drove herself home.

She found Kathryn on the back porch smoking and reading a newspaper in the dim evening. Alice appreciated that as she became more capable of moving about she had taken to smoking outside.

Alice let her bag fall to the counter and found the kitchen spotless, a plate of food had been left for her atop the stove. Had Kathryn cooked dinner that evening? She picked it up and uncovered the foil, taking in the delicious aroma of a home cooked meal. She grabbed a fork and made her way to the back porch, to where Kathryn sat in the lamplit evening.

"Hey there." Kathryn blew smoke from the side of her lips, watching Alice as she sat down in the chair beside her.

"You made this?" Alice marveled as she held up the dish.

Kathryn shrugged, "Chantelle helped." And then she smiled.

"Looks delicious."

Kathryn tapped off her cigarette and watched as Alice took her first bite of mashed potatoes and collard greens. "My God, it is good." Alice sighed, feeling self-conscious under Kathryn's watchful eye.

"You deserve a home cooked meal every now and then." Kathryn seemed pleased.

Alice had missed her cooking. She had forgotten just how good she truly was at it.

"How was filming?" Kathryn asked as she put out her cigarette and then folded the newspaper she'd been reading.

"As well as always." Alice was enthralled with the mashed potatoes. She hardly noticed the way Kathryn was looking at her as she lit a fresh cigarette. "I got a pretty good laugh – like a real one, you know? Not one of those stupid producer generated laughs. That was nice. It hasn't happened for a while. Probably because the script is usually awful. But this week I figured it out. I really worked on this moment and it worked."

Kathryn was smiling at her. "I look forward to seeing it."

Alice looked at her. "You…you watch it?"

Kathryn shrugged. "I have."

Alice felt suddenly shy. "Oh."

Kathryn laughed. "It's good, the show. It's about damn time they gave a black woman equal screen time. It's ridiculous, you know, in this day and age that there aren't more black people on television. And she's attractive, isn't she?"

"Jeanette?"

"Yes, your colleague Jeanette." Kathryn nodded.

Alice felt as if she were on trial for something but she couldn't decipher what. "I suppose she is."

"You're close?" Kathryn flicked her cigarette.

"Close? Why yes, yes. We're close. She's a very dear friend." Alice mumbled. "Oh," she looked up at Kathryn. "Not...not like..."

"I see." Kathryn nodded and smoked, staring somewhere far, far away. "Well, I wouldn't blame you." Kathryn exhaled a cloud of smoke.

"It's not..." Alice sat her plate aside and rubbed at her forehead. "I'm not running around with every woman I work with."

"I never said that." Kathryn held up her hands, as if in mock surrender. "Forget I mentioned it. I was only saying how very beautiful she is."

"Well, she is. Very beautiful. But we're not...I'm not..."

"All right then." Kathryn put out her cigarette and reached for another.

Alice curled and then uncurled her fingers. "I'm tired. I'm going to take a bath and go to bed."

"Alice." Kathryn's voice sounded frightened, stopping Alice in her tracks.

Alice turned to face her.

"I didn't mean to upset you. I'm...I'm sorry." The words were foreign coming from Kathryn.

Alice took a deep breath. She moved to Kathryn, placing her hand gently on her shoulder. "It's all right. I am really very tired." And she leaned down and pressed her lips to Kathryn's cheek, inhaling the scent that was intrinsically her.

Kathryn patted her hand and Alice slunk away, retreating to her room, to a bath where she sank into its recesses and fought back confusing tears.

She awoke the following morning to the smell of breakfast

and then thought of the late-night phone call she'd made. A feeling of guilt wrapped itself about her.

She emerged from her room and padded toward the kitchen, finding the act of living with Kathryn – actually inhabiting a space with her day in and day out – still so baffling. How she had dreamt of it all those years ago, and now here they were so many years later. In this imperfect arrangement.

Kathryn was at the stove flipping pancakes and sipping coffee.

Even now, undone as she was, she held a beauty that mystified and enraptured Alice. Her hair was a graying blonde color, her hands aged, wrinkles about her eyes, her lips – and yet she was as beautiful as she had been all those years before.

"Morning sleepy-head." Kathryn teased as she stacked perfectly round pancakes neatly onto a plate that she held out for Alice.

Alice stared at the plate in her hands. "Oh, I shouldn't…"

"Just a bite." Kathryn urged, walking with her slight limp to the kitchen island where she pushed the butter and syrup in Alice's direction.

"They smell amazing." Alice was still marveling as she sat at the counter.

"They'll taste even better." Kathryn winked and poured Alice a steaming cup of coffee.

And true to her word, they tasted better than anything Alice had allowed herself in a long while.

"They're good, right?" Kathryn watched her as she ate.

"Delicious." Alice agreed. And then the guilt returned.

Kathryn was leaning against the island, weathered hands wrapped about her coffee cup, watching Alice as she ate.

"I…I have some, uh, errands to run today." Alice sipped the coffee and was surprised that it tasted better than when she made it.

"Ah." Kathryn straightened, limping her way around the kitchen, cleaning as she did, looking anywhere but at Alice.

"I…I'm sorry."

"Why?" Kathryn asked breezily without turning around. "You're just running errands."

Alice felt her cheeks warm.

"Is there anything I could help with? You know I'm not enjoying being a kept woman." Kathryn tried to joke.

Alice laughed, wiped at her lips and stood. "No, no. You needn't do anything. Except perhaps have Chantelle work with you more on that leg of yours. Does it still hurt to walk?"

Kathryn shot her a piercing look. "It's just fine."

"Kathryn." Alice sighed as she sat her plate in the sink.

"All right, I'll have her work with me more." Kathryn conceded all too quickly nowadays.

Alice looked at her again and had the sudden urge to kiss her.

But she caught sight of the clock. "I…I'll be back. Later."

Kathryn nodded.

Alice got into her car chastising herself. Why was she feeling so guilty? There was nothing to be guilty about. Nothing at all.

And yet as she pulled into the now familiar driveway and met the woman at the door, her stomach knotted.

Her errand kissed her on the lips and ushered her inside.

"I made some coffee." Robin said, but it wasn't as good as the coffee Alice had just left at home.

They sat on the couch and Alice blew across the steaming mug. "How's the real estate market going?" Alice thought to ask.

"I sold a rather outrageously priced mini-mansion in Malibu yesterday and already have a very interested buyer right here in Palos Verdes. I have a showing later today." Robin let her elbow rest against the back of the couch – a slightly sad smile playing at her lips despite the rather impressive news of her winsome week.

"That's wonderful news. Congratulations." Alice smiled.

Robin looked pleased as she sipped her coffee. "But I don't think you came here to talk about my work."

"Oh?" Alice's eyebrows raised.

"That roommate of yours is really getting to you, isn't she?"

Alice's lips parted. "Well, it is rather odd to be…living together. After all this time, but I…well, I didn't intend on coming here to talk about her."

"She ends up being all that we talk about."

"That's…that's not true." Alice considered this. Was it true? "I'm sorry…I didn't mean…"

"I can understand it. After what you've told me…"

"But I'm not…I'm not interested in…"

"Don't fool yourself, Alice." Robin laughed.

"I'm serious. It's in the past. I've dealt with all of that."

"Have you?" Robin was looking at her pointedly.

Alice fiddled with her thumbnail. "It was all a long time ago. A very long time ago."

"But she's here now. She's living with you."

Alice felt tears welling in her eyes. "She has no one else. I…"

"You care about her. It's very admirable." Robin commended her, but it felt like a jab.

"I suppose, but I don't…I don't know what I'm doing. And I'm…I'm angry. I'm really angry that she…I mean she doesn't just get to come and go out of my life as she pleases. I don't know what she's going to do next – if she's going to disappear again and…and…She doesn't know…"

Robin let her hand fall gently over Alice's. "You love her."

"No." Alice shook her head and felt a tear spill messily down her cheek.

"I'm not going to lie and say that this is easy for me, but

I've come to the realization that perhaps I'm just…in the way…"

"No…no…I can't love her. Not after…" Alice cut in.

Robin took hold of both of her hands and Alice saw the light gleam of tears reflected in the other woman's eyes. "Alice, I can't be this person for you when I know your heart's not in it. I thought I could, but I…I can't…"

"No, Robin…" Alice shook her head. "You're the…" she felt a sharp pain in her chest. She didn't want to lose this. "I've never been with anyone like you before. You're…you're the best…"

"Shh," Robin pulled Alice close to her, pressing her lips to her forehead. "I know. It doesn't make sense to me either. But, honey, I can't compete with her."

Oh, Kathryn. Oh, Alice hated Kathryn.

"I'm sorry. I'm so, so sorry."

Chapter Fifty-Two

Kathryn

Kathryn's finger skimmed over the impressive collection of books on Alice's living room book shelf.

The Bell Jar, *The Feminine Mystique*, *Sexual Politics*, *I Know Why the Caged Bird Sings* (with a handwritten note on the inside front cover from Jeanette), *The Female Eunuch*, *The Second Sex*, *The First Sex*, *Witches, Midwives, and Nurses: A History of Women Healers*, *The Women's Room*, *The Group*, *The Fountainhead* (ah, Dominique).

"Well, well." Kathryn felt her lips pulling upward at the titles. Alice had certainly been getting an education. Kathryn pulled *The Women's Room* from the shelf and limped over to the couch where she lit a cigarette – because she had the back door and a window open, and Alice seemed to never be coming home again.

She was supposed to be icing her knee after Chantelle had put her through her paces that afternoon, so she propped it up on a pillow and brought the ice pack Chantelle had made for her over the offending appendage.

After adjusting her glasses she opened the book and took to reading while smoking, smoking because she needed something to *do* with herself.

"The blank eyes, the empty faces, the young bodies that ten minutes earlier had paced its length, were gone. It was these that, passing her without seeing her, seeing her without looking at her, had driven her into hiding. For they had made her feel invisible. And when all you have is a visible surface, invisibility is death."

Kathryn laughed darkly to herself. "Too true," she murmured.

And she became so enthralled with the novel she did not hear when the front door opened and closed. It was not until she heard a voice calling out that she nearly dropped the cigarette from between her fingers and ash scattered about her lap.

"Mom? Mom, are you home?"

Her heart beat wildly in her chest as she closed the book and put out the cigarette.

"Mom? Are you…smoking?" His voice preceded him into the room, and Kathryn waved her hand about the air as if she could do anything about it now.

"Smoking, yes, but I'm afraid I'm not your mother." Kathryn spoke as a young man she recognized from his image plastered all about Alice's home appeared in the sitting room.

"Who…" His confused look told her Alice had not informed him that she was currently residing with her. "Wait…you're…you're Kathryn Anderson."

He was very handsome in person from what she could tell from her spot on the couch. "I'm afraid so."

"But what…" Jack was looking at her, confused.

"Your mother has taken me in. For the time being anyway."

"I see." He had moved closer to her. Curious. As she was

curious about him. "I was, you know, sorry to hear about your accident."

"I guess I take pleasure in shooting myself in the foot." She shrugged.

Jack was wringing his hands, uncertain what to do with himself. "I didn't mean to barge in here…"

Kathryn waved him off. "It's your home more than it is mine."

"Will she be back soon?"

"Your guess is as good as mine." Kathryn straightened her shirt, wiped the ash from her lap, then looked up to find Jack still looking at her. Uncomfortable, uncertain, almost afraid of her. Was she so imposing? "What? I won't bite. I know! Why don't we go outside and you can tell me all about yourself. I knew you, you know, when you were in diapers. You were a darling baby."

Jack's cheeks flushed at this, a shy smile played on his lips that reminded Kathryn of Alice's.

"But you might have to help me up." Her knee had gone numb with the ice.

Jack quickly jumped to help her. She leaned against him as he led her to the back patio, where he helped her down onto the patio chair. She extracted a cigarette and lit it as he sat down in the patio chair beside her. She looked at him as she did so. "Do you smoke?"

He shook his head. "No, never have."

"Good for you. I wouldn't recommend it." She smiled. He was so like Alice. She sank into the patio chair, savoring the last rays of daylight. "So tell me, Jack, have you had a good life?"

He laughed for the first time. "The best."

"I can only imagine. Alice is one hell of a mother."

"I couldn't have asked for a better one."

"She tells me you're in law school."

"Yes, I'm only a semester away from graduating."

"It's good. You're smart. Just like her." Kathryn felt a warmth spreading itself through her body. A happiness at what he had become. A pride, as if she had had a hand in it.

If only she had been able to…

And yet she had done what was necessary. For her. For him.

"You worked with my mother when I was born…didn't you?" He had sunk into the chair beside hers and was staring up at the evening clouds.

"Yes." Kathryn nodded.

"I've seen the show. Don't tell my mom, but I liked you best." He admitted sheepishly.

"Really? But everyone was always in love with your mother. She was the real star of the show." Kathryn blew smoke from the side of her mouth.

"Nah, you were just as good." Jack assured her.

She shook her head in disbelief.

"What was she like back then? Was she…happy?" Jack turned to look at Kathryn, startling her with his question.

Happy? Oh, had Alice ever been happy? Had any of them ever been truly happy?

"Oh, Alice was…" Kathryn thought about it. There had always been a sadness to her. A great seriousness and sadness that abated only in those moments when they were alone…

She turned to look at Jack.

"You don't think she was happy?"

Jack shrugged. "She doesn't really talk about then. I've tried to ask her, but she…she just looks sad."

"Well, I'm sure she was happy. At least some of the time, I'm sure of it." Hadn't Kathryn made her at least momentarily happy?

"Did you know my dad?" Jack's question held a fearful quietness to it.

Kathryn felt her stomach drop. She scrunched up her face, took a deep drag of her cigarette. Oh, she had not been prepared for this. How she did not wish to remember his father. "Yes."

"Was he…kind to her?"

Kathryn took a deep breath. "Shouldn't you ask her?"

Jack looked down at his hands. "She won't tell me anything."

Kathryn scoffed. "She's tight-lipped, isn't she?"

Jack nodded. "I wish she'd just be honest with me."

Kathryn took a deep breath. "Honesty. Well, now that can be quite difficult. Sometimes the truth hurts more than not knowing."

"I'd still rather know the truth."

Kathryn pointedly looked at him. "Are you always truthful?"

Jack balked at the question. "Well…I try to be."

"Bullshit." She blew a cloud of smoke into the sky. "None of us are ever truthful all the time. You're going into law, aren't you? Isn't that all a bunch of smoke and mirrors?"

Jack stared at her wide-eyed, shocked and then they were looking at one another and he started to laugh and she laughed, and the tension dissipated between them.

"You're different than I imagined." Jack finally said.

"Yeah, what did you imagine?"

"You just seem…"

"Unapproachable? An ice queen? A deluded old starlet? A wild, reckless addict?" Kathryn guessed for him.

"No, you're none of those things."

"Well…"

"You're wise and kind and funny, and I like you." He smiled.

"I like you, too." Kathryn smiled and stubbed out her cigarette. "What do you say we make some dinner for your mom?"

He helped her up and back into the house where they

went to work making pasta and tomato sauce with garlic bread.

And it was during a conversation of how Jack perceived the second film Kathryn had made with Peter – "…but she did attain power over everyone in the end." "She was only powerful within the confines of her home. Outside of it she was no one." "But you never feel that during the film." "She never left the goddamn house! She might as well have been trapped!" "But is that what he intended?" "Well, sure. Peter always likes the idea of trapped women." – that Kathryn looked up to find Alice lingering in the living room doorway, watching them.

Their eyes met, and Kathryn couldn't help the tug of her lips upward at the sight of her.

But almost instantly Kathryn could sense that something had happened, that Alice was not herself. Her eyes were red, face puffy as if she'd been crying.

Kathryn's brow furrowed in concern.

Jack was stirring the sauce as he said something – another of his speculations about one of her German movies – when he realized they were no longer alone. He turned to follow Kathryn's line of sight to his mother.

"Mom?"

"Well, I see the two of you have met." Alice let her purse fall from her shoulder and wiped at her cheek.

"Yeah, why didn't you tell me she was staying here?" Jack probed.

Oh, Jack. Now was not the time to give her the third degree. Alice looked as if she were barely holding it together as it was.

"I'm sure she had her reasons." Kathryn answered for Alice.

Alice gave her a curious look.

"Why don't you go freshen up – dinner's almost ready." Kathryn suggested to Alice, offering her a chance to escape.

Alice faltered for a moment, as if uncertain what to do with herself.

Kathryn could tell that Jack was also looking at her with concern.

Alice finally nodded, "okay. I'll...I'll just be a minute." She bit her lip and tried to smile at Kathryn and then briefly looked to her son. "You're all right, baby?"

Jack smiled. "Yeah, it's nothing. We can talk later."

Alice smiled but it hardly reached her eyes. "Okay."

Kathryn watched Alice turn and disappear down the hall to her bedroom.

"Why don't you set the table? I've got it from here." Kathryn said, trying to bring back the ease they had found before Alice's arrival.

Jack nodded at her and set to work with the plates and silverware.

Kathryn stared down at the pasta sauce, wanting to know just what was going on with Alice.

Alice, who was eluding her.

Chapter Fifty-Three

Alice

She could see Kathryn smoking on the patio through the window over the sink.

Jack had left with a plate of food for Bobby, having claimed it was the best thing he'd eaten in years.

Alice was loathe to admit that she agreed with her son.

Oh, Jack. Oh, Jack with Kathryn.

His eyes had shone with such admiration for Kathryn as she had carried the conversation throughout dinner, distracting and entertaining her son with wild anecdotes. The two of them were like peas in a pod.

And oh, how she had dreamt of it all those years ago. A fairy tale that seemed too good to be real. A strange but perfect family that had served as a nighttime fantasy for Alice as she'd raised him single-handedly.

But seeing the two of them together, the reality of it, had only evoked a simmering fear within her.

Kathryn was very beguiling. People so easily became

enraptured with her. There was something about her that drew people in, making them believe every word that dripped from her pretty mouth.

But the image was a house of cards. At one moment so real, and present, and then on the slightest whim, at the very suggestion of a light wind, shattered and destroyed.

It frightened her.

Perhaps this had all been a terrible idea. To bring her here.

First Robin…now her son…

She watched Kathryn bring the cigarette to her lips, inhaling as she stared into the darkening evening thoughtfully.

What was she thinking?

The tea kettle whistled, startling Alice.

She wiped her hands on the kitchen towel before pouring boiling water over tea bags. She took the mugs out into the cool evening, not certain why she was so nervous to speak with Kathryn just then.

Kathryn put out her cigarette and smiled up at Alice as she accepted the tea. "Thank you."

Alice settled onto the other patio chair and cupped the mug in her hands. "I suppose I should thank you."

"What for?" Kathryn sat the mug down so that she could light another cigarette.

"You were very kind. To Jack."

Kathryn exhaled a cloud of smoke. "He's a darling young man. I can't believe…well, all these years. He's grown so much."

Had her voice shaken with tears? Alice couldn't be sure in the dim light. "He certainly has."

"I can remember holding him in my arms as if it were yesterday and now he's almost a lawyer." Kathryn bristled. Lifting her hand to her face, she smoked.

Alice's stomach twisted.

"I'm happy, Alice, happy that he's had such a good life. I can see it." Kathryn was trying to assure her.

Alice nodded. Wishing, wishing…but what had wishing ever gotten her?

She laid her head back on the patio chair and looked up to the sky, trying to make out the stars above them.

A tear slid unexpectedly down her cheek.

"He asked me if you had been happy." Kathryn's voice was quiet.

Alice bit her lip. "Why would he ask that?"

"Were you?"

Alice laughed. "Of course." Another tear slid down her cheek. "At times, of course I was." Hadn't she been? Hadn't there been moments of happiness interspersed amongst all the unhappiness?

She tried to remember and only caught momentary flashes of color, of memories she wasn't even sure had truly happened. Had they been dreams?

But Kathryn had been real. All those years ago, she had been…at least some of the time.

They sat in silence.

Kathryn smoked and sipped her tea.

Alice let tears trail down her cheeks. Kathryn wouldn't be able to see without her glasses, would she?

"You're seeing someone." Kathryn's dark, husky voice broke the silence.

Alice sat a little straighter in her chair, wiped at one cheek. "What?"

"It's all right. I don't blame you. Not one bit." Kathryn went on. "I hope you know that I don't expect anything."

"Oh, no…" Alice looked to Kathryn and found her eyes trained upon her. Her heart beat roughly in her chest.

"So you are seeing someone?" Kathryn smoked, stared at her.

Alice shook her head. "I...I was. But...but not anymore." She curled her knees up to her chest.

"Oh, Alice." Kathryn sighed.

"No..." Alice held up her hands. "No – I don't want to talk about this with you."

"But you're upset..."

"Kathryn..." Alice stopped her.

Kathryn looked at her, baffled and hurt.

Good, she thought.

Then she felt terrible for taking pleasure in hurting Kathryn.

But hurt was something she was far too familiar with feeling when it came to Kathryn.

"I'm going to bed." Alice uncurled herself from the chair and left Kathryn sitting soundlessly perplexed on the patio.

She went to her room, closed the door and let the tears come messy and hot down her cheeks as she fought her way out of her clothes and started the bath. She climbed into its warmth and sank down below its surface to stare at the ceiling through a watery haze.

She stayed beneath the water until she could no longer breathe and then surfaced, gasping for air, pulling it greedily back into her lungs.

She went through her nightly routine of lotions and potions as she tried not to think of what it was she wanted to think.

She laid down in her bed and felt so utterly alone. Alone as she had not felt in years despite having fallen asleep alone for decades.

She listened as she heard footsteps down the hall, another door closing. And then silence again.

She was not alone.

And yet she was.

She turned off the light and rolled onto her side, grabbing at a pillow, holding it close to her chest. She jammed her fist into her mouth, not wanting to sob aloud. Tears did not come, but sadness overtook her.

All those years, those days and nights after…

What had they become?

She lay awake for what felt like hours.

Twisting to the right. Then the left. Then flat on her back.

Anger was swirling inside of her. Anger she had not felt for years. Anger at *her*, at them, at all that had been.

All that time wasted.

And look at what it had done to *her*. Look at what had become of *her*.

If only…

Alice sat up with a grunt and looked at the clock.

Only an hour had passed since she'd gotten into bed.

She groaned and stood up, wrapping a robe about herself as she walked to the bedroom door. She stepped out into the hallway and found that no light came from beneath the guest room door.

Was she really sleeping? How could she sleep when Alice was feverish with rage?

Alice opened the door.

Kathryn was laying on her back, staring at the door. As if she had been expecting her.

"I'm so angry with you." The words slid rapidly from Alice's lips. As if she might not say them if she didn't say them right then.

"I don't blame you." Kathryn struggled to pull herself halfway up on her elbows. "I'm angry too."

"You…you…" Alice tightened her fists at her sides and then released them. "I want…I want to trust…"

"I know."

Alice felt the anger dissipating from her at the sight of Kathryn reclining there on the bed before her. Moonlight and street lights filtering in through the blinds, illuminating her beautiful, tired features.

Alice was overcome with exhaustion, and her own bed seemed so far away and so very cold.

They stared at one another.

Kathryn, exhausted from holding herself up, lay back on the bed and patted the spot beside her.

Alice let her robe slip from her arms. She tossed it atop a chair in the corner and crawled into the bed beside Kathryn.

Kathryn gave her space, staying to her side.

But their hands found each other's beneath the sheets in the night.

Kathryn's hand was warm and soft.

Chapter Fifty-Four

Kathryn

"No, I upheld my end of the bargain." Kathryn stood at the patio door, phone held between her shoulder and ear as she lit a cigarette.

"Meine Süße, you can't just…verschwinden."

Kathryn chuckled darkly. "Watch me."

"But you are my wife, are you not?"

Kathryn rolled her eyes to the heavens. "Oh, Peter."

"Ich brauche dich hier. Bei mir, damn it."

"Nein, Peter. Not now. Nicht jetzt."

"I have a movie for us, meine Süße."

"Peter." Kathryn exhaled a stream of smoke. "I'm tired. I'm really tired. I don't want to do this anymore. Ich kann das nicht mehr." She whispered.

"We have a deal, Kathryn."

"I have to go." She stubbed out the cigarette she'd lit and turned to hang up the phone to find Alice standing in the kitchen doorway, clutching her script to her chest and staring directly at her. Kathryn could still hear Peter on the other end, yelling, trying to call her attention back to him, so she had to follow the cord back to the receiver to disconnect the overseas call.

"I'm sorry." Alice was suddenly fascinated by invisible lint on her pants.

Kathryn waved her hand in dismissal. "It was nothing." She looked at Alice, always so timid in her presence now.

Timid as she'd been for the past few days. As they teetered on the brink of something.

Alice always taking one step forward only to retreat ten.

Kathryn was keeping a respectable distance.

"Only, I will owe you for the long-distance call. I apologize." Kathryn sighed as she sunk down onto the end of the couch.

Alice shook her head. "Please, don't worry about that."

Kathryn looked Alice over. "You're home early."

"It was a short rehearsal day. Someone was out sick." Alice sank onto the other end of the couch and let her script fall onto the table.

Kathryn studied her from across the couch. Her hair was illuminated in the fading light of day, lit up like a flame, but it seemed to be the only thing glowing. Her eyes were tired. Her face long.

She turned to look at Kathryn and something ignited in her golden green eyes. "How'd you learn to speak German?" Alice shyly asked.

Kathryn chuckled. "From my parents. They were German immigrants."

"I didn't know." Alice was looking at her with heightened curiosity.

The things they didn't know. The things there had never been time for before, the usual pleasantries of origin and personal history. Kathryn realized how little she knew of Alice and how little Alice knew of her.

But she had only ever wanted to protect Alice.

Or was it herself?

Kathryn took a deep breath. "They came to America the year before I was born. My father got work in a mine in Pennsylvania but was more interested in drinking." She raised an eyebrow at the irony.

"What happened?" Alice had curled a leg up beneath herself, was hugging a pillow against her stomach.

Kathryn eyed her. "You don't really want to…"

"I want to know, Kathryn." Alice's eyes were piercing.

Kathryn shrugged. "He died. When I was five. He went to work drunk off his ass and the rocks crushed him in the mine."

"Jesus." Alice's eyes widened.

Kathryn toyed with the seam of her pants. "I think I've always wanted to protect you."

"From what?"

"Me." Kathryn exhaled, longing for a cigarette.

"Oh Kathryn. I never needed protection from you. I made my choices. Eyes wide open."

Kathryn looked at her through watery eyes. "I wish…"

Alice leaned forward and put a hand on her thigh. "Then tell me."

Kathryn wiped at her eyes. "I need a cigarette first."

They ended up out on the patio, sitting on the same lounger, an open bag of Oreos between them, a fresh cigarette smoking between Kathryn's fingers as she twisted a cookie apart.

"Siblings?" Alice inquired, before licking the cream from her cookie.

Kathryn watched her pretty pink tongue. "A younger brother. He came two years after me. Kurt. His name was Kurt. God, I haven't said his name in ages." She smoked.

Alice waited.

"But you want it all, don't you?" Kathryn tried to smile.

Alice nodded.

"Well, after my father died - my mother was really very resourceful. You know, she mended clothes for everyone in town. So we got by for a while. We managed. And you know, I always admired her for being independent. But she wanted something better." Kathryn stared down at her half-eaten cookie. "When I was nine she met a man." Kathryn brought the cigarette to her lips and inhaled shakily. "He was so charming, you know, one of those really honest do-gooder types. He was kind to my mother and he promised her…he promised us he would take care of things. That we could live in a big house and she would never have to work again." Kathryn glanced out at the pool's glassy surface. Oh, how she had never told this story to anyone. Charles had known, but not the whole of it.

"He was nice to all of us equally when we moved into his big home in a nearby city. But then I started noticing him paying more attention to me. I didn't think anything of it because he had this way of making anyone he was talking to feel really special. He would ask my mother if he could take me places. Like the store or the park or just…out driving. It started so innocently." Kathryn's voice had grown soft.

She could feel Alice looking at her, could feel that she was holding her breath, though Kathryn had no idea a tear was already trickling down her cheek.

"And you know, I liked the attention. I always liked when older people gave me attention. It made me feel like, oh God, like I was seen. Like *someone* could see me and that I was *someone*." Kathryn was diverting, but she had to in order to make it through. "I was in love with my English teacher in high school. Oh, I know it's horribly cliché, but I loved her. Miss Gallagher. She was beautiful and so…kind. And she'd let me come over on the weekends because I was her brightest student, and I would do just about anything to be with her. To be away from him. It was like she knew…somehow, she *knew*." Kathryn smoked again, all of it coming back to her.

"I knew what I had become, what I looked like. And I knew how people looked at me. How *he* looked at me. It started with little touches here and there. A lingering hand on my back, on my thigh. And my body started to respond to it, like it wanted that. But I hated him. And I think he knew it. I think that made it better for him. When he touched me, I thought of her. And that first night it happened, the first time he slipped into my bed, I went running out the back door and all the way to Miss Gallagher's house, and she took me in and bathed me and laid me next to her. I told her I had liked it. Oh, not him, but the feel of it..." Kathryn shook her head. "She told me that what he had done was wrong, that I should come to her, that she could protect me."

"A year later I was seventeen and pregnant with his child. My mother kicked me out of the house when I started showing. I didn't know what to do. My brother tried to protect me, but he was just a kid. I went to Miss Gallagher's and she let me stay and we...we became very close. And I liked that too." Kathryn shrugged. "But I couldn't stay forever. There was so much talk in town. Everywhere I went I was a slut or a whore and Miss Gallagher nearly lost her job when they found out where I was staying. So after the baby came - my baby, my little girl, my...my Vivian...I left her at my mother's doorstep and I fled for New York." Kathryn felt the tears running down her own cheeks, still unable to look at Alice.

She put out her cigarette and reached for a new one.

Alice stayed quiet on the other side of the lounger.

"I met Charles in New York and...well, you know the rest. My savior, blablabla. I think he just liked me because I was a loose woman who liked fucking." Kathryn laughed as she lit the cigarette and then wiped at her cheeks.

"I...I had no..." Alice was crying in earnest.

"Oh, darling. It was all so long ago." Kathryn looked to her for the first time since they'd convened outside.

"It's not…it's terrible…"

"Terrible was what happened to my baby brother." Kathryn exhaled. "You wanted it all, didn't you?"

"My God." Alice looked as if she were bracing herself for the worst.

"He went into the army during World War II."

"Was he killed?"

Kathryn shook her head and reached for another cookie. "No." Kathryn puffed at her cigarette then broke the cookie in half to eat one side and then the other. "He was running these night air raids and they wanted their pilots sharp. So they gave him amphetamines. He came back hooked. Shot himself right between the eyes a year later."

Alice was silent. And then there was a gasping "Oh!"

Kathryn felt the strangest sense of lightness overcome her. As if by sharing all the old hurts and pains it had eradicated the wound, made it clean and whole.

She took Alice into her arms and held her as she cried, finding that she too was also crying.

"It's all right now." Kathryn assured Alice. "I'm all right."

And she was, wasn't she? At least then in that moment.

At least here, now with her arms wrapped about Alice and the night washing over them.

They sat like that forever and for no time at all, Alice falling onto the lounger beside her so that they both looked up at the sky together.

Alice living it all for the first time, and Kathryn allowing it to fade away on the evening wind.

Chapter Fifty-Five

Alice

"I'm sorry. I shouldn't have…"

"No." Alice sat up and peered down at Kathryn's face in the dark. "I'm glad that you…thank you."

She had never heard Kathryn speak so much and so openly about herself.

It broke Alice open and apart. It shattered her, making her long to hold Kathryn there with her forever.

But would Kathryn stay?

"What is it?" Kathryn had clasped at her wrist, was looking at her curiously. "I didn't tell you my story to get your pity, you know. I can full well see the wrongs I have done in my life, all the mistakes, and whether my childhood was good or bad it doesn't right the wrongs."

"It's not that." Alice shifted a little, taking Kathryn's hand in her own. "Are you going back to your husband?"

Kathryn laughed at that. Alice wasn't sure why that was funny.

She watched as Kathryn brought the nearly finished cigarette to her lips to inhale and then exhale away from Alice. Her other hand was about Alice, tracing mindless patterns on her back as if they were still intimate together. Her fingers slipped beneath her shirt, errantly caressing Alice's bare skin, setting her nerves on fire.

"It sounded as if he wanted..." Alice went on when Kathryn did not immediately respond.

"He's hardly a husband." Kathryn interrupted. "He was a kid with financial backing enough to make films, and he needed a name and he worshiped me. We had an arrangement, a marriage to get me to Germany, to get me into his films." She shrugged. "He's a fucking faggot; he's never touched me." Kathryn smoked at the end of her cigarette and leaned ever so to butt it out in the ashtray.

Alice couldn't help the relieved laugh that escaped from her lips.

Kathryn peered at her curiously, hand stilling on her back as if she'd just realized what she was doing. "What's so funny about marrying a queer?"

Alice sighed. Laid back to stare at the sky again, breathing as if for the first time. "You won't go then?"

Kathryn hummed. "I have no pressing plans." She sat up suddenly, startling Alice. "We really should eat something, don't you think? Oreos do not a dinner make."

Alice watched as Kathryn stood up and then held out a hand for her.

She took the hand and supported Kathryn inside. They ordered from a local Chinese place and sat on the couch eating, though when Alice looked up she found that Kathryn was not so much eating as watching her eat. "You're okay, aren't you?" Kathryn finally asked.

Alice was self-conscious then. She stared down at her noodles and bit her lip. "I had...have an eating disorder. I'm sure you knew."

Kathryn nodded.

"It's better but…sometimes…"

Kathryn's hand fell over Alice's. "I wish I had a good stiff drink right now but…well, we all have our demons."

Alice considered this.

"But what about you?" Kathryn began picking at her rice again.

Alice looked at her.

"Your second marriage. I followed the papers, I knew, at least as well as the rest of the world, what happened, but…"

"Oh." Alice nodded. It was only fair. Kathryn had given her so much.

It was a doorway she did not often open. A time that had been so confusing and painful to her and yet she had gotten her son back. So it had been worth it, hadn't it?

"Ken." She hardly thought of him now. He'd died some years ago in a car accident. "He really liked women. Too much. They wanted to settle him down after he ended up knocking up Susan Kenney, you know she was married to Tom Woodruff at the time. So he was getting himself some bad press, and I was apparently the perfect Band-aid for the whole situation."

"Fucking Charles." Kathryn's eyes were furious. "He didn't…Ken didn't…"

Alice raised an eyebrow and swirled the noodles around. "That's what's so interesting. He wasn't interested in me, and I wasn't interested in him. Our wedding night he went out on the town and I watched television in the hotel." She laughed at the memory of that night. How she'd sat in front of the hotel television set until *The Valley* had come on. The show Kathryn had done after *The Wes Goodwin Show*. It had filmed in New York and Kathryn had played a terribly unimportant wife character. But Alice watched it religiously and every second Kathryn was on the television she drank her in and imagined…

And that night, the night of her honeymoon, Alice had touched herself while watching. Consummating what could never be and then she'd curled into a ball and had cried herself to sleep.

Oh, all these years.

But Kathryn was before her now. Waiting...

Alice felt warm beneath her shirt collar, held by Kathryn's enraptured gaze.

"I was so relieved." She went on. "I thought we could make it work somehow. And I got my Jack back." Alice smiled. The one redeeming thing that had happened. "Ken adored Jack, too but he was gone enough that he didn't really interfere. But the stories started getting out. He was picked up for soliciting prostitutes, for being in the wrong place at the wrong time.

"I think we could have just gone on like that, in fact, I thought maybe it would work since he had all the women he wanted, and he left me alone. But he actually fell in love with one of those women. I couldn't keep him to myself. It would have been selfish." Alice sighed. "We divorced so he could be with Marcia Gleason." Alice marveled at the woman who had stayed by Ken until his dying day. She still wondered if he had ever strayed from Marcia as he had from her. But theirs had been such a different relationship.

"I was afraid Frank might try something after the divorce but he died. He had a massive heart attack about a year later." Alice curled her legs closer to herself. "He left all the money – all *my* money to his sister. But what did I expect? And what did it matter? I was making enough then, and I had Jack." The only missing piece had been Kathryn.

"It worked out then." Kathryn was looking at her with her own relieved expression. And then she was fixated on her rice. "That whole time...you never..."

Alice took a deep breath and shook her head. "No. No...

not until..." She looked down at her food. She'd lost her appetite.

"Only recently?"

Alice nodded. "I wouldn't have gone out, but Jeanette suggested it. Thought it might take my mind off...well, I didn't intend on meeting anyone anyway. And then..." Alice shrugged.

"A woman?"

Alice slowly nodded her head up and down. "Robin. She's really wonderful."

"I'm sorry." Kathryn offered.

Alice scoffed. "No you're not."

"I am. I want you to be happy..."

Alice shook her head.

"What happened?" Kathryn prodded.

"She said we shouldn't see each other anymore." Alice stared at the couch between them.

"I see." Kathryn poked again at her rice. And then as if she wished to abandon the subject altogether, Kathryn asked, "What about your mother? Did she stay away, too? She didn't bother you anymore?"

Alice was relieved at the change of subject. "She never really spoke to me again after everything that happened. My father told me to give her some time, but he ended up dying. Cancer. And then she died a year later. And..." Alice felt a pull of tears she hadn't felt for a long time. How apathetic she had been at her mother's funeral.

"My God. Is that all we have to look forward to?" Kathryn sat her take out box on the coffee table.

"I certainly hope not." Alice also put her food down, feeling exhausted from the evening. Exhausted and elated and confused.

"I wish you would have..." Kathryn whispered.

"You were gone by the time I got divorced." Alice knew. Alice wished.

Kathryn laughed darkly.

"And you were gone long before that, too." Alice felt emboldened to say.

"What do you mean?" Kathryn's expression sobered.

"Something happened…you were so different in the end."

Kathryn moved to stand, reaching for her cigarettes. "I was trying to protect you."

"I didn't need your protection." Alice sat up.

Kathryn laughed coldly. "I'm going out for a smoke."

And Alice watched her walk away, out to the patio where she stood at the edge of the pool and lit a cigarette.

Alice missed her presence, mourned the loss of intimacy they had finally shared. There were things Kathryn was not telling her, but it could not all be revealed in a night. It was only a start, wasn't it?

Alice reached for a blanket and followed Kathryn to the patio.

Kathryn was staring at the moon's reflection in the pool.

"Robin ended things with me because she knew I was still in love with you." Alice found herself saying.

The cigarette paused on its ascent to Kathryn's lips.

"I always have been. It's never gone away."

Kathryn stood stock still, not moving an inch.

Until her shoulders sagged and Alice knew she was crying.

Alice watched, uncertain. Until her head lifted to the sky above them.

"Oh, Alice. I love you, too."

And Alice moved toward her, wrapping her up in her arms and the blanket and holding her, inhaling the scent of her through the back of her shirt, the scent that had lingered all around her ever since Kathryn had come back into her home, into her life.

"I'm so scared."

"Me, too." Kathryn confessed brokenly, holding Alice's hand in her hand, pressing Alice tightly against her.

Alice pressed her ear against Kathryn's back so she could hear and feel the pulse of Kathryn's heart beating rapidly. "What do we do now?"

Chapter Fifty-Six

Kathryn

She spat toothpaste into the sink and, glancing up, caught sight of herself in the mirror.

The lines only grew deeper with each passing day. The work Peter had had her do in Germany was only a Band-aid. Nothing could possibly stop time from marching forward.

But wasn't there a beauty to each of her wrinkles? As if she had earned them and somehow she was coming out of the fight victoriously, beautifully.

She turned off the light in the guest bathroom and walked to the hallway.

Alice's door was open, light from a lamp flooding out from inside, warm and inviting.

Kathryn stepped inside and looked about. She had yet to see the room but it was all Alice. The walls were a soft white. The bed was large and looked plush and warm. There was a fig leaf tree in the corner before large windows that overlooked the pool.

It was tranquil and calming, and Kathryn felt at ease despite the warm excitement and anticipation that had curled within herself.

Alice came out of the bathroom rubbing lotion on her hands. Her silk robe fluttered out behind her, hair unpinned and down about her face. She was still glorious, hardly looking a day older than she had all those years before...

Kathryn wanted a drink but wanted even more to bury her face in Alice's neck, to inhale the scent of her. So familiar and so missed.

Alice was appraising her, looking over the nightgown she'd pulled on, soft and silky and black. "Well." Alice's pretty mouth formed the word.

Kathryn moved closer, taking Alice in her arms.

Their lips met, slow, tentative.

There was time now as there had never been time before. No husband would show up, no show would get derailed by a liaison, there was no publicity to be concerned about. It was only the two of them, lost to the rest of the world in that moment.

The kisses deepened, Alice's arms going about Kathryn. "I've missed you." She murmured against her lips and Kathryn trailed her kisses down Alice's neck, nipping at the skin with her teeth.

They found the bed and unraveled each other. A kiss to the shoulder blade, the strap of a gown removed, a pert pink nipple unveiled before lips covered it.

Alice responded so beautifully, so wantonly. Kathryn had forgotten the little purrs the auburn-haired woman would emit, the contented sighs, the slight quickening of her breath at each kiss, each caress. Kathryn delighted in the way she inhaled if her hand brushed at her hip bone, if her lips were to linger there. Time had changed her, and yet nothing had changed.

Kathryn remembered every curve, every freckle, every marking.

Alice sighed in release and then her fingers were buried between Kathryn's legs as she rolled her over so that she was on top. Kathryn's eyes slid closed as Alice's fingers worked against her. As Alice's lips pressed against her cheek, her forehead, bowing to suck her nipple. Alice, Alice, Alice.

Her whole body released into submission.

She was clutching at Alice, helpless moans slipping from her lips as her release came.

They grasped at one another, limbs held tight and close.

Kathryn's eyes slid wide open, and she could not believe it. Was it a dream or was it truly happening?

But Alice bowed to kiss her and she knew. Oh, she knew it had happened.

Her body shook as if she were cold.

"Are you all right?" Alice was looking at her with concern.

"I...yes." Kathryn smiled up at Alice. A tear slid down her cheek, warm and wet. "I never thought..."

"Me either." Alice was teary-eyed.

And then Kathryn was laughing. Elated at it. "You're marvelous."

Alice flushed, bowing her head briefly to kiss Kathryn's sternum. She let her weight fall down atop Kathryn, resting her ear against her chest.

Kathryn stroked her hair and held her close.

The need reared its ugly head and Kathryn kissed Alice's forehead. "I need to..."

"Oh." Alice slid from her. "I'll come with you."

"You don't have to." Kathryn chuckled as she slid to the edge of the bed, searching for her nightgown.

"I want to." Alice insisted, sitting up as if her body was as limber as ever.

Kathryn lit a cigarette on the patio and pulled the throw

blanket she'd stolen from Alice's bed tighter. The night had grown frigid.

Alice was sitting near to her, caressing her leg. Kathryn's hand found Alice's. Neither wishing to be apart now that it had come full circle.

But, Kathryn could tell over her cigarette, Alice was pensive.

"What is it?" Kathryn whispered.

Alice looked down at their combined hands. "Why…" she hesitated.

Kathryn tugged at Alice's hand encouragingly.

"Why did you go back to Germany?" Alice leaned forward, rubbing at her face as if annoyed that she had asked the question.

Kathryn tapped ash off the side of the chair. "There was unfinished business…I…" Did she have a good excuse? That she couldn't bear the thought of Alice taking her on like she was a charity case.

It had hurt her pride and yet she'd come running back despite it.

She knew all too well that Alice was good for her.

Could she be good for Alice?

The thought raced through her mind, frightening her.

"I didn't want to…impose."

"You wouldn't have been. You're not now…" Alice insisted.

"Yes, I am. You're…you're doing everything for me…"

"I'm not." Alice firmly stated.

"I don't need to be looked after like a child." Kathryn huffed, trying to pull her hand away but Alice grabbed it back.

"I know you're not a child and I know you will make your own decisions. But, Kathryn, I want to help." Alice spoke resolutely.

"I don't need help." Kathryn snapped.

Alice laughed sharply and their hands fell apart. "You're just afraid. Don't do this, Kathryn." And Alice stood up. "Don't ruin this."

Kathryn turned from her, unable to look at the pain on the other woman's face.

"Please come back to bed when you're done." Alice said and then turned on her heel to go back inside.

Kathryn lit another cigarette and wiped tears from her face.

Shouldn't love make it all easier? And yet within the freedom there had now come a horrible fear.

This was real. Alice still loved her. Despite it all. She still loved her.

And Kathryn was ruining it.

She stubbed out her cigarette and went to brush her teeth and wipe her face clean before slipping back into Alice's bedroom.

Alice was looking at her when she entered, watching her as she went to the other side of the bed and slid between the sheets.

Kathryn's body was wired and unsettled.

Alice slid closer, stroking her arm, her chest.

Her eyes appeared above Kathryn's face and their lips met in a brief kiss that turned into something more languorous. An absolution. Something taut between them but when Kathryn reached between Alice's legs, Alice stilled above her.

Kathryn retreated, rejected.

"Kathryn…" Alice was trying to pull her back.

"No," Kathryn turned on her side away from Alice and pulled the blankets up around herself.

"I…I want to…" Alice's voice shook. "But you don't have to appease me with sex. Can't I just…can't I just hold you? All those years we never got to simply….be."

Kathryn scrunched her eyes tightly shut and then open again. The tears slid from eyes, irritating her already dry skin.

Sex, sex had always been to appease, to please, to get what she needed.

But Alice was not asking her for this.

Alice never would. It would be a mutual activity. Not used to persuade or pacify.

She slowly turned around to face Alice.

The smaller woman pulled her into a tight embrace, and Kathryn cried against her chest until she fell asleep.

Chapter Fifty-Seven

Alice

Glistening with sweat from her early morning barre class, Alice rummaged through the back of her freezer for the pint of hidden ice cream. She had decided to throw it out on the way back from the gym but upon discovering it and the fact that it was nearly full, she made the split decision to skim some off the surface before tossing it.

She'd gained ten pounds since Kathryn's return.

Kathryn didn't seem to mind one bit when she wrapped her arms about her in the night, but *she* certainly minded the larger numbers on the scale.

But she had just gone to barre class and the ice cream was sitting there untouched.

She scooped up a spoonful, relishing the cold rush and sticky sweetness that melted on her tongue.

She decided another spoonful couldn't hurt because it was not only the weight gain that preoccupied her mind.

Kathryn would be attending the live taping that very evening.

Alice scooped another bit of ice cream up but just as she stuck it in her mouth, she heard a cough and turned to find Kathryn standing in the doorway from the hallway, bedraggled and sleepy-eyed, watching her intently as she stood with the spoon shoved in her mouth.

"Well, I think there's nothing wrong with dessert for breakfast." Kathryn's voice was always so deliciously low in the morning.

"Oh," Alice sat the spoon in the sink and put the lid firmly back on the ice cream. "I was going to throw it out. You know, turn a new leaf and start again. I haven't been able to fit into anything comfortably for the past month and so I went to barre class this morning and I was going to…you know…"

Kathryn had come up behind her and wrapped her arms about her, pressing her lips against her neck. "I missed you in bed when I woke up," her smoky voice murmured as she nipped Alice's ear.

"Oh, Kathryn." Alice sighed, bracing her hands against the edge of the sink as Kathryn's hand wandered where it wanted over her body.

"You look gorgeous to me." Kathryn whispered as her hand slid down into Alice's spandex tights.

"Kathryn," Alice tried to sound threatening – unaccustomed to having sex in her kitchen, or even in the morning (though Kathryn seemed to be rewriting all the rules and she was so easily persuaded) – but only succeeded in moaning the name.

It was in the moment that Kathryn turned her around so they could face each other – and Alice's lips were just about to hungrily seek out Kathryn's – that Alice noticed someone standing in the doorway. Watching.

"Oh!" Alice shoved Kathryn away and Kathryn, still

unsteady on her leg, nearly fell backward. Alice reached for her just as she braced herself with the kitchen island.

"What the hell…" Kathryn muttered.

"Jack? What are you doing here?" Alice's voice was alarmingly high, even to her own ears.

Jack's cheeks flushed a deep shade of red. "I…uh…I'm sorry…I should…"

"Oh God." Kathryn groaned.

Alice wanted to bury herself beneath the sheets of her bed and never come out again.

What a way for him to see…for him to know…Oh, Jesus.

Alice took a deep breath. "Jack…don't…don't go."

Jack couldn't meet her eyes.

Would he be disappointed in her?

"Mom, I mean I get it. She's hot, but like…God. I didn't think…I should have knocked. I should have rung the doorbell. I'm sorry." Jack was apologizing now.

Alice waved him off. "No, I'm sorry, I didn't mean for you to find out like…that."

"Coffee anyone?" Kathryn had busied herself at the coffee machine.

They ended up all sitting at the patio table with coffee, Kathryn with a cigarette, smoking nervously as Alice, nervously, tried to explain it all carefully to Jack.

"You mean to tell me…" he looked between the two women. "That you were together when I was born?"

"Uh, well…I mean, yes. Your mother's water broke at my house. I drove her to the hospital." Kathryn laughed, as if delighted by the memory.

"So you've always…shit…"

"Language." Alice chastened automatically.

"Oh, lay off him. He's probably scarred from what he just witnessed. Who wants to catch two old ladies going at it?" Kathryn deadpanned.

"Kathryn." Alice buried her face in her hands. "Jack, I

am sorry that you had to see that. But yes. We do have a long, complicated history together. And we just recently…rekindled that."

"So have you…always been gay?" He asked them both, his voice small, the question holding within it some inner need to know something.

Alice took a deep breath. "Well, I'm not sure I ever thought about it that way. I feel more comfortable with a woman. I always have." She tried to answer honestly because she could tell it mattered to him.

"I always liked both men and women. Sexually. But I think I prefer the companionship of a woman to a man." Kathryn tapped off ash from her cigarette.

Jack looked down at his lap.

"What is it, baby?" Alice was worried he might be upset with her, that he might pull away at this revelation. She had never shown him this side of herself before.

Her heart was beating so terribly fast.

He offered a brief smile without looking up. "Oh, I feel as if I always knew somehow. About you…but I…"

Kathryn sat forward, uncrossing her legs. Alice gave her a curious glance.

"I have something to confess as well." Jack's brow was furrowed. "I…I like men."

Alice nearly laughed and then stopped herself, afraid he would think she was laughing at him. But it was only relief that flooded her. That he should tell her now, finally. She had known – and perhaps he had known about her – for so long. She had wanted him to embrace it, but maybe she hadn't made it easy for him.

Oh, she wished he would not have to look so scared to tell her.

"Oh, honey." Alice took his hand in hers. "Oh, baby. Thank you for telling me. For telling us. I…I had my suspicions, but…oh, I'm proud of you, baby."

"You are?" He perked up at that.

"Of course I am!" Alice squeezed his hand. "You'd better bring that Bobby over here for dinner one of these days."

Jack startled at this.

"Don't think I don't know about him." Alice was smiling at her son, thrilled that they could speak candidly now.

Kathryn was smiling at the both of them. "Well, then it's settled. I suppose we're all one big gay family now."

Jack laughed.

Alice turned to smile at Kathryn, but she had a distant look in her eyes. She was puffing at her cigarette as she lowered her gaze. "I mean, as long as you both want me here."

Jack took Kathryn's hand in his. "I haven't seen my mother this happy in years. Thank you."

And when Alice looked at Kathryn she found that Kathryn was smiling through delighted tears.

It was settled then. It was all out in the open, and a warm relief furrowed deep within her.

She was so tired of hiding, of anyone having to hide. The way Kathryn so easily showed her affection when they were at home felt so natural and yet as soon as they would be out in the world it would all change, wouldn't it?

Alice would have to hide externally forever.

She thought about this as she drove to the studio that evening, Kathryn all put together and radiant in the seat beside her. Their hands found the other on the seat between them.

"Are you nervous?" Kathryn was studying her.

Alice turned a corner and glanced in her direction. "Of course."

"Are you always or because of me?"

Alice laughed. "Both."

Kathryn laughed, squeezed her hand. "Well don't you worry about me."

"How can I not?" Alice smiled.

Kathryn rolled her eyes and leaned back.

"Do you miss it?" Alice asked.

"Oh, I've been enjoying this time of having no demands, of not having to constantly learn lines and rehearse and kowtow to everyone, but..." she stared out at Los Angeles passing by. "Of course I do."

When they pulled into the studio lot, Kathryn hung back to smoke and Alice ran into Jeanette inside the stage door.

"Well, well, well." Jeanette was looking at her with an unreadable expression.

"What?" Alice, already nervous, felt she could not take one more surprise that day.

"I suppose you've mended things, then?"

"What are you..." and just as she spoke, Kathryn appeared in the doorway behind her.

The three women regarded one another before Kathryn smiled easily and stepped forward to extend her hand to Jeanette. "Jeanette Jenkins. I'm Kathryn Anderson." She said as she placed her hand on the small of Alice's back – Alice's cheeks flushing hot red at the contact.

"I'm aware." Jeanette took her hand and they shook.

"It's nice to finally meet you."

"Likewise." Jeanette fluttered her eyelashes. Alice grimaced inwardly. Knowing just what Jeanette felt for Kathryn – the contempt she had for all that Kathryn had put her through.

But couldn't she see it was all right now?

"Listen," Kathryn spoke and Alice felt a migraine coming on. "I want to thank you for being there for Alice. I know it's been hard on her...all my shit is a lot for anyone. But I hope...well, I hope I can change your mind about me."

Alice looked, surprised, from Kathryn to Jeanette.

She saw a slow smile curl its way on Jeanette's lips.

A challenge.

"I hope you can."

Chapter Fifty-Eight

Kathryn

The phone was ringing in her ear. Kathryn twisted the cord about her fingers, heart beating.

The phone connected on the other end, startling Kathryn.

"Hello?" The voice was familiar but deeper, warmer than it had been. The woman had come into her own.

"Vivian?" Kathryn said before she thought to hang up and abandon this ill-conceived idea.

"Kathryn? Is that you?"

"Y-yes." Kathryn murmured and fiddled with her lighter, longing to be outside where she could smoke freely because her nerves were unsettled now.

"I've been – we've been trying to get in touch with you." There was an urgency to Vivian's voice, a fearful sadness.

Kathryn stood up straighter. "What for?"

"It's mother. She's…she's not doing well. They released her from the hospital. They say there's nothing more they can do. She's going to..." Vivian's voice trailed off. "Won't you come?"

Kathryn found it hard to breathe. "I had no idea...I..."

"Kathryn, please come." Vivian's firm voice insisted.

"It's been so long...I..."

"She asks for you."

Kathryn leaned over the kitchen counter, clasping at the edge with her free hand.

"Kathryn? Where are you?"

Kathryn wiped at the tears falling messily from her eyes. Was this how it ended? Everyone dying? She had been so angry at her mother for so many years and now...

"Kathryn?"

"I'm here, I'm...I'm in Los Angeles."

"We heard...we saw the news...are you all right?" Vivian's voice was timid, unaccustomed to speaking with Kathryn, to knowing anything about her. She sounded more the mother to Kathryn's irresponsible child.

"I'm okay." Kathryn assured her.

"Please, won't you come?"

Kathryn worried her lip.

"Is it money? I can have Bill send you a ticket. We'll take care of everything. You don't have to worry."

"Oh, Vivian." Kathryn balked. Did she really think she was destitute? She'd made sure she was paid for the last film before she'd left Germany. She had not come on nothing. Sure, it was tight, but she was not in the poor house.

Vivian must have thought she had fallen far.

"Okay." Kathryn breathed before she could say no.

"Oh – oh, really? But you'll come soon? She doesn't have long."

Kathryn was nodding up and down. "Yeah, yes."

Kathryn moved frantically to the patio, finding she was down to one of her last packs of cigarettes and she longed to smoke her way through the day, to perhaps get so high that she might mask the pain shooting through her.

She lit cigarette after cigarette until she heard the door to the patio open, and Alice appeared with a cup of coffee and some toast.

Alice stilled when she saw Kathryn's face.

Kathryn wiped at her cheek and lit another cigarette. "It's my mother. She's dying." She said around the cigarette.

"Oh, Kathryn." Alice sat at the edge of the lounger.

"I called….fuck, I called Vivian to…I don't know….I thought maybe we could, you know talk, and then she tells me that mother's dying. She's at home. Dying. They want me to come." Kathryn puffed irritably at her cigarette.

"Kathryn," Alice placed her hands about Kathryn, steadying her. "Are you all right?"

Kathryn looked tearfully at Alice. "No."

"Do you want to go?"

Kathryn shook her head wildly. "No, but…but I need to. I need to." And then Kathryn grasped at Alice.

"I think this is important, Kathryn." Alice trailed her fingers down Kathryn's cheek, brushing her hair from her face.

"Do you want me to come? I could…I could rearrange the show schedule, I could…"

"No." Kathryn shook her head. "No, let me do this."

"You'll be okay?" Alice was looking fearfully at her. Distrusting. Kathryn hated that. Hated that more than anything.

"Yes."

"You'll call me if…if anything happens…"

"You'll be my first call." Kathryn assured her because there was trust to be mended. And because she wanted a drink right then. And it all scared her.

She worked it out to leave the following day. Alice would

take her to the airport in the morning, and on Sunday she would return to Alice again.

The worst of it was the plane. Stifling without a drink.

The hostess smiled prettily at her and asked for her drink order. Kathryn eyed the miniature bottles of liquor hungrily but asked for ginger ale. She watched, enviously, as the man beside her downed not one but two bottles of vodka while she sat smoking and drinking the overly sweet ginger concoction.

It did little to calm her. She was jittery beyond belief when they landed in Connecticut. She limped off the plane, hips stiff from sitting, knee still recovering.

And then, standing before her was the shocking image of a beautiful, blonde woman flanked by two teenaged children and an attractive dark-haired man behind her.

She was glorious, a mirror image of what Kathryn had once been.

She moved toward Kathryn as Kathryn slowly walked toward her.

They met in an embrace, and Kathryn felt her tears falling freely, no longer caring if anyone saw the great and forgotten Kathryn Anderson falling apart in the Bradley International Airport.

They lived in a small suburban town in commuting distance from New York for Bill's work. Bill seemed amiable enough. Kathryn spoke to him as he drove to the quaint neighborhood with sprawling homes tucked away from the road, hidden by trees.

The children were well mannered. The oldest was a girl, Molly, and the younger a boy, Will. They looked at her with fascination and a bit of awed trepidation.

Vivian smiled at Kathryn, as if relieved by her presence. Relieved that perhaps she would not have to go through this alone.

Kathryn could sense this.

Bill pulled into the driveway of a beautiful two-story home and dutifully took her luggage.

Kathryn stood, staring up at the house.

"She'll be so happy to see you." Vivian came to stand beside her, the children having already followed their father inside.

Kathryn sighed, lit a cigarette to help settle her nerves. "I've spent so many years being so angry with her."

"I know." Vivian shifted on her heels, following Kathryn's line of sight to the second story of her home. "It was so different back then. I think…well, I like to think she did her best. And I know…I know she loves you."

Kathryn grimaced. If she loved her then she should have protected her.

"Shall we go inside?" Vivian asked, watching as Kathryn finished her cigarette.

Kathryn nodded, extinguishing it beneath her shoe. It was now or never. She had already come this far.

Vivian led her into the impeccably designed and perfectly cleaned home. Not a single thing was out of place. She caught sight of Bill pouring himself a snifter of brandy and longed for some.

Instead she was led through the home towards a back bedroom. It smelled of death. Her mother was not long for this world.

The room was dark, and she could hardly make out the form of her mother tucked beneath the blankets.

"Mother, Kathryn is here." Vivian spoke softly, turning on a side lamp.

The form in the bed shifted, turning to look. Her face was so sunken, as if the life had already begun to drain from it. Kathryn felt her knees go weak. She couldn't do this.

"Katarina! Meine Tochter. Meine Kind. Komm her." The old woman was reaching weakly for her, her voice a faded, hoarse whisper.

She went to her mother, sinking to the floor at the bedside so the woman could cup her cheeks, could look at her.

"Es tut mir lied. Ich liebe dich, Katarina."

"It's okay, mother. It's okay." Kathryn was sobbing.

"Vergibst du mir? Bitte, meine Tocher." The woman grasped at Kathryn, a great sadness gathered about her, a heaviness that Kathryn realized only she could dispel.

Kathryn bowed to kiss her mother's cheek. "Yes. Ich vergebe dir. Yes."

"Oh, Katarina!" Her mother clasped at her.

She grasped at her mother, sinking into relieved sobs. Oh, how she had hated this woman, how she had vowed to never forgive and now seeing her as she was…only a woman. A woman who had done her best. Oh, she loved her more now than she had ever loved her.

But she would lose her now.

She lay with her mother until darkness overtook the room. Vivian had slid out at some point.

Kathryn made sure her mother was asleep before she kissed her on the cheek and stood. She was lightheaded from not having eaten and she craved a cigarette.

She left the room in search of her purse and found a spread of food waiting in the kitchen.

"Are you all right?" Vivian asked from where she was putting the final touches on dinner.

Kathryn nodded up and down. "Going out for a smoke." She stole an hors d'ouerve from a plate and slid out to the back deck. She lit the cigarette and listened as the back door opened behind her.

"I know." Vivian's soft voice came then.

Kathryn turned to look at the woman. "What?"

"She told me everything." Vivian put her hands on the back of a patio chair.

"Oh." Kathryn felt her stomach knot. "Well…"

"I don't blame you. Or her." Vivian went on. Remarkable

Vivian who seemed untouched by it all. As if she were content in knowing the truth of it.

"I'm…I'm so sorry." Kathryn felt fresh tears slipping down her cheeks.

"I think, if I'm honest, I always knew."

"Can you forgive me?" Kathryn sunk down onto a nearby seat.

Vivian moved toward her, sitting down next to her. She put her arm about her. "It was never your fault."

Kathryn nodded up and down, as if she had known that, but she realized she had not. She had always blamed herself. Blamed herself for letting it happen the way it had. It *had* been her fault.

But here was Vivian, her daughter, telling her just the opposite.

Kathryn put her head in her hands and wept, Vivian running her fingers in soothing circles across her back.

Chapter Fifty-Nine

Alice

She was eating Oreos nervously and watching late night television when the phone rang.

Her heart was pounding in her chest, not knowing what to expect.

"Alice." The voice on the other end sounded normal enough. She could not detect a slur, any hint of inebriation. "She died."

"Oh." Alice put a hand over her mouth.

"She just…slipped away while we were sitting there." Kathryn said. Almost matter-of-factly. "She…she asked for my forgiveness. It was as if…she needed it. So she could die." Kathryn exhaled on the other end of the phone.

"I'm so sorry."

"Alice." Kathryn's voice sounded worried. "I…I had a drink. I found some brandy in a cabinet and I…"

"It's okay, Kathryn." Alice whispered. "It's okay."

"It was just one. I…"

"I know."

"I feel sick."

"That's okay. That's to be expected."

"I don't want to be like this." Kathryn groaned.

"You've just had a shock. It's okay. It's normal, what you're feeling." Alice assured her, stomach knotting.

There was silence on the other end. An inhale, an exhale. She was smoking.

Kathryn hummed. "Viv…Vivian knows. She knows that I'm her… She already knew." Kathryn coughed. She was smoking too much.

Alice took a deep breath. "You're all right?"

There was silence on the other end.

It was the sad realization that Kathryn struggled, Kathryn had sadness, Kathryn had pain, Kathryn was as human as anyone else that shot through Alice then. Kathryn could break.

She was broken now.

Alice's love for her swelled infinitely.

"No." Kathryn whispered, tears strangling her voice. "Yes. Yes, I'm okay because – God, I love her. I never thought…oh, it's such a relief." She was laughing. "All these goddamn years. Why…why couldn't it have…"

"Shh." Alice warned her.

"Oh God." Kathryn sighed.

"When is the funeral?" Alice stared at the television as *The Wes Goodwin Show* started playing. It came on every evening at eleven. She picked up the remote to change the channel but stopped.

She remembered the episode clearly enough because it was the evening Kathryn had kissed her behind the set.

Kathryn had been standing there in the wings right before Alice's first entrance. Alice had been so nervous around Kathryn the weeks prior to it, had started to shake ever so slightly when she was in the older woman's presence. Alice hadn't understood it until Kathryn's lips had brushed against her own in the dark.

Kathryn had wanted her just as she had wanted Kathryn.

She understood it then and even more so now as she watched.

"The funeral is Saturday." Kathryn's voice came to her. Older, hoarser, smokier than it had been all those years before on *The Wes Goodwin Show*. "Alice, would you…could you come?"

"Of course. Of course, I'll be there. I'll take the red-eye after filming. I…of course." Alice felt a warmth spreading out across her chest. Kathryn wanted her there. She wanted her to meet her family to know…to support her.

"Thank you, Alice."

Alice flew into Connecticut bright and early Saturday morning. Her eyes were puffy; she hadn't slept a wink since Kathryn's call.

When she stepped off the plane, she was greeted by Kathryn, sunglasses shielding her eyes, all in black save for her shock of white blonde hair. She was smoking a cigarette and looked unsettled despite the smile that curled her lips upward when she caught sight of Alice.

"My darling!" Kathryn cried, reaching for Alice, pulling her close to her. "Thank you." She whispered into her ear, and there was a certain relief that it was only the smell of smoke and mint on Kathryn's breath and nothing more than that. She was okay, she was okay. "Vivian's already cooking up a storm at home. Come, come on! I can't wait for you to meet her. She's…oh, she's divine. A dream!"

Alice nearly felt jealous of Kathryn's newfound love for her daughter. She smiled and allowed Kathryn to help her with a bag. It was strange how her knee seemed more improved than before. She was walking straighter.

They got into a car that Alice presumed belonged to Vivian or her husband, and Kathryn leaned over before she pulled away and kissed Alice like there was no tomorrow. "Oh God, I've missed you." They pulled out of the airport parking lot.

Alice laughed. "Do they…do they know?"

Kathryn shrugged and rolled down her window to light a cigarette. "I told her you'd be sleeping in with me. There was no way I was going to let her put you in the room where Mother died." Kathryn almost laughed at her own morbid joke.

"Oh, Kathryn." Alice sighed at her crudeness. "I could have gotten a hotel."

"Nonsense. She *wants* to meet you." Kathryn insisted.

Alice's bravado was fading by the time they pulled into the driveway of an elegant home in a peaceful suburb. It was stately and calm. Vivian was as beautiful as Kathryn had said. The children were bright and curious. They adored Kathryn. They sat near to her, smiling when she came in, eyes bright and wide.

They took to Alice too, but she wondered if they knew. Wondered if when Vivian was smiling at her she knew the full truth of why she was there.

The service was simple and sweet. Alice surreptitiously held Kathryn's hand as she cried at her side.

Alice tried not to bring untoward attention to herself, hiding behind a veil, knowing full well her face was tired and puffy and perhaps she wouldn't look like herself. But afterwards, when Kathryn went out to smoke, several women in attendance discreetly inquired about autographs and Alice acquiesced.

"It's so nice of you to support your colleague." An older woman told Alice.

Alice simply nodded, watching as her *colleague* reappeared through the door, looking for her.

Kathryn spotted her and came toward her, taking hold of her wrist. "Let's get out of here."

And Alice could do nothing but obey.

They drove back to the empty family home and Kathryn tore at Alice, pouring all of her grief and sadness into making passionate, unrelenting love to Alice. Burying herself inside of Alice, seeking, seeking, seeking.

Alice came over and over until they heard the door opening downstairs followed by familiar voices.

"I love you." Kathryn held Alice's face in her hands, wanting her to know, to understand.

And Alice, weak and contented and full just nodded. "Love you, too."

"I'll go down. Come when you're ready." Kathryn slid from the bed, fumbled for her clothes and her cigarettes. She kissed Alice again and disappeared from the room.

It took time for Alice to catch her bearings. She snoozed for a while, and then finally groggily pulled her weak body from the bed, moving to the en suite bathroom to shower.

Once she had herself and the room back in some semblance of order, she walked downstairs and found Vivian in the kitchen. Beyond that she could see Kathryn deep in conversation with Bill. She smoking a cigarette and he puffing at a cigar.

"Oh, Alice. You're awake. Kathryn told me you were exhausted from the flight." Vivian smiled warmly. She could have been just as intoxicating as her mother, but there was a gentle passiveness to her that Kathryn had never possessed.

"Yes – sorry. I...I just needed to sleep a little. I...the funeral was...beautiful." Alice was not ready to face Kathryn's daughter alone.

"Thank you. I'm just happy Kathryn was here." Vivian smiled. "Are you hungry? Let me fix you a plate. Sit, sit down." She motioned toward the bar stools across from herself and started piling food on a plate. "I'm glad she has you."

"What?" Alice startled out of her dreamlike trance.

Vivian smiled softly. "She always thinks I haven't a clue about anything. What would I know about homosexuality?" There was a playful slant to her lips.

Well, she was a little bit like her mother after all, Alice mused.

"I saw her German movies and knew. I just knew." Vivian laughed. "It all made sense. And this makes sense. I've seen all those old *Wes Goodwin* episodes. My goodness, if the world knew…"

"Well, I'd prefer…"

"Oh, no. I would never say a thing." Vivian held up her hands.

"No, I didn't think…" Alice cleared her throat. "I do love her. And I want…oh, I want her to be happy."

Vivian smiled at her as she placed a plate full of food before her. "Me, too."

They smiled at one another.

Alice looked down at the food. "This looks delicious."

"Eat, eat." Vivian urged.

Alice stabbed the green beans with a fork but paused, staring again at Vivian. "And you…you're happy?"

Vivian nodded, smiled reassuringly. "I am."

The door opened and Kathryn came flooding back in. "Oh, look who decided to join us."

Alice smiled at her, at the happiness that being here with her daughter gave Kathryn. And then Kathryn touched Alice's back – making her shudder – and was once again carried away on some discussion of the world economy with Bill. "It's no fucking different here than over in Germany. It's just as bad, not near enough jobs but the prices…"

"The prices will always rise!" Bill was debating her after stealing a piece of turkey from a tray.

Vivian and Alice looked to one another, eyes rolling in acknowledgement of the futility of the disagreement.

It was the following day, as they sat on the airplane to Los

Angeles, Kathryn smoking away while engrossed in a newspaper and Alice half-reading a novel, half staring at Kathryn, that Alice turned to Kathryn.

"Did you mean it?"

"Mean what?" Kathryn looked up, glasses slipping down her nose.

"That you missed the business."

Kathryn laughed a little. "Well sure, but what the hell can I do about it now? Howard was very clear. I'm through here."

"Well," Alice shyly reached into her bag, pulling out a script. She handed it to Kathryn.

"What is this?" Kathryn put out her cigarette and took the script. "It's an episode of your show?" She looked it over.

"Yes, in two weeks. And there's a part...here..." Alice opened to the second page, pointed. "It's for you. If you'd like it."

Kathryn looked up at her, eyes wide. "Oh, Alice."

Alice could not be certain if she was pleased or upset. "Well, I just thought that maybe...it's only one episode, but you know it's something and perhaps..."

Kathryn's hand fell over Alice's and squeezed. "Thank you."

They looked at one another, Alice's concern morphing into a pleased smile that matched Kathryn's. Their eyes doing the work that their lips could not so freely.

Chapter Sixty

Kathryn

Los Angeles, 1982

"All right, break for lunch." An assistant director called out.

Everyone dispersed and Kathryn reached for her cigarettes, lighting one.

"I like what you're doing today, Kathryn." The young man, Colin, who was playing her grandson brushed by her as she inhaled on her cigarette.

"You, too." She looked him over, amused by his amusement with her.

"Hey, can I bum one of those?"

She scoffed. "I don't think you're old enough to be smoking."

"I'm nineteen." He insisted.

She laughed again and turned away from him, heading toward her dressing room.

How she'd managed to land this gig was still astonishing,

but the network had liked her on Alice's show. They seemed to remember she was good at acting and thought she'd be the perfect matriarch for their newest show *The Harrisons.*

Matriarch. Ha.

But it was a job. It was something to do, and she relished it.

She tossed her script and pack of cigarettes atop her dressing room table and then nearly had a heart attack when she glanced for a second time in the mirror.

"Meine Süße." He purred and she felt her balance go off kilter, falling against the edge of her dressing table.

"What the hell are you doing here, Peter?" She turned to face the man sitting on an armchair in the corner of the dressing room.

He was casually smoking a cigarette, long legs crossed, holding a manila envelope.

"What is this about some silly papers, my darling?"

Kathryn sat down at her dressing room mirror. "You haven't signed them?"

"Why should I?" He was taunting her.

"Because I want out, Peter. Jesus." She put her cigarette between her teeth and picked up her comb to fluff her hair.

He looked sadly at her. "No you don't."

"I do!" Kathryn insisted, slamming her comb atop the dressing room table. "Damn it, sign the papers."

He was still smiling and she wanted to punch him.

"You cannot possibly be happy here, meine Süße. This is some…how do they say? Second rate bullshit commercial television. This isn't what we do. This isn't art."

"Oh, come off it." She rolled her eyes to the ceiling. "This pays the bills, my dear."

But something caught her eye in the reflection of the mirror.

Peter was holding something in his hand.

Showing it to her.

She swallowed.

"Goddamn you." She turned again to face him.

"Come on, meine Süße. Come back to me. You know you want this. I have a lot more. The last movie was a great success."

Kathryn shook her head back and forth. "No. Get out. Get. Out. Now."

He stood up but did not move to leave, simply came toward her, holding out the baggie.

She did not move.

He pushed the door closed.

"Peter, stop it." She quietly begged.

He leaned over to grab a mirror and she stood up.

"I'm not doing this. It's over, Peter. It's…" she watched him cut a line, voice shaky. "It's…"

"You want to come back to me."

She shook her head. "I…I have to…"

He grabbed at her wrists, pulling her toward him. "I can't do this without you, Kathryn."

"You can. You can, Peter."

"Have a line with me, Kathryn. Come on." He turned her to face the perfectly cut line of white powder tempting her atop the dressing table.

How she knew it would make her feel.

But her heart was pounding fast and hard in her ears. Thumping away in her chest.

"No." She fought at his strong embrace. "No, please. Let me go."

"What happened to my Kathryn? Hmm?" He held her tight and brushed her cheek gently with his free hand.

She spit at him in shock.

He released her and she pushed past him, opening the dressing room door, stumbling into someone blindly. "Help." She whispered, feeling choked. She couldn't breathe. She kept walking, people looking at her with concern, but she breezed past everyone, moving closer and closer to the exit door. She needed air, she needed…oh…

She staggered into the bright sunlight of Los Angeles. She'd dropped her cigarette somewhere. She was confused. What had happened?

She heard voices behind her, people calling out to her, but she kept moving down the backlot road.

She walked past several sound stages, moving with deaf ears and tunnel vision.

How dare he do this to her?

She had been good. She had been so good.

Fuck him.

She hated herself for wanting it as badly as she did in that moment.

But she kept walking away from it.

Walking until a familiar sound studio sprung into view. She slid into a side door, and someone tried to stop her but she kept going.

The rehearsal space was clear save for Jeanette and someone else on the set. They were rehearsing a scene. She tried to see, to know if it was who she was looking for, but Jeanette's scene partner was not who she wanted.

Where was she?

Kathryn moved as if in a dream, panic welling inside of her.

"You can't be here." Someone loudly whispered, but Kathryn disregarded the threat.

She needed, oh how she needed…

She kept looking, walking through shadows in search of the only person who would make sense in that moment.

She kept looking and looking…

Until, there…there in the shadows she noticed the familiar figure. Standing just out of sight in a dark corner, watching the rehearsal through a slit in the stage.

Kathryn walked closer, walked until the figure noticed her and turned, looking, startled, at her.

"Kathryn…are you all right?" Alice whispered. Looking beautiful, beautiful and angelic where the light from the stage filtered through the crack in the wall and illuminated her face. Oh, she was a breath of fresh air, she was oxygen itself.

Kathryn shook her head.

Alice wrapped her up in her arms. She smelled like home. "What happened?"

"Peter…Peter was…was…in my dressing room…he had…he had…and I wanted…and he won't sign…fuck." Kathryn was incoherent, but Alice seemed to understand.

"It's all right. You're safe now. You're safe." Alice was holding onto her in the darkness of the sound stage. She pressed her lips to Kathryn's.

Reassuring.

Kathryn's whole being calmed in Alice's embrace.

Safe.

Epilogue

Alice

Los Angeles, 2003

"I think a little more blush. Yes, that's fantastic." Gigi was running the show as she always did. "Alice, you look gorgeous," she gushed in the girlish way she had. Alice tried not to fault her for trying so hard to appease an old woman who knew how many wrinkles she had to cover up for the television.

"You're sure you're ready?" Jack was holding his daughter Katlyn's hand. Katlyn was staring at her grandmother with big, wide eyes.

"Of course." Alice turned from the make-up artist and looked down at the girl. "What do you think, Kat?"

"You're gorgeous." The seven-year-old repeated what Alice's assistant had just said.

Alice laughed and opened her arms for the girl.

"Alice, you're on in five. Everything all right?" A stage-hand ducked his head in.

"Yes. I'm ready when you are." But her heart was pounding roughly in her chest and she had not slept the previous night. She released Katlyn and turned to look at herself one more time in the mirror.

The ruby about her neck shone in the dressing room lighting. She fingered the necklace. Wishing.

She kissed her granddaughter and son and followed Gigi and the stagehand to the soundstage where a chair was waiting for her across from the interviewer.

Alice allowed them to mic her, and she smiled at the young woman sitting across from her. She looked relaxed.

If only she could be so relaxed.

"It's an honor to meet you, Alice." The woman, Barbara, extended her hand.

Alice took it, patted it. "It's nice to meet you as well. I do hope you'll go easy on me."

Barbara winked. "I'll certainly try."

There was a countdown, some ridiculous intro that detailed Alice's long career in television and film, and then Barbara was looking at her, smiling.

"And now you've decided to do a rather controversial film. Can you tell us more about *Her Secret Life?*"

"Well, I was instantly besotted when I read the script and knew it needed to be made. I think it's important we normalize relationships that are not only between men and women - as we've seen in movies and on television since the beginning of the medium."

"So this is a movie about being gay?"

Alice bristled. "No, it's a movie about life. About the limitations a woman has placed on her that keep her from her true desires."

"Do you think those constraints are still placed on society? On women in particular?"

Alice's eyebrow rose. "I would like to say no. We are now in a new millennium and I see things changing all around me. I see the way the business has changed, what is now possible, especially for women, but to say that people – women specifically – are suddenly free to express themselves and live the way they want…no, I don't see that a whole lot has changed."

"That's why this is an important film. Is it strange for you, at your age, to be playing a woman who loved another woman?"

Alice fingered the necklace about her neck. "Strange? Not at all. And I think anyone at any age can love someone. It doesn't just well up and die as you get older. All the feelings are still there."

"This film explores a woman who has come to terms with her life and wants her daughter and granddaughter to finally know her truth. Why do you think people have to wait so long to be open about themselves?"

"Well look at the world around us. Not so many years ago it was a crime to be gay. People lost their jobs, their families, their lives if they wanted to be who they truly were. It's not easy to live outside the bounds of what society deems acceptable. I think this movie is brave because my character, Martha, no longer wants to hide who she is from the world. She's waited too long already to be who she is, for people to really know who she is, and I wanted to show that it is never too late to do that."

Barbara sat back, re-crossing her legs. "You've been an avid supporter of many LGBT organizations right here in Los Angeles, is that correct?"

"Yes, as you know my son, who is here today, has a lovely partner and they now have a seven-year-old daughter together. I think we need to see more of this in the world. We need to help show people it is normal and acceptable and beautiful. I volunteer at a center where they help LGBT youth who have been kicked out of their homes for being who they are. I've listened to their stories, I've heard their struggles. These stories need to be told. I think it's time that movies reflect the real lives of people and not just what Hollywood thinks the general public wants to see."

"Was there trouble finding support for this film?"

"Oh yes. No one wanted to touch it. We had to go outside Hollywood to film. We actually went to Canada and hired a crew there."

"Most of the funding came from…"

"Me." Alice laughed. "I was an executive producer. And I hired as many women as I possibly could to help make this. It is by no means a great big Hollywood blockbuster, but it's important. It's an important movie with an important message and I know it will reach the people it needs to reach."

Barbara was looking rather wide-eyed at her. As if she did not expect a woman of Alice's age to be so open about current day affairs. "What about your rather conservative fan base who still remember you as Kay on *The Wes Goodwin Show*? Are you worried about how this film might change their perception of you?"

Alice dryly laughed at the question. "No. They can think what they want of me."

Barbara gave her a slight smile. "I think many viewers may want to know – have you ever loved a woman?"

Alice smiled. "Of course, who hasn't loved a woman?"

Barbara laughed.

But Alice knew she could not avoid the inevitable forever. Though her personal life should not have had to be brought up or mentioned during this press circuit, they had decided that if it did, she would not shy away from it.

The movie was personal to her.

"Is it true that you became very close again with your co-star from *The Wes Goodwin Show*, Kathryn Anderson, after you were on a reunion show in the 80s? She guest starred on your show *Different Threads* and then went on to be remembered for her starring role on *The Harrisons*."

Alice picked at a thread on her pants. "Yes." She swallowed, her mouth dry. "Yes, we were very close. She was a wonderful person. Despite everything that happened, she really was wonderful."

"She died some years ago…"

"Yes, she died in 94'."

"I can't believe it's been that many years."

Alice shook her head. "Me, either. You know she was doing really well toward the end. She had her ups and downs, but she was doing really well until they found the cancer and…" a tear slid past her eyelid, trailing down her cheek. She wiped at it. "It wasn't fair. But she did the best she could right until the end."

"And you loved her?" Barbara was looking at her with such empathy.

Alice looked from Barbara to where her son stood in the shadows holding his daughter. And she smiled at them. "I…I loved her, of course I did." Alice peered back at Barbara, laughing. "I think all of America loved her. But I…yes, I loved her."

And she always would.

Acknowledgments

This probably would not have happened without Lina and her support and encouragement.

Thanks to Rae who conceived of this idea with me all those years ago. I'm sorry I've messed with it so many times, but I really like where I've taken it and I know its original heart and soul are still intact. Thank you for the words when I couldn't find them!

Many thanks to my best beta reader, Lorrie! You helped reform this novel and encouraged me forward. Thanks for always brainstorming with me.

To Laura, the best adopted aunt I could ask for, who loved the story and edited it - thanks for taking out all my added 'thats' and 'thens' and other extraneous words.

To all the fanfiction reviewers who urged me along throughout the years and left me wonderful reviews. I was encouraged to create something of my own and so I have.

About the Author

Anna Woiwood is a writer of mid-century Sapphic stories. Her debut novel, The Veracity of Lies, was a finalist for a 2023 Golden Crown Literary Award in historical fiction and A Tiger in Suburbia was a 2024 Golden Crown Literary Ann Bannon Popular Choice finalist. She lives in Kansas City with her small cat son, Walter. Find her on Instagram @anna.w.writes

instagram.com/anna.w.writes